THE CASE OF THE CURSED COTTAGE

A WISE Enquires Agency Mystery

by
Cathy Ace

FOUR TAILS PUBLISHING LTD.

PRAISE FOR THE WISE ENQUIRIES AGENCY MYSTERIES

'...a gratifying contemporary series in the traditional British manner with hilarious repercussions (dead bodies notwithstanding). Cozy fans will anticipate learning more about these WISE ladies.'
Library Journal, starred review

'If you haven't read any of Cathy Ace's WISE cozies, I suggest you begin at the beginning and giggle your way through in sequence.'
Ottawa Review of Books

'...a modern-day British whodunit that's as charming as it is entertaining...Good fun, with memorable characters, an imaginative plot, and a satisfying ending.'
Booklist

'Ace spiffs up the standard village cozy with a set of sleuths worth a second look.'
Kirkus Reviews

'Sharp writing highlights the humor of the characters even while tackling serious topics, making this yet another very enjoyable, fun, and not-always-proper British Mystery.'
Cynthia Chow, Librarian, Hawaii State Public Library in Kings River Life Magazine

'...a refreshing departure from standard mystery fare... Cathy Ace does a remarkable job making (the women of the WISE Enquiries Agency) three dimensional and believable...'
muttcafe.com

'A brilliant addition to Classic Crime Fiction. The ladies (if they'll forgive me calling them that) of the WISE Enquiries Agency will have you pacing the floor awaiting their next entanglement... A fresh and wonderful concept well executed.'
Alan Bradley, New York Times Bestselling Author of the Flavia de Luce mysteries

Other works by the same author

(Information for all works here: **www.cathyace.com**)

The WISE Enquiries Agency Mysteries
The Case of the Dotty Dowager
The Case of the Missing Morris Dancer
The Case of the Curious Cook
The Case of the Unsuitable Suitor
The Case of the Disgraced Duke
The Case of the Absent Heirs

The Cait Morgan Mysteries
The Corpse with the Silver Tongue
The Corpse with the Golden Nose
The Corpse with the Emerald Thumb
The Corpse with the Platinum Hair
The Corpse with the Sapphire Eyes
The Corpse with the Diamond Hand
The Corpse with the Garnet Face
The Corpse with the Ruby Lips
The Corpse with the Crystal Skull
The Corpse with the Iron Will
The Corpse with the Granite Heart
The Corpse with the Turquoise Toes

Standalone novels
The Wrong Boy

Short Stories/Novellas
Murder Keeps No Calendar: a collection of 12 short
stories/novellas
Murder Knows No Season: a collection of four novellas
Steve's Story in "The Whole She-Bang 3"
The Trouble with the Turkey in "Cooked to Death Vol. 3: Hell
for the Holidays"

For Shirley, in Port Eynon

WEDNESDAY 25th JANUARY

CHAPTER ONE

Henry Devereaux Twyst, eighteenth duke of Chellingworth, was terribly worried about his son. *His son!* Henry's heart swelled at the mere thought that such a person even existed. Yet he did. And he was perfect. At least, that was what Stephanie, his beloved wife, kept telling him. It was not in the least alarming, she said, that their son had a slight rash on his cheeks. There was nothing out of the ordinary about the number of hours he seemed to spend doing little but screaming. His sleep patterns were absolutely to be expected. Stephanie kept repeating these reassurances, yet Henry feared his son was suffering in some way; surely an infant shouldn't appear to be so perturbed all the time?

Whenever he held his son, he was terrified he might hurt him: he felt clumsy, all the time; he feared his hands were so large they might snap the tiny fingers which wrapped themselves around his suddenly sausage-like thumbs; he suspected his clothes might be rubbing too roughly against his child's delicate skin.

Despite all these concerns, Henry couldn't help but marvel at his son's perfect little fingernails, and his wonderful toes, which seemed to each have a life of its own. And those cheeks – albeit with a little rash on them – were magical.

Yes, Henry was concerned about his son's general health and well-being, and feared he might always be so, but he was even more worried that the child didn't even have a name, yet.

Devereaux should have been the choice, as the names Henry and Devereaux had been interchanged for the firstborn son within the Twyst family in recent times.

However, the sudden death of his older half-brother Devereaux, due to an undiagnosed dose of the measles, had soured the name for Henry. There were several other names that had been used within the Twyst line for generations which provided options, but Stephanie had complained that their son didn't 'look like' any of them.

With Frederick, Algernon, Devereaux, Henry, and Charles all up for discussion, his wife had immediately discounted Henry, claiming she couldn't be expected to cope with two Henrys at Chellingworth Hall. Henry himself had spoken out against Devereaux, and Stephanie had also been dead set against Frederick. Charles? They both felt there were enough Charleses in the world already. Their conversation had become circular when considering Algernon; both liked the diminutive 'Algie', but when Stephanie's mother had pointed out that – for some – that might suggest an unpleasant growth on the hull of a boat, they'd set it aside, too. Harold, the fourteenth duke's name, had then come under consideration, but Stephanie's father had made his opinions about that quite clear, and they were far from positive; it appeared he couldn't rid himself of the image of Harold Steptoe, or even Harold Wilson.

So they were stuck with no name for their son at all, which was irking Henry. 'My son', 'the boy', and various other ways of referring to an as-yet-unnamed male infant, were grating on his nerves. And his mother's assertion that this lack of decisiveness was all Henry's fault wasn't helping. She'd suggested that he and Stephanie looked into all the names used by every one of the previous seventeen dukes, which they had done – the Chellingworth Bible allowing them to find them handily listed in one place.

One name had rather taken Henry's fancy, but Stephanie had baulked at Cadwaladr, or even Cadwalader, so Henry had been giving the matter some thought – to try to stop himself from being so worried about the rash on his son's cheeks – which was why he was sitting alone in the library.

A dozen books were laying on the desk in front of him, all having been perused, then set aside in frustration.

Edward, his butler, was suddenly at his elbow. Henry jumped; he had no idea how the man managed to walk across a room so silently.

'My apologies, Your Grace, I didn't mean to startle you. Her Grace has asked if you will be joining her for tea in the small sitting room today.'

Henry checked his watch. How on earth could it be almost four o'clock?

'Yes, I shall join her in a few moments, thank you, Edward. Though it might take me a little longer than that to replace all these volumes.'

Edward cleared his throat discretely. 'I would be happy to do that for you, Your Grace, if you have finished with them all.'

Henry sighed. 'I have, thank you. Though I've made no headway.'

Edward picked up an ancient, leather-bound volume. 'The history of the Tudors is an excellent book, Your Grace. And, with this family having been granted its land and title by Henry VII, it would offer an excellent source for choices of names for your heir.'

'Indeed,' said Henry heavily. 'However, Cadwalader seems a step too far for the duchess, though it's a wonderful name from the history of our original benefactor.'

As he reached to replace the volume on a shelf Edward noted, 'I believe Henry VII's father's name was Edmund. With a "U" not an "O". I know it's not very Welsh; in fact, I believe it comes from two Anglo-Saxon words meaning "rich protector". But, since Her Grace is English, and you are Welsh, maybe an English name from within the lineage of the Welsh Tudor kings and queens would be acceptable?'

Henry paused, turned, and said, 'Edmund? Have I ever known an Edmund? No…no, I don't think I ever have. Which is useful – because one knows so many people who are less than pleasant, and their name then becomes associated with one's feelings toward them. No, not an Edmund anywhere in my life. That's a useful suggestion, Edward. Thank you. Her Grace and I shall certainly contemplate it.'

'You're most welcome, Your Grace. And Edmund Tudor's father's name was Owen, or Owain, if you wished to consider the Welsh form.'

'Owain? Might people think we're trying to align ourselves with Owain Glyndwr by using that name, I wonder? Probably not the best move for a Welsh duke…or is it?' Henry decided to give the names a little more thought before he opened the discussions about them, thanked his butler, and headed to join his wife, and their son, for tea.

As he entered the Great Hall, there was no doubt that his son was already in the small sitting room. He – Edmund? Yes, that felt comfortable – was loudly screaming his displeasure about something or other. But, as his wife kept telling him, that was normal.

Henry sighed. 'Normal' was a word that had lost all meaning since his son's arrival; sleepless nights, Stephanie being constantly exhausted, his mother- and father-in-law always being…wherever he wanted to be, and the seemingly endless need to feed, change, or pacify a tiny human being made the use of the word moot. Indeed, he suspected he might never refer to anything as 'normal' ever again. Which was, thought Henry, a great shame, because he'd rather enjoyed his 'normal' life.

Stephanie was in the process of handing his wriggling son to her mother when he joined the family group. Sheila Timbers looked so confident holding the baby; Henry wished he felt that way, but reconciled himself to his wife's mother having been through all of this before, when Stephanie had been born. This was Henry's first time to have any involvement with an infant – his sister, Clementine, had been almost invisible to him at that age, spending all her time in the nursery with Nannie.

As he thought of his sister his heart sank a little; she'd not been heard from since she'd been informed of his son's birth and had sent her best wishes in the form of a large bouquet of blooms for Stephanie. While her being out of touch meant a peaceful life, it didn't usually bode well. Probably getting into all sorts of trouble with her dubious artist friends, he suspected.

As he thought of artists, his mind drifted to his own art studio, a Christmas surprise created by his wife in a delightful folly that sat on the little hill behind Chellingworth Hall. He'd spent no more than a few hours there, because his son had been born on January the second, just a day before he and Stephanie had been due to head off to London to be close to her preferred doctor and hospital. Henry had been relieved that the uncomplicated birth – though doubtless a painful experience for his wife – had taken place without any problems whatsoever at the local hospital, so at least his son had been born in Wales, something for which he'd always been grateful, himself.

'But, even so, no…not Owain.'

'Did you say something, Henry?' Stephanie looked tired, but happy. Henry hoped the sparkle would return to her eyes soon.

'No dear. Just musing.' Henry thought it best not to mention the Edmund option.

'Tea? Cake?'

Henry nodded. 'Not too much cake, though.' He patted his tummy.

'Good idea to watch out for that,' said his mother-in-law knowingly. 'Once this one starts running about the place –' she nodded at his finally-silent son – 'I dare say you'll find the weight dropping off, but you'll need to exercise some willpower until then.'

'Indeed.' Henry felt this was his safest response.

Henry gazed at his son. Was it the angle at which his mother-in-law was holding him, or did he really have a head that was shaped differently on each side? Or was it just unusually long? Henry bobbed about to try to decide.

'Are you alright, dear?' Stephanie sounded concerned.

'Just wondering about the shape of Edmund's head,' said Henry.

'Who on earth is Edmund?' John Timbers sounded confused.

'I have no idea, Dad,' replied Stephanie. 'Who's Edmund, Henry?'

Henry bit his lip, cross with himself that he'd let the potential name slip…then realized that he not only liked the sound of it, but that he felt it suited his child.

He straightened his back. 'The Twyst family owes everything to Henry Tudor, whose father's name was Edmund. I wondered if we might consider that as a name for the next duke. Edmund Twyst sounds rather good, don't you think? Mother couldn't protest, due to the Tudor family connection, and it's not a name that carries much baggage for me personally nor, as I consider it, in the broader sense. What do you think?'

He looked at his wife, his mother-in-law, and his father-in-law, searching their faces for emotions.

'You're right,' said Stephanie. 'I don't think I've ever known an Edmund, so there's that – which is good.'

'Edmund Hillary – first to reach the summit of Everest,' said John.

'Edmund Blackadder – that might be a problem,' said Sheila.

'Who's he?' Henry didn't have a clue.

'He's a comedy character on television, dear,' said his wife, 'though I have to admit it had never really registered with me that he was called Edmund. I always think of him as just Blackadder.'

Henry was interested. 'Is he…was he funny? In a good way?' He wondered how he could find out more.

'Pathetic, and fawning.'

'Annoyingly pompous.'

'Scheming, but always failing.'

Henry didn't think his family's replies sounded promising. 'How is any of that funny?' He was truly puzzled.

Stephanie smiled. 'You're right, it doesn't sound funny, but it was. We'll find some episodes for you to watch. But I have to say that – now Mum's mentioned that particular use of the name – maybe it wouldn't be a good choice for our son, after all.'

Henry felt crestfallen. Names from the family were out; names of people he'd known and didn't like, or that Stephanie had known and didn't like, were off the table; now names of television characters were also being discounted. He wondered if there were any names left at all. Which worried him.

CHAPTER TWO

Gemma Thomas was a small, neat brunette in her late thirties, presently wearing a pinched expression. She was sitting silently, hugging her knees, hadn't touched the tea and biscuits on the coffee table in the office of the WISE Enquiries Agency, and wasn't making eye contact with any of the four women who ran the business. Indeed, as potential clients went, she didn't seem to be prepared to be forthcoming about her requirements at all.

Mavis MacDonald had called the entire team who ran the agency to their office, housed in a converted barn on the Chellingworth Estate, because – when she'd spoken to the woman on the phone the previous day – she'd requested an urgent, face-to-face meeting. Now Mavis was wondering if the potential client was having cold feet; it was something she'd seen happen before.

Her colleagues were also no strangers to a client needing a little time to gather their thoughts before divulging what could sometimes be delicate personal matters, so Mavis wasn't surprised to see they'd all adopted an appropriate air of being patient, and considerate of the woman's needs.

Christine Wilson-Smythe was the youngest of the group, only in her late-twenties; while she appeared calm – her attractive face creased into a warm, welcoming smile – her eyes were telling Mavis she had something on her mind. Given the way she was twirling her brand new engagement ring, Mavis guessed that Alexander Bright, her fiancé, was it. Then Mavis saw a fleeting change in her colleague's expression; she knew that her father, an Irish viscount, was texting Christine much more than usual these days – was there something odd about that? She wasn't sure. Maybe she should try to find out.

Annie Parker sat beside Mavis, and she looked uneasy; Mavis wondered why.

Maybe it was because she had insisted that Annie had to shut her delightful, but too-playful, black Labrador puppy Gertie in the apartment above the office while the meeting took place, or maybe her colleague was thinking of who everyone was finally acknowledging as her partner, Tudor Evans. He ran the only pub still open in the village of Anwen-by-Wye, the Lamb and Flag, and Annie had mentioned several times, recently, that business wasn't too good for him. Mavis wasn't worried about Tudor, but she was concerned about Annie; she was the member of the group of four who'd been least happy about the move from London – where she'd been born and raised – to the Welsh countryside just over a year earlier, and who had, therefore, made most changes to her life and lifestyle. It seemed she'd settled, especially now that she and Tudor were an 'item', but Mavis couldn't help but think Annie was still a little restless, in some way.

Carol Hill, on the other hand, had been absolutely delighted to be able to move back to her homeland of Wales, and she, her husband, and infant son, had settled into a delightful Georgian house overlooking the village green in Anwen-by-Wye as though they'd always been there. Mavis didn't want to mention the stain she could see on the shoulder of Carol's dress while the potential client was there, but made a mental note to tell her about it when they were alone; the after-effects of burping babies was something with which Mavis had – long ago – been familiar, having two grown sons of her own back in what she still referred to as 'home' in Scotland.

As Mavis thought of her sons and grandchildren, she realized she needed to snap her attention back to Gemma Thomas, who was still sitting there mute. She decided to adopt her best cajoling tone; her decades as an army nurse, and then matron, had allowed her to develop a range of skills designed to persuade many a recalcitrant patient to explain their symptoms. She glanced at her three colleagues before she spoke, which they all knew meant she was about to take the lead.

'So, Mrs Thomas, are we to take it you'd like us to look into something connected to the cottage you own? You only gave me very broad details on the phone; I can assure you there's no' many things that would shock or surprise us, so please, feel free to speak openly. Nothing you say will go further than these four walls.'

Gemma picked up a biscuit, which crumbled to pieces in her nervous fingers.

Carol leaped to her feet. 'Don't you worry about that – just leave the bits on the floor. Annie's puppy Gertie is upstairs; we'll bring her down when you've gone, and she'll take care of that. There you are.'

Carol handed the nervous woman a napkin, which she used to soak up a tear in the corner of her eye. Having dabbed herself dry, she reached into her handbag and placed a photograph of a rather attractive cottage on the table. All four women leaned in to get a better look.

'This is the cottage my husband and I own, in Gower. Sea View Cottage. It…it looks so lovely.'

The four women all exchanged a meaningful glance: Gemma Thomas's tone suggested dread rather than delight.

'And there's some sort of problem there?' Mavis ventured a reassuring smile as she spoke.

Gemma nodded, swallowed hard, and said, 'It…it murdered one of our guests, and now it's tried to kill my husband.'

The apprehensive silence that followed the woman's bizarre statement allowed everyone to clearly hear a particularly plaintive whelp coming from the apartment above.

Annie Parker looked up, her expression betraying her concerns about her beloved Gertie being shut away.

Gemma Thomas's eyes followed Annie's gaze. 'Oh please, don't think you have to lock away a dog on my behalf – I love dogs. You can let it out to join us, if you'd like.'

Annie was out of her seat in a heartbeat. 'Ta, she doesn't like being shut away, doesn't Gert. I'll bring her down.'

Mavis was pleased to see that the arrival of the puppy, with her wagging tail, and gangly legs, seemed to relax the potential client.

A great deal of petting took place before Gertie settled herself beside Annie's feet, then Mavis said, 'You were saying, Mrs Thomas, that someone has died? Because of your cottage? A murder, you say? I would have imagined that would be something the police would have looked into. It's no' a matter for a firm of private investigators, like ours. Have they been involved? Made a determination of murder?'

Gemma Thomas squared her shoulders and said, 'Yes, they have been involved. But they said it was an accident, as did the coroner. However, I still believe the cottage killed the man, and then it tried to kill my husband. And I suspect it played a role in my uncle's death too. It's a killer cottage, that's what it is. Because of the wretched curse. And I want it stopped.'

'But a cottage can't really kill, can it? It's inanimate. And what do you mean by saying it's a cursed cottage?' Annie dared to ask.

'Witchcraft,' hissed Gemma. 'Witches used to live there, and they cursed it.'

Annie sat back in her chair and said, 'I see.'

'I knew you'd understand,' said Gemma, looking relieved. She picked up her cup and gulped down tepid tea. 'Thank you. No one else believes me, see? The police think I'm *twp*, completely doolally. You will help me, won't you?'

Mavis cleared her throat, glaring at Annie. 'Help you do what, exactly?'

'Stop it killing people – and trying to. I'm desperate to sell it, but I can't put it on the market knowing what I do about it; I'd be signing someone else's death warrant. I've got to get it sorted out. Can you help me? Please say you can. I've heard some very good things about you, which is why I'm here…and you're all women, which should help too.'

'And why do you think that would help?' Mavis asked politely.

'It only kills men, so you'd be safe there…investigating.'

To Mavis's ears, Gemma Thomas's tone was peculiarly matter-of-fact; she had no doubt the police wouldn't have taken kindly to a suggestion that a recent death was due to a cottage.

Christine Wilson-Smythe leaned forward, the gleam of curiosity in her eyes. 'I'm so sorry to hear about your guest, and your husband, of course…maybe we can help. Please, tell us all about it.'

It was as though the floodgates had opened: Gemma Thomas hardly drew breath for the next ten minutes as she listed a seemingly endless litany of problems that had occurred over the past couple of years at the cottage she'd inherited from her late uncle, and had renovated to become a rental property. She finally spoke, more hesitantly, about the tragic death of a guest, named Brian Kelly, whose electric bicycle – his own bicycle, she emphasized – had somehow managed to send him careening down a steep hillside, to his death. Her husband had suffered a close call when he'd unplugged a coffee maker, which had basically exploded into his face.

She concluded, 'And I'm sure, now, that it killed my uncle, too; he was found dead in his chair – carbon monoxide poisoning. To be honest, even I thought that was just an accident at the time. But now? Now I know better. It has to be stopped. The cottage is cursed; I've heard rumors, but never believed them. One of the neighbors told me there were two witches living there years ago, but I thought it was all rubbish. However, now I think they're right – and I need someone to break the curse. I even asked the local vicar to perform an exorcism, but he said he didn't do that sort of thing. Now it's all around the village that I'm not just an absent owner – which was bad enough – but everyone seems to think I believe in ghosts, too. Which I don't. But I do believe in evil, and that cottage is evil. I've cancelled all our future bookings, and I want shot of the place – but I can't put it on the market until I know it's safe, see?'

Mavis sat back on the sofa. 'I dare say we could take a look…'

Gemma pounced, 'Oh yes, please. And the sooner the better.'

Mavis replied, 'If you'd leave that paperwork with us, and give us a chance to discuss the matter as a team, I could email you later today with a proposal and a quote. How would that work for you?'

Even Gertie picked up on Gemma's relief and excitement, leaping to her feet and wagging her tail furiously.

Gemma Thomas stood and shook Mavis's hand with great vigor. 'Thank you – that would be wonderful. And…and thank you all for not laughing at me; I've had quite enough of that, recently. I look forward to hearing from you.'

Mavis closed the door behind the potential new client, and turned her attention to her colleagues, who were handing around the photograph of the cottage, even as Carol was opening up online pages and references for the place.

Annie Parker began pacing, nibbling her lip. 'Sorry, Mave, I know I could do the job, but I just don't feel comfortable about going back to Gower again. Not so soon, anyway. Maybe Chrissy or Car could do it? Or even you. But me? Nah – too soon for me, Mave; I don't even need to talk to my counsellor about this one. Yeah, not for me. Sorry.'

Mavis nodded her head slowly, and hooked her gray, bobbed hair behind one ear. Annie looked truly reluctant, she judged, and she had to allow the woman to follow her instincts. The work Annie had been doing with her counsellor to address her emotional response to a case that still haunted her was progressing well. Mavis had more than a passing awareness of the significant impact that could be made upon a person by a psychological trauma, so understood it was critical that Annie not be pushed too far, too fast.

Mavis nodded. 'Aye, well, that's fair enough. I dare say it would be a no from Carol, too, what with needing to be away from her son and husband to be able to do it. Whether we share our potential client's fears and beliefs about the cottage being a danger to males – quite specifically – or not, we shouldnae take any chances, so I'd be unhappy about baby Albert going with her. What about you, Christine? I'm of the mind that the only way to get to the bottom of this would be to stay at the cottage itself. Mebbe for a week or so. I dare say Alexander could join you for some, or all, of the time – just as long as your fiancé's presence wouldn't distract you from the case itself, or maybe you feel it would be too dangerous for him.'

Christine smiled brightly. 'A week in a seaside cottage that's possibly cursed and kills men? What could be lovelier? And in January, too. Yumm.'

Mavis squared her shoulders. 'You'd be warm and comfortable, I'm sure. Mrs Thomas explained how they invested in their renovation to have it all set up as one of those high-tech "smart homes" – all the mod cons.'

Carol added, 'I just sent you all the link to the online listing of the cottage. Take a look. It's lovely. The website listing refers to it as Sea View Cottage, but they've also included the fact that it was once the village post office. There's a little more history as you click through the listing; seems it was built in the mid-1700s, but I'll let you read it all for yourselves.'

Christine twirled her long, chestnut ponytail as she scrolled through the gallery on her laptop. 'Oh, yes, it looks grand,' she remarked thoughtfully. 'Tastefully furnished, and modern.'

Mavis took her chance. 'You'd be happy there for a week or so, wouldn't you? Settle in, talk to the locals, find out what they all think about the place. Annie's right to assume she'd be our first choice for this, because, as we all know, chatting to people and winkling information out of them is her forte, but you're no slouch at that yourself, Christine, so how about it? As you know, we need to respond to Gemma Thomas today.'

Christine looked up from her laptop, and Mavis noted how broad her smile was when she said to Annie, 'If you wanted to come with me, I could be on hand to help if you got the collywobbles. You know – maybe you should get back up on the horse that threw you, so to speak. The Gower peninsula is gorgeous; you don't want to never be able to go there ever again, do you? Your Tudor's from Swansea, isn't he? You're bound to want to go there with him at some point. Right?'

Mavis held her breath; how would Annie respond? She watched as her friend and colleague gave Christine's offer some serious thought; she could tell Annie was conflicted because of the way she was nibbling her lip.

When Annie spoke, it was without her usual verve. 'I could, I suppose. But…you know I can't drive, so, if it all got a bit much for me, would you be prepared to get me out of there and back to somewhere I feel…safe? If I need to. Not saying I will, of course.'

Christine beamed. 'You know I would. I don't want you to do anything you really don't want to – but it would be grand to spend some time just the two of us together…we've never really done that, have we?'

Mavis knew how tight the bonds were between Annie Parker and Carol Hill – they'd known each other for many years before the WISE women had come into being. And Carol and Christine had also known each other quite well for some time before they'd all met up, when Mavis had still been Matron at the Battersea Barracks. But the links between Annie and Christine were still…tenuous, felt Mavis. They hit it off well enough, and their skill sets complemented each other's, but they weren't really 'close'. This case could change that, she reckoned.

'Me without Tudor, and you without Alexander, then?' Annie sounded a little more like her usual self.

Christine nodded. 'Yes, how about that? Now that Alexander's put a ring on my finger, and we've made a real commitment to each other, maybe we should learn to spend a little time apart. Oh heck – that sounds wrong, but I know what I mean. It's a trust thing. But Annie…will Tudor manage alright without you? I see that dogs are allowed at the cottage – so you could bring Gertie. How about that? Long walks on the beach. And we can pump all the locals for information about the cottage.'

Annie nodded, and gave the idea two thumbs up.

'Excellent,' said Mavis, feeling relieved. 'The village is called Port Beynon, and the cottage is up on a hillside, just a short walk down to the village proper. It doesn't sound as though it's as big as Anwen-by-Wye, and that's small enough, so I think you'll be dealing with a community that's a manageable size.'

'It's probably a bit posh,' observed Carol. 'I can tell from a quick glance that the house prices down there would make your eyes water, so a lot of outsiders might have moved in, over the years. Maybe the rumors are being fuelled by the locals because the Thomases are asking too low a price, and they're afraid it'll affect the value of their own houses? That might be one avenue to follow.'

Mavis added, 'Gemma Thomas told me when we originally spoke on the phone that there was a fair bit of bad feeling about her renting out the cottage when she started to do so, but now she reckons the locals have all come to accept it, because she made it plain she does her best to rent it only to "nice" people. Maybe they don't want someone else buying it to rent out to just "anyone"? Or maybe it's the price, as Carol says. Maybe it's something we cannae even imagine...that'll be your job to find out. As well as getting to the bottom of why this so-called "curse" exists at all. Is it just some recent local twaddle? Or does it go back a long time? What's the real, down-to-earth reason for all the plumbing, electrical, and other dangerous problems? And you'll need to take a closer look at the motor accident that killed the renter, Brian Kelly: dig deep into that. The police down there should have valuable insights, I'd have thought. Could this be a chance for you to use your goodwill with the folks in that part of the world, Annie? It sounds as though they've not been prepared to accept Gemma's concerns, which I cannae say surprises me, but could you speak to your contact there?'

Annie was nibbling the end of her thumb. 'DCI Carys Llewellyn? Hmm...it's been a while since we spoke. I could...yes, I could try.' Mavis felt less concerned when Annie stuck out her chin and added, 'Leave it with us, Mave, we'll get to the bottom of it all. Right, Chrissy, doll? Our biggest problem will probably be who's going to do the washing up.'

'There's even a dishwasher you can program to take care of that while you're out,' said Carol.

Christine mugged wiping her brow. 'Disaster averted,' she said. 'We could suggest us two staying for a week or so, whenever the client...becomes a client.'

Annie added, 'She said she's cancelled all her future bookings, and it shouldn't take either of us long to be able to get down there. As you know only too well, Mavis, neither of us is working on another case at the moment.'

'If she agrees to our terms,' noted Mavis firmly.

Everyone nodded.

Carol said, 'The website for the cottage says there's a satellite dish, broadband, and wi-fi with boosters throughout – needed because of the thickness of the walls, and the fact that all the smart systems are run that way – so you should be able to keep in touch with us, which is good. But if as many things go wrong there as Gemma has said, just make sure you've always got a fully charged battery for your mobile, and be certain of where you can get a signal, so you can reach one of us if needed. I happen to know that Gower is renowned as having poor mobile phone reception. Oh, and don't forget the chargers you can use in Christine's car, okay?'

Christine and Annie nodded.

Annie said, 'Just so we're ready if it all happens quickly, could you email everything Gemma gave you, please, Mavis? I'll read it when I can. It would be nice to have a head start.'

Carol added, 'And I find the historical side of things interesting, so why don't I get some links and notes sorted about the cottage, and about the area, too? It know it a bit – we went there on Sunday School outings when I was little. There's a big hall – or, at least, there was one, right on the front, just behind the sand dunes that run along the bay. It's smashing…a great place to blow off the cobwebs. And I seem to recall there being a fish and chip shop – though that might have closed by now, or be shut for the winter. I'll find out and send the info through to you. In fact, depending on when you're there, maybe I could drive down to visit you – with David and Albert coming for the ride, but staying away from the cottage itself, of course.'

Annie laughed; Mavis judged she did it a little too heartily.

Christine said, 'Very funny, Carol. None of us believe the place is really cursed, like none of us believe it's a "killer cottage", but there's been a recent tragedy, and we have a potential client who sounds as though she'd be prepared to pay us to demystify the place sufficiently that she feels comfortable selling it…which is grand. I, personally, hope she agrees to our terms, because a week by the seaside with Annie and Gertie sounds excellent. Mind you, I'll be keeping my fingers crossed there's a pub, as well as a fish and chip shop. All the ingredients for the best *craic*, eh?' She winked at her colleagues.

Carol's fingers were flying across her keyboard. 'It's changed a lot since I was there last – I can tell that much right off the bat. Looks like there's a seasonal youth hostel…and, yes, a fish and chip shop, *and* a pub – so you won't starve, and you've got at least a few places where you can quite naturally engage the locals.'

Mavis concluded the meeting with meaningful looks directed at her two colleagues. 'Hopefully Gemma will say yes to our proposal; I'll let you know. Then it sounds as though Tudor and Alexander are going to have to cope with virtual billing and cooing for a while, eh?'

Annie laughed. 'Oi, I'll have you know that Tudor and I have never once billed, nor cooed, ta very much.'

'And Alexander's not given to either…except under extraordinary circumstances,' giggled Christine. 'But, look, if it's okay with everyone now – and, as if to prove we're both liars – I've promised to drive Annie to the Lamb and Flag where she and Tudor are having dinner in his flat above the pub early, because he's got tables booked for this St Dwynwen's Dinner he's been going on about for weeks.'

Annie leaped up. 'Oh heck, yes, look at the time. I said I'd be there by four…we'll be late if we don't go now. I did warn you, Mave.'

Mavis nodded. 'You did, and I know it's important to him, and you. I think it's rather nice that he's making so much of the Welsh equivalent of St Valentine's Day. Remember last year? That was when Ian Cottesloe was all over the place announcing the engagement between Henry and Stephanie. Now look at them – happily married, and a healthy baby. Just lovely.'

Christine stood, having turned off her laptop. 'Careful, Mavis – don't you go getting any ideas; I know Alexander and I are engaged to be married, but we haven't even set a date yet, and I have absolutely no plans to have children…at least, not that we've discussed in any case. Please don't make me feel there's a clock ticking somewhere.'

Carol smiled broadly. 'You're not even thirty yet, Christine, so you've got time to decide about children; but don't put off talking about it forever – we never know what life holds for us. There was me and David trying to get pregnant for years, while Stephanie and Henry only needed a couple of months. Plans are all well and good, but the hand you're dealt isn't always the one you'd have chosen. Full of surprises, is life. All you can do is make the most of them.'

Annie pulled on her coat as she replied, 'Well, I hope The Case of the Cursed Cottage doesn't hold too many surprises for us two, because I need a bit of stability for a while. As long as things don't start going bump in the night, I'll be alright. But now? Let's go, Chrissy – there's a roaring fire, a bowl of lamb stew, and the warm embrace of a lovely man waiting for me. Yes, Gert, I know…you can play with Rosie soon; how on earth does this dog know when she's off to be with her littermate?'

Mavis replied, 'I dare say she picks up on you looking forward to seeing Tudor. Now off with you all, and let me phone Gemma Thomas. I'll text you with any news, and I'll close up the office for the night. Will you come straight back here, to your flat, Christine?'

'No, Alexander's meeting me at the pub – then we'll both come back to the apartment later…he's driving up from London for the night.'

'This St Dwynwen's got a lot to answer for, though I'll admit I'd never even heard of her until we all moved here to Wales. Funny the things that pass one by,' said Mavis to Carol as Annie and Christine headed out. 'Will you and David be marking the occasion in some way?'

Carol grinned. 'You bet. David's cooking "something special" for us, and I spotted a bottle of bubbles at the back of the fridge – by mistake, of course. So, yes, a lovely evening should be had by all…as long as Albert decides to be a good baby and go to sleep. He's been a bit better this past couple of weeks, which is a relief; David and I were beginning to believe we'd never get more than a few hours of sleep at a time for the rest of our lives. What about you, Mavis? Dinner with Althea at the Dower House – just a normal evening?'

Mavis nodded. 'Aye, if anything with that woman can be called normal. She's in fine form at the moment, though she seems a little obsessed by her grandson – which is to be expected when it's your first, I dare say. Though I don't recall having been that way with mine.'

Carol smiled. 'Well, enjoy it, and give her my best. Good luck with the client; text me if I can help, but – otherwise – I'll do a bit of desktop browsing, send everyone what I find, and let's talk tomorrow about the online search I'm doing for Rhodri Lloyd about that bricklayer who's suing his client. I'll have something back from my enquiries by then, I'm sure. Bye.'

Mavis sat in the empty office and organized her desk, and her thoughts, before she began to type up the quote for Gemma Thomas; she had a good idea of costs, a plan to move ahead, and hoped the agency would have a new client before the end of the week.

CHAPTER THREE

Tudor Evans beamed when Annie walked into the pub, which did her no end of good. She'd managed to put on the brave face she knew was expected of her when she'd agreed to go back to Gower, but she needed to talk to someone about it, and Tudor was the right one for the job. She also knew she could bring it up at her appointment the next day with her counsellor, if she felt the need.

Tudor lifted the opening in the bar so Annie could slip through, and gave her a peck on the cheek as she passed beneath his arm.

'As you can see, it's as lively as a graveyard here at the moment,' he observed wryly, 'so I'll be up in about five minutes when I'm sure Aled knows what he's to do to keep an eye on things in the kitchen. You go on and settle yourself.'

Annie pecked back, and allowed Gertie to drag her toward the stairs as she called, 'Right-o, don't be long. I'll put me feet up and drop off otherwise…this one had me up before six this morning. If you want me awake, you'd better hurry. Yes, alright, Gert, don't pull so hard, you'll hurt yourself.'

Tudor's flat smelled wonderful – the lamb stew had obviously been cooking for hours – and looked welcoming, too; Annie had added several touches of décor over the past few months, and the place finally looked as comfortable as the man who lived there.

Gertie and Rosie greeted each other with great enthusiasm; the sisters were always delighted to spend time together, played nicely – usually – and often snuggled down, completely entwined, for naps. Annie loved the way that Gertie's glossy blackness intermingled with Rosie's almost buttery yellow fur, which was already a good bit longer than Gertie's. She was glad that Gertie's fur was as short and sleek as it was; it looked as though Tudor might be in for quite a few more hours of grooming duties than Annie as the years passed.

With the pups settled, Annie moved a few items around on shelves, and sniffed the kitchen.

She didn't dare lift the lid on the pot of stew – Tudor always knew when she'd done it and didn't like it one little bit, so she kicked her shoes into a corner, before curling up in Tudor's big armchair in front of the fire.

Convinced she hadn't nodded off, she was startled when Tudor appeared and rubbed the top of her head as he stood over her.

'My three favourite girls, all snuggled up and warm,' he said, smiling. 'If you could set the table, I'll bring out the stew. And there's a little surprise in the fridge, if you fancy checking in there.' He grinned impishly as he headed to the cooker, so Annie scampered happily to the fridge, where a half-bottle of excellent champagne and two champagne flutes were already well-chilled.

Half an hour later, they were both sitting back in their seats with full tummies, and empty bowls and glasses.

'That was – even by your standards – absolutely fantastic,' said Annie, reaching to kiss Tudor, who helped her out by leaning in.

'There was something different about tonight's lamb stew, but I can't put my finger on it.'

Tudor mugged an innocent face. 'I cannot imagine where I got the idea from, but I put a bit of hot sauce into it – just a bit, mind you – and I think that's made all the difference to the umami.' He blew her a kiss.

Annie smiled. 'My hot sauce? My good St Lucian stuff that I always carry about with me?' Tudor nodded. 'Hang on a minute…did you nick mine, or buy your own?' She gave him a playful push – which almost sent him sideways off his seat.

'Bought it online. I knew I could trust the brand because you, and your mum, swear by it, so I took a chance. Ordered four bottles. It was a good deal.'

Annie was amazed. 'You bought something online? Put hot sauce in your lamb stew? Gordon Bennett, what next? Getting a coffee machine that makes cappuccinos for the pub? Offering baked goods down there too? We'll make a twenty-first century, cosmopolitan man of you yet, Tudor Evans.'

Tudor laughed. 'Don't faint, but I have, in fact, been doing a bit of research into those fancy coffee machines; I've been thinking it might not be a bad idea to try to bring in the sort of person who'd go to a coffee shop or tea shop. There's nowhere in the village for people who don't want to be "in the pub", so how about I make a part of the pub a bit less pub-like? The Snug, was what I thought; dress it up a bit, have nicer cushions, vases, flowers, even tablecloths…you know the sort of thing. Look what you've done up here. I know you helped me out a bit in the early days, before we were even "us". But now? Well, now I think it's time I got a bit more serious about it.'

Annie stood and urged Tudor to do the same. As she hugged him tightly, Gertie and Rosie roused themselves from their positions guarding the fire, seemingly expecting there to be plates that needed to be licked clean at any moment. And there were, followed by Tudor announcing he'd have to get down to the bar in ten minutes, so they'd better do the washing up quickly, but then they'd leave everything to drain.

'First though, a final toast,' he said, pouring a mouthful of champagne into each glass, emptying the half-bottle. 'To St Dwynwen, true lovers, and the lovelorn, wherever they may be. *Dwi'n dy garu di*, Annie…I love you.'

Annie didn't attempt to repeat the Welsh, but said, 'And I love you too, Tudor.'

At the kitchen sink, she passed dishes and Tudor washed them. They chatted as they worked, with Tudor's main topic of conversation being about his 'plans' for the snug. 'Oh, and I forgot to tell you,' he said, wiping his hands on the tea towel, 'Marjorie Pritchard was in here late this morning. I don't know what that woman expects; I gave her a coffee from the drip-thingy and she moaned about it something rotten she did – which is what made me spend a bit of time looking online at better coffee machines to be honest with you, so maybe her whining will pay off for once.'

'What was she on about today? Other than the quality of your hot beverages, that is.' Annie was sure there'd be any number of things Marjorie felt in need of her particular type of attention.

'Oh, this and that. Came in to tell me that Iris Lewis is considering standing down from the village's social committee when we start the new year for it on Ash Wednesday, then went off at a tangent about her hands.'

Annie was puzzled. 'I get it that Iris might want to take things a bit easier these days – she's getting on, and there was that problem she had before Christmas. But what's wrong with Marjorie Pritchard's hands?'

Tudor hung up the tea towel, sighing. 'Well, to be fair, they did look a bit of a mess. She's got a friend from years back who's going through treatment for breast cancer, so Marjorie had taken her to some local day spa place, out at the Ash Court Country House Hotel. You know, that fancy place between Builth and Brecon?' Annie nodded; she'd heard of it, though had never been there. 'Well, this was a week or so back, and Marjorie is convinced they infected her fingers when she had a manicure there.'

Annie knew nothing about manicures, never having been keen on anyone touching her at all – except for medical, or possibly romantic, reasons. 'If it was that long ago, couldn't she have picked up the infection some other way? How does she know it happened there?'

'Apparently, her feet are the same. Had a mani-pedi, she said. Came in here wearing her gardening clogs because she's had to bandage her big toes, so now none of her other shoes will fit, it seems. And she was really worried about her friend – the one with cancer; her immune system is a mess, see, so Marjorie was scared in case the same thing had happened to her, but it seems she's alright, which Marjorie admitted was a relief. Anyway, she was going on and on about how she can't get even an apology from the woman who runs the spa, and is planning to make a formal complaint. Of course, in the interim, she rehearsed complaining to me. If I ran the place I'd apologize just to shut her up.'

Annie petted Gertie and Rosie, and gave each dog a treat. 'So would I, but then they might be admitting liability, I suppose. You have to be careful with a thing like that. Maybe Marjorie had a problem before she went to the spa, but just didn't know it?'

Tudor shrugged.

Annie continued, 'Or maybe she was allergic to something they used on her...one of the...products? Oh heck, I don't know, I've got no clue what they do to a person at places like that – other than things that look like torture, and cost an arm and a leg.'

'Not everyone needs beauty treatments,' said Tudor, gathering Annie to him. 'Like you. How could they improve upon bright eyes, perfect skin, and a smile like that?'

Annie chuckled. 'Yes, I'll come and check on the pups; yes, I'll put away the washing up; yes, I'll stay and help in any way I can downstairs tonight. Happy now? You haven't got to butter me up for me to do all that, you know.'

'I know...but I mean it. You're perfect the way you are.'

Annie broke the mood as she said, 'Come on then – let's go and make sure that any lovebirds coming here to celebrate the Welsh version of St Valentine tonight have the best evening possible.'

'Let's. But, before I go back to my duties, I just want you to have this.' Tudor reached into one of the cupboards under the kitchen counter, and pulled out a slightly lumpen, gift-wrapped...something.

Annie smiled, but felt a catch in her throat. 'I didn't know we was doing presents, Tude. I haven't got anything for you. Is that a thing, then? Presents on St Dwynwen's Day? I'm sorry – I didn't know.' She felt awful.

Tudor's face fell. 'No – no it's not a thing...but I wanted to give you this because it's our first one together, as a proper couple, and this is traditionally a gift a man gives to a woman to show his feelings for her, so there's absolutely no expectation on my part of any sort of reciprocation. Don't feel that – please don't...or you'll make me feel bad about doing this.'

The couple broke into laughter as they realized how the situation had spiralled.

Annie said, 'Right, then, I'll shut me gob and be grateful. Thanks, Tude. Can I open it now?'

Tudor nodded, grinning, so Annie pulled at the wrapping paper in a determined fashion.

Struggling with the tape, Annie glanced at him, and his expression reminded her of Gertie when the cupboard where her treats were stored was being opened.

Finally able to see what Tudor had given her, Annie was delighted, and amazed. 'Oh, Tude, it's beautiful.'

Tudor all but exploded, 'It's a love spoon, all carved from one piece of wood, if you can believe it…even that Celtic knot cage thing at the top. Magnificent, isn't it? I have no idea how the people who make them do it – but there's no question it's a work of art, right?'

Annie nodded, allowing herself a moment to take in all the details – two hearts intertwined, a double-bowled spoon at one end, the globe-shaped cage Tudor had described at the other. 'Oh Tude, it's lovely. Ta.'

'It's a tradition going back many hundreds of years in Wales for a man to give a spoon like this to the woman he loves…and this is the best day for me to do that: our first St Dwynwen's Day together.'

Annie wondered if she could smile more widely, or if her face would break if she did. She hugged Tudor as tight as she could, then said quietly, 'I'll cherish it forever.'

THURSDAY 26th JANUARY

CHAPTER FOUR

Althea Twyst, dowager duchess of Chellingworth, had eaten scrambled eggs, a sausage, two rashers of bacon, a tomato, and a pile of mushrooms for breakfast. Mavis MacDonald had nibbled on a piece of toast and marmalade, watching Althea munch her way through the feast as though she hadn't eaten for a week. Mavis wondered where she was putting it all – she wasn't aware that Althea had a hollow leg.

'That should keep you going for a wee while,' was all she said when Althea sat back in her chair looking smug, and satisfied.

'Is there any toast under the napkin, dear? Good, I'll just have half a piece,' was Althea's surprising response.

Mavis wondered why the octogenarian was so peckish; they'd enjoyed dinner together the previous evening, and Althea hadn't eaten any less than usual at that time.

'Where's this appetite coming from?' She knew she might as well be direct; since becoming Althea's housemate at the Dower House about a year earlier she'd always found it best to be forthright, and didn't see any reason to change.

Althea's dimples showed as she smiled. 'I have no idea. I woke up feeling ravenous, and can't think of a good reason to not give in to that feeling. I spoke to Cook first thing, and I'm so pleased she made as much as she did; I enjoyed every mouthful.'

'Good,' said Mavis, trying to not sound as though she were passing judgement. 'Are you away up to Chellingworth Hall for lunch with the new baby, today?'

Since the arrival of the currently nameless heir to the Chellingworth title, Althea had spent a good deal more time at the Hall than usual.

Mavis was pleased, because it obviously gave Althea great joy to spend time with her grandson, though she wondered how Althea's desire to be an actively attentive grandmother was being received by the baby's parents, and other grandparents. Reassuring herself that this wasn't, thankfully, her problem, Mavis realized she'd missed something when she heard Althea tutting.

'Sorry, dear, I was miles away,' said Mavis. 'What did you say?'

'I asked you what you thought of the name Eustace.'

'For the bairn?'

'Yes, for my grandson. I think it has a ring to it, and, though it's not a family name, I don't think it's a bad one. It has a bit of substance to it, don't you think?'

Mavis didn't need to give the name much thought at all. 'He'd be called Eustace Twyst – is that fair?'

Althea looked crestfallen. 'Ah, yes…it is a bit of a mouthful, isn't it? Though, of course, when one has a title one is so rarely referred to by one's given names. Henry's just "Chellingworth", usually. Hardly anyone uses "Twyst" for any reason, except within the family, and friends.'

Mavis considered Althea's worried face. 'Aye, but there'll be school, and you know how cruel children can be. I think maybe Eustace is no' the best name to go with Twyst. Let's keep trying, eh?'

Mavis had been fielding suggested names since the moment word had reached the Dower House that Stephanie had given birth to a boy, and even more so since it had become clear that choosing a name for the child was proving a challenge for his parents.

'How did you choose your boys' names, dear?' Althea was finally folding her linen napkin beside her empty plate.

Mavis chuckled. 'Ah now, that was easy. The first one was always going to be James, after both his grandfathers; my father was always known as Jimmy, while my father-in-law was always Jamie.'

'How strange,' said Althea.

'No' really, no' in Scotland, dear.'

'I think that's rather sweet,' said Althea, distractedly.

'Anyway, Duncan was my father's middle name – his other grandfather didn't have one – so that was our second boy done and dusted. Has "James" been discussed yet, by the way?' Mavis suspected it had been.

Althea nodded absently. 'Far too Scottish for a Welsh duke, we've all agreed that.'

'And you've all discussed "Edward", I suppose, him being the only son of Henry VIII. I know how important the Tudors are to the Twysts.'

Althea nodded. 'Yes, but he died so young, poor thing, that Stephanie didn't care for it. Arthur's been discounted too, Henry VIII's older brother; like poor Devereaux, he died before taking the title, leaving the younger son to step up, like Henry did...my Henry, not Henry VIII...who also did – if you see what I mean. Personally, I rather liked Arthur, but Stephanie's mother said it made the baby sound like an old man, and Stephanie said he doesn't "look like" an Arthur. I've always been quite taken by Arthurian legends myself, so think that's a shame. But, there we are, I'm just the dowager; it's nothing to do with me.'

Mavis wasn't going to allow the conversation to take a turn, so said, 'You'll be off there for lunch, and we'll dine together, as usual?'

'Indeed. There's still a lot to do. There are the godparents to be agreed, the date of the christening, and I shall be proposing that I furnish the child with his christening mug. I have no idea if the Timbers want to be the ones to do that, but it's a tradition within the family, and I'd like to maintain it. Henry's was crafted by a celebrated silversmith to a design created by my own dear, departed Chelly. Clementine's was one the silversmith had already made – much more feminine, and flowing in design. Chelly said he wasn't good at that sort of thing, which was why we picked one they already had. The one he designed for Henry was quite plain, almost severe.'

Mavis had never seen the point of christening mugs, or cups, or spoons, though she'd been grateful to be given them when her boys had been born by those to whom such things did matter.

Of course, she'd passed them on to her sons when they'd moved into their own homes.

She suspected that mugs had more or less died a death as traditional gifts for babies, though realized things would be a little different, and much more traditional, when it came to all the palaver that was likely to surround the arrival of a future duke.

'Have you got a whole load of christening mugs up at Chellingworth, going back for hundreds of years?' Mavis wondered what it would be like for a child to never leave the home into which they were born, and couldn't imagine it.

Althea looked thoughtful. 'I have no idea, to be honest. Indeed, I don't even know when the giving of such an item began within the family. I must look into that. I know Chelly always used his mug for his toothbrush. It was an ugly thing – rather blackened silver, lumpen, heavily embossed with figures, birds, and lettering. It even had a lid with a great big crown on top. He kept that in a drawer, because it was always catching on things.'

Mavis laughed. 'And did his own father design that for him?'

'Oh no, dear, it was given to Chelly's grandfather by Tsar Alexander III when they were on a yachting holiday together. Chelly's grandfather had been invited to Denmark by Prince George – the one who became George V later on – and they bumped into the tsar and his Danish wife there.'

'As one does,' said Mavis, trying to hide a smile.

'Indeed, as one would have done,' said Althea, dimpling. 'They spent some time on the Imperial yacht, and I recall Chelly telling me his grandfather helped the tsar, somehow, when some sort of storm blew up. That's all I know, really, but it resulted in the tsar giving Chelly's grandfather the silver cup. By then, Chelly's father had already been born so it wasn't passed to him; instead, it was given to Chelly as his christening mug. It was rather large, I recall. I wonder what happened to it. I dare say it's about the Hall somewhere. I wonder if this child might like that one?'

Mavis shrugged.

Althea continued, 'No – that's not fair. I shall have a new one commissioned, or maybe I could find something I like that already exists. I want to give something to my grandson that will be his, outright, even if he chooses to add it to the general Twyst pile after his time.'

Mavis couldn't help but say, 'Will the bairn no' grow up surrounded by enough stuff?'

Althea didn't quite tear up, but Mavis suspected she was on the verge of it. 'I understand why you say that, Mavis, and – coming from a humble background myself, not born to this sort of life – I recall thinking that very thing when I arrived at Chellingworth Hall as a bride. But what I've learned since then is this: the dukes of Chellingworth don't really "own" the Estate or the Hall in the way normal people own their homes. Nor do they "own" the paintings, objects d'art, furnishings, or even the books in the library. No, they are simply caretakers, ensuring that all they inherit is handed down the generations safely, securely, and with its historical relevance being recorded. It's a strange life, to be so blessed with wonderful material objects, yet to also be chained to them. I'll not complain, Mavis, because – heaven knows – there are so many people who have so little; I absolutely understand my privilege. But I also understand the responsibilities that come along with it. I saw how they weighed upon my dear Chelly, and I see the same happening to Henry – though Chelly was rather better equipped to deal with them, having known from his earliest days they would, in fact, be his responsibilities to bear. Henry wasn't expecting it; I know he feels the loss of his chosen path as an artist very keenly. I'm rather hoping he finds his new role as a father to be transformative. He needs – somehow – to learn to see the world through fresh eyes. To truly understand the blessings of his position, rather than just its burdens.'

Mavis nodded slowly. 'I cannae disagree with you on that point,' she said quietly.

Gathering herself, Mavis added with more vigor, 'Now then...I know you let me live here for next to no financial contribution, but I still have expenses, and that means I have to earn some sort of living. I also have a role to play in three others being able to do the same, so I'd best get away to the office. We've a potential new client I'm hoping to hear from, and I need to organize a few things I have arranged for next week, too. Enjoy your planning of the christening – and don't forget, it's no' a military operation, and it's really up to the parents to decide about the godparents. Right?'

Althea dimpled. 'Of course, dear.'

CHAPTER FIVE

Carol's calico cat, Bunty, slinked around her ankles as she stood at the Aga warming her hands; she'd been outside hanging up some washing, and the air was chilly. It was due to be a clear morning with rain by the evening, so the forecaster had said; she hoped the clothes would be dry before the rain came – she hated having clotheshorses all over the place. Albert seemed to get through so many little outfits; other mums she knew had warned her that would get even worse once he started walking. Scooting about on his bum managed to get him grubby enough, and now that he was pulling himself up to be able to stand, she wondered when he might take those first magical steps…though she knew it could be some time yet.

'Not long now until you'll be having your first birthday, is it?' Carol bounced Albert on her hip as she cooed at him. He grinned and gurgled happily, delighting his mother. 'Well, a few months, anyway. You've been out of me now for as long as you were growing inside in me, and just look at the size of you. Who's a big boy, then?'

'Me,' said David as he appeared at the kitchen door. 'And this big boy needs some coffee. Any in the pot – or has your mam drunk it all, already, Albert?'

Carol laughed as her husband kissed the top of her head, then his son's cheek.

'There's loads there,' she said. 'I've only managed one cup. But I did get the clothes on the line, and this one's clean and fed – ready for his dad to take over.' She looked up at the kitchen clock. 'I've got a meeting online in half an hour, and I need to check a few things beforehand. Can you keep an eye on him while I go in the other room to do that?'

'Yeah, put him in his cage, and he'll be fine.'

'It's his safe play area, David. Come on now, it's not a cage.'

David looked askance at the playpen in the middle of the kitchen floor. 'Just pop him in there, throw in some raw meat, and he'll be fine for days, I'm sure.' He laughed. 'Once the caffeine's kicked in, and I've shoved some cereal into me, I'll give him a proper cuddle while his mam's working.' He lifted Albert from Carol's arms, plopped him into his playpen, tossed in a few cuddly toys, and headed for the coffee pot. 'See you when you've finished. Will we be having lunch together?'

Carol pushed herself out of the kitchen chair, pulled her cardigan around her shoulders and called, 'That's the plan. Hopefully with no interruptions, today.' She headed into the dining room, where the table was covered with papers, and her two laptops.

By the time Mavis and Christine appeared on the camera set up at the office, and Annie appeared on hers, Carol had reached a good place in her note-taking, and was ready to give the team her preliminary report.

Mavis opened the meeting by saying, 'I've no' heard back from Gemma Thomas, so it's over to you, Carol. If you could bring us all up to speed, that would be helpful. And, by the way – Annie's taking this meeting at her cottage because she's got an appointment which means she'll be leaving in an hour, so let's be focused.'

Carol shrugged. 'I was planning to be,' she said, feeling a bit judged. 'I hope you've all read the notes I sent,' she began. Knowing Christine well enough to be able to interpret her expression, Carol immediately realized at least she hadn't, so added, 'In case you haven't, here's a summary: Rhodri Lloyd, solicitor, is our client in this instance; he has a client – Mark Morgan – who has asked Rhodri to act on his behalf because he is being sued for one hundred thousand pounds by a bricklayer – Ben Stirling – who undertook some work at the Morgan home, where he claims Morgan caused him to fall from his ladder while building a wall in the Morgans' garden.'

'Oh heck, 'said Annie. 'What happened?'

Carol sighed, 'The claim states, specifically, that Morgan caught a rope with his foot that pulled the ladder to one side, causing Stirling to fall approximately eight feet.'

'Nasty, said Annie. 'Badly hurt, was he?'

Carol replied, 'It is not disputed by Rhodri's client that paramedics attended, and that the bricklayer, Stirling, was discharged from hospital with a "suspected sprain" of the cruciate ligament in his left leg. The incident took place four months ago. Stirling is claiming he is still unable to work, and has sued Morgan for loss of earnings which he estimates to run to the stated one hundred thousand pounds, far beyond that which is covered by his own accident insurance.'

Christine said, 'I didn't think we'd become such a litigious society.'

Mavis shrugged. 'Aye, well…it's an ill wind, Christine.'

Carol continued, 'Mark Morgan is, as Rhodri put it, "incandescent", and wants to countersue. First, he's questioning Stirling's diagnosis; with such soft-tissue injuries, it's often difficult for medical imaging to be conclusive. Secondly, he's questioning the amount being claimed; he says there is no way Ben Stirling could have reasonably expected to have made that amount of income in that time period. Thirdly, Morgan has paid Stirling in full for the wall to be built, but the work remains incomplete. This has led, in turn, to Morgan not having been able to move forward with the sale of his house, because the wall needs to be completed before it's presented to the market – or so says his estate agent. Thus, Morgan is asking Rhodri to countersue on his behalf citing lost potential income due to fluctuations in house values during the past few months. All in all, it's a bit of a mess, especially since Morgan absolutely refuses to pay another builder to complete the work Stirling began; it has become a matter of honor, he says. Rhodri, being the sort of person he is, has pointed out to his client that he might achieve a better outcome if he can prove that the original injury to Stirling is no longer preventing him from fulfilling his contract.'

'A case of Stirling swinging the lead?' Annie's tone was dismissive. 'Has he pulled anything like this before?'

Carol smiled. 'Just what I've been looking into. But it's complicated. First of all, of course I can't access any of Stirling's medical records, so I have no idea if he's "suffered injuries" before.'

'Bet he has,' said Annie, tutting.

Carol pressed on, 'Secondly, he's a sole trader, but has operated under at least ten different business names over the past seventeen years or so. I have found one instance where a ruling was made in favour of a company with a name that matches one he used to have, and am awaiting the arrival of some information – which is taking longer than I'd hoped – that will allow me to be certain it was him. The case in point was a similar sort of situation, but – even if it turns out it was him on that occasion – maybe it could be argued that two similar accidents over the length of his career might not be, given his job, that unusual. However, on balance, I think Stirling is – as Annie so elegantly put it – swinging the lead, but there's nothing to go on, other than my gut.'

'That sounds like a lot of business names to have had over the years,' agreed Christine. 'Fishy, if nothing else.'

'Mebbe just a way of getting out of uncomfortable positions regarding debts, or even taxes,' said Mavis, 'but it sounds, Carol, as though you're suggesting we move to stage two, as we agreed with Rhodri we might have to ahead of taking on this case.'

Carol nodded. 'I do. An eyes-on operation is needed, with the aim of gathering hard evidence of Stirling not being as incapable of work as he's claiming.'

'Is he saying he needs to use crutches or a wheelchair? Anything easy to spot like that?' Annie asked hopefully.

'Knee brace and a walking stick, he says,' replied Carol.

Annie said, 'That's a shame; he could be wearing a brace under his trousers and we'd be none the wiser…and he could always say he'd forgotten his stick. We've all heard that old chestnut before when we've done surveillance jobs for other attempted frauds like this.'

All four women nodded thoughtfully.

Carol said, 'Rhodri Lloyd agreed that we could put three days into the observation – but we all know it might be fruitless. That said, the bricklayer, Stirling, lives relatively locally, in Builth Wells, so it shouldn't be too difficult for any of us to do it.'

'Handy, at least,' noted Mavis.

Carol added, 'I've already trawled his social media and there are no recent photos showing him sprinting about the place – in fact, there are quite a lot showing him using the stick, and looking pretty miserable. He lives with his wife and son; plays for the darts team at a pub called the Screeching Owl, which has a room with a small stage where they specialize in heavy metal bands, it seems; he's an enthusiastic member of the local motor club, which has been around for a hundred years, believe it or not.'

'Who'll be doing the watching?' Christine was the only one brave enough to ask, thought Carol. 'If Gemma Thomas comes through, me and Annie will be down in Gower, and you can't do it, can you, Carol? Sounds like you're it, Mavis.'

Mavis sighed. 'Aye, well you know I'm never at my happiest when I'm on watch duty, but at least I have a couple of excellent audio books I can be listening to while I do it. I'll run everything past Rhodri Lloyd first, of course – and check that circumstances havenae changed since he briefed us. But it sounds as though I'll be taking this one forward. Have you named the case for us yet, Annie, by the way?'

Annie offered, 'The Case of the Invalid Invalid?'

Carol grinned. 'Oh, I like that one, Annie; isn't the English language wonderful? Two words spelled the same way, but pronounced differently, and with different meanings. No wonder it's so hard to learn.'

'We could call it The Case of Stirling the Lead-Swinger? Nah, that's no good. Or what about The Case of the Belligerent Bricklayer?' added Annie brightly. 'Maybe that's better?'

Carol said, 'Nothing I can find out online about Stirling suggests he's that way inclined, so maybe it's best to not make assumptions?'

Mavis said, 'Ach, I for one hope he doesnae turn out to be belligerent – so let's no' tempt fate. We'll go with The Case of the Invalid Invalid, and enjoy the play on words, eh?'

The women all agreed, and Carol made a note of it in her report.

'I'll get all this over to you, Mavis, so you can talk to Rhodri about it, okay? Mavis?' Carol couldn't see Mavis any longer. 'Are you still there?'

'Aye, I'm here,' said Mavis, reappearing. 'My mobile was just out of my reach, thanks for passing it, Christine. There's a message come in from Gemma Thomas: she's signed the contract, and she'll get the cottage in Port Beynon ready for Christine and Annie to arrive on Saturday. That alright with everyone?'

Christine beamed. 'That's grand. How about I pick up you and Gertie at your place about ten on Saturday morning, Annie? Okay?'

'Lovely, doll. Gert's quite happy in the back of your Range Rover, in't you Gert?' Carol saw Annie's head disappear as she reached to – presumably – pet Gertie. 'And she's got her own little wheelie bag for everything she'll need – the one I give Tude when she stays with him. It'll be nice to be able to take her with me, for once. And good cover, too, I'd have thought…dogs and winter beaches go together like fish and chips, don't they? And I look forward to lots of both. I'll get back to looking into the place now we know we're going. That stuff you sent through will be very helpful, thanks, Car.'

Carol always rose to the bait…eventually. 'It's Caro*l*, Annie, though why I still bother correcting you after all these years I don't know. Right then – I hope we're all sorted, because I have a son and husband who could do with my attention…after I email everything to you first, of course, Mavis.'

'Thank you. I have nothing else,' replied Mavis. 'Anyone got any other business leads? Anything they'd like to discuss?'

Annie waggled her hand, making Carol smile. 'I've already had a good, long chat with Tude about me going back to Gower, and I'll talk about it at my session today, too. I just want you all to know I'm certainly up for it, even if I'm a bit…unsure of how I'll feel when I get there. That's all, really.'

Christine said, 'I'll have your back, Annie. That's what friends are for. And I bet we won't have any problems…you know, of the sort you had last time.'

'Flippin' well hope not,' said Annie, then she was gone.

Carol did as she'd promised and sent a lengthy email to Mavis, then toddled into her kitchen, where she found her husband holding her son on his lap while Bunty sat on the table, leaning forward and sniffing at Albert's toes…not something Carol had ever seen Bunty do before. She took a mental snapshot – and her heart was full.

CHAPTER SIX

Stephanie was in the morning room with her son cradled in her arms, her mother and mother-in-law at her side, and her butler looking on, as she examined the Chellingworth christening gown he'd just handed to her in a large box.

'Oh dear,' she said, 'it could do with a little attention. It's extremely old, incredibly precious, and far too fragile for a baby to wear, don't you think? Shouldn't it be preserved somehow? We could find something new – and maybe more appropriate for the twenty-first century – for my son's christening.'

Stephanie noted the surprise on the dowager duchess's face as she said, 'I don't recall it looking this bad when Clementine was christened – though, of course, that's over fifty years ago. In my recollections of her day in church, and Henry's, this gown was white, not this biscuity beige. Where did you say it's been kept, Edward?'

'I understand that the box was located in a wardrobe in the old nursery, Your Grace.'

Althea said, 'That makes sense, I suppose – the gown being connected with the children. I'm racking my brains to remember what happened to it after Clemmie's christening; I vividly recall she was sick on it, poor child. But, yes, you're quite right, it looks to be in a rather sorry state, despite all this…oh! I remember! It was sent to London to be specially cleaned and packaged. I don't recall the name of the place, but I dare say the records will be somewhere about.' Althea peered at the gown. 'To be fair, they seem to have done rather a good job with the lace – that seems to be intact, and not too brittle-looking. But the silk? That colour is all wrong, and it looks almost as flimsy as the tissue paper with which it's been padded. Dare we touch it, do you think?'

Sheila Timbers finally spoke. 'You want my grandson to wear that ratty-looking thing? How old is it?'

Stephanie did her best to keep her cool. 'It's all written down – there's a document inside the lid of the box. Go on, Mum, have a read.'

As Sheila Timbers opened the envelope embossed with the Chellingworth crest, Althea squared her small shoulders and said, 'It was made for the sixteenth duke's christening in...um...1874, I think,' she said proudly. 'It's been worn by every Twyst child since then.'

Shelia said, 'There's a list of names in this note: Devereaux Twyst, Camille Twyst, Henry Twyst – would that have been your husband, Althea?' Althea nodded. 'Then there's a Charlotte Twyst, Devereaux Twyst, Henry again, then Clementine.'

Althea smiled wistfully. 'Camille was my dear, departed Chelly's aunt. He spoke of her as an ethereal figure, who lived...well, in the rooms Clementine uses when she's here, actually, those being the traditional living quarters for the eldest daughter of the family. Camille never married, and died when Chelly was very young, he told me. Then Charlotte was my Chelly's younger sister; she married a French count, and drowned when she fell from his yacht off the coast of Amalfi. I never met her, because she'd died before I ever met Chelly, though I always wished I had – she sounded most vivacious. The most recent Devereaux would have been Chelly's firstborn, of course, and then there were my Henry and Clementine.'

Stephanie noticed that Althea had become a little misty-eyed as she spoke, and was irritated when her mother snapped, 'High time for a new gown, then, I'd have said.'

Althea looked shocked. 'But there wouldn't be time. The Twysts have always been christened very quickly. It would take months to have a new gown made.' She looked at Stephanie with surprise, 'Surely you've set a date for the christening.'

Stephanie could feel the blood pumping through her temples and suspected her blood pressure was climbing, which she knew wasn't good for her. She told herself to stay calm.

She replied as evenly as possible, 'No, Althea, we haven't set a date; Henry assured me the only reason there was a tradition of rapid christenings came about as the result of great tragedies in centuries past when quite a few infants…didn't last very long. Not even when they were the child of a duke. We're in no hurry. These days, some people wait until the child is one, or even two, years old.'

She didn't dare look at Althea who said very quietly, 'Oh, I see.'

Her mother didn't help when she said quite happily, 'Even so, I'm sure they've got some very nice choices for a new gown in London. Maybe Harrods?'

Stephanie was sure she saw Althea shudder…she certainly saw her mother-in-law's little fists develop white knuckles as she said, 'If this gown is no longer fit for purpose, another should be created to match it. I believe we should do all we can to preserve the traditions of the line. There are dressmakers who will be able to find suitable lace and silks to be able to recreate this gown. It is the Chellingworth gown, and there should be a new Chellingworth gown for this child's christening, and for this child's children to use…and theirs, down the generations yet to come. I don't think that something one might buy in a shop – even if it was once a very nice shop – would do at all. That is my opinion. The Chellingworth gown must be recreated.'

Stephanie and Althea finally made eye contact as Althea continued, 'And I believe that this child should be christened within the next few weeks, or at least within the next two months. What about St David's Day? March the first, your wedding anniversary, Stephanie. That would be suitable, don't you think? The patron saint of Wales's day, and one year after your wedding. Yes, it would be most appropriate.'

Scrolling on her phone's screen, Sheila Timbers snapped, 'It's a Wednesday.'

'So?' Althea sounded puzzled.

Sheila said, 'You can't have a christening on a Wednesday; no one would come.'

Althea stood. 'It's the christening of a duke's heir; whatever the day of the week, those who are invited will attend,' she said firmly.

Sheila harrumphed.

Althea continued, 'I shall, of course,take responsibility for the recreation of the gown, and I shall see to it that this child receives a suitable christening mug to commemorate his baptism, too.'

When Henry sauntered into the room, Stephanie said, 'I wasn't expecting you, dear. How lovely of you to join us.' Relief washed over her.

'He's like the Spanish Inquisition, but without the soft cushions, or the comfy chair,' said Althea sharply.

Stephanie explained to her mother, 'Althea's a great fan of Monty Python.'

Sheila's eyebrows shot up and her tone became dismissive. 'Never saw what all the fuss was about, myself. Just a lot of privileged university boys writing silly skits, inventing excuses to be able to dress up as women as often as possible. Like a posh panto.'

Althea tutted, then said to her son, 'The Chellingworth christening gown has been inspected and found wanting, Henry, and I was just talking about your boy's christening mug, a tradition for we Twysts, as you know.'

'Ah yes, the good old christening mug,' said Henry, joining the family group with a spring in his step and a smile on his face. 'I used mine to hold my pencils on my desk in the nursery, as I recall. I say, I wonder what became of it. You always used to tell me how father had designed it for me himself, didn't you, Mother?'

Stephanie watched as her husband kissed his mother's cheek, then paused, and looked at each of the three women in turn. 'Is everything...alright?' As she'd feared, the atmosphere in the room was tangible; it had to be if even Henry had noticed something was awry.

'The Chellingworth christening gown needs to be replaced, Henry, so I shall see to it,' said Althea rising. 'And I shall also be the one giving your son his christening mug.'

Stephanie could feel her temples thump as Althea straightened her back, the way she always did when she was being...assertive.

The dowager continued, 'By the way, Henry – yes, your father put a great deal of thought into the one he designed for you; it would be nice to think you have more of a connection to it than your poor recollection of where it might now reside suggests. And I'd like to take your father's mug back to the Dower House with me. Where might it be – do you know?'

Stephanie's heart went out to her poor husband, who looked as though he realized he'd stepped onto a landmine, and now didn't know what to do for the best except to stand stock-still and stare into space, helpless with panic.

'Your mother's just suggested March the first as a potential date for our son's christening, Henry. How do you feel about that?' Stephanie hoped her husband would repeat what he'd said to her on more than one occasion, about being quite happy to wait for at least a few months before the service. However, as soon as she saw the expression on his face as he looked at her, she knew he wouldn't.

'St David's Day? Our first wedding anniversary? Oh yes, that sounds splendid.' Henry rolled on the balls of his feet.

'It's a Wednesday,' said Sheila Timbers flatly.

Henry looked puzzled. 'Would that make a difference? I cannot imagine that it would.'

'Exactly,' said Althea quietly, glancing at Sheila.

Stephanie decided the situation called for action. 'I wonder if you'd all excuse me. Our son needs feeding, Henry.' She stood, and gathered her child to her bosom.

Henry looked puzzled. 'But surely you just fed him? I saw you do it.'

Stephanie knew he wasn't catching on, so said firmly, 'Well he didn't feed satisfactorily, so I'll take him upstairs where both he and I will be quiet and calm. I might join you all for lunch, but please, don't wait for me.' She nodded her head, hoping Henry would follow her – and was relieved when he did.

As she crossed the Great Hall, Henry walked beside her. 'Are you quite well, dear? You seemed a little…frazzled in there,' he said.

Stephanie paused and hissed, 'Yes I am frazzled, Henry. Your mother is taking over. The christening gown, the christening mug, the date for the christening…she's trying to impose her will on me. On us. And I won't stand for it, Henry. Granted the Chellingworth christening gown is too old and fragile to be used again, but shouldn't *we* be the ones to replace it? And wouldn't *you* like to design a christening mug for your firstborn, like your father did for you? Though she's quite correct that you should know where yours is. And if she wants your father's blessed mug for the Dower House, then at least find that one and give it to her. Good luck with those two at lunch – and, be warned, my mother's not going to want your mother to take the lead in everything – so you'd better make sure war doesn't break out over the cheese souffles. You're a father now, Henry – a father. Time you began to act like an adult at least. And tell Edward I'll have my luncheon in our private sitting room upstairs, thank you.'

Stephanie concentrated on walking up the staircase with her precious cargo, but managed to catch sight of Henry as she did so. He was doing a very creditable impersonation of a fish, his mouth working, but no sounds coming from it.

CHAPTER SEVEN

Annie had left Tudor to attend to his duties at the pub, and was crossing the springy, emerald grass of Anwen's village green, allowing Gertie to gambol at the fullest extent of her lead. She sometimes thought she should pinch herself when she looked at her picturesque, thatched cottage. One of only three that sat on one side of the green, she knew she was lucky to be able to rent it from the Chellingworth Estate for next to nothing, and she'd formed a surprisingly deep attachment to it in the year she'd been living there.

'Young Gertie's taking you for a quick walk before the rain gets here, is she, Annie?'

Annie's heartrate quickened as she heard the voice of Marjorie Pritchard; having earned her reputation as something of a tartar over decades of committee meetings in the village, Annie hoped Marjorie wasn't going to try to get her to volunteer for…something. Annie was always happy to help, when she could, but hated the idea of making a regular commitment.

Hoping to reach the safety of her front door as quickly as possible, Annie's spirits sank as Marjorie stopped beside it; there was no escaping her. She sighed and slapped a smile on her face. 'Let's get it over with, shall we, Gert?' she whispered, then added more loudly, 'She deserves a bit of a romp, she's been a good girl, and if she tires herself out now she might just need a short walk when it's wet later on.'

The two women greeted each other with smiles at Annie's doorstep; Marjorie had to look up at Annie who, at six feet, towered over her. Annie could see dark circles beneath the woman's eyes – not normal for her. Recalling that Tudor had warned her that Marjorie was in a bit of a state about her hands, Annie wondered if she dared ask after the woman's health, but politeness dictated she should, so she did.

'No, I'm not alright, thank you for asking. Look at these.' Marjorie Pritchard pulled her hands out of her pockets, then carefully peeled off one of her white cotton gloves. 'Look. It's a miracle I'm not dead. It shouldn't be allowed. Won't even offer me my money back. Did Tudor tell you what I've been going through?'

Annie nodded as she tried to stop Gertie from wrapping her lead around both women's legs. 'He said you'd been to the day spa at the Ash Court Country House Hotel, and didn't have a very good experience. How's your chum, by the way? She's not got any infections, like you clearly have, has she? That could be dangerous, given her illness.' Annie sounded concerned because she was; just because she thought manicures were a complete waste of time and money it didn't mean you shouldn't be able to have one safely if you wanted. And there was no question that Marjorie's hand looked a right mess – it had to be horribly painful.

Marjorie sighed, and gingerly pulled her glove back into place, wriggling her fingers gently, and wincing. 'Thank heavens she doesn't. No problems at all. Small mercies, and all that. I was telling Sharon at the shop just this morning that I might talk to someone about suing the place. They won't take any responsibility at all for what they've done to me. I mean, what if more people end up like this? The doctor's given me some cream, and some antibiotics, but I could be this way for weeks. It's very uncomfortable. What do you think?'

Annie hated being asked for advice; she'd just spent a good part of her day seeking counsel from a professional, making her even more uncomfortable about being asked to dole it out…and to Marjorie Pritchard, of all people, who was usually the first to give everyone advice about everything, whether she'd been asked for it or not. But Annie knew that Marjorie had a good heart, and often did what she did for the best of reasons, even if she managed to be incredibly irritating when she did it.

'Would it help if the WISE women looked into it for you? You know, before you go spending money on solicitors.'

Annie couldn't believe what she'd just heard herself say; Carol might have said something like it, or even Christine – but her? Maybe fortnightly sessions with a counsellor were softening her to the point where her hard, outer shell would just dissolve.

She panicked and hastily added, 'I'd have to get the rest of the team to agree, of course…and we might get no further than you would, of course.' How far could she backtrack, she wondered?

Marjorie pounced. 'Oh, that would be lovely. If it wouldn't be too much trouble, of course.' She lifted her handbag with the crook of her elbow. 'Have a look in there – go on. There's a leaflet in there from the place, and I've written the names on it of the manager of the spa, and the manager of the hotel – though she gave me the brushoff, saying that the spa runs as a totally independent business, just renting the space from the hotel. Covering her backside, she was.'

Annie rummaged inside Marjorie's handbag until she managed to pluck out a rather crumpled glossy leaflet. She squinted at Marjorie's scrawl.

'That's what got me into this state,' said Marjorie vehemently. 'That offer they had of two mani-pedis for the price of one, if you booked between those specific times. I thought it would be a nice treat for Denise, my friend with cancer. No good deed goes unpunished, they say, don't they? Well, it seems that's true, for me.'

'Does this say Willow?' Annie couldn't make out Marjorie's handwriting at all.

Marjorie tutted. 'Can't even write properly, can I? Yes, Willow Richards. I don't think it's her given name, but that's what the manager of the spa is called, and that's the name the manager of the hotel told me to use if I was to put anything in writing. Foreign that one is – the hotel manager – I believe, though I've never met her face-to-face.'

Annie smiled, 'And Willow herself?'

Marjorie nodded. 'I've met Willow, of course, because she's actually at the spa greeting you when you arrive. To be fair, they've got a lovely reception area, and she's – well, she's got a presence.'

'How do you mean?'

Marjorie's brow furrowed, 'Tall thing she is, like you, but she's not proper black like you – you know, not born that way. No, she's just dark brown, which you can see quite clearly is because she tans, not because it's natural. And her hair? That should have set the alarm bells ringing for me, I suppose; white it is, not even blonde, with green streaks in it. Oh, listen to me – as I'm saying it out loud, I'm realizing she looks like a willow tree. Oh, yes, very clever. I see. Anyway, a young thing she is, can only be in her mid-thirties, and she's running the whole spa; all I can say is she doesn't know how to keep the place clean, and safe. If nothing else there must be some sort of health bylaws or something she's breaking.'

Having opened her mouth to offer help, Annie thought she'd better take the matter seriously. 'How about you come indoors and I'll make you a cuppa – you can tell me everything you've done so far, and I'll take notes. Then I'll be fully informed before I talk to my colleagues about it.'

Marjorie literally licked her lips. 'A cup of tea would be lovely. Parched, I am. Sharon didn't even have time to boil a kettle let alone make a pot when I was over there just now – people popping in all the time. Not for much, of course, but that's not what going to the shop is about, is it?'

Annie couldn't imagine why you'd go to a shop unless you needed to buy at least something, but knew how Sharon's reputation as the fount of all knowledge in the area drew in her local devotees, who wanted to make sure they weren't missing out on some juicy local news.

With Gertie making it plain that she knew she was due to be fed, and Marjorie standing there with her tongue all but hanging out, Annie stuck out her chin, pulled her keys from her bag and unlocked her door saying, 'Right then, you settle yourself, I'll feed this one, and we'll share a pot and some crumpets. It's about the right time of day for crumpets, I'd say.'

Marjorie beamed. 'Oh I love a toasted crumpet, me. Any Marmite by any chance?'

Annie chuckled. 'If not, I'll pop over to Sharon's because she's bound to have a jar there.'

'She'd hardly be able to claim to know her customers if she didn't have any Marmite on the shelves,' agreed Marjorie, as Annie closed the door behind them.

FRIDAY 27th JANUARY

CHAPTER EIGHT

Annie sat at her desk in the office smiling brightly at Carol on the screen, whose expression was betraying her surprise as she sat at her kitchen table in the village.

Carol said, 'You actually offered to help Marjorie Pritchard? Without someone threatening to chase you with a pack of wolves as you ran naked through Brecon if you didn't?'

Annie nodded. 'Yeah, well, I had a weak moment and felt sorry for her,' she said softly. 'And having shared a pot with her, I feel even more sympathy for her now. She could hardly hold a cup because her hands are so bad, poor thing. Imagine being like that for who knows how long? And all because she had a manicure. They must have broken some rules, or laws, surely? I tried a bit of Googling last night, but everything seemed vague. Don't suppose you could have a bit of a poke around, could you, Car? Car*ol*. Sorry, doll.'

Carol gave Annie something that started as a withering look, but shifted to a warm smile. 'I'll have a bit of a look-see while you tell us all about it. I can listen and search at the same time. I've got the time to do a favor for Marjorie, haven't I, Mavis?'

Mavis shrugged. 'Aye, well, you've sent me everything about Stirling the bricklayer, you've sent Annie and Christine all you could find out about the cottage in Port Beynon, and those are our two cases at the moment so, aye, I dare say you do. Fire away, Annie, and have at it, Carol.'

Annie referred to her notepad, and talked through all the information she'd gathered from Marjorie. No one interrupted, and she'd taken good notes.

By the time they all had empty tea mugs, Annie concluded. 'So that's it. She says the place looked clean, which was why she was happy to have the treatment she did. The only good thing is that her friend wasn't hurt in the same way, and – to be fair to Marjorie – while I could tell she's in pain, and rightfully angry, I do think that's her main concern…that no one else gets the same sort of infection. So – have you got anything to add, Carol?'

'A bit. You need a business licence to run a nail bar, or do massages or other therapies, as you'd expect,' said Carol. 'Each county in the UK has different rules about health and safety, so that's a local government thing. Here, in Powys, they use the standards laid down in the Health and Safety Executive's "Control of Substances Hazardous to Health" guidelines – COSHH, for short. There are detailed regulations about all sorts of aspects of nail bars, hairdressers' premises, massage and other treatments, too. But the thing is, it all seems a bit…well, I don't get the impression there are inspectors breathing down the necks of the practitioners or businesses offering these services on a daily basis…or even at all, unless it's when they start up, or if there are a lot of complaints about a place.'

'I dare say it's one of those "not enough people to keep an eye on things" situations,' said Mavis sagely.

'Surely it's all got to come down to management, and wanting to have a good, clean reputation for a good, clean spa,' said Annie. 'Which is why I'm surprised they haven't been more accommodating of Marjorie. I mean, you'd think they'd do at least something to…well, maybe they can't help her now, because that's up to her doctor, but they should have been able to spot the fact she's the type of woman who's not going to lie down and take this sort of thing quietly.'

Christine nodded. 'You're not kidding. Maybe her reputation hasn't reached as far as the five-star luxury of the Ash Court Country House Hotel, but anyone with two brain cells can tell Marjorie Pritchard is not the sort of woman you can brush off.'

Mavis said, 'Aye, well if she said it looked clean, and her friend's not been affected, maybe it wasnae just what they did to her, but maybe she did something to herself either before or afterwards that caused this infection. Annie – was she quite certain she'd done nothing out of the ordinary before or after the manicure? Not been touching something out of the ordinary? It might be that she had wee breaks in her skin – which would no' be unusual if they'd been working on her cuticles, for example. Some substance that she didn't encounter at the salon itself could have infected her that way.'

Annie chuckled, 'Oh no, Mave, she was absolutely, one hundred percent certain that she'd done nothing out of the ordinary in the day or so following the manicure, after which her symptoms set in.'

'Do you think Marjorie's the best judge of how a place like that is supposed to be kept clean?' asked Carol. 'A friend of mine in school had a Saturday job at a hairdressers' in Carmarthen's town center, and she seemed to spend her entire day cleaning stuff; sweeping up, wiping down, sterilizing equipment, that sort of thing. Said the place stank, and she always had to have a bath when she came home because she reeked of the chemicals. I can see there's a good deal in the COSHH details about protecting workers from the harmful short- and long-term effects of coming into contact with, and even just inhaling, all the chemicals used in the beauty business, these days. It doesn't sound as though those regulations either existed, or were enforced, back then. Maybe they aren't enforced now. We don't really know, do we?'

'You're right,' said Mavis. 'I believe we all agree that Marjorie isn't the sort of person who'd lie about any of this, but I dare say we could also agree she's no expert when it comes to workplace hygiene; someone who knows what they're looking for should visit the place in question, and find out what they can.'

'I need my hair cut,' said Carol rapidly.

Annie laughed aloud. 'Nice one, Car. I've never seen you volunteer to do a bit of undercover work as quick as that before.'

Carol looked wounded. 'You know how hard I work to juggle everything here. But it's true, my hair desperately needs at least a good trim. I'd have to get David to be with Albert to get it cut anyway, so why don't I go to the spa at the hotel to get it done there? Then I can have a good old nose about the place. I'll read up on what I should be on the lookout for before I go. How about that? Maybe the company could pay the difference between what it would cost for me to have a cut, wash, and blow dry there instead of at my usual place in Builth? It can't be that much. I know we're not flush, and we don't have a client who's covering expenses…but…'

'With all the hours you're putting in to support our fieldwork, Carol, I think you deserve it,' said Christine.

'Go on, treat yourself, Car,' said Annie.

'Aye, go on then, it's a good idea,' said Mavis. 'Will you phone for an appointment and get that sorted out yourself then, Carol? And Annie, why don't you tell Marjorie what we're doing, so she knows we're taking her plight seriously.'

Annie nodded. 'Yeah, I'll give her a bell a bit later – I can only cope with Marjorie in small doses.'

'There – it's done. I've got an appointment with someone called Caz at three this afternoon. A cancellation. I just booked it online,' said Carol.

Christine looked surprised. 'You've booked a haircut online, in thirty seconds, with someone you've never met? Isn't that a bit…reckless?'

It was Carol's turn to laugh. 'I've been trimming my own hair since Albert was born, because I haven't been able to justify taking the time to go and get it done by a professional. Unless they hack at it with a knife and fork, I suspect they'll do a better job than I manage with nail scissors in front of the bathroom mirror.'

'You've been trimming your own hair?' Christine sounded amazed. 'But it always looks so lovely – those loose, blonde, corkscrew curls of yours are wonderful. You've no idea how jealous I am of your hair. Mine is so thick it has a mind of its own. Yours always looks as though you've just left the salon.'

She paused, smiled, and added, 'But…I must remember the Sisterhood, and not be jealous, or angry, or covetous.'

Annie chuckled. 'You lot have no idea, do you? This?' She rubbed her hand over the fuzz of hair on her shapely head. 'This in't a choice as much as a necessity. Try to grow it more than this and it just breaks off. I can treat it, oil it, nurse it along like it's the world's rarest orchid…and it still won't grow. You lot have no idea how lucky you are to be able to choose how long to have your hair, so think on that. And as for finding a hairdresser who has even the first idea of how to deal with my kind of hair? Good luck with that, especially around here. Cardiff would be the nearest place where they'd be used to dealing with it, is my bet, which is why I always drop into my mum's hairdresser when I'm in Plaistow. Knows what's what, she does; takes one look at me, then at it, and just tells me how to look after it at home because there's not much she can do but massage it for me.'

Carol smiled sadly. 'Funny, isn't it, how we're never content with what we have? I'd love to have a short, short cut like you, Annie, and I hate the curls you envy me for, Christine – they've been the bane of my life since I developed them aged two.'

Mavis held up her hands as if in surrender. 'Aye, well, hair can be something we end up spending far too much time worrying about, all round, I'd say, so let's move on and discuss…no, let me take this, it's Gemma Thomas.'

Christine motioned to Annie asking if she fancied more tea, then poured her colleague a cup; Carol took the chance to pop to the loo; and Gertie got not just a special bit of petting, but a chance to lick up the biscuit crumbs Annie shook from her sweater onto the floor.

Mavis had stood to take the call, and walked briskly around the large office as she spoke; she'd announced that one of her resolutions for the year was to walk whenever she could, and being on the telephone was one of those situations, so she was walking in laps as she spoke. 'I understand, of course,' said Mavis. 'They are here with me now, and we'll confer. Please don't worry, Mrs Thomas, and please extend our best wishes for a speedy recovery to the gentleman concerned. Yes, I shall, goodbye.'

'What did she want?' Carol retook her seat at her kitchen table just as Mavis sat down again at her desk.

'That's not a good look, Mave – what's up?' Annie was concerned.

'I know you and Christine were due to drive to the cottage at Port Beynon to take up residence tomorrow morning,' began Mavis, 'but I'm afraid that will have to be pushed back to Monday. Will that be acceptable to you both?'

Christine nodded. 'It means I can spend some time with Mammy and Daddy – and Alexander, of course – in London this weekend, which would be lovely,' said Christine, 'so it's better for me. But why do we have to put it off? Has something happened? Is everyone okay?'

Mavis shook her head. 'As I believe I told you, Gemma Thomas uses a management company to ensure that the cottage is ready for renters; they come in when guests leave, clean the place, reset it for the next arrivals, and so forth. It appears that, recently, Mrs Thomas has stipulated that only females should be sent to the cottage – her beliefs being what they are about the cottage curse only applying to men, as you all, no doubt, recall.'

'Oh no, Mave, something bad's happened, hasn't it?' Annie's tone was ominous.

Mavis nodded slowly. 'The company sent a couple, a married couple, who work together; the cottage hasn't been occupied since it was last deep-cleaned, so a light dust, polish, and rinse was all that was asked for. The wife was cleaning the bathroom, the husband the kitchen. He's sustained some quite severe burns to his hands; the water from the kitchen sink was unexpectedly hot – boiling, in fact – and it scalded him. He'll have to receive special treatment. Skin grafts might be in his future.'

The mood in both the converted barn and Carol's comfy kitchen in the village shifted.

'We'd better be careful when we're staying there, Chrissy,' said Annie.

Christine swallowed hard and nodded. 'You're not kidding.'

CHAPTER NINE

It was ten to three when Carol pulled up in the area of the car park set aside for 'Day Spa Guests' as opposed to those who were staying at the Ash Court Country House Hotel itself. Despite the fact she wasn't one of those shelling out a laughable amount of money to be able to sink into the luxurious four-poster beds or wallow in the waffly robes enjoyed by overnight guests, she was allowed to enter the building through the main portico and doors. Thus, she was able to be delighted by the marbled hall, soaring atrium, and hushed elegance of the reception area, which was a symphony of muted tones, exotic rugs, and tables whose sole purpose seemed to be to hold massive vases full of elaborate fresh floral displays.

Carol stifled a smile; she'd become a regular guest at Chellingworth Hall over the past twelve months or so, and couldn't quite come to terms with the fact that she now found this exquisite building a little…underwhelming. It was grand, and it would have been – not long ago – what she'd have thought of as the epitome of poshness. Now? Now she knew better, and saw it for what it was: a lovely old manor house, set in a few well-maintained acres, that had been primped, then stuffed full of luxury baubles designed to deliver value for money to those for whom the eye-watering prices needed to be justified.

The receptionist looked Carol up and down, then said, 'You'd be here for the spa, would you? Mrs Hill, three o'clock, is it?' The receptionist's tone was polite, if a little patronising. Carol nodded.

The smartly-suited young woman ticked off what Carol presumed was her name in a ledger on the podium, then wafted a balletic hand gesture toward a brass-encased sign with an arrow that pointed toward the Ash Court Luxury Day Spa. Carol reckoned that if the spa was anything like the sign, she'd be in for a posh time of it.

Carol realized the woman could probably spot an outfit comprising pieces all picked up at High Street shops, or even where she bought her groceries, as opposed to the designer get-ups the guests were likely to be wearing. However, she felt she'd been judged extremely rapidly, so held her head high as she marched away from the stairs and lift, and all the other areas that could only be rightfully accessed by those who had a key card to a room. Carol suspected her key card would have to be made of solid gold, and non-returnable, if she was ever going to spend that sort of money in a place like this.

A marbled corridor led her past a small lounge where velvet-upholstered chairs were dotted about, then she took a turn toward the rear of the building, where the lighting became gradually more dim, and the walls were clad in what appeared to be bamboo. The entry to the spa itself was heralded by a smoked-glass door with gold lettering, which only allowed a hint of a view of what was beyond.

She pushed, entered, and was almost overwhelmed by the aroma of sandalwood, surprised to hear birds chirping, and sensed a dramatic change in temperature – the place was warm, and relatively humid. None of these were good signs: Carol didn't like the smell of sandalwood; abhorred recorded birdsong; and certainly didn't care for humidity – and neither did her hair. She wondered how long it would be before it bounced out, the way it always did in the damp, and what that might mean for any reasonable job to be made of it being well cut. She sighed, and reminded herself she was at the spa in her professional capacity, and that – if any disasters befell her – her hair would grow back quickly, which was why she was constantly trimming it.

A tall, overly-tanned woman of about Carol's age – or at least not yet forty, Carol judged – approached from behind a desk emblazoned with the spa's logo.

'You must be Mrs Hill. How wonderful to meet you. I'm Willow Richards, the manager here. May I take your coat? Please have a seat, your stylist will be with you shortly.'

Carol thanked her.

She continued, 'There's cucumber water on the side table, and I invite you to use one of our specially prepared towelling hand wipes; they've been infused with a blend of ingredients selected for their natural cleansing properties.'

Carol surrendered her coat, popped her handbag across her body, and picked up one of the aforementioned wipes, which was chilled, refreshing, and left her hands smelling woody and lemony. The décor suggested Asian influences, mixed with the minimalism of the Nordic countries…and an operating theater. It was an oddly soothing mixture – the browns and soft greens of natural woods, bamboos, and linens, with seamless, high-gloss, white surfaces of molded plastic in between. Carol was surprised by how far she sank into the plush seat beside the table covered with neat rows of magazines, then immediately began to worry about how she'd ever get up again.

The wall beside the reception desk was bedecked with framed certificates. Taking her opportunity, Carol asked, 'All your practitioners are qualified, I see.' She nodded at the wall.

Willow followed Carol's gaze and smiled beatifically. 'Indeed. We wouldn't retain anyone not fully accredited to deliver the services they provide. It can take quite some time to find the right person for the job, but this is such a wonderful place to work, we're able to attract the people we want.'

Carol grinned in the way she hoped a real client would. 'Good,' she said, 'I know it'll grow back, but I'd like my hair to look as good as possible.'

Willow flashed a smile that didn't quite reach her eyes, then Carol saw her expression change to one of relief. 'Ah, here's Caz now. She'll be looking after you today, Mrs Hill. Caz, this is Mrs Hill, your three o'clock.

Carol turned to greet the woman to whom she was about to entrust her hair, and froze: stark, black eyeliner; magenta quiff to one side, shaved head the other; several holes in her nose, and at least two dozen in her ears, though none sporting any jewelry.

The young woman wore the same pristine, high-necked white tunic as Willow, but Caz's was stretched over her large, muscular frame. Carol reckoned she was in her mid-twenties, and knew exactly how intimidating she looked. Her heart sank.

She managed to utter a brave, 'Pleased to meet you, Caz.'

'G'day. I enjoy meeting new victims.' There was an Australian twang, and the young woman roared with laughter at her own joke.

Willow spoke firmly. 'Ignore Caz's manner, Mrs Hill. She's the best stylist and cutter around, or we wouldn't have her here. You can trust her, whatever she might say. Or look like.'

Carol hoped Willow was right, because she felt as though she were being led into the lion's den, rather than to a black leather-upholstered seat in front of a well-lit mirror.

Once Carol was settled, and the seat adjusted to the height Caz wanted, the young woman stared at Carol's reflection in what Carol felt was a most accusing way, then she began to pull at Carol's hair, stretching out her curls in every direction, and letting them bounce into place.

'This is all natural, right?' Caz was direct, if nothing else. 'No color, no perms, no products?'

'Nothing at all; just shampoo and conditioner.'

'And you've either been cutting it yourself, or whoever did this to you should be shot.'

Carol didn't just feel herself blush, she could see her cheeks glowing in the mirror. 'I've got a baby who's not a year old, yet. I haven't had time to go to the hairdressers' in ages.' She wondered if she might get another withering look.

'No worries. I can sort it. You want it so you can wash and go, right?'

Carol nodded.

'Good. It's wonderful hair. People spend a fortune to get this blonde color, and these curls. You're lucky – though I bet you hate it, right?'

Carol smiled, gradually warming to Caz's personality. 'I always have, but it is easy to look after. Since it won't do anything but this, I don't bother trying any more. And that's a good thing, with a baby.'

'Right, let's get you washed, and I'll cut it so it frames your face better. With all that weight you're carrying, you'll want it to hide as much as possible around the sides of those cheeks.'

Carol realized she wasn't being asked a question, and felt terribly disappointed that this young woman seemed to have so quickly assessed many of her issues when it came to self-image. 'Can't seem to shift the baby weight,' she said quietly.

Caz leaned in. 'They've got some good classes here that could help you drop it. You should try them. Ask for the special offer. Can't hurt, right? Get you sweating off a few pounds before you know it. They've got a nutritionist too, and a woman who'll give you a facial that could even out your skin tone a bit – and get rid of some of those blackheads.'

Carol felt as though any vestige of self-confidence she might have had was being chipped away with each scathing remark. By the time she allowed Caz to position her to lean back into the washbasin, she was close to tears. How had she let herself go so much? What must David think? No wonder her mother had given her all those sideways looks at Christmas. She was a mess…a big, fat, unhealthy, pimply mess.

As Caz checked the temperature of the water on her own wrist, she said to Carol, 'I'll get one of our manicurists to pop some wax onto those hands of yours, then you can sit wearing warming gloves while I give you a cut and blow dry; that should sort out those ragged knuckles and cuticles for you.'

Carol sighed, and focused on the ceiling above her, deciding it was best to say nothing; she'd grit her teeth and allow this girl to decimate her self-worth…and be even more keenly on the lookout for ways by which she might be able to point to a lack of general hygiene in the place.

Unfortunately, on that front, she'd drawn a blank so far. The seating, the basins, the hoses, the towels, everything screamed 'I am clean' at her. She'd even seen Caz wash her hands before she so much as touched the equipment at the basin.

'I'm going to use this shampoo,' said Caz, holding the bottle so Carol could see it. 'It's all natural, no parabens at all, and I think you'll find it'll make a difference to the texture of your hair. But using it just once won't help in the long run; that would need a sustained effort on your part. Like everything – we can only do so much; in the end it's up to you to keep doing what you know you should be, to look and feel your best.'

She reeled off every ingredient in the bottle; it sounded as though she were about to wash Carol's hair with an entire farm-to-table vegan menu, not a vanilla-scented, creamy shampoo. Once Carol confirmed she wasn't allergic to anything on the list, Caz spent the next ten minutes giving her the best – well, the first – scalp massage she'd ever had in her life. Carol felt dazed as she wandered back to the styling chair, and flopped into it, only able to half-focus on her reflected face and turbaned head.

'I'll leave you wrapped in that warm towel for five minutes,' said Caz brightly. 'Your scalp can relax, then I'll tackle that hair. You can relax, too, let me recline the back, and you can just *be*. Try a bit of meditative thinking, if you can. I'll have a word with Jasmine about doing something with those hands while I'm working on your curls.'

Carol felt as though she weighed almost nothing, cocooned in the comfortable curves of the padded chair as she lay there, eyes closed…drifting off…

The whispering wandered into her consciousness as if from a dream. 'Out like a light, she is. Look at her, poor cow. Those clothes she's wearing? Supermarket stuff. And her skin? Can't believe she's ever done anything but wash it with soap. I think I can sell her on the shampoo and conditioner, but you have to make out how you can save those shovels she's got for hands, Jasmine.'

Carol didn't like what she was hearing – not one little bit; she could feel her temper rising inside her as listened.

Forcing herself to remain as still as though she were fast asleep – which she suspected was what Caz would believe to be true of a woman in the sort of state she clearly believed her to be – she fumed, silently.

Caz continued, 'Once I've finished with her, then you come by and tell her about the deal on three free months at the gym if she signs up for a year, Willow. Alright? Come on, girls, we're a team. Let's hook this one. God only knows where she'll get the money from, but if we can beat her down a bit more, then promise we can build her up, we can land her, I know it. We've got to hit our targets for this month. We didn't do as well as we could for St Dwynwen's Day, did we? And Valentine's Day isn't for weeks; let's hope more couples are going out for posh meals then, so the women want their hair and nails done to look their best, right?'

Carol's ears were out on stalks; Caz's tone had changed – it had hardened, and sharpened. It was also clear that, while Willow was the nominal manager of the place, Caz was the ringleader.

Carol pondered her options: the first thing she did was tell herself off for allowing herself to feel less confident about the person she really was, just because she didn't look as glamorous as she might; then she wondered how she could find out more about the schemes Caz was talking about; finally, she decided that she needed to fully understand what was going on at the spa not just because Marjorie Pritchard had been somehow infected there, but also because of what Caz had made her feel about herself, which was unforgiveable.

She waited patiently until the stylist roused her with some gentle words. 'How are we feeling now? Ready to start? Jasmine's here to give you a nice hot wax coating for those hands before I get going. Here you are, Jasmine; I'm sure Mrs Hill will be very grateful for you doing this as a favor for her.'

Carol smiled at the girl who'd just arrived.

Caz bent to Carol's ear and whispered, 'A fiver in her pocket would be a nice thank you for her, wouldn't it?' Then she stood again and concluded, 'I'll be back shortly.'

Carol suspected Jasmine was about eighteen, or at least looked it. Birdlike, with massive brown eyes, she had a strong accent hailing from one of the Swansea Valleys, and looked as though she was terrified of Caz.

Carol put her plan into action, and became the silly, bubbly woman who was out to spoil herself because she'd come into a bit of money. She hinted at, but didn't specifically mention, bingo.

By the time Caz reappeared, Carol had learned a great deal about Jasmine's family, her time at college gaining her beautician's qualifications, the way the spa was run…and – although Jasmine never said the words – how Caz did, indeed, rule the roost.

'All done here? Good. I'll be half an hour, no more, then you can come back and peel it all off for Mrs Hill, unless you're busy with another client, in which case I dare say we'll manage, won't we?' Caz loomed over Carol as she raked her hands through the curls she'd just released from the turban.

Carol was amazed; her hair had lost what she'd always thought of as its natural frizz, and was hanging in loose, perfectly formed ringlets. It already looked better than she could remember it ever had done. Fifteen minutes later Caz had snipped, pulled, combed, and snipped again, and Carol had managed to pump her for as much information about the spa's history – and her own – as possible.

Then Caz brought a piece of equipment on a stand that looked like something out of a science fiction film; it had a halo of bright lights, and a hand-held device like a small umbrella blew gently onto Carol's hair as Caz rubbed it through her curls. Everything was dry in a few minutes, and then Carol's hair looked…magnificent. It glowed; it flattered the contours of her face; her curls were even, bouncy, and gleaming. Carol couldn't hide her genuine delight as the stylist adjusted a handheld mirror to show her the back of her head.

Caz said, 'That'll hold you for about six weeks. You'll need a trim then, but you might be able to push it to a couple of months if you use the shampoo and conditioner I recommended.'

Carol nodded. Her curls actually bounced.

Caz continued, smiling, 'Why not ask Willow for a bottle of each when you leave, and make an appointment for eight weeks' time? We get busy, so it's best to book now. We'll text, or email you, to remind you about it. Oh look, there's Willow now. What do you think, Willow?'

Willow arrived, did a bit of ooh'ing and ah'ing, then went into a pretty heavy-handed sales pitch for the gym – to which Carol's response was: 'I'd love the chance to have a look around it before I sign up for anything. Could I do that now?'

Caz intervened with a hearty reply. 'Of course. Willow can show you around, but let's get that wax off you first, eh? There you go – no need to bother Jasmine after all. It's coming off in one piece. Look at that – like a new pair of hands, right?'

Carol had to admit that her hands felt softer and smoother than they ever had, and they smelled divine…fresh and lemony, with a hint of lavender.

'Lovely,' she said, 'I might have to come back for a proper manicure, and even a pedicure, but let's see the gym first, eh? Then maybe your nail bar area?'

Willow became her guide throughout the premises, which extended beyond the compact but well-appointed gym, to three treatment rooms, and another containing an upright capsule.

'That's the sunbed,' explained Willow. 'We don't really offer it, it's just there if people ask. Quite a lot do – it gives a person a nice healthy glow, especially at this time of year. And a lot use it before they go off to get some winter sun – to get a base tan going, you know? Or maybe you don't – you're very fair-skinned, aren't you? Do you usually burn?' Carol nodded. 'Yes, I can see you would. My sister's like you – skin so white it's almost translucent. But me? I like to have a bit of color, me.'

Carol hadn't needed to be told that; indeed, she wondered if other people ever had the chance to use the tanning pod, because it looked as though Willow was in there on a frequent basis.

Carol made her face look as though she was giving the idea some serious consideration.

'Maybe if I can knock off a few pounds, and get my other parts sorted out a bit, then I could think about that.' Carol tried to sound as pathetically hopeful for a total makeover as she knew Caz had represented her as being. 'Oh, what's that?' She peered into a small room with a water feature, which wasn't running, a single wooden chair in the center, and an exotic rug on the wooden floor.

Willow closed the door. 'It's where we used to have our Indian head massages done,' she said quietly.

'You don't offer them any longer?'

Willow smiled – nervously, Carol judged. 'No, not these days. The person who did them…left. We decided we'd withdraw the service until we can find the perfect replacement.'

'Caz gave me a pretty good head massage when she washed my hair,' said Carol brightly; she noticed the look of irritation that Willow tried to hide, and the fact she had stopped her constant jabbering.

Indeed, the woman said nothing, until she announced, 'And this is Jasmine's domain. Pedicures over there, of course –' she waved at a couple of padded seats set up high, with receptacles for bowls at kneeling level – 'and manicures over here.'

Jasmine looked up from the hand to which she was applying a French manicure. The heavily made-up, red-headed woman wearing cat's-eye glasses turned to look at Carol, and smiled, graciously, over the thick collar of her waffly, white robe.

As they walked away, Willow said, 'So, what about it? Want to take advantage of the deal on the gym membership?'

Pausing at the reception desk, Carol said, 'I'll take the shampoo and conditioner, and I'll book a trim for eight weeks' time. I'd also like to book a manicure and pedicure, and I'd like to spend an hour in the gym before I make a commitment. That would all be alright, wouldn't it?' She beamed her most winning smile, and was pleased when everything was agreed.

Sitting in her car a while later, admiring her hair in the rearview mirror, then telling herself off for her vanity, she phoned Mavis.

'Aye, Carol, and how did it go?'

'I think something's definitely off at the place, and I'll write up a report explaining why I feel that way. But I'll have to come back to do a few more observations; can the company budget stretch to a mani-pedi?'

'How much?' Mavis was never backwards in coming forwards when it came to money.

Carol had managed to keep a straight face when she'd paid for the styling and hair products, but when she totted it all up for Mavis, including the treatments she'd already booked, Mavis nearly blew a gasket. The women agreed they couldn't imagine how some people could afford to use a place like the spa on a regular basis, then Mavis capitulated, agreeing that Marjorie Pritchard was a pillar of the community and they should always help when they could, though it irked Mavis to use the company's money to do so.

On the drive home Carol wondered how her 'new look' would be greeted by David; she hoped he'd like it, because she did, and she'd made up her mind that it was quite acceptable to like a new hairdo, after all.

MONDAY 30ᵗʰ JANUARY

CHAPTER TEN

Annie and Christine had agreed that telling a senior detective about the so-called 'cursed cottage' in an email probably wouldn't get the result they wanted – which was a bit of help. Unfortunately, Annie hadn't been able to arrange a face-to-face appointment with Detective Chief Inspector Carys Llewellyn of the Swansea police until Tuesday. Knowing that was set up, the pair had allowed themselves to enjoy their drive from Anwen-by-Wye to Swansea, then on to the Gower peninsula, listening to music – when they could agree what to listen to – and generally chatting about everything, and nothing, as well as discussing the finer details of their cover story.

The fun of that conversation, wherein some absolutely ridiculous backstories had been bandied about, concluded with the decision that they were two old friends from their time working in the City of London, though Annie had now moved to Anwen-by-Wye, while Christine had stayed on in London. This week's getaway was a chance for them to catch up and make some new memories together. They'd agreed that sticking to backgrounds as close to their real lives as possible would be helpful, since they were likely to be interacting with a good number of people over a fairly lengthy time period, and both knew – from experience – that could be a dangerous situation to be in; complex lies could trip up a person all too easily.

The final approach to the village got Annie in a bit of a lather, because she'd never seen such narrow, winding, so-called 'A' roads before, not even around Anwen-by-Wye, where, frankly, they were frightening enough for her.

At least in that part of the world the roads usually accommodated two cars at a time, but the road into the village wasn't much wider than Christine's vehicle, often with stone walls on each side, and the so-called 'passing places' didn't suggest your paint would be safe if you used them as such.

It was at times like these that Annie was pleased she didn't drive, though she noted that Christine managed to keep moving along at quite a pace.

Following one especially tight corner, Annie blurted out, 'Shouldn't you slow down a bit? I mean they've painted "slow" on the road in English *and* Welsh, so I suspect it's more than a suggestion.'

'I learned to drive on lanes like this back in Ireland. If you don't attack them, you'll never get anywhere.'

Annie gripped the hand rest on the door. 'As long as we get there in one piece, that's all that matters.'

Once they'd survived the lanes, their arrival at the cottage itself was a relief, and a delight; parking was easy, because there was a gravel-covered area large enough to accommodate at least three cars beside it. The place itself had a charming exterior: whitewashed stone walls; glossily painted old windows; a protective wall surrounding the entire front of the cottage; the gated entrance made all the more welcoming because of a lovely arch above it; and – on the little bank set against the wall – was a weathered, glazed, wooden noticeboard where folks could pin information about local events.

With her hands full, Annie nodded toward the redundant old post box in the wall, 'They've blocked that up, I see,' she observed, 'and someone's bothered to put a note about there being "no collections", which is thoughtful. Mind you, the post's so bad these days, who'd notice?'

Christine chuckled as she dragged her suitcase through the gate and over the step. 'Let's get in; I need the loo, and you can put the kettle on. I'm gasping, so I am.'

Annie smiled warmly. 'You know you get more Irish when you're angry, or in a panic, don't you?'

Christine fiddled with the keypad in an attempt to open the smart lock, and eventually flung the door open, shouting over her shoulder, 'While it's impossible for you to sound more like the Cockney you are,' as she dropped everything and ran up the stairs.

Annie paused at the threshold because the door swung closed in front of her, so she had to push it open with her foot. 'Gordon Bennett, another place where they didn't design doors for six footers,' she said, ducking her head to enter. She dropped her handbag, and stood up her wheelie case, giving herself a moment to take in the cottage that was about to become her temporary home.

It certainly didn't look cursed; it looked inviting, despite the fact that ahead of her was a wooden staircase so steep it was almost like a ladder. Its narrowness made her wonder how on earth anyone had ever managed to get any furniture up it.

To her left was a decent-sized kitchen; it had whitewashed stone walls, modern wooden cabinets around its perimeter with open shelves above them, and a round table with six mis-matched wooden chairs at its center.

To her right was a sitting room, into which she stepped. There were a couple of antique wooden rocking chairs, and two comfy-looking modern sofas. They'd been upholstered in a restful dusky blue, one placed either side of a coffee table that had been made from what appeared to be a slice of a large tree. There was a small window looking out into the tiny front yard, then to the road beyond.

It was a lovely room, but what took Annie's breath away was the magnificent view through the set of four, folding glass doors that formed its entire back wall. Outside, she looked across a slate-slabbed patio toward a lawn that disappeared down a slope. Beyond that, the sandy beach beckoned, and the sea glittered beneath the wintry sun to the gray of the horizon. The view was so enchanting she almost didn't notice that she'd probably have to duck every time there was an ancient wooden beam crossing the whitewashed ceiling.

Christine bounded down the creaking stairs. 'That's better.'

Stepping into the sitting room she said, 'Your turn...oh, what a view.'

Annie sighed, and stared.

Christine bubbled, 'You can't really tell from the road, can you? I'd never have guessed we'd be able to see all the way down to the beach. I wonder if the garden goes right to the sand; that would be quite something, wouldn't it? To be able to just walk from your house to the beach.'

Annie smiled. 'Yeah, it would…and it's all ours for a little bit, so let's make the most of it. I'll just pop upstairs to the bathroom, then I'll check what we'll have to do to keep Gert under control, and safe, while she's here. If there's no fence at that bottom bit, that could be a bit of a problem – though the brochure says dogs are allowed, so there must be some way to keep them confined.'

'Maybe they expect them to be a bit more likely to come to heel when they're called than Gertie is?' Christine winked.

'Oi, she's only a puppy,' said Annie, hauling herself up the steep staircase, using the thankfully sturdy handrail.

'It's straight ahead of you,' called Christine. 'Be prepared for the world's smallest bathroom.'

'You're not kidding about that bathroom,' said Annie when she rejoined her friend. 'Good for them for managing to fit in a shower, but I can't imagine I'll have fun in there. These elbows need space, and I'll have to bend me knees to get me shoulders wet, the showerhead's so low.'

'I've just been downstairs to the sort of basement bit, that's built into the slope; there are two more bedrooms down there and a much bigger bathroom. It's got a shower over the bath. Maybe you'd better use that one?'

Annie agreed. 'I'll have a look, but, before that, let's see how we can keep Gert safe, okay? Fancy walking the perimeter of the garden so we can see how far that fence really goes? It looks good and sturdy down both sides, but I want to see what happens down on that slope. Gert'll be alright on her own in the car for a few more minutes…or I can do it on my own, and you can get the kettle on.'

'Give me a sec, I'll see to the kettle and come with you; we're here to get to know the place after all, and it's not raining at the moment, so let's make the most of that.'

With the kettle sorted, Annie and Christine hauled open the massive, glazed doors, and set off along the fence, one each side of the garden – which was the width of the cottage, plus the parking pad beside it.

They each checked the fence for breaches, or weak points. When they met up again at the far end of the garden, Annie was feeling relieved.

'I'm glad they kept the fence going all the way around, and the gate down here looks sturdy, though I still don't fancy the idea of Gert being able to run all the way down here, where I can't keep an eye on her.' The two women looked back toward the cottage, which was now completely hidden by the steep slope of grass. 'Come on, let's get her out of her crate so she can run about for a bit.' They headed up toward Sea View Cottage.

Theirs was the only building on the side of the narrow road that offered direct access to the beach, and there was only one other dwelling opposite it; it was a squat, wide structure, set at an angle – its front not looking straight at the sea. Annie reckoned the rental cottage was likely to obstruct most of its view.

'Surveillance, over there, at two o'clock,' said Annie. 'In that fancy conservatory,' she said. 'They just shut their blinds on us. I have to wonder how they got planning permission to stick that Victorian design onto the side of such an old, rustic cottage. I mean it's nice…but jarring, don't you think?'

'Probably like a fridge in the winter, and an oven in the summer, with that glass roof it's got,' said Christine, 'but I see what you mean. It looks…well, not exactly ugly, but certainly not sympathetic to the building itself.'

Annie agreed, 'Yeah, but when you've got even a partial glimpse of a view like this, I dare say you'll do whatever it takes to make the most of it.'

Christine said, 'Here we are then. I'll sort the tea, you get Gertie. I brought a packet of chocolate digestives as well as some good, strong teabags, in case the stuff Gemma said was supplied wasn't good tea. But I forgot milk. You okay without it?'

Annie chuckled. 'Tea with no milk it is – it'll be lovely, as long as it's strong.'

'It'll be that.'

Gertie was delighted to be freed, and made the most of the next half an hour running about the garden, sniffing at everything, and bounding back to Annie for reassurance between excited discoveries. Annie and Christine nursed their mugs sitting on the patio chairs, which Annie had wiped down with one of the thoughtfully supplied and labelled 'DOG TOWELS' she'd spotted hanging on hooks in the entryway.

The view was amazing; the patio formed a 'roof' for the newer part of the cottage which housed the extra bedrooms and bathroom, and, while it provided no shelter from the stiff breeze blowing off the sea, at least it allowed them to take in the rest of the small hamlet that had built up around the area where the road met the beach and the public car park below them.

'That's got to be the pub,' said Annie, 'it's the biggest building around.'

'Except for that church we passed, with the massive statue of a seaman. There was something in Carol's notes about that – it honors some lifeboatmen lost at sea in some dreadful tragedy.'

'Do we have a plan? Now that we're here, but know we can't meet with Carys Llewellyn until tomorrow.'

Christine checked her watch. 'Before we do anything else, let's sort out signing into the wi-fi here, make sure we're up to date on work stuff, then get everything put away? I hate unpacking, so I like to get it done as fast as I can, and we need to get a few things into the fridge. Sorry about the lack of milk.'

'No worries, it's an excuse to go down to the seafront to find the shop.'

'Great idea.' Christine sighed. 'Sorry. I thought I'd brought everything we'd need, but I had to forget milk, of all things. Ah well, we'll not die because of that, will we?'

'Funny, ha-ha,' said Annie.

Christine grinned. 'Oh heck, given where we are – yes, sorry.'

Annie said, 'I dare say you don't usually have to think about things like milk…but you must have to pack and unpack a lot, what with using the flat above the office, your flat in Battersea, and staying with your parents at that big old pile they've got in Fitzrovia. How do you ever know where anything is? Have you got different toothbrushes in every place, or are you constantly lugging everything between Wales and London?'

Christine chuckled. 'It's not so bad. For example, Mammy and Daddy need me in posh frocks quite a lot, so they all stay at their house, because I rarely need to dress up that much anywhere else; my clothes for work are at the flat on the Chellingworth Estate, and my flat in Battersea? That's full of a lot of stuff I don't seem to use much these days. To be honest, when I've been in London recently, and not staying with Mammy and Daddy, I've been at Alexander's place more than my own. And, yes, I have toothbrushes in all four places; toothpaste too, and all the other basic toiletries. I dare say, if you put it all in one place, it would make a great big pile. Oh! What was that?'

Both Annie and Christine jumped, having heard a loud, banging noise. Gertie began to bark furiously, then darted to the side of the cottage where the fence prevented her from reaching the parking pad. Annie rushed behind her pup and found herself staring out at a woman in her sixties wearing a waxed jacket, wellies, and sporting a hurricane-proof, more-salt-than-pepper perm beneath a loosely tied headscarf. She was holding a plate covered with plastic wrap.

'I'm Amy Francis, from across the road. Gemma Thomas has said it's alright if I bring over one of my tarts whenever she has guests. It's apple, from the trees in our garden. Nothing fancy, but it gives me an excuse to bake.'

Annie wondered if Gemma had told Amy about them. 'How did you know we were coming, to be able to make it in time?'

Amy smiled coyly. 'It's not hard to work it out; the cleaners always come when people leave and, if there's been a gap between guests, they always come again before someone arrives.'

'Good to know,' said Annie, thinking a renter would say as much.

Amy continued, 'This time they came twice – on Friday and yesterday. Something happened that meant one of them was carted off to hospital on Friday…but I mustn't speak out of turn.'

Annie could spot a gossip a mile off, and immediately realized that Amy Francis might prove a valuable resource in terms of gathering information about the cottage.

She decided upon her exact plan of attack, and said, 'Yes, Gemma told us there'd been a bit of a problem, but she wasn't specific; we were due here on Saturday, in fact. I tell you what, I'll come through and let you in, then why not join me and my chum for a cuppa and a slice of what I'm sure will be a delicious tart, and tell us all about it?'

Amy hesitated, then said, 'That would be lovely, thank you. No one's ever invited me in before and, you know, a person is always curious about what's been done to a place.' She turned and waved to a figure at the window of the house across the road. 'My husband, that is, at the window. He says I shouldn't do this. You never know who might be here, he says, but it's nice to welcome people…let them know they're wanted. All you visitors are good for the local economy, see? So that wave should reassure him I'm just fine, and that you don't look like axe murderers.' She turned again, motioned to the plate, then at the cottage. 'He'll understand, I'm sure. I'll meet you at the front door.'

When Annie opened the door, Amy Francis was gesticulating wildly at the person now clearly visible as an elderly man in a cardigan, who was shaking his head and wagging his finger. Annie waved and smiled, but he dropped the net curtain and disappeared.

'Would your husband like to join us?' Annie thought it best to ask.

Amy looked horrified. 'Oh no. He won't set foot in this place ever again, he's said. It's far too dangerous…oh, that's me all over, opening my mouth and putting my foot in it. Don't take that the wrong way…um…?'

'Sorry, I'm Annie Parker, and this is Christine Wilson-Smythe. Come on in, Amy – and do tell me more. Have we rented ourselves a "dangerous" cottage, then? Is it haunted?'

Annie and Christine exchanged a conspiratorial grin.

Anne said innocently, 'The woman we rented it from never mentioned such a thing. Chrissy said it looked as though it could be, but I don't believe in ghosts.'

Amy accepted a seat at the kitchen table, and Christine hunted out plates and cutlery, and even found some jolly lemon paper napkins in a drawer. Eventually, they all had a slice of what Annie was relieved to discover looked to be a delightfully moist apple tart in front of them.

Christine had refreshed the pot, and they all ate, while Amy happily regaled them with stories about the cottage they were sitting in, as her own home, across the road, and the hamlet at the seafront.

She spoke conspiratorially, yet freely. 'When the old Gorst sisters who used to live here died, we were living up in Killay. But we always knew we wanted to be down here – it's such a lovely spot. Anyway, when they went, the cottage was stuck in probate for years and years. Every time we'd come down to Port Beynon as a family – to the beach, and what not – you could see it deteriorating. It was a terrible shame. Then the Overton's bought it and did it up a bit. There's an Overton family still down the hill there a bit, but this was the mother and father. He had a nasty accident at the bottom of the garden, so he moved in with his son down the road. They decided to rent it out after that. That was when Glyn and I moved in. Llew too – he'd have been about five then, I'd say. Loved it here, we did – except that we always had to keep an eye on Llew. Off to the beach to hunt about in the rockpools he was, every opportunity. He even used to sneak down there at night, sometimes, when the moon was bright. Oh yes, we had a bit of a time of it with him. But there…boys, you know?'

Annie and Christine smiled as though they did.

'Were you here for long?' Christine had finished her tart and tea.

Amy gave the matter a moment's thought, then said, 'A good while, I suppose. They were happy times.'

She looked around the kitchen wistfully. 'We liked it here. Not that it looked like this then. Much simpler back in those days. Not all shiny and new like it is now.'

'It's delightful now,' agreed Christine.

'What was it like then?' Annie adopted her innocent expression.

'Then? Not bad, just not…like this. We were here until Llew was about thirteen, and we had all we needed here. Then the Overtons put it up for sale, but there was no way Glyn and I could afford it. Mind you, we found a nice little place back in Killay to rent. Then, a few years later, the house we live in now came onto the market, and we had enough for the deposit. We've been there twenty years now, and not a day goes by that I'm not grateful to our Llew.'

Annie was puzzled. 'Your son bought you a house?'

Amy smiled. 'No, not really, but he helped out a bit. He made an app thingy for the Internet, you see – all the way back then, when he was just a teenager – and some bloke in California bought it off him for a tidy sum. That meant we could buy the place we're in now. Like a miracle, it was, because we all agree we're just as happy there as we ever were here. It was just a shame it couldn't have all happened a few years earlier, then it would have been us who bought this place, not Ted Thomas and his wife. But, there, what's meant to be, will be, I always say.'

Amy Francis leaned in and continued in a whisper, 'His wife went first, poor thing, then him. Stroke then a heart attack for her, it was. But him? Oh, now that was a shock, I can tell you. We were first on the scene, you know. Well, sort of second, really, because Llew called us over when he spotted him through the window – but we came as quick as we could.'

Annie poured more tea. 'Oh, that must have been awful for you. What happened?' She reckoned no self-respecting owner of a rental property would have told a mere tenant how their uncle had died.

Amy nodded sagely. 'Carbon monoxide poisoning, they said, and he was bright red, alright. No alarms, see. We had them put in our place right afterwards. Awful thing to happen to him.'

'And we heard a rumor that someone else died here not long ago,' said Christine, adopting a conspiratorial air. 'Was that the same sort of thing?'

Amy sat back. 'Oh, you mean the poor man who was staying here? Yes. He did die. Not right here, inside the cottage – I don't want you to think that.'

'Oh good,' said Annie, the way a tenant would.

Amy added, 'No, not him, not here. Bad enough poor old Ted dying in his old armchair in the other room. No, this one went on the road outside. Down the hill a bit, actually. Of course, I didn't really know him, but it shakes you up all the same, doesn't it? Someone dying like that, I mean. I came over with my tart when they arrived, but he said he couldn't have it in the house because his wife was allergic to nuts. I told him there weren't any in it, but he said they couldn't risk it. Fair enough, I suppose.'

'Didn't you ever meet her?' Annie leaned forward.

Amy nodded, 'I saw her on the beach one day; out for a walk, they were. She was wrapped up like a mummy; didn't look as though she was at all happy though she was hanging onto him, holding hands. Thin and pasty, she was. We had a little chat, you know, and she said she'd managed to fix the Internet, because it hadn't been working, which showed she had a bit of gumption in her, if nothing else. He didn't seem to be the type who'd have gone to do it.'

'So you met him too? What was he like?' Christine took her turn to ask.

Amy's face suggested she'd sucked a lemon. 'Him? Well, he was a bit rough and ready, if I'm honest. Florid. Horrible temper on him. I couldn't believe the way he shouted at her – and out in public, too. Terrible. Two minutes they were here, and we were glad when they'd gone. Oh dear, what am I saying? Sorry – not to speak ill of the dead, you know.'

'We understand, though it really is always best to tell the truth about these things, isn't it,' said Annie, hoping Amy would do just that. 'So, not a nice bloke?'

Amy looked around, as though someone might overhear, then added in a whisper, 'You know how drinkers get a red nose? Well, he had one of them. Which isn't to say he was drunk when he went out on his cycling contraption, but the hill down to the beach is deceptively steep, and the bend up above us isn't well engineered, says my Glyn. And that's where he lost control. The one who died. Went right over, somersaulting, like, several times, they said. Broke almost every bone in his body they reckoned.'

'You spoke to the paramedics?' Annie wondered how reliable Amy's information might be.

'Me? Oh no, I couldn't have got close to a mess like that. Glyn did, though. One of them who came is the granddaughter of a bloke who used to come to church here, even when he'd moved up to Clyne Common. He's dead now, but she's done very well for herself. That's who told Glyn. Said she couldn't work out how he'd managed to do what he'd done…said those bikes don't usually do somersaults like that. Which you'd hope they wouldn't, of course.'

Annie and Christine agreed that was the last thing you'd want them to do.

'Did anyone examine the bike to try to work out what had happened?' Christine leaned in as she asked.

Amy shrugged. 'No idea. A big lorry with a flat bed thingy came to take it away. Right palaver that was, they even had to shut the road again. Don't know where they took it. I know it sat on the bank for a few days, in the rain, before they came for it. Mangled, it was. No wonder the poor man died. It looked like a bus had run over it.'

'But no other vehicles were involved, were they?' Annie realized she didn't know.

Another shrug. 'No one said so, but it was about one in the morning when it happened, so there wasn't anyone about. They didn't even find him until Jason from the pub was off to his food suppliers' early the next morning. That's what's so awful; all night he was there, on his own, in the dark – and so close to the cottage. Mind you, they said he'd have died right away, though, so it's not as if he was lying there in agony for hours, I suppose.'

'Didn't his wife miss him?' Christine sounded truly puzzled.

'Of course she did – but what was she going to do? Been up to some sort of thing at the airport on Fairwood Common, he had – that was why they were here, something to do with a flying club. When he didn't come back to the cottage all she could do was phone his mobile, which I know she did, because she kept saying it over and over when they were taking him away.'

'What did the police have to say about it?' Annie was genuinely interested.

'The police? I don't know. They were there in the morning when it was all going on, of course; had to shut down the road, which is a real problem because there's only the one way in or out of the place, but I never saw hide nor hair of them after that. It was only the man driving the lorry who came to take the bike, on his own. They'd tied a load of tape around it, on the bank, though. Reflective, so you couldn't miss it.'

'In the days after the accident, didn't the police come to your door asking if you'd seen anything on the night that it happened?' Christine looked puzzled.

Amy looked as though the idea hadn't occurred to her. 'No. What would be the point? Everyone was in bed at the time.'

Deciding to try another tack Annie asked, 'Any more tales of disaster about this place?'

'Recently, no, though there's been talk – since that poor man – about the old rumors. The way there's been a bit of a curse on this place since the two old, weird Gorst sisters used to live here.'

Christine topped up Amy's cup, and said, 'Do tell.'

So Amy did, through two more pots of tea, and another slice of tart each.

When she'd left, Annie and Christine made a plan.

Christine cleared everything in the kitchen – which involved working out how to fill what seemed to be an unnecessarily complicated dishwasher – while Annie headed to the sitting room to send some emails.

First, she sent an email to DCI Carys Llewellyn about the death of the tenant, whose name she knew had been Brian Kelly, then sent another to Carol asking her to find out what she could about the two Gorst sisters Amy had just been talking about whose names, she had informed them, were Lil and Bess.

When they'd both done their jobs, they agreed that allowing Gertie to sleep in her bed in the kitchen – which she'd been doing for most of the time Amy had been there – would be fine, as long as they shut the door to stop her running unsupervised around the rest of the cottage, while they walked down to get some supplies at the village shop, and maybe gather some more local insights.

CHAPTER ELEVEN

Mavis had steeled her soul, and prepared the bag of supplies she'd need to sit in a car outside the house of a possibly malingering bricklayer for an entire day. It wasn't that she minded doing watch duty, but had to admit that she was no longer able to stop worrying about toilet arrangements on jobs like this; it was about the only time in her life she felt she'd prefer to be a man.

In one way, she was glad she'd be out all day; Althea was in a peculiar mood, but not sharing any reasons why that might be the case, and Mavis had decided she couldn't always be fretting about her. Althea was as good as could be expected for a woman of eighty who'd now just about fully recovered from recent hip-replacement surgery, and she was even continuing with the exercises she'd once baulked at undertaking, recognizing they kept her a little more supple than might otherwise be the case.

Mavis told herself she worried about Althea so much because once you were a nurse you could never go back to being an objective observer of those you loved and cared about ever again – or even of complete strangers, for that sake. She'd had to catch herself a few times lately when she'd been about to give unasked-for advice to a person she didn't know at all, but who was doing something that had the potential to damage their health or well-being. That was nothing but a slippery slope.

Mavis sighed as she dumped her bag into the back of the small, red car she'd rented for the day. She'd had to explain to Rhodri Lloyd, their client, that spending money on car rental was a good way to remain undetected by a target; it meant they were less likely to have their suspicions aroused by seeing the same vehicle in their area on multiple occasions.

Rhodri and his client had agreed to the expenditure surprisingly quickly, which had both pleased and surprised Mavis.

As she gave the matter some thought, Mavis reckoned that Rhodri's client had long-ago passed the point where he was worried about incurring costs to allow him to, hopefully, reveal the fraudulent behavior of the bricklayer who was suing him. Indeed, she reckoned he'd be happy to spend almost anything to prove the man was lying; it was now a matter of principle, not about getting value for money as far as a new wall was concerned.

Mavis sighed as she, once again, checked her destination on her GPS screen. Her research had told her that the semi-detached house where Ben Stirling lived was close to the end of his street, which meant she could hopefully park around the corner and still get a view of his front door. She'd also already established, by using the satellite images on online maps, that there wasn't any way she was going to be able to see the rear of his house, or his back garden, without gaining access to one of the houses in the street which backed onto his. She and Rhodri had agreed that might be needed, but to hold that approach in reserve; neither of them fancied the idea of getting the neighbors involved.

Finding herself in luck, Mavis parked at the end of the street around the corner from the Stirling household, and was satisfied she had as good a view of the entire front of his house, as well as his double garage doors, as she'd have had if she'd been parked right outside. She placed her custom-made windscreen cover in position. She could see quite well through the mesh, and she'd cut small holes in it that allowed her the chance to look out properly, and even take photos when needed. She'd discovered, through experience, that the dark gray color allowed her to sit and not be noticed, but it wasn't sufficiently noteworthy that anyone walking past the car would remark upon it.

The concept was something she'd seen displayed at an exhibition of surveillance technology she'd attended with Carol – though she'd preferred to take the idea and make her own version, rather than pay the ridiculous sum that had been asked by the so-called inventor.

It had taken her quite some time to find a cover that wasn't either reflective, or emblazoned with a pair of giant sunglasses or some witty saying, but she'd persevered, and had ended up with a workable solution that had cost less than half the amount being asked for the ready-made version. An all-round win, in her book.

She plugged in her earphones, turned on her talking book, and settled into the not-yet-uncomfortable seat, her eyes glued to the front door of the Stirling house, her digital camera at hand on the seat beside her.

She'd been there for not quite an hour, when there was action: a gangly youth exited the front door, and opened the garage doors wide. He was wearing the teen uniform of a hoody and jeans, so she couldn't see his face clearly, though she took several photos as he went about his business. He wheeled a motorcycle out of the garage, and set it on its stand in the drive. She reasoned this must be the subject's son, Stuart. Knowing her photos would have the time and date information in their data, she concentrated on watching, rather than note-taking, and had turned off her book, pulling out her earphones in case there was something useful she might hear.

Unfortunately, the boy set the engine of the motorcycle running, and revved it, using the handlebar controls. A moment later, Ben Stirling himself walked out through the front door. Mavis snapped away, but realized immediately that the man was limping heavily, and relying upon the stick he had in his left hand a great deal. So far, so bad. She watched and snapped as he pointed at the motorcycle, his son fiddling about on the side of it that Mavis couldn't see. Lots of revving, fiddling, pointing, and more revving followed, until the son turned off the ignition, and wheeled the motorcycle back into the garage. He joined his father, and they both entered the house.

Mavis checked her photos, made some notes in her notepad, recording times and activities, then resumed her watchful stance, resisting the temptation to have a cuppa out of the Thermos she'd brought; as soon as she drank, she'd be on the path to needing a loo, and she didn't want that.

Settling to her task, Mavis acknowledged that, sometimes in these situations, she wished she was a good enough knitter or crocheter to be able to create some sort of useful garment without having to take her eyes off her target. But she wasn't, and knew she'd probably look down at a dropped stitch at a critical moment, which would be most unprofessional, so she plugged herself into her book again and settled down.

The front door opened, and a slight woman walked out, heading to the garage. She was wearing a short, belted mac over a skirt, with high boots. *Not likely to be getting on a motorcycle*, thought Mavis. A couple of moments later a small, pale-lemon Mini – of the original style and size – left the garage. Mavis hadn't seen one like that in many a year; she'd driven a brown Mini for some time herself, decades earlier, but this lemon color? She'd always liked that. Her estimation of at least Ben Stirling's wife rose.

As the woman edged toward the end of the drive, her husband came out of the front door. Mavis reckoned he seemed a little less doddery on his feet, and noticed that he used his left hand, with the walking stick in it, to push the garage doors closed. Was this a sign he really didn't need his cane? She snapped furiously until he, once again, disappeared into the house.

She'd just settled again, when her phone rang. It was Althea. Mavis considered not answering, but knew how that panicked the dowager, so she said brightly, 'I'm a bit busy, dear. Is this urgent?'

'We can't find Chelly's christening mug, and Henry can't find his. He should be able to, don't you think?'

Mavis sighed. As was quite often the case, Althea had begun a conversation at what felt like its mid-point. She gathered her thoughts. 'The Case of the Missing Christening Mugs, eh? Do you think they've been mislaid, or stolen?'

Althea didn't respond immediately, then said quietly, 'It hadn't occurred to me that they were anything but mislaid. One of them was large and quite ugly, and one was custom-made…neither very appealing.'

Mavis said, 'But both silver. Solid silver?'

Althea agreed. 'I dare say they might both be worth tidy sums, if only for the weight of the silver. Oh dear. But why on earth would anyone bother to steal two christening mugs when we have so many other…things? Besides, since that new security system was installed last year I don't think a mouse could get a piece of cheese out of Chellingworth Hall without half the village knowing about it. Those claxons? Those lights? Any potential thief would be deaf and blind before they got out again.'

'Aye, that's the point, dear. Scare them out of their wits – once you've done your best to no' let them get in in the first place, of course.'

'Henry said no one's tried to rob Chellingworth since…well, you know when. But so very many people are welcomed into it each season, when the Hall is open to the public, that I dare say there's a chance someone might have spotted the mugs and has taken them. Though, of course, the docents and security people are there to make sure that sort of thing doesn't happen. Yes – maybe that's it. I hadn't even thought of theft until you mentioned it. I just assumed it was Henry being careless, or forgetful. Again.'

Mavis saw the front door of the Stirling home open, so said, 'I've got to be off now, dear. Have you asked Clementine about the mugs? You've often mentioned how she tends to take things to her rooms at Chellingworth, or back to the family pile in London, without mentioning it. I'll see you later – must go.'

Mavis disconnected, picked up her camera and snapped rapidly. Bob Stirling had shut his front door behind him, and was now wearing a jacket. Mavis wondered where he'd go. Acknowledging he was still limping heavily, she began to get concerned when he turned out of his garden and headed toward the corner of his street. Luckily for Mavis he stopped at a sludge-colored hatchback, and got inside.

As she continued to photograph him, and the car – in such a way that she captured the number plate – she wondered if a knee brace would allow for driving, and made a mental note to find out.

She dumped her camera, and slid down in her seat as he passed her, then she ripped off the windscreen cover, and got going. She managed to turn the car around and follow him, but she got stuck at a set of traffic lights, and he'd disappeared before she was able to follow his lead.

Cross with herself, Mavis did the only thing she could; she drove to a local garage to use the facilities, then returned to her prime spot at the corner of his street and settled in to wait, but at least – this time – she had some work she could do, and she didn't have to keep staring at the front door of the man's house.

TUESDAY 31st JANUARY

CHAPTER TWELVE

Annie wasn't looking forward to revisiting Swansea police headquarters, but she didn't say as much to Christine, who she felt was a bit down. Thwarted in their attempt to get a bit of shopping done and glean some more insights into life in Port Beynon the previous day – the shop having closed early due to 'winter hours' – they'd had toast for breakfast, tea with no milk, and were now, therefore, both relieved to be clutching small buckets of cappuccino as they waited for DCI Carys Llewellyn to join them in a meeting room.

'It's a bit grim for a meeting room,' noted Christine.

'There used to be a plant in that corner, but even that's gone now,' replied Annie. 'And you can see two hundred and twelve bricks through that window. I once counted them.' She kept telling herself she didn't need to feel as though the seat was disappearing beneath her…that she should focus on the positive aspects of her return to this particular location, and not allow herself to dwell on the reasons she'd been there before. That was what her counsellor had suggested when Annie had told her about her assignment, so she clung to that…as she tried to stop her knee from bouncing uncontrollably beneath the table.

Carys Llewellyn finally entered the room and looked exactly as Annie remembered her: navy trouser suit, white shirt, lowish heels, well-coiffed, unfussy hair. She greeted the two women with a wide smile as she shook hands with Christine, and hugged Annie with a surprising amount of enthusiasm.

'Lovely to see you again, Annie, though I wish the circumstances could be better. But, there, with me doing what I do, and you doing what you do, unless we bump into each other in a pub somewhere, we're always going to be meeting up because of some sort of tragedy, aren't we?'

'True,' said Annie. 'Just like your brother. Because he's the chief inspector in our part of the world, we only ever see him when there's a problem. Though he did come to a village event at Christmas where we all had a chance to meet his wife, and we got to see him in something other than his uniform.'

The DCI chuckled quietly. 'I'm going to put money on the fact he was wearing a jumper that was suitable for the golf course, because that's all he seems to own. Goes from one uniform to another, does that brother of mine. Family get-togethers are a hoot, not. But, there, this meeting isn't about me, or Carwen, or his oh-so-lovely wife, it's about your dead man, Brian Kelly, isn't it?'

Annie sensed that Carys Llewellyn didn't get along too well with her sister-in-law, but the detective was quite correct, the women weren't meeting to explore family dynamics – she and Christine were hoping for some insights into the death of one of Gemma Thomas's tenants.

Carys opened a folder and spoke without looking up at Annie and Christine. 'I don't expect you to comment upon the fact this is the second time I've told you that a case I've queried, that's being handled by uniform, has left me disappointed. Sadly, I have to say that I believe the circumstances surrounding the death of Brian Kelly should have received more attention. Reading the file, the facts are all there, but there's no follow-through. The medical records tell me massive trauma was sustained by most of the body, though not the head, ironically, because Mr Kelly was wearing a better-than-regulation helmet.'

She paused, then shook her head slowly. 'It seems his heart was punctured by a rib, and that's what killed him. Fast, which is good, I suppose.'

She read silently for a moment, then added, 'Time of death was put at anywhere between midnight and three in the morning of the day he was found, which was at half six, by the way. Nothing could have been done for him if he'd been found earlier, which I suppose is a relief for his loved ones, at least. There was an examination of his…vehicle…I'm never sure what to call those bikes that are pushbikes with an electronic motor attached. This file tells me the correct term is an e-bike, and that's what Brian Kelly had.'

She read silently again, then rattled off the details of the exact model. 'It was a folding type, and it's noted here that the wife – Sara Kelly, they'd been married for six years – told the attending officers it was a bike he used every day; he took the train, then cycled to work, right through the London traffic. The couple hail from Liverpool, but moved to the outskirts of west London several months ago. Amersham. She told the officers that it wasn't a new bike, he maintained it well, and he was an experienced rider. The file tells me that the examination of the bike was "inconclusive", which is irritating. It says there was so much damage to the entire thing that it was impossible to tell if any part of it had failed, to cause the accident. I understand the widow was given all the information gathered at the time, and while – of course – she's not "happy" about it, she's accepted the verdict of accidental death.'

Annie and Christine exchanged a knowing glance as Carys Llewellyn closed the folder. She looked at each woman, in turn, then added, 'So why should I consider this to be anything other than just that? It was an unfortunate, and very nasty accident, that happened on a remote road, in the middle of the night, and led to a tragic end. Wasn't it?'

Annie felt Christine press her knee against hers under the table, so cleared her throat. 'Our client owns the cottage where Brian Kelly was staying at the time of his death,' began Annie. Even she knew she sounded hesitant.

'And they're feeling guilty for some reason?' Carys's tone was dismissive.

'No, not guilty in that way...well, not really in any way, I suppose...' Annie felt lost.

'Gemma Thomas and her husband inherited the cottage from her late uncle,' said Christine firmly. 'She's got it into her head that "the cottage" killed her uncle, killed this Brian Kelly, and even tried to kill her husband a little while ago. She wants to sell up, but won't until she knows the place is safe. We're staying there to try to prove it is safe – though, to be honest, quite how we're going to do that we aren't sure. She reckons the place is cursed, you see, and it's almost impossible to prove a negative; if she insists upon believing something that cannot be disproved, then I think we're onto a bit of a non-starter, to be honest with you. That being said, we're game – so we're starting with trying to find out all we can about the two deaths she's focussed our attention upon; this poor Brian Kelly being one, and her uncle being the other. We met a neighbor who lives across the road from the cottage yesterday, and she mentioned local rumors that the cottage was cursed by two spinster sisters who lived there until their deaths. Apparently, they hated men and did some witchcrafty mumbo jumbo stuff so that men would never be safe there. Which is all rubbish, of course, because Gemma's uncle lived there quite happily for donkey's years all fine and dandy, until he died of carbon monoxide poisoning.'

Carys leaned forward. 'So...the cottage did, in fact, kill him.'

Annie shrugged uncomfortably and jumped in. 'In a way. But Brian Kelly? We wanted to prove to our client that his death was in no way connected with her cottage. But, if the reason for his accident was never discovered, then we can't go much further along that path, can we? There is one thing though: the neighbor we were talking to told us that the police never did any house-to-house interviewing or questioning after Kelly's accident. They didn't seem to make any effort to find out if there were any witnesses. And I wondered why that might be. Do you know?'

Carys stroked her jawbone, stared up at the ceiling for a moment, then replied, 'I don't, but I shall. I'll be talking to...the appropriate person...later today.'

'Do you know them? Will they help? Annie asked.

Carys smiled wryly. 'Tried yesterday, but was told it wasn't a priority. I then bumped into said person on the stairs, and made it clear it was a priority for me. We're meeting at two. Prompt.' She checked her watch.

Annie smiled. 'Good for you,' she said quietly. 'Maybe you'll be able to tell us something, after that meeting?'

Carys didn't reply, but instead asked, 'Did the neighbor you spoke to give you the impression that someone might have seen the accident – or something pertaining to it? Anything…suspicious?' A gleam in her eyes suggested to Annie she was already planning what she'd say at her two o'clock meeting.

'She said that everyone would have been in bed, asleep, at that time of night,' said Christine heavily, 'and we reckon she's a pretty reliable source. Classic village gossip; she's the sort who'd know if you told a fib in your silent prayers, so she would…and she'd tell anyone she could about it, too. Makes a very good apple tart though, to be fair to the woman.'

'And her name is?' Carys had a pen at the ready.

'Amy Francis. Husband is Glyn. Live in…sorry, don't know the name of the place, but it's directly opposite Sea View Cottage, which is the one we're staying at,' offered Annie. 'And Chrissy's right about her; fount of all local knowledge is Amy, and only too happy to share.'

Carys smiled. 'Sounds like exactly the sort of person I expect you'll get chummy with, all in the name of gathering local intel. The sort of woman our lot should have been talking to as well – which is what I'll be suggesting this afternoon. But, enough said about that. What was the uncle's name, by the way? And any idea when exactly he died?'

Annie hadn't expected that Carys's interest would be piqued to such an extent, so she pulled out her phone, opened an email, and scrolled quickly. 'Ted – or Edward, I suppose – Thomas. Oh, that must mean Gemma didn't change her name when she married.'

'Or else she married another Thomas,' said Carys, scribbling. 'That sort of thing happens a lot around here. A friend of mine was Morris in school, she's on her second husband, and she's still, and always has been, Morris. Married two of them, she has. And, no, before you ask, none of them were related at all…not unless you go back a couple of hundred years, I dare say. Anyway, do those notes of yours tell us when Ted Thomas died?'

Annie shook her head. 'Sorry, no. All our client said was…hang on, let me work this out…he died, they took possession of the house and got the builders in for about a year, and she started renting it out right away, and that was a couple of years ago. So he must have died about three years ago. I hope that helps – or would you like me to ask her for the actual date?'

Carys tapped her pen. 'I don't want to get anyone's hopes up, or get them worried either – so let me look into it first. If there are too many Edward Thomases recorded as having died in the general timeframe, or if I can't work out which one he is, I'll text you to ask her. Anything else? I've got a spare few hours…not. So, seriously – is there anything else you feel you should tell me? Like why did your client think the cottage tried to kill her husband?'

'A coffee maker exploded in his face,' said Christine. Annie could tell she was trying – rather unsuccessfully – to stifle a giggle.

'Most unfortunate,' said Carys. 'And do we have a date for that? Anyone look into why it happened?'

'About three weeks ago, and no,' said Annie. 'Oh…and there was the cleaner, too, of course.'

Carys looked up from her note taking. 'What cleaner?'

Annie told her about exactly when and how the cleaner had been burned by hot water.

Annie noticed Carys's brow furrow. 'And only the male was affected, eh? Is it usually women who do the cleaning there?' Annie nodded. 'So, unusual for a man to be there on that occasion. Any other tales of woe, or unexplained accidents happening to men there?'

Christine shrugged. 'To be honest, by the time she came to us, I think Gemma would have thought it was "the curse" if a man staying there had so much as stubbed his toe, and she did regale us with a whole list of "accidents" that had happened at the cottage, as well as telling us about innumerable breakdowns that needed fixes, having caused some inconvenience to guests – though she didn't mention any serious injuries. However, it's clearly not something that happens every time a man dares set foot in the place – whatever Glyn Francis or his wife might think. I honestly believe that it's all nonsense, and we'd hoped you could help us prove that in some way, though, of course, it seems you can't, at least when it comes to the accident that befell poor Mr Kelly.'

Carys looked at her phone. 'I must be going, but I promise I'll give this some time. I know what questions to ask which people, and I'll tell you whatever I can…whatever I'm allowed to. But I'll ask this of you: please tell me what you find out, especially when it comes to the fatalities of Mr Thomas and Mr Kelly. I need to know if any concerns or suspicions are raised that an outside party is involved. Got it?'

Annie and Christine nodded.

'Thanks for doing this for us,' said Annie, as all three women rose.

Carys smiled. 'I wouldn't say this to most people, but you were a great help with that case a while back. Thank you. I said I owed you, and I do. This is me paying back that debt of gratitude.' She leaned in and repeated, 'Paying it back in full – okay?'

Annie grinned.

The return trip to Port Beynon took a little longer than the outward journey, because Annie and Christine decided to pause at Swansea Airport on Fairwood Common so they could then follow the route back to the cottage that would have been taken by Brian Kelly. It was fairly direct, and they noted that very few parts of the road had any lighting to speak of – except as pubs or a few collections of cottages were passed. The road was sound, if winding.

Once again, Annie couldn't help but grab onto whatever she could as Christine drove too fast – as far as Annie was concerned – and she only managed to relax when they ended up having to follow a tractor for some distance. Finally able to enjoy the scenery, she felt a bit disappointed because there wasn't as much of it as she'd hoped; the road was bounded on both sides by tall hedges, all trimmed back to stubble, blocking any views or vistas of the coastline and its famed beaches.

When they arrived at the cottage, Annie finally sighed with relief.

'About ten miles,' said Christine, 'so twenty for the round trip. A long ride for someone used to shorter ones across London. Maybe he was tired out by the time he reached the village?'

Annie was puzzled. 'There's no charging thing at the cottage – would he need one of those for an e-bike, do you know?'

Christine shook her head. 'No. I've got a friend with one of those bikes; he has a charger thingy he carries with him, plugs that into an ordinary wall socket, then plugs his rechargeable battery into that. It's easy.'

Annie unbuckled her seat belt as she said, 'I wonder why Kelly was where he was, though. Amy said he was down the hill a bit. Why would he have gone past the cottage?'

Christine paused, her door already open. 'Maybe he lost control up the hill and was trying to regain it, but overshot the cottage?'

Annie sighed. 'Who knows? Not the police, by the looks of it. Though maybe someone around here saw…something. It's not as though anyone's asked them.'

'Talking about overshooting the cottage, do you think Gertie will be alright if we drive down to the shop before it closes?'

'Nah – she's been on her own too long already. She's not used to it. I'll let her do her business, then walk her down the hill – you can drive if you want. I know it looks like rain, but I don't mind getting wet. I've got all my walking gear with me.'

Christine chuckled as they headed to the front door. 'Remember when you first got to Anwen-by-Wye? You only had trainers. And look at you now – dressed like a real country gal. You've made a lot of changes to your life in a short time; you should be proud of yourself.'

Annie ducked as she walked through the front door, and heard Gertie's excited yelps in the kitchen. 'You're not kiddin', doll. But all for the best. I was treading water in London – now I've got a different life in front of me. You too. Did you all discuss your wedding when you were with your mum and dad at the weekend?'

They were almost overwhelmed by Gertie when Annie opened the kitchen door, which allowed Christine to get away with a quiet reply. 'Not you, too.' Then the subject was dropped, and the threesome set off for the village shop.

WEDNESDAY 1st FEBRUARY

CHAPTER THIRTEEN

Mavis got up with a bad back; two days of sitting in two different cars outside Ben Stirling's house had proved fruitless. Though she'd managed to successfully follow him when he drove himself to a betting office the previous day, she still had no evidence that he was not as incapacitated as he claimed. She'd also discovered that his car was an automatic, and her research into knee braces told her there was no reason why a person with one on their left leg – which he claimed he had – couldn't cope with driving a car without a clutch pedal, which had been very disappointing.

Her hire car *du jour* was an unremarkable dark blue saloon; not something Mavis would have ever chosen for herself, but a red car, followed by a brown one, then blue, meant she hoped she was much less likely to be spotted.

Having failed on the previous two days, Mavis set out with a heavy heart but a determined spirit on her third, and – even before lunch – was delighted that there was more action than she'd seen before. All three members of the Stirling family had things to do outside the home that day, it seemed: the son set off on his motorbike; the wife set out in her Mini, and, finally, Ben himself hobbled to his car, which he'd managed to park outside his house. Mavis was ready to follow him, and eased into the suddenly-busy traffic along the main road just a couple of vehicles behind him.

Annoyed that his car was such a sludgy color, she kept her eyes on him constantly as he drove steadily out of the town, and onto the quieter roads.

Concerned he might spot her with so little other traffic about, Mavis told herself it wouldn't be odd for one car to be behind another for some considerable distance, there not being many alternative routes to…anywhere.

As they continued, it seemed to Mavis that Ben Stirling was driving a little erratically; he'd slow down for a while, then go back to the speed limit, then a little over it. It was annoying. Eventually he pulled into a garage, where Mavis noticed the petrol was just a few pennies cheaper than at other places. She had to drive past, or draw attention to herself, but was delighted to spot a pub not far along the road – so she pulled in there, parked facing the road to allow a quick getaway, and waited. And waited. After twenty minutes Mavis decided her best course of action was to drive back to the garage and pass it, to see if Ben's car was still there. It wasn't.

Ah well, she'd taken a gamble that he'd pass her when he left the garage, and it hadn't paid off. Mavis realized her only option was to drive back to the Stirling house, hoping Ben had returned home. Would he really have driven all that way just to save a few pennies on petrol?

Not even I would do that, thought Mavis to herself, as she pulled into what she was now thinking of as her parking spot. Yes, Ben's car was outside his house again, and he was still sitting inside it, which she thought odd; he must have been there for some time, unless he'd stopped somewhere else on the way home.

Mavis made notes of the route she'd taken, mileage driven, and times. She also took photos of Ben sitting in his car, as she had done of the garage where he'd stopped. About ten minutes later, Mavis wondered if the man had dropped off to sleep where he sat; he wasn't moving, and didn't appear to be talking to anyone on the phone.

Another quarter of an hour passed before Mavis made up her mind that something was wrong.

Annoyed that she might have to break her cover, she wrestled with her conscience: should she walk to the man's car to see if he was alright, or should she give it a bit more time, hoping his son or wife would come home? Or maybe they were already inside their house, and hadn't noticed that he had returned?

She couldn't decide what to do for the best…then finally plumped for putting on a pair of sunglasses and driving past his car as slowly as she could.

Checking for traffic – both the street she was parked on and Stirling's street were clear – she pulled out slowly and passed as close to the side of his vehicle as she dared. She stopped. Ben Stirling's head was lolling back, his face gray, his eyes closed. Mavis pulled off her sunglasses, leaped out of her car and banged on his window. Nothing. No response. She dialled 999.

CHAPTER FOURTEEN

Carol's day had started well, then it went downhill rapidly; David wasn't feeling well – headachy and blocked up, plus a dodgy tummy – and Albert was unusually grizzly. A man cold and a new tooth coming through were Carol's diagnoses, so she told herself the pair of them would be fine together, as long as David didn't drop off or feel too poorly to tend to his son. He took some pills that were guaranteed to dry him up, ease his aches and pains, and keep him awake, then assured Carol he was able to fulfill both his parenting and professional duties for the day.

Out of the house by eleven, Carol drove as fast as she dared to make her appointment with Selina, the trainer at the spa's gym, and arrived just in time. Once again, she went through the process of having her name checked at the hotel's reception desk – this time by a blonde, as opposed to a brunette, but that was the only perceivable difference between the two receptionists she'd met so far. Out of breath just getting to the entrance to the spa, Carol couldn't help but wonder how she'd fare being put through her paces by a personal trainer, so she pushed open the smoked-glass door with trepidation.

Once again she was greeted by Willow Richards, and then handed off to Selina, who was lean, with honey-hued, smooth skin…of which there was a great deal on display.

Carol followed the young woman and said, 'I haven't got any clothes like you're wearing, so I thought these old things would do. If I decide to sign up, I could maybe invest in something a bit more snazzy.'

Selina turned, looked Carol up and down, and replied, 'We sell exercise-wear here, but I think we're out of your…size. I've got a catalogue you can look at. We could always order it in for you, though it might take a while; they usually only have the most popular sizes in stock.'

Carol bit her tongue; she wasn't surprised people like her didn't make more use of gyms if they were going to be made to feel like hopeless cases. She contented herself with a sigh, and a mental reminder that she was doing this for work purposes.

'No Caz today?' They'd reached the gym and she'd neither seen nor heard the woman whose hairstyling talents had – according to David in any case – made Carol look ten years younger, and happier than he'd seen her in a long time. Carol touched her hair as she spoke, knowing it looked and felt great.

Selina turned, hands on hips. 'Off sick. A cold, or a tummy bug, I think. They're both doing the rounds.'

Carol was just about to tell Selina about how challenging the start of her day had been – by way of engaging her in a conversation that might lead to some useful information-gathering – when Selina started to bark at her.

'We've only got an hour, and I can't imagine you're familiar with the equipment we have here, so let's start with the safety briefing, shall we?'

Carol was taken aback, but dutifully followed Selina as she explained what various pieces of equipment did, how they were to be used, and how they were not to be used. She said she'd be with Carol for the whole hour, so she didn't need to worry about changing the weights on anything. Indeed, she went further, telling Carol that all she'd be using that day was the equipment's lowest possible setting. She added, in no uncertain terms, that Carol wasn't to touch any of the plastic-encased dumbbells that weren't yellow – the lightest ones.

They headed to the sauna next; Selina suggested Carol might find it useful if she wanted to drop a few pounds, but added that the effect would only be temporary because it only helped get rid of excess fluids, adding that most of Carol's weight wouldn't be that easy to shift.

Carol felt as though she were being pummelled as she took yet another knock to her self-confidence, then reminded herself she was already aware of the hard-sell techniques Caz encouraged at the place.

Selina calmly explained that the use of it was included in the gym membership package, as was the swimming pool, though that was a hotel facility spa clients could take advantage of, rather than vice versa.

As they headed for the door to the pool, a woman appeared from the direction of the gym, looking lost. She stopped in her tracks. She was wearing a black swimming cap, goggles, a waffly robe, and flip-flops revealing rather prominent bunions, and toenails painted with a metallic purple varnish that Carol thought quite spectacular.

'Not hotel?' She looked around, confused; at least, Carol suspected she was confused; the goggles made it hard to be sure.

'This is the spa. Are you wanting to return to your locker in the hotel changing room?' Selina shouted.

The woman replied just as loudly, 'Hotel. I want hotel. Where is hotel?'

Carol reckoned she had a Russian, or Ukrainian accent – something from that part of the world, in any case.

Selina stepped forward, ushered the woman back into the pool area, and pointed to a door at the far end of the enclosure with the word HOTEL printed above it in letters two feet tall.

She pointed at the door. 'Hotel,' she shouted.

'Thank you,' screamed the woman back at her, and headed off.

'Does that happen often?' Carol was intrigued.

Selina shrugged. 'People don't read signs, it seems. Sometimes we find hotel guests wandering about in the spa looking for their clothes in our locker room – which is green, as you've seen – whereas the hotel locker room is white. You think they'd notice the difference, wouldn't you?'

Carol nodded, then gave her attention to the pool itself, which was appealingly turquoise, and centered in a room encrusted with iridescent mosaic tiles on one long wall, the opposite wall being entirely made of floor to ceiling mullioned windows.

She was surprised that it didn't smell of the horrid chemicals she associated with the public swimming baths she'd encountered in her youth; instead, she noted a light fragrance that was both refreshing and relaxing – it reminded her of perfect summer days on the beach.

'That's it,' snapped Selina. 'Now you've had the tour, let's get going. A bit of cardio to start, I think, so I can gauge your fitness levels.'

Carol's reverie cut short, she plodded back to the gym and applied herself, as instructed. Thirty minutes later she was pink in the face but feeling good; she'd used every piece of equipment without incident, and had quite enjoyed it all.

'We'll finish with some exercises you can do at home, with tinned foods if you haven't got weights. Just grab the yellow dumbbells, then place your feet as far apart as your hips, on the mat over there, and we'll begin with some gentle lifting and stretching.'

Selina bent to pick up a set of blue dumbbells from the rack – which held about forty sets of weights in all. The blue ones were much bigger, and heavier, than the yellow ones Carol was already holding, which she noticed were – for some reason – damp. She saw Selina's well-developed arm muscles flex as she picked up the first one, but, before she could pick up its partner, the entire rack collapsed, sending dozens of weights cascading toward the two women. Carol leaped backwards, but Selina wasn't as quick, and she was struck by several of the large, black weights that had been on the lowest couple of rungs. She screamed and fell backwards.

There could be absolutely no doubt that Selina's shinbone was broken.

Carol wasn't sure if it was Selina's agonized screams, or her shouting, 'Help – someone come to the gym to help!' that brought both Willow and Jasmine running, but she was glad they did, because her phone was shut away in the locker room, so they were able to call the emergency services on behalf of their badly injured colleague.

CHAPTER FIFTEEN

'Tea is being served in the small sitting room, Your Grace,' said Edward as he helped Althea with her coat.

'Who's there?' Althea whispered.

Edward cleared his throat. 'Their Graces, the duke and duchess, with your grandson, Your Grace. Her Grace's parents are about to come downstairs to join the party, too, I believe. They have been advised that tea will be served early today, to accommodate the…um…feeding schedule Her Grace has outlined to us, Your Grace.'

Althea thanked Edward, who vanished with her outerwear, leaving the dowager and McFli to make their way, together, to greet her family. She was grateful she might at least snatch a few moments with her grandson without her daughter-in-law's parents being there, too.

The scene that met Althea's eyes when she entered the room where tea was being served beside the roaring fire was idyllic. She was so happy for her son; both she and Henry himself had reached the point – when he'd turned fifty, she recalled – where neither of them had believed he'd ever know the joys of fatherhood. However, she reminded herself that, almost as soon as Stephanie Timbers arrived at Chellingworth Hall to take up the role of public relations manager several years ago, she'd liked the young woman, and she'd done a few little things along the way to give Stephanie and Henry the opportunity to work together on several projects.

Now here they were; her son didn't just have a duchess to stand beside him through life, but a son and heir, too, which was both wonderful and something of a relief for Althea.

Greeting her family, the dowager was happy to sit, settle McFli beside the fire, then take her grandson in her arms, holding him close, and giving her attention to him completely.

When Sheila and John Timbers arrived to take tea with them all, she decided there and then that she'd hold onto her charge for just a little longer than she usually did; she could have a slice of Victoria sponge any old time, but didn't have too many chances to cradle her grandson.

The conversation revolved around the child, of course, and Stephanie was able to inform everyone that the latest medical examination of both mother and baby had gone swimmingly, with both getting full marks for recovery, and development.

With this excellent news being digested, along with cups of tea and slices of cake, Althea cooed when the baby's eyes peeled open and he smiled at her, then began to wonder how such a small bundle could become so heavy, so quickly.

Relinquishing her grandson when his mother suggested he be returned to his carry cot so that everyone could enjoy their refreshments, Althea watched and listened as Sheila and John chattered about what they'd been watching on television before they'd come to join the group. From what she could gather they'd been engrossed in something where people allowed so-called experts to grub about in their attics trying to find items no one even knew were hidden away there, that were then dusted off, and sold at auction for what the participants were frequently delighted to discover was quite a lot of money.

Althea couldn't imagine having unknown people rummaging about in her home, and said as much, then added, 'But, I dare say if we'd all done a bit more rummaging over the years, at least we'd know where your christening mug, and your father's, were, Henry.'

She took her son's heavy sigh to be one of annoyance and prepared herself for an onslaught of whining that would be his way of justifying why not knowing where those two items were hiding was absolutely not his fault at all. Standard Operating Procedure for Henry – but that wasn't what happened at all.

'Actually, Althea, Henry's been quite active on that front,' said Stephanie. 'Go on, Henry, tell your mother what you've been up to.'

Althea put down the plate she'd been holding under her sponge, making sure to brush the crumbs onto the rug as she did so – knowing that McFli was sitting waiting for them. Then she attended to her son, who was displaying his usual reluctance to speak.

'What have you been up to, Henry?' Althea could always tell when he needed a prod.

Henry stood beside McFli at the hearth, and rocked on his toes a little. 'I began with the records made by the insurance people who come every year, in the Estates Office. Bob Fernley and I dug out everything from the files, and Edward kindly had them installed in the library. I've been perusing them there, ever since.'

'With what purpose, dear?' Althea couldn't imagine.

Henry looked rather pleased with himself when he replied, 'Well, you see, Mother, those documents list the items here at Chellingworth Hall. All of them. So, every time I found a mention of a silver mug, or silver cup, of some sort, I got one of the staff to go to the room where it was listed as…residing…and to bring it to me, in the library.'

Althea smiled. 'How terribly clever of you, Henry.'

Stephanie glowed. 'I know, it was, wasn't it? And we really thought the missing mugs would come to light that way, didn't we, Henry?'

Henry nodded. 'Thank you, Mother, Stephanie. Indeed, one had hoped that would have flushed them out into the open, so to speak, but we were disappointed. We did, however, manage to amass a great number of silver items in the library that I had absolutely no idea we possessed. Some of them are rather delightful, though some – I must say – leave something to be desired.'

'Tastes change over time,' said Sheila, sounding sage. 'Take this dress I'm wearing; it's perfectly fine when it's just family, for tea, but I couldn't wear it out – it's very "five years ago".'

Althea felt the woman had, once again, missed the point of the conversation entirely. 'So we still don't know where the missing mugs have got to?' She felt exasperated.

'Hang on, Althea. Henry didn't leave it there, did you?' Stephanie was smiling and nodding at her husband in an encouraging way.

'Indeed not, dear. I would not be thwarted,' declaimed Henry, using what his mother recognized as his rendition of a Churchillian tone. 'I then undertook a thorough search of all the private rooms used by the family.'

Althea had always been amused by the way her son stuck his thumbs into his waistcoat pocket when making what he felt to be an important point; she had no doubt he'd no recollection of the fact that his late father had done much the same thing. She smiled to see how her son's small idiosyncrasies were, sometimes, so similar to those of her dear Chelly.

'And did you find them lurking at the back of somebody's wardrobe, Henry?' She was genuinely interested.

Henry deflated a little. 'I'm sorry to say that I did not. And I really was most meticulous in the way I worked through every drawer, every cupboard, and every nook and cranny. I made a little map of each room before I began, and worked my way around each wall, one at a time.'

'Oh dear,' said Althea.

'I am now absolutely certain that those mugs are not here. Anywhere.' Henry sounded triumphantly defeated, if such a thing were possible.

'Do you have any more plans to try to locate them?' Althea couldn't imagine what they might be.

Stephanie jumped in. 'He has, and he's taken action on that front already, haven't you, dear?'

Althea couldn't help but be heartened not just by how incredibly resourceful it appeared her hitherto somewhat lacking son had become, but how unusually proud of him his wife was being.

'The idea of theft occurred to me,' said Henry, thoughtfully. 'Of course, we have one of the best types of security systems for our sort of set-up, but I did wonder if there might have been a slip-up somehow.'

Althea tried to not roll her eyes, because she didn't want her son to suspect she thought this a foolish statement…at least, she hoped it was.

Henry continued, 'Then I remembered how Alexander Bright and the chap who runs that antiques business he's involved with, Bill Coggins, are always being sent information about stolen goods by the police. I recalled him telling me about lists they are sent, and photographs too, just in case something is presented to them for sale, illegally.'

'But you haven't reported the mugs as stolen, Henry,' said John Timbers.

Althea was always startled when he spoke, because he only did so very infrequently. On this occasion she nodded toward him graciously, silently agreeing with his observation.

Henry replied patiently, 'I agree, but if they have been stolen, and we've been unaware of that, they might turn up at Alexander's place – so I hunted high and low to try to find some photographs of the two mugs in question.'

'Good heavens, that must have taken some doing.' Althea had an inkling of just how many family photograph albums existed, and couldn't imagine facing the task of combing through them all.

'I was able to help with that part,' said Stephanie proudly. 'It was fascinating, to be honest. Unless I'd had to do this, I might have gone for many years without seeing all the family members who've lived here at Chellingworth and many of the events it's hosted in the past. It was a gift, in a way – and we found just what we needed, too, didn't we, dear?'

Henry returned to the table when Edward brought two more pots of tea. He poured, as he said, 'Indeed we did. I found a photograph of me in the nursery, with my christening mug on my desk with my pencils in it. I was wearing that navy-striped two-piece, Mother. I dare say you recall that. I seem to think I was especially fond of it.'

Althea nodded and said, 'Ah yes, I remember it well. As you say, a favourite of yours, and mine, too.' She didn't mention that Henry had stuck both points of a compass into his hand to see if it would hurt, had bled profusely over said striped outfit, and that it had been destroyed.

'I also found a snap of Father at his bathroom door – with his christening mug in the background of the photo. Might that have been a shot you'd have taken, Mother? It seemed an odd place for there to be a camera.'

Althea smiled, feeling wistful. 'Was your father in shirt sleeves with his braces off his shoulders. Half shaved, with foam still on his face?'

Henry nodded, looking impressed. 'Gosh, what a memory. Yes, that's it exactly.'

Althea smiled silently, then spoke quietly. 'That was the summer when we…you were small, and we'd not yet had Clementine. Those were…very special times.' Althea had absolutely no intention of saying anything more.

'Well, just as well you took the photo, Mother, because both it, and the other one of me in the nursery, are with Alexander. He and Bill are going to check to see if they, or anyone else "in the trade", has seen the pieces. What do you think of that?'

Althea could tell that it wasn't just she who was impressed, so replied, 'Henry, you are my son, so – of course – I am proud of you every moment of every day, But, on occasions like this, when you come up with such clever ideas and prove you have the ability to follow them through, I am more than proud of you, I am proud *for* you…because I've always believed you need to be challenged to have the opportunity to show you can in fact rise to meet most tasks.'

Her son said, 'Thank you, Mother, that means a great deal.'

'You're welcome, dear. Now, might I have another piece of that wonderful sponge, please?'

CHAPTER SIXTEEN

Annie woke hoping to see the sea, but all she got was a face full of fog. She'd commandeered one of the bedrooms on the lower floor, feeling unable to cope with either the low ceilings or tiny bathroom upstairs; she managed with those same challenges at her cottage in Anwen-by-Wye, and had to admit it was nice to be able to enjoy rooms with proportions more accommodating of her height. She'd got out of bed, had a wonderful stretch, and had opened the curtains ready to enjoy the lovely view, but was disappointed to discover she could only see a few feet across the lower patio; beyond that the grassy garden faded to nothing.

She felt a little claustrophobic for a few moments – keenly aware of the fact that it looked as though the rest of the world had disappeared entirely – but then revelled in the simple luxury of being able to slide open a glass door and walk out with her puppy, while still wearing her pajamas, with a jacket pulled around her shoulders. She loved the fact she didn't need to be properly dressed to go out, as she had to be in the village, which was another problem with her little home – there was nowhere for a dog to relieve itself.

She kept a grip on the lead as Gertie hunted about for the perfect spot to do her business; Annie didn't want to lose sight of her, because then she wouldn't know where she needed to clean up. Finally able to get to the bathroom herself, she prepared herself for the day, pulling on thick leggings and socks, ready for what had been decided as the plan: get out, and stay out until contact had been made with the locals. The trip to the shop the day before had been fruitless: the son of the family who owned it was behind the counter, and getting him to utter a single word had been like pulling teeth; the rest of the village had been deserted – the rain, that had soaked both Annie and Christine to the skin, had seen to that.

'The weather forecast didn't mentioned fog, but at least it's stopped raining,' said Annie as she and Gertie joined Christine in the kitchen.

Christine checked her watch. 'The tide's in – so it's probably a sea mist.'

'How do you know when the tide's in?'

Christine chuckled. 'I checked last night, because Alexander asked me about it.'

'How is he? Missing his fiancée yet? You must be missing him. I know I'm missing Tude. He's become such a big part of my life. Oh, sorry – I was asking you about you, not telling you about me.'

Christine looked Annie up and down with a quizzical look. 'That's okay – conversations are allowed to wander between friends. Anyway, he's missing me a bit, I suppose. But, come on, let's not chatter here – we said we'd go for a good long walk on the sands, so let's get going, as soon as we can. I've already filled a thermal mug with coffee to take with me, because tea never tastes right out of those things. Shall I do one for you while you have that piece of toast I don't want?'

Annie looked at the toast hungrily, and agreed to the plan of action.

Finally out of the cottage, the two women strolled down the hill, with Gertie ahead of them both. Annie gripped her lead and kept her close; she didn't think she'd see anything or anyone coming toward them, though she hoped she'd at least hear any cars. Finally at a part of the road where there was a pavement, she relaxed a little; eventually, Gertie was allowed to run at the full extent of her expanding lead when they reached the sand – not that there was a great deal of it, the tide being high.

'Along in this direction there's an arc to the beach, with dunes,' said Christine, leading the way.

'You've been doing your homework,' remarked Annie. 'Did Alexander ask you about that too?'

Christine looked bemused. 'Alexander? Ask about the beach? No. Not really. He's tied up preparing to bid for a new project at the moment. Got a lot on.'

Annie noticed a strange tone in Christine's voice. 'Everything okay? Between the two of you, I mean.'

No answer.

'I knew a girl, once, who'd been living with her boyfriend for six years. They got married, and she walked out on him and the marriage on their honeymoon. Making a commitment can change things, I know.'

Christine paused, rubbing the sand with the toe of her rugged walking boot. 'It's weird. Of course, I've never been engaged before, and I do believe he and I are right for each other...but...I didn't know that being an engaged person would feel...like this.' Annie noticed her twisting her massive engagement ring through her knitted glove as she spoke.

Annie took her chum's arm, as Gertie barked at a clump of grass on the side of a dune. 'I'm not able to give any advice. Sorry, doll. Never been engaged myself, though I thought I was coming close to it once upon a time – before he died, and I found out that he was still married. Nah, no use on this one, me. But tell me what you mean. What *does* it feel like?'

Christine battled with some stray hairs that had blown into her mouth. 'I always thought being engaged would be a thing in its own right. But it doesn't feel like that. Everyone's asking us when we're going to get married, and I hadn't expected it, though I know, now, that I've been guilty of doing that myself in the past; someone's bubbling with excitement when they show you their ring, and you immediately ask if they've set the date. It's as though a person's not allowed to enjoy being engaged...as though it doesn't exist as a recognizable state. You're no longer *just* a boyfriend and girlfriend, you're a couple on a journey to the altar...without being able to pause and enjoy the scenery along the way.'

Annie pondered Christine's words. 'Maybe a short engagement is the way to go, then? You know – if you're going to do it, just do it.'

Christine chuckled darkly. 'Get the wedding sorted quickly? That's not going to happen. You've no idea how Mammy's been. It's frightening, so it is. Such a palaver.'

'Do your parents want you to get married in Ireland, by any chance?'

Christine shook her head. 'Been up one side and down the other on that one, so we have. No way am I asking a couple of hundred people to go to Ireland for it, and I've said that. Quite plainly. Besides, the house there isn't in any fit state to host a wedding…Daddy's got people working on almost every part of it come the better weather, so he has.'

'A couple of hundred guests? So many?' Annie was gobsmacked.

Christine nodded. 'And that's likely to grow as we all remember people we've forgotten. That's what we did last weekend – write lists of people who *have* to be invited, who *should* be invited, and those we actually *want* to invite. The only short lists were those of the people Alexander and I want there; the others all go on for pages.'

Annie didn't know what to say. Christine's father was a viscount, and he'd made a fortune in the City of London – those two factors alone would mean he'd have to invite a lot of people to his daughter's wedding, or risk putting their noses out of joint, she reckoned. Then there'd be Christine's friends and acquaintances, not to mention all the people Alexander would need to have there for both business, and personal, reasons. Though, for him, there'd be no family at all, of course.

'Elope?' Annie grinned.

Christine said quietly, 'It's occurred to me on more than one occasion these past couple of days. I'd thought that being engaged would be fun. It turns out it's not. Even Alexander's gone a bit…well, sort of off the boil.'

Annie didn't fancy venturing into waters of a deeply personal, and private, nature, so said noncommittally, 'You haven't seen much of each other over the past few weeks, really, have you? And, like you said, he's got a lot on his plate at the moment. Maybe he's just…a bit too tired for it.' She left it at that.

Christine laughed, and shoved her friend playfully. 'I don't mean like that. I mean he's gone a bit quiet about the whole "engaged to be married" thing. He doesn't want to talk about it, then he does.'

Annie was composing a suitable reply, when Gertie went off at such a pace that she almost got pulled over. 'Oi, Gert,' she called, tugging at her lead.

The reason for the puppy's enthusiasm came into sight – a rather overweight pug with its tongue hanging out, its bulging eyes looking quite happy. The dog was followed by an equally round-eyed, rotund man, who Annie reckoned was not quite five feet tall. The overall impression of the man being the human version of his dog was made all the more noticeable by the fact he was wearing a dun-colored, sheepskin jacket with leather-covered buttons that were under some strain.

'Winnie, come back, Winnie,' he shouted. The dog took as much notice of him as Gertie was taking of Annie. None. Their leads got tangled as both dogs greeted each other with enthusiastic sniffing.

'Sorry,' the man said, sounding out of puff. 'She likes meeting other dogs. Will yours be alright with her?'

'Gert? Yeah, she loves to socialize,' said Annie, proudly looking down at how nicely the two dogs were getting along. 'A bit enthusiastic, but she's still a puppy. Means no harm.'

'They do nip though, don't they? Puppies.' The man looked concerned, and kept tugging on the battered old lead he was holding.

Christine stepped in. 'Let me get you four untangled – no, you two stand still, and I'll sort it out.' As she struggled with the writhing dogs, she said, 'Good morning, by the way. My name's Christine, and this is Annie. The puppy is Gertie. And did you say yours is Winnie? Nice name.'

'She's Winifred the Third. I call them all Winnie.'

Annie didn't think the man sounded terribly friendly, so decided on a full charm offensive. 'We're staying at a place up the hill for a while. It's so beautiful here – even when you can't really see anything, it's lovely. Are you local? It must be wonderful to live here all the time.'

'I know who you two are. Amy told me. I'm Cadog. Cadog Smith. Lived up behind the Francis house, over by the fields, all my life, I have. So, yes. Local. Proper local. I'm even named for the church.'

Annie was trying to work out what the man was talking about. 'Named for the church? Sorry, I don't understand.'

Finally gaining control of Winnie, Cadog said, 'The church on the hill. St Cattwg's. Cadog, see? He founded a church there himself, back in the sixth century. Not a lot of places can say that. Mind you, the building you see now has only been there since the twelfth century, and they carried on sticking new bits onto it in the fifteenth and sixteenth centuries, then opened it up a bit inside back in the eighteen hundreds. New windows from last century are nice – though they're a bit modern for my tastes. Will you be attending the service on Sunday? I'd be happy to point out the leper's window they blocked up in the wall, and I can tell you all about the water stoup that was given by a Spanish sea captain in gratitude for the locals saving him. Got good voices, have you? We always enjoy it when visitors with good voices come along.'

Annie and Christine stiffened, though neither commented upon the man's extraordinary manner. As he spoke, he smiled broadly and tilted his head as though looking just above them – though he couldn't possibly see anything, because his eyes were closed tight. When he stopped speaking, he opened his eyes again, and smiled even more manically.

Annie found it very off-putting. Hesitantly, she replied, 'We're not quite sure of our plans for the weekend, yet, but we're all for joining in with community activities.' Hoping to engage him further she dared, 'Does anything else go on around here that we could throw ourselves into?'

Both Winnie and Gertie had decided they might as well lie down on the sand if their humans were going to chat, so Annie gave Gertie a 'Good girl', hoping the man would come up with something.

'There's the pub quiz tomorrow night. That's very popular in the winter. Good chance for everyone to get together.' He beamed.

Annie beamed back, knowing he couldn't see her.

He continued, 'My wife was very keen on it – one of the founders, in fact. Not up to it now, I'm sorry to say, but she insists that I go.'

'Are you a member of a team?' Annie wondered how it all worked.

'I pair up with someone. You only need two for a team – so you could join in with that. It's free – though it's only fair for the participants to buy a few drinks during the evening, you know? Any good at quizzes, are you?'

Annie chuckled. 'Depends on the prizes.'

'Now there you're in luck, because it's always meat. Good meat, too. None of your sausages. Proper roasts. Local, of course. Lamb, usually, but sometimes beef. A couple of the local farmers donate it. Then they try their best to not let anyone else win it. The atmosphere can become quite competitive – though it's all good fun, really.' He smiled cheerily as he spoke, blindly.

'Sounds right up our alley, doesn't it, Chrissy?' Annie nudged her friend.

Christine enthused, 'Oh, I should say.'

'Excellent. It starts at seven, but you have to be there to sign up by half six. And they do a good lamb stew so don't eat before you get there. But, if you want that, you should get there for about half five, because he'll sell out of it. Always does.' Cadog paused, opened his eyes, then closed them again. 'I have no idea why he just doesn't make more.'

Annie was still in chatty mode. 'I'm always saying that to the landlord at the pub in our...I mean my...village. He does a very good lamb stew, too. I'll be interested to find out how this one measures up to his.'

'And what part of England is that in, then?' Cadog turned his head toward Annie as he spoke, nodding gently, as if to a child.

'I live here in Wales. Anwen-by-Wye, in the Wye Valley. Do you know it?'

Cadog shook his head. 'There are so many little places around there. All lovely. We used to drive that way when we were younger, of a weekend, me and my wife. Not now, of course. And that's where you live? How extraordinary. Are there many English people there? It's not so far from the border, I suppose. You're both English, aren't you?'

'I'm Irish, actually,' said Christine, 'though I live in London now – as I'm sure your neighbor told you. Annie's the one who lives in Wales, I'm in Battersea. Do you know it?'

Cadog shook his head. 'Went to London once. Didn't like it. Too many people, all in a hurry and looking miserable. Not for me. Nor my wife. We agreed on that. This is our place.' He waved an arm, just as weak sunlight pierced the clouds.

Annie noticed how the droplets left by the fog on the dune grasses glistened like jewels, and, above her, the seagulls' cries sliced through the background rumble of the surf on the beach. She liked the place; it felt…right.

'It's wonderful,' she said – aloud, as it happened – then gathered herself. 'Right then, lamb stew and a quiz night it is for us, Chrissy.'

'Absolutely. I can hardly wait.'

'You can bring her, too,' said Cadog, nodding at Gertie. 'Dog-friendly the pub is now, which isn't a bad thing. I can't bring Winnie though – she's always got a bit of a dicky tummy in the evenings, and I can't inflict that on anyone, in public, like. Besides, she's company for the wife. Right-o, I'll be off home now then. Want to get in before the rain comes,' said Cadog, urging a reluctant Winnie to get up.

Annie looked at the sky. 'Rain? Really? It looks as though the sun's coming out.'

Cadog shook his head sadly as he headed toward the hill. 'Take my word for it, cats and dogs within the hour, whatever those weather forecasters might say. I can spot it a mile off, me. And you two be careful at that cottage – they don't say it's cursed for no reason, you know.'

As he trudged off, Annie and Christine gaped at each other, then agreed to follow Cadog as he went on his way; this was too good a chance to miss.

'Come on, Gert,' said Annie, 'let's go.' Gertie was happy to comply, and soon the dogs were trotting along together with Annie one side of Cadog, and Christine the other.

'Amy mentioned something about the place being cursed,' said Annie, 'but we'd love to hear more. What do you know about it? Were there two witches who used to live there?'

Cadog seemed pleased to have the chance to chat, and Annie was delighted to notice that he kept his eyes open as he walked; he looked straight ahead, not at her or Christine.

'Oh, she mentioned them, did she? Two sisters, they were. I knew them both, in passing. Didn't go out much, and they were already old even when I was young. Both died in the place, back about fifty years ago. Must have both been in their nineties by then. One went, then the other one not long after. Never came to church. Didn't mix at all. Didn't ever have any visitors. Didn't drive. Got everything they needed in the village. Or delivered. Back in those days a van would come around with all sorts. And they gardened, grew their own stuff, see? Right up until the end. Both of them. Must have been fit, I suppose. Both Gower women, but from Slade Cross originally. Not here.'

'Where's that?' Annie was trying to keep Gertie under control.

'Along the way. This is Port Beynon, then there's Horton, then a little bay, Slade. Farms up above it, and a few cottages. Moved here when their father died, I think. Had a farm, couldn't run it. Sold it, bought that cottage. Plenty big enough for the two of them. Lovely little place, isn't it? Running right down to the beach like it does. Magic. And there they stayed.'

'But not witches?' Christine pressed.

Cadog shrugged. 'Got to ask yourself why they never came to church, haven't you? Heart of the community, it is. Especially back then. My father was Church Warden, and we always went three times every Sunday. Them? Never. Now that does not speak of God-fearing people. So – maybe not witches, but godless, that's for sure.'

'But why would they curse the cottage?' Annie was hoping for something.

Cadog's reply surprised her. 'Hated men, they did. I saw both of them spit as men walked past. Horrible, they were. Nasty pieces of work, both of them. One was taller and thinner, the other short and round. Had a mole on her face like a big sultana. With hairs growing out of it.'

Annie was taken aback by how personal Cadog's words seemed. 'But a curse? Why? So that men wouldn't be happy living there? Didn't the current owner's uncle live there for a long time?'

'Yes, Annie's right,' said Christine. 'Trust me, being Irish I know of enough places where curses are believed in so strongly that people give a house a wide birth forever. But the cottage has been more or less constantly inhabited, with no major disasters befalling those who've lived there – or are there things no one is telling us, because we're paying tenants?'

Cadog stopped to catch his breath; they'd reached the steeper part of the hill, and were huddled at the side of the road, the pavement having disappeared. He took a good look at Annie, peered at Christine, then snapped his eyes shut. 'Some places aren't good places. That's all I'll say. I've heard that all sorts of things go wrong at the cottage, all the time. Maybe the Thomas family's luck at the place has run out – or maybe having all those workmen in the place transforming it just brought out the bad in the walls. I know what I know, and I'll say no more.'

They walked on, finally approaching the cottage. Before they reached it, Cadog turned and waved. 'I always cross the road here. It's best. Maybe see you tomorrow night. Nice to meet you. Bye.'

'Well, he's cheery,' said Christine as she opened the front door.

'And knows more about this place than he's saying. I got the impression that one of the boys the two old sisters spat at was him – didn't you?'

Christine agreed. 'I wonder if Carol managed to find out more about them – I'll check with her. Salad for lunch? Or shall I open a tin of soup?'

'Soup for me, ta, doll,' said Annie. 'And it'll be my turn to cook dinner tonight – so how about pizza? I like to plan ahead, just so I can get my mouth in shape.'

'Okey doke. Now, let's get some lunch in us, and get on with some work. I've got loads of people to talk to who've come here to repair and replace things, and I know you do too.'

The rest of the day flashed past as far as Annie was concerned, and – with a tummy full of pizza – she fell into a deep sleep, dreaming of Tudor, with whom she'd had a lovely chat in the afternoon.

It was just before midnight when a noise woke her. She didn't know exactly what it was, but it was definitely inside the cottage, and it was…yes, creaking. Annie sat up slowly, and swung her legs out of bed. The noise was getting closer. Her toes found her slippers, and she stubbed her feet into them. With the curtains closed, and in unfamiliar surroundings, Annie couldn't quite get her bearings, and the next thing she knew she'd bumped into something, yelled as she banged her knee, the something clattered onto the floor, Gertie leaped up and started barking…then there was a blinding light.

'Are you okay?' Christine was standing in front of her with a torch pointing into her eyes.

'Turn that thing off, and turn the lights on. Switch on the wall, just inside the door,' said Annie, rubbing her knee.

With the lights on, Annie could see that she'd knocked over the small bedside table, and the mug of water she'd had on it. Luckily the mug hadn't broken, but she was amazed at how far half a mug of water had managed to spread. She and Christine mopped it up with a towel from the bathroom, and then – with everything back where it should be – she asked, 'How did you get here so quickly?'

Christine looked guilty. 'I was just outside your door when you shouted. I thought something was wrong.'

Puzzled, Annie asked, 'Why were you outside my door? And why the torch?'

Christine sat on the edge of the bed. 'I could hear…something, Annie. I was lying in bed, and I could hear something.'

'Where?'

'Well, it wasn't on the floor I was on, nor above me, so I got my torch and went into the kitchen and the sitting room. It had stopped by then, so I waited about a bit…then I heard it again. I was sure it was coming from down here. So I came down – I was as quiet as I could be, so I was. I didn't want to wake you. But even these new stairs creak, though not as bad as the old ones.'

'What sort of sound was it?' Annie hardly dared ask.

Christine looked worried. 'It was like…crying. Not like cats when they sound like babies, but sort of…mournful crying. Terrible it was. Got me right here.' She clutched at her chest, and Annie could tell her friend was really shaken.

Annie sighed. 'It's alright, doll, don't worry about it. Probably Gert was whining in her sleep – she does that sometimes. Runs marathons when she's asleep too. I've got used to it now, so it wouldn't wake me. But to you it could easily sound like…well, what you described.'

Christine nodded, but looked unconvinced.

'Tell you what,' said Annie, 'use the bedroom across the hall for tonight, and we'll both keep our doors open. If Gert goes at it again, she might wake you, but at least you'll know what it is. How about that?'

Christine perked up and agreed.

Finally back in bed – having let Gert out for a quick nature break – Annie snuggled into her pillow and tried to sleep. She hoped the noise that Christine had heard *had* been Gertie up to her tricks, and not…something else. She squeezed her eyes shut, and tried to control her breathing. Yes, it had to be Gert's fault.

THURSDAY 2nd FEBRUARY

CHAPTER SEVENTEEN

Mavis had woken up feeling as though someone had wrung her out and left her on an icy clothesline to dry overnight. Having got to her bed at three in the morning, after spending hours at the A & E with Ben Stirling and, eventually, his family, she'd allowed herself a lie-in, but felt as though she'd hardly slept at all.

Once she'd gathered her thoughts, and prepared her body for the day ahead, she sat at the desk in her room and phoned Rhodri Lloyd; it was going to be a difficult conversation, but it had to be done.

Preferring to get unpleasant things over with quickly, Mavis reported the events of the previous day as pithily as possible. When she disconnected, Mavis thought she'd done as good a job as possible under the circumstances, and also felt Rhodri had been…well, understanding – eventually – though flummoxed to start with. He'd promised to get in touch with her after he'd received more instructions from his client.

Believing the most difficult part of her day was behind her, Mavis descended to the dining room to share lunch with Althea. She was hoping her case wouldn't be the main topic of conversation, because she was in a bit of a pickle as far as that was concerned, but Althea's mood wasn't the best – as was evidenced by the fact that she complained about the consommé, then hardly touched her poached egg with salad.

Finally exasperated, Mavis said, 'Right, out with it. You've played with what was perfectly good food on your plate until it's almost inedible, so tell me what's going on or I'll be worried about you. Why are you off your food? Why so snappy with Cook? It's no' like you. Are you feeling unwell?'

Althea shook her head sadly, then looked across the table at Mavis with moist eyes. 'I don't think my son likes me, and I'm certain his wife and in-laws don't. They're trying to stop me being involved with my grandson's christening. My own family is ostracizing me. What shall I do?'

The matter now out in the open, Mavis could tell that Althea was truly upset, and not just putting it on…as she sometimes could.

Mavis pushed aside her empty plate, having enjoyed her luncheon very much indeed, it having also been her breakfast. 'Tell me all about it.' She reached out and patted Althea's small hand where it lay on the crisp, linen tablecloth.

Dragging a hanky from her pocket, Althea dabbed her eyes. 'I think I got everything off on the wrong foot because of the christening mugs.' She nibbled her lip. 'I could have handled that differently, I know. But I do want Chelly's here with me, and I do think Henry should know where his is. As should Clementine, of course – but she's nowhere to be found, and has probably got hers with her at the house in London. But Chelly's and Henry's are missing. Properly missing. It's very sad, and now that I've made such a fuss about them, Henry's become rather cross with me. As have Stephanie and her parents. I wasn't trying to take over everything. I just like things done a certain way, because they always have been. And I do think it's within my role to be the keeper of family traditions. And I do speak my mind. But I'm not a steamroller.' Althea sobbed gently, then added, 'I'm only small. How could I be a steamroller?'

Mavis weighed her response. Althea had mentioned the matter of the missing christening mugs days earlier, and had been chirping excitedly about several other aspects of the impending christening of Henry's heir. But she wanted to be clearer about exactly what had happened to make Althea feel she was being marginalized when it came to the organization of the event. As Mavis knew only too well, the devil was always in the details, and Althea's perspective sometimes wasn't as clear-eyed as she would have folks believe.

Mavis began. 'So how certain are you that the mugs aren't at Chellingworth Hall?'

The dowager sniffed and replied quietly, 'Henry organized a search.' She nodded as she added, 'To be fair to him, he's done a surprisingly good job of it. You know that sort of thing isn't his forte, but he made a plan – which struck me as very sensible – and carried it out.'

Mavis listened as Althea told her the steps Henry had taken. 'A good use of resources…for Henry,' she said, when Althea had finished.

'Exactly,' agreed Althea. 'Stephanie was ever so proud of him, as was I. And I told him so. It was a lovely start to our tea.'

'And Henry did this all himself, you say?' Althea nodded. Mavis was even more impressed. 'Good for him, especially for searching the private areas – because I dare say items can be moved about more readily when rooms are in use all the time, as opposed to most of Chellingworth Hall which seems to house a great number of collections, in a great number of rooms, that no one uses any longer.'

Althea sighed. 'Gone are the days when the family was large, the Hall being home to the entire extended version of it. Back then, the duke and duchess had time to indulge passions and hobbies; poor Henry and Stephanie seem to go from meeting to meeting these days. Did you know she's set up a committee to consider possible ways to revitalize Anwen-by-Wye?'

Mavis admitted she didn't.

'Neither did I, until yesterday afternoon,' said Althea sadly. 'She got it going last autumn, apparently, but no one said anything to me about it. Of course, once she mentioned it I offered to do anything I could – but she declined. Said she'd move ahead without me.' A sigh rattled through the dowager's small body. 'Another thing I'm not needed for. I know I possibly grumbled a little about my duties before Henry married, but I believe I always said I was grateful for the way Elizabeth Fernley, the estate manager's wife, stepped up to take on a lot of the day-to-day matters when it came to running the Hall. However, in the past year, I've felt my role in the life of the seat shrinking. And now? It seems they want me to do nothing…all day…every day.'

Mavis suspected Althea was about to wallow, and wasn't having any of it. 'So the mugs are gone. You've already told me there've been no break-ins, and, if a member of the public managed to, somehow, find them and walk off with them, there's no way of you knowing that.'

'Henry had another bright idea on that front,' said Althea, smiling. She told Mavis about Henry's recruitment of Alexander and his insider's knowledge of the antiques trade. 'Even Sheila and John Timbers were impressed with that one,' she concluded.

'As am I,' said Mavis, amazed at the duke's ingenuity. 'Now you say you cannae get hold of Clementine, to see if she can throw any light on the matter?' Althea shook her head. 'Is that a cause for concern?'

Shrugging, Althea replied, 'I don't think so, dear. It's not as though any of us are usually in touch with her on an ongoing basis. We might not hear from her for weeks, and the same could be said of her hearing from us, I suppose. It's only because I want to speak to her that I know I can't, if you see what I mean.'

'Aye, I dare say she could be anywhere. She went off on that tour of Egypt and didn't tell you until the topic happened to come up at Christmas, so maybe she's away somewhere that's warmer than it is here.'

'I don't think so, dear, her passport was one of the things Henry found in her rooms at Chellingworth. Which we all remarked was odd. When I reach her, I must mention that – she might wonder where it is. But I'm not really terribly worried about her. My main concern is that it's not just the old ones, you see? There's the new christening mug for the baby, too. Henry's doing that, he says, I'm not to get involved.'

Mavis felt her head spin. 'Meaning?'

Althea puffed out her cheeks, 'I suppose that was my fault too, in a way. I reminded Henry how Chelly had designed a silver mug especially for him, and now he's decided he wants to do the same for his son. Which is lovely. And he told me after tea that the silversmith he's talked to has said it can be done in time, which is good, but I'd thought I could be the one to get the new mug.'

Althea sniffed into her hanky, then added. 'It's rather a disappointment.'

Mavis said, 'How do you mean "in time"? Has a date been set?'

Finally smiling, Althea said, 'Yes, the first of March, as I suggested. Which I do believe is the perfect day for it.'

'At St David's church, in the village?'

'Yes. Reverend Roberts is quite excited, because it will be his first, and – given his age – probably his only time to christen someone who'll one day be a duke.'

'You're no' getting the bishop in to do it then?' Mavis didn't bother to hide the fact she was teasing her chum, just a little.

Not sensing the friendly jibe, Althea's expression was serious when she said, 'I'd already spoken to him about it, but Henry said he'd prefer not to have the bishop, so I had to phone him back and tell him to stop polishing his miter – if that's the sort of thing a bishop does. I suspect he thought it a most peculiar turn of events.'

'I dare say,' said Mavis, hoping she'd managed to keep any suggestion of mockery out of her tone. 'But you'll still be the one in charge of clothing the bairn, right? The replacement christening gown will be overseen by you, you said.'

Althea's cheeks developed small pink spots. 'Stephanie has now…informed me…that Megan Davies in Bridgend, will be making it. She's the young woman who made Stephanie's wedding dress, if you recall. Of course I understand that using her to make the christening gown would be an emotional link with the wedding, and, thus, the seat. The original christening garment has been photographed; it managed to survive that process, at least, which is a relief. And we all saw how wonderful Stephanie's gown was at the wedding, so I dare say the woman will make a good job of it.'

'And no' let it be stolen from her workshop, I hope, like Stephanie's dress was,' observed Mavis dryly.

'Obviously,' replied Althea, rather tartly, thought Mavis. 'And Cook Davies will be working with Stephanie on the menu for the gathering at Chellingworth Hall following the church service.'

Mavis reckoned she knew where this was going.

Althea sighed heavily. 'And no one is taking any notice at all of my suggestions for the boy's name. So there. I am not needed. Superfluous to requirements. Completely unnecessary. Utterly—'

Mavis interrupted, 'I understand, dear. It seems we both find ourselves without purpose at the moment.'

Althea looked surprised. 'I thought you were busy stalking that man who says he's got a bad back but hasn't.'

'It's no' a bad back, it's a bad knee, and I've no' been stalking him, but watching him...following him. But that's my job, so it's quite different, though I dare say it sounds the same. Anyway, I cannae do that any longer, because now he, his wife, and his son, all know my face and my name. I spoke to Rhodri Lloyd about it before lunch. It's a difficult situation, and I'm no' happy about it.'

Althea giggled. 'Oh dear. Did you "blow your cover" somehow?' Her eyes sparkled wickedly.

Mavis felt herself bristling. 'A man's well-being had to come before the case.'

Althea's mouth formed an 'O'. 'What happened? Is that why you were out until the small hours? I didn't like to ask...but I was curious.'

Mavis resigned herself to a full retelling of the day she'd had; Althea was an attentive listener, until the point she told her about finding the bricklayer unresponsive in his car, when Althea burst out excitedly, 'He was dead? In his car? And you'd been taking photos of him all that time? How awful for you. And his family, of course.' She paused, then added, 'But, if he's dead, what do you mean by saying he knows what you look like?'

'If you'd just let me finish telling you, you'll understand. He wasnae dead. I could see a vein pulsing in his throat, phoned for an ambulance, and got into the passenger seat of the car with him while I waited for them to arrive. To me, it looked like a heart attack, and the paramedics confirmed my diagnosis.'

'But of course they did, dear,' said Althea.

Mavis continued, 'I followed them to the A & E, and waited until they'd been able to get hold of his wife.'

'Good idea,' said Althea.

'I felt...I felt someone should be there for him, you see? Not that he'd have got less attention if the medical staff had believed no one cared about him – but it happened on my watch, quite literally, so I felt...well, no' responsible, but – as you said – I'd been watching the poor man, when I could have been administering some sort of first aid. As it was, the operator who hung on with me made it quite clear that I was no' to touch him and, to be fair, the ambulance was with us quickly.'

Mavis sighed, recalling her time alone with Ben Stirling, sitting in his car outside his house; it had allowed her to ponder too many instances in her past when she'd watched over someone as they used up the last moments of their life.

Mavis reckoned she must have given away her inner turmoil in her expression, because Althea put on what she recognized as her 'soothing' voice as she said, 'Good for you for finding him, for acting as you did; you probably saved his life. If it hadn't been for you, he might have been in that car for hours, unattended...just gradually drifting away.'

Mavis knew that Althea was trying to help, but she still felt wretched about not having gone to check on the man sooner than she had.

She sighed, and said, 'They managed to get hold of the wife, but no' until she'd returned to the family home. She and the son arrived at the hospital at about the same time as each other; she'd phoned him to tell him to meet her there.'

'Very sensible, under the circumstances,' observed Althea.

Mavis felt she had to agree, knowing she'd said as much at the time.

She continued, 'Once they knew it was me who'd found him, they were very grateful, of course, for what I'd done. I managed to convince them that I was just a passing motorist who'd noticed something was a bit off. But, even though they don't know I was watching him, if they see me again they'll recognize me. So I'm not going to be of any use in that respect.'

'Oh dear,' said Althea quietly.

'Not that Ben Stirling will need watching for a wee while – he'll be kept in hospital for a bit; stents, medication, observation. It was a very mild attack, and eminently treatable, they said.'

'A relief for all concerned,' observed Althea. 'And how did your client react? I know you've quite taken to this Rhodri Lloyd person, but does this mean the agency is off the case, or just you? Is there even a case any longer? Oh, I say – you don't think the man's heart attack had anything to do with his fall, do you? Might he end up suing your client's client about that too? See – I do listen when you talk to me about your cases; I take it all in. Though I don't think you've told me the name of your client's client.'

She dimpled at Mavis, who couldn't help but smile. 'Aye, you do listen, I know that. Which is why I bother talking to you in the first place. My client's client is Mark Morgan. The bricklayer, as I just mentioned, I believe, is Ben Stirling.'

Althea said, 'Got it. Mark Morgan. Thank you. And, of course I wouldn't forget Ben Stirling's name. How could one? He is a most unpleasant man, with unpleasant manners, and given to unpleasant outbursts. Have you spoken to the head gardener up at Chellingworth about him, yet? Ivor's had more than one run-in with him. Sent him packing once, when he was supposed to be carrying out some repairs to the brickwork surrounding the walled garden; called himself a "master bricklayer" and turned out to be nothing of the sort. I seem to recall Ivor saying the man had done more harm than good.'

Mavis was taken aback. 'You never cease to surprise me, Althea. Why have you no' mentioned this to me before?'

'You only just told me the bricklayer's name,' Althea sounded quite put out.

Mavis acknowledged that her friend was quite correct, then added, 'Mebbe I should begin all my enquiries with you – you seem to know so much about so many people…and about so many things.'

Althea beamed. 'Thank you dear. Yes, you probably should, it might save you a lot of time and wasted effort.'

Mavis couldn't help but smile.

Althea added, 'Now, if only my family thought as highly of my usefulness as you do, my world would be a brighter place.'

Mavis smiled indulgently. 'I dare say it would, dear. Now, I'll no' waste any time, I'll be off to the Hall to catch Ivor before he finishes for the day. And thank you.'

'You're welcome. Always happy to help.'

CHAPTER EIGHTEEN

Annie and Christine had taken their laptops to the kitchen and sitting room, respectively. Neither had slept well, both had got off to a slow start, and each had agreed that a little 'personal' time was called for before they got going with their work.

Annie chatted with Tudor for about an hour, while Gertie and Rosie barked at each other over the video call. She was pleased to hear that village life was continuing to jog along nicely without her – or was she? – and was relieved to hear that Marjorie Pritchard's hands were healing well. Afterwards, she spoke to Carol, who filled her in on the disaster that had befallen Selina, the trainer at the spa's gym, the previous day.

Annie said, 'I'm sorry to hear that, doll. I hope she'll be alright, and I'm glad you're okay. Just as well you're more nimble than you look.' Carol's silence suggested to Annie that she'd said something wrong, but she couldn't imagine what that might be. 'You alright, doll? A bit shaken?'

Carol snapped, 'Not shaken, but it was a dreadful thing to happen. I've made an appointment to meet the manager of the hotel tomorrow; I think I've worked out how to gather some information that I can't ask for at the spa without tipping them off that I am who I am, and that I'm doing what I'm doing. And I'll be going back in for a mani-pedi, hoping I can get something out of Jasmine. She strikes me as a better bet than Willow...or Caz, if she's back from sick leave.'

'You'll sort it, I know you will. If anyone can work out what's going on there, you can, Car...*ol*. Did you manage to find out anything a out the Gorst sisters who used to live at this cottage, by the way?'

Carol shook her head. 'I'm so sorry, I really haven't had a chance to do more than a cursory search. Nothing so far – I promise I'll do it properly, and I'll email you. But now I've got to make a move; Albert's stirring, and he needs his mum.'

Annie smiled. 'Alright, doll, no probs.'

Carol added, 'By the way – okay if we pop down to see you on Saturday? I've done all that research into Port Beynon and it's made me want to see it again – as an adult. We'll probably get there about ten, alright?'

Annie smiled at her chum on her screen. 'Lovely. Let's hope it's dry then, eh?'

'Yes, fingers crossed. Take care – oh and good luck at that pub quiz you're doing tonight. It might be fun.'

'I don't know about that. Those things always have questions only clever people can answer, but I'll do my best.'

'You know loads of stuff, you just don't know you know it. Talk soon. Bye.'

After her personal calls, Annie settled to the list of companies that had provided staff to fix and repair things at the cottage over the past couple of years. It was repetitive and frustrating work, but she plodded on diligently, and made copious notes.

Christine had managed three short conversations with Alexander as he'd been driving between various construction sites he had on the go, then one more before he went into his 'big meeting'. He was putting forward a bid on some property owned by a local authority in south London, proposing a mixed-use development of workshops and retail outlets for small businesses on the ground floor, with flats that would be renovated to accommodate, quite specifically, large families, above. Christine knew it was his passion project.

Wishing him good luck for the umpteenth time, Christine said enthusiastically, 'Slay them, Alexander. You know exactly how to make people want what you want. So just kick the charm machine into top gear, and go for it.'

'Right,' he replied, sounding a bit odd to Christine's ears, 'that's exactly what I'll do. Thanks for the pep talk. Speak later,' and he was gone.

Christine realized she'd missed several texts from Mavis, so eventually worked through them, and decided it was best to phone her.

She invited Annie to join the video call, because the tone of some of Mavis's texts had worried her. The two women huddled over the coffee table in the cottage, the rain streaming down the wall of windows that offered a view of more rain beyond, and listened as Mavis recounted all that had happened with Ben Stirling, including the tip-off she'd received about him from Althea.

'I'll wait to hear from Rhodri about next steps, of course,' concluded Mavis, 'but I'll talk to Ivor up at the Hall tomorrow; he'd left by the time I got there today. Off to the dentist, they said, though, to look at his teeth you'd no' think he'd ever even met one, let alone sat in their chair.'

'That's a bit sharp for you, Mave. You alright, doll?' Annie didn't like the way Mavis looked at all; just like Gertie when her ears were down.

Mavis sighed, far away in the Dower House. 'I feel I should have done more – gone to see to poor Ben Stirling sooner than I did.'

Annie's heart went out to her friend and colleague. 'Having had this conversation about a hundred times with my counsellor, Mave, I'll tell you what she always tells me about "survivor's guilt"…well, the gist of it, anyway. And bear in mind, you're not the only survivor – he's one too, thanks to you. But, look, you couldn't have done anything to change the situation the man was in, and, when you found him, you did what you could, as fast as was possible. You're not to blame for him having a heart attack; it would have happened with or without your presence. Constantly replaying possible alternative scenarios leading up to the point when you found him isn't going to change anything for him, but it can change things for you: it can stop you moving forward, because you're stuck in a cycle of making yourself feel guilty all over again. That's what you can change, Mave – the future. You can't change the past.'

Mavis nodded thoughtfully. 'Thank you, Annie. And thank your counsellor. I shall think on what you've said. Now, away with you both – you've work to do. Keep sending your daily updates through. Bye for now.'

Annie and Christine cleared the kitchen of the detritus that had accumulated through a day when both of them had preferred snacks rather than eating properly. Finally, they pulled on their wet weather gear, made sure the torches they each had were working properly, and set off down the hill, with Gertie being excited to join them.

By the time they reached the entrance porch of the pub they were both dripping, and Gertie managed to make them even wetter by shaking herself; she looked quite proud. Annie dragged out the dog towel she'd stuffed into the small backpack she'd carried, did her best to get the wriggling pup in a bit of a better state than she was, then they plodded inside in their wellies, hoping they didn't make too much of a mess as they did so.

'It's not quite what I'd expected,' said Christine quietly, as they hung their dripping jackets on a couple of hooks inside the door.

'Me neither,' replied Annie, 'though, frankly, the fact that the name of the place is "the pub" should have been a clue. Not one single capital letter? To me, that always reeks of somewhere that's far too up itself to be really interesting.'

The stone-built pub had looked solid, ancient, and traditional from the outside, with 1785 chiselled into a marble slab above the porch proudly celebrating the date when it had been opened. However, inside, it had bright, white walls, marble-topped tables surrounded by modern stainless-steel chairs, the floor was made of large slabs of slate, and the bar? Well, it wouldn't have looked out of place in a posh restaurant in London: spotlights made the hundreds of glasses hanging above it glitter like a long chandelier; dozens of bottles of spirits were stacked on backlit shelves, looking colorful, if a little lurid.

'Look at how many beer pumps they've got,' noted Annie. 'Tude's only got four, and one of them hardly ever gets used. There must be about a dozen along that bar. And see the amount of different bottled beers they've got in all those gleaming chiller cabinets over there? Those must be the special glasses for all that lot. Gordon Bennett – that's quite something.'

Christine pulled at Annie's arm. 'Come on, there's a table beside the wall. You can tuck Gertie into that alcove, which looks as though it was once a very large fireplace. What a shame they painted over it. She won't get under anyone's feet back there. I tell you what, that smell is grand; my mouth's watering already. Let's get settled and order something to eat. You sort Gertie, and I'll go to the bar. What do you fancy? G & T? Or a beer? Should we take it easy? You know – so we're alert for the quiz.'

'Don't know what I fancy, yet. You get what you want, then I'll decide.' Annie juggled her backpack, Gertie's lead, and Gertie herself, until she managed to get into a chair, and tried to convince her pup that the spot she was showing her was where she should settle down. In the end, she threw the damp towel onto the floor so that Gertie could make herself a nest, into which she curled quite happily.

Christine returned to the table holding two items. 'Menus,' she announced. 'This one's for food –' she held up a small, laminated card – 'and this one's for drinks.'

'That one looks like a small paperback,' said Annie, reaching for the drinks menu, bemused. She leafed through it. 'Well, I've seen things like this in London, but I wouldn't have expected it here. There have to be forty-odd beers listed, and each one with its own detailed description. I'm surprised they haven't named the person who grew the ingredients.' She read a bit further. 'Oh, come off it. Who wants to drink a beer with "hints of grapefruit and chalk". What a ridiculous thing to say. "Chalk"? What does that even mean?'

'It means it has a slightly drying effect on the tongue,' said a voice behind the pair.

Annie and Christine looked up to see a man who…seemed to go on forever.

'Good evening, ladies. I'm Jason, pub manager, and your host for the evening. I'll be responsible for making sure you have the best possible time while you're here. I dare say you're Annie and Christine? Cadog mentioned you when I ran into him on the beach this morning.'

Jason was in his late thirties, something over six feet tall and well-built – though in a way that was proportionately perfect for his height. His muscles were clearly visible beneath the rolled-up sleeves of his plaid shirt and through his tight tee shirt, which displayed the logo of a surfing company. He had chocolate brown eyes, a full dark beard, and hair that brushed his shoulders. Both women stared, then shut their mouths, simultaneously.

Christine managed to gather her wits more quickly than Annie, and said, 'Nice to meet you, Jason. I'm Christine, and this is Annie. That's Gertie. Cadog told us that dogs were allowed. Will she be alright there?'

'Of course she will.' He beamed. 'And it's my pleasure to serve you with your first refreshments of the evening; I brought this bowl for Gertie, and a couple of T.R.E.A.T.S. are hidden in my pocket, if she's allowed.'

Annie chuckled. 'She can spell that word already, but thanks for trying.' Gertie proved she was as clever as Annie said by standing to attention and wagging her tail. 'Go on then, but just a couple. She'll take as many as she's given. Managed to get into a bag of them once and made herself thoroughly sick.' Annie wondered why she was babbling.

Jason allowed Gertie to take the treats from him, which Annie was pleased to see she did nicely, not trying to take his hand off, as she often did to Annie herself, or even with Tudor.

'Now then, ladies, what can I tempt you with today? Will you be eating? I heard from Cadog that you have an interest in lamb stew. That's available, of course, but you might also like to consider the chicken chasseur, or even the duck stir-fry. They're all excellent.'

Annie said, 'I'm for the lamb stew, thanks. What about you, Chrissy?'

'Duck. I'd like to try your duck, please Jason.' Christine did something with her eyebrows that Annie had only ever seen her do when speaking to Alexander.

'Trying the duck is always a good choice. I'll see to that for you,' he replied.

Annie tutted.

The pub's manager continued, 'Now, have you decided what you'd like to accompany your food? We have a good selection of wines, as well as beers and spirits, as you can see. But there's something I like to do – I like to guess people's favorite drink…may I?' The women both nodded. 'I'd say you're a G & T, all the way, Annie, but for you, Christine, I'd say your tipple of choice would be…yes, you're a champagne girl, aren't you?'

Annie looked at Jason, then she looked at Christine, and decided to be the voice of reason. 'Very clever, Jase, but we're doing the pub quiz so we want clear heads. I'll have a beer that tastes like a beer, please, and Chrissy here will have one too. Won't you? No fruit flavors. No fancy glasses. Just beer.'

'Stout for me,' said Christine. 'Duck…and a velvety, dark stout. Thank you.'

Jason nodded graciously. 'Very well. Lamb and a beery beer, and a duck, with velvety stout.' He headed toward the bar.

Annie thumped Christine. 'You were flirting. Stop it. You're engaged. And how on earth did you mange to make choosing your meal and your drink sound so…smutty? You're awful, you are. And he's no better. I mean, I'm not blind – he looks as though he's stepped off the cover of some steamy romance novel, I can see that – but all that flattery? Just to get us to spend more money, that's what that is. Can you imagine what he's like when all the young things are in here half undressed in the summer? I bet they drool over him. He's trouble, him. And you've got Alexander, who's enough trouble as it is. Can't help yourself, can you? You've got a type, it seems.'

Christine had the good grace to blush a little. 'Oh, come off it, Annie. I'm engaged, not dead. It's just a game. The oldest one there is. A little dance, where no one gets hurt, but everyone gets to smile and feel good about themselves. It's fun.'

Annie tutted, and was surprised when a girl who looked barely old enough to be working in a pub brought their drinks to the table.

'Don't we come to the bar? Are you bringing our drinks to us because we're eating?' Annie wasn't used to being served in a pub.

The girl looked cross. 'Yes. I mean no. Everyone comes to the bar, for everything, and you pay when you order it, and get it, at the bar. But Jason asked me to bring these over, special, and he's told me your food and these drinks are on him, so you're set for now. But, yes, you come to the bar for your drinks. And pay for them there and then. It's…well, it's a pub.'

She flounced off, leaving Annie and Christine smiling.

Savoring their drinks, the women enjoyed a moment of silence, then Annie said, 'Did you find out anything useful from all those companies you contacted today? I hope you did, because I came up more or less empty. I don't know whether everyone I spoke to was as thick as two short planks, but all I got was a load of mumbling about appliances that "shorted out", or pipes that got "blocked by foreign objects". One woman with a posh voice, but the personality of a box of hair, told me "these things have to be expected at older properties". It got annoying in the end. Mind you, I dare say they were all just telling me whatever was on the paperwork the people who actually did the jobs had submitted.'

'It's funny you mentioning that catch-all about it being an old property, because I talked to the company that installed all the smart home systems. They were at pains to point out how modern everything was, and how it would mean the homeowner wouldn't have exactly those sorts of problems. And it's true – the entire cottage was rewired, all the appliances are only a couple of years old, and the smart house system that controls them hasn't even been updated at their end yet, so it's as technologically advanced as you can get. The only thing they didn't do was install solar panels, and that was because the local authority wouldn't allow it on such an historic building. Oh, by the way, did you know that Sea View Cottage was once a famous smugglers' haunt?'

'You in't read any of those notes Car made, have you? All over that she was. You should look at them; links to all sorts she gave us.'

Christine shrugged. 'I did glance at them, but it was all so…I don't know, I just couldn't settle my mind to them, I suppose. Thinking about…other things all the time.'

Annie continued, 'Well, yes, I do know it was a smugglers' home, and that there were secret cellars dug into the hillside under the place – which is where the new bedrooms and bathroom are now. I also know that, when the smugglers were found out, there was a bloody fight there with at least half a dozen dead by the end of it. The smugglers' bodies were hung up for weeks, as an example to all. But it seems this area was full of people only too ready to beat the tax man…and it was the sailors on the boats themselves who'd sail into the bay to offload their goodies. Then they'd say they'd been robbed, and the smugglers would sell the stuff for a tidy profit – but at prices people could actually afford.'

Christine looked impressed. 'This place must have bee awash with rum at one time, I suppose.'

'And salt. And soap,' replied Annie.

'Soap?'

'Yeah, apparently the taxes on soap were nuts. When you see portrayals of all the poor people looking dirty back then, it might not have been because they didn't want to wash, but because they couldn't afford soap. Makes you think, doesn't it? Lucky, aren't we?'

Christine nodded, and was just about to ask more about smuggling, when the same irritated server who'd brought their drinks plonked a bowl of lamb stew in front of Annie and a bowl of glistening vegetables, noodles, and duck, in front of Christine.

'The cutlery's over there, if you can manage to get it by yourselves,' she said, then headed back to her sulking station, behind the bar.

The meals were both delicious, as the mmm'ing proved. Annie and Christine each tasted the other's choice, and agreed they'd both picked the right thing for themselves. They weren't halfway through when Jason appeared again.

'Is your meal as good as you'd hoped, Christine?'

'Most satisfying duck I've had in a long time,' she replied.

Annie almost spat out her lamb when she heard Christine's tone, then she kicked her under the table.

'My lamb's good,' she said – maybe a little too loudly. 'But it's missing…something. Lacking…umami, in some way.'

Jason looked surprised. 'Lacking umami, is it, Annie? Well, I'd better have a word with the chef about that. No, no…he doesn't know what you mean. That's a good lamb stew, that is.'

Christine put down her cutlery and gazed up at Jason. 'You're the chef too? You cook all this yourself? My, but you're talented. Might I have the recipe for this dish? Or is it a secret?'

'If you get it, you could cook it for your fiancé, couldn't you, Chrissy?' Annie made the remark as pointed as possible.

'Ah yes. The ring's hard to miss. He's a lucky man,' said Jason with resignation.

Christine fluttered her eyelashes demurely at the compliment, but Annie wasn't having any of it. 'He is, and he knows it. And she's lucky too, because he's one in a million. In't he, Chrissy?'

'He is,' admitted her friend, still doing the annoying fluttering thing.

'Pleased you're enjoying the food, but I must get back to my other patrons, if you'll excuse me. You're staying for the quiz?' Both women nodded. 'Good – it's always fun. That's Eddy in the corner – sign up with him.'

With meals finished, and drinks polished off, Annie went to the bar for another round, then stayed with Gertie while Christine signed them up for the quiz.

Returning to their table, Christine announced, 'We're the Power With Style team, aka PWS – our initials. They needed a name, and it was the best I could come up with. Here are our answer sheets and pencils. It all seems quite well organized. Eddy said they'll start promptly, so to be sure we have drinks to get us through half an hour of questions, because no one likes it if people go to the bar when the quiz is taking place. Sounds a bit…serious, if you ask me.'

Annie expressed her opinion with a look that would have stripped paint, and applied herself to her beer, and petting Gertie. 'Organized fun is always serious,' she observed.

At seven sharp, Eddy tapped on a microphone – and a sudden hush fell across what had become a more or less completely full pub. Annie didn't have a good feeling about how the evening was going to work out, but, much to her surprise, the question session was fun.

The half an hour flew past and, at the end of it, she and Christine felt they'd done a decent job with their answers. There was a fifteen-minute break – when the bar was completely swamped – then a second round started, in which the pair didn't feel they performed quite as well. Neither of them knew much about sport, so they'd guessed those answers, and the science questions were challenging too; entertainment, history, geography, and current affairs were all topics that, between them, they seemed to know a fair bit about.

Answer sheets were passed to the adjoining tables for marking, and there were groans and cheers as teams recognized their disasters and mini triumphs. At the end of it all, the PWS team came third out of a total of fourteen. Their good placing wasn't exactly welcomed by the locals, but there were generous compliments as the post-quiz rush to the bar, and the loos, got underway.

In the ladies' toilet, Annie bumped into Amy, who bubbled with enthusiasm about the PWS's performance. 'My Glyn was surprised how well you did. Come and say hello on your way back to your table, will you? And I'd love to introduce you to our son, Llew. He's the one who always teams up with Cadog, since Cadog's wife's not able to come any more. Always good on the science and geography, is Llew. Ever so bright he is.'

Annie asked, 'Does he still live in the area?' Amy had mentioned he'd been a teen when he'd made the money that had allowed them to buy their house, but assumed he'd moved on. Yet, if he was regularly at the pub quiz, he had to have remained reasonably local.

'When we moved into our place we assumed he'd be gone in a few years, but he went to Swansea University, so commuted, and he's never really seen a reason to leave. Does apps, now, all the time, in his room.'

Annie grappled with idea. 'He lives at your place, and he's what – an app designer?'

She used apps all the time, and had read about how developers had made fortunes from them, but hadn't ever really considered who those people might be.

That one would be living in a tiny Welsh seaside hamlet hadn't occurred to her. Or was Llew Francis just a dabbler?

She said, 'I know you told us he'd sold an app when he was young, but is that still what he does? And he works in his bedroom?'

Amy laughed. 'That sounds so funny, when you say it like that. He's got a nice sitting room-cum-study across the hall from his bedroom, so he's quite independent of us, really.'

She paused, then leaned in and added, 'Except for me doing the cooking, and cleaning, and his washing, you know? But there, I'm his mam, and I'll always be that. Besides, he's not quite forty yet, so there's plenty of time for him to be thinking of getting his own place. I'll introduce you, now.'

Annie had only seen the person sitting beside Cadog from a distance, but found he was quite a sight, up close. The image of his mother – except that his mass of hair was naturally curly, rather than chemically induced to be so; he was short, wiry, bespectacled, and had a surprisingly deep voice for his stature. He spoke politely, with a much less pronounced local accent than his mother, and wore a tee shirt under his bottle-green hoodie that proclaimed him to be a fan of *Star Trek*.

Annie wasn't surprised to discover, when Amy introduced her to Glyn Francis, that his father also had a deep voice and wore glasses. Llew was definitely his parents' son. He wasn't the chatty type, though, so it was Amy who did most of the talking. Annie got the impression that – while his mother didn't really have a clue what his work involved – she was incredibly proud of what she kept calling his 'potential' which, Annie thought, was a bit of a stretch when it came to referring to a man in his late thirties.

Finally returning to Christine and Gertie, Annie said, 'Now's our chance to mingle, set up some beach-walking or coffee dates with the locals, so we can try to get some more insights.'

'We're meeting Cadog on the beach for a stroll around eleven tomorrow, then Jason's coming for tea after his lunchtime "rush" here – probably about three'ish, and...'

'Hang on,' said Annie, 'when did all this happen?'

'You've been gone for ages. I don't hang about, you know.'

Annie sulked for a moment, then added, 'And Jason thinks it's safe for him to come to the cottage, does he? Given what everyone around here seems to believe it does to men?'

Christine chuckled. 'He doesn't believe all the gossip any more than we do. And remember what Carys said? He's the one who found poor Brian Kelly's body; he might have some information he doesn't even know is important.'

'And Cadog knows such a lot about…well, such a lot, so that's good. Let's hope he knows more about the Gorst sisters than he's told us already, because Carol can't seem to find out anything about either of them.'

'Fingers crossed.'

Annie agreed.

FRIDAY 3rd FEBRUARY

CHAPTER NINETEEN

When Carol arrived at the Ash Court Country House Hotel for her third visit, she felt she made an impression. A better one. Instead of tired old exercise clothes, she was wearing her new, beautifully tailored tweed coat over what she'd always known to be a flattering navy dress, which she held in reserve for situations where she needed to be viewed as a consummate professional. It was from her time when she'd overseen a large team of computing specialists at a massive firm in the City of London, but that had been before she'd had Albert, so it was more snug than it once had been, but still spoke of quality.

The receptionist did a double take that Carol found most satisfying, then asked her to wait in the lounge where the manager of the hotel would meet her.

Els van Beek was slim, smart, neat, and had intense blue eyes that looked even more startling because of her snow white hair. Carol reckoned she was somewhere around her own age, so in her mid- to late-thirties, and she noted that she carried herself with the air of someone who felt completely at ease in their surroundings, and their skin. Carol felt her dress clinging to her as she followed the effortlessly put-together woman to her office, which turned out to be much plainer than Carol had imagined it would be. Much smaller, too, with only one tiny window.

Sitting in the cramped space, Carol explained herself: she told the efficient-looking woman about Marjorie Pritchard's injuries, about the WISE Enquiries Agency, and the accident that had happened in the gym.

The Dutch woman assured Carol that the hotel bore no liability for anything that happened at the spa. – in impeccable English, with only a trace of a delightful accent.

She then surprised Carol by adding, 'I think it must be very exciting to be a private detective. Is it? Or do you often end up in small offices, talking to people who cannot help you? You see, I have nothing whatsoever to do with the spa. I do not really know the people who work there, under whatever terms, nor do I have access to any of their client records. It is a completely separate entity.'

Carol chuckled at what she took to be the most polite brush-off anyone had ever tried on her. 'It can be fascinating being an enquiry agent,' replied Carol, 'especially when people who think they can't help us end up finding they're able to contribute important information to one of those enquiries. Especially in cases like this where, even if the relationship is at arms' length, there's the potential for a set of circumstances that is impacting one place of business to – directly or indirectly – sour the reputation of another.'

'Touché, Mrs Hill. What exactly do you think I can do for you?'

Carol explained. 'When I've come to use the spa, your hotel receptionist has checked my name on a list. I would like access to those lists, so that I can find out who's been visiting the spa. And you probably have lists of the people who have worked at the spa, going back some considerable time, for the same reason – so they can be allowed access via the hotel.'

Els van Beek wrote on her notepad. 'And?'

'Have you received any complaints about the spa from your hotel guests?'

The Dutchwoman's eyes grew steely. 'If any such complaints had been received, I could not tell you. Our guests value our discretion.'

'I wouldn't need names, just…occurrences. I'm trying to spot any patterns, find out if our friend is the only one who's been unfortunate enough to suffer as she has, or if there's something amiss at the spa.'

Els van Beek studied Carol with narrow eyes. Carol didn't care for the feeling it gave her.

Carol pressed on, and explained, 'I have to be honest and say that the unexpected collapse of a large metal frame holding hundreds of pounds of weights is not the same as an infected hand, but it's something that shouldn't happen. That's what I'm after – information that can help me build a picture. But I don't think I can manage to spend enough time at the spa, nor wait for a long enough period, to be able to spot such a pattern. And, if I ask for such information from them, they'll know they are being investigated. I can only give you my word that we at the WISE Enquiries Agency understand discretion. We couldn't stay in business if we didn't.'

The hotel manager's pen hovered above her pad. She surprised Carol by standing, smoothing down her skirt and saying, 'I shall be gone for about five minutes, to collect the names of people who are to be allowed access to the spa and the pool that are kept at the hotel's reception desk. When I return, I shall run them through the photocopier for you...over here.'

She puzzled Carol by moving to stand beside the copier on a small desk beneath the window.

She added, 'Come and see, I've been busy here all day. I'll allow you to enjoy the view of the gardens, while I fetch those lists.'

On top of the copier was a folder titled: 'Spa complaints'.

Carol said, 'Thanks.' As soon as the door closed behind the woman, she pulled open the file. Inside were individual sheets detailing complaints, but someone had already blanked out the names of the complainants in thick black pen. Carol pulled out her phone, flicked each page, and snapped. By the time Els van Beek returned, Carol was carefully examining a pot plant that appeared to be in dire need of...something.

'I'm no expert,' said Carol, 'but this doesn't look very healthy.' She nodded at the plant.

Els busied herself at the copier, making sure to get each page of the book she'd brought from reception properly aligned before she made each copy. Carol silently applauded her diligence.

Glancing at the plant Els said, 'That? Yes, it's in a sorry state. My ex-partner's parting gift to me.'

Carol couldn't hide her surprise.

Els must have seen her reaction. 'She'd already half-killed it, and I think that's why she gave it to me; the irony was not lost upon me – our relationship had needed life-support for some time, but didn't survive. I'm seeing if I can do better for this plant. It would be a small triumph.' She handed the papers to Carol. 'Do you have everything you need, now?'

Carol smiled. 'Almost, thanks. You've been most helpful. But there is one more thing, if you don't mind.'

Els hovered by the door. 'Ask.'

'Is there anyone you can think of who might bear a grudge against the spa, or the hotel? For example, a disgruntled past employee?'

Els checked her watch, tensely, and answered rapidly. 'I cannot speak for the spa. For the hotel? We have many members of staff, and our turnover is high. It's always the way in this business: hours are long, expectations are high, guests can be unthinking. Of all the people we have had to let go during my tenure, there is no one person who stands out as having a particular grudge against the hotel, though I dare say many would speak less than happily about their time here, and about some of the management who, understandably, sometimes have to crack the whip, so to speak. But their bark is worse than their bite, unless a staff member proves themselves incapable of improvement, in which case we let them go. There are many other establishments where expectations are less demanding that ours. We have a reputation to maintain, so only the best will do for our guests. I'm sure you understand. That being said, I can tell you we recently lost several members of staff – across the board – due to a syndicate winning the lottery. It wasn't a huge jackpot, and not everyone involved gave up working here – just those who were a little older, or earning less. It has been an unexpected challenge, I must admit.'

Carol had a thought. 'Was the person who used to give the Indian head massages at the spa a member of that syndicate?'

Els smiled, and tilted her head slightly as her eyes glinted. 'He was. How did you know that?'

Carol shrugged. 'I used my detective's skills.' She winked, comically. 'Did anyone else from the spa leave?'

Els shook her head. 'Not that I'm aware of but, as I say, they are not my concern; I happen to know about Mike because he is the flatmate of another of the winners who reported to me. They have pooled their money to buy a house, and both have left. As I said, it wasn't the biggest jackpot, and it was divided among many, but it will make a difference to all the winners' lives, in varied ways, I'm sure. Now, is that all? I hope you understand that I have a pressing need to be…elsewhere. Thank you for coming. I would appreciate you sharing any relevant information about the outcome of your enquiries.'

Carol was being dismissed, and knew it; once again, the hotel manager had been nothing but polite, and yet she'd shut Carol down, and had – basically – kicked her out of the door. Despite that, Carol felt happy that Els had shared so much information with her…then couldn't help but wonder why she'd done it. Had that all been a bit too easy?

Carol decided against an exorbitantly expensive coffee in the lounge, so scurried back through the sleety rain to her car, where she popped the papers she'd protected under her coat onto the passenger seat, and headed home.

By the time she got there the sun had, inexplicably, come out, and David claimed he might feel a bit better if the fresh air could only clear his head. Carol wrapped up Albert, and didn't complain when the two of them set out to see the ducks at the pond, because she knew she could do with an empty house to allow her to sort through all the information she'd just acquired.

First, she uploaded the photographs she'd taken of the information Els had left lying about onto one of her laptops, then scanned in all the sheets the hotel manager had copied for her; she always found she was better able to assess data when it was on a screen, rather than in paper form.

She scrolled through the complaints made to the hotel about the spa to begin with, and made notes as she read, summarizing the nature of the problem, and the date it had occurred.

Carol loved spreadsheets, and the result of her efforts was that she was able to spot a pattern in an instant: hotel guests who were staying at the weekends seemed to never have made any complaints referring to the spa. Indeed, over the several years covered by the records there had only once been a complaint that referred to an incident that had taken place on a Saturday or Sunday, which was interesting, if not particularly illuminating. What was interesting, was that the overall number of complaints had significantly increased over the past couple of months.

The other thing she was able to discern was that the complaints concerned every type of service and treatment being delivered by the spa, not just one or two. Could every single staff member be incompetent? Carol didn't think so.

Pondering that, she decided that the only way to be able to sort and make sense of the lists of names of spa and pool users was to type them all into their own spreadsheet. She really didn't fancy that; it would take hours, and she hated copy-typing…but she couldn't see a way around it. The other challenge was that all the lists were handwritten, presumably by Willow ahead of a day full of spa clients arriving. Sadly, the sheets didn't tell Carol why a person was going to the spa, and she wondered if that might be helpful to know…but, faced with her mammoth task, she settled herself and set up a new spreadsheet to allow her to type, and type…and type.

As she squinted, and typed, she almost laughed at the idea that being an enquiry agent was an exciting job. Then her son and husband arrived at the back door, and she was in heaven again.

CHAPTER TWENTY

Mavis sat at the dining table in Chellingworth Hall and looked around, wondering – not for the first time – how this had become her life. She was about to be served what would doubtless be a wonderful lunch, her tablemates being a duke, his mother, a duchess and her parents, an infant who would, one day, become a duke…and a woman who'd once been a television personality, but now ran a bookshop specializing in her own field of endeavor and expertise of cooking.

It never ceased to amaze Mavis that this was now quite normal for her, but she allowed herself a moment to take in the beauty of the low sunlight glancing off the silverware and crystal, the massive portraits on the damask-covered walls, and the furnishings which were all worthy of being placed in museums.

Mavis smiled to herself, then perked up as Val Jenkins, once known as The Curious Cook because of her television series of the same name, said, 'It's lovely to see you, Mavis. First time this year, isn't it? I hope you're keeping well. You look it. As does the dowager. I understand from Stephanie that she's quite her old self again – picked up where she left off before her hip surgery. I bet that's thanks to you.'

Mavis wasn't one for false modesty. 'Aye, well, she put up a fair old fight, but I got her exercising, and she's as strong and nimble now as she's likely to ever be. And you're looking a picture of health yourself. Have you done something with your hair?'

Val smiled coyly. 'I'm not very good at looking after myself. One of the things I hated about doing the telly stuff was all the primping. Of course, as a cook, you have to be mindful of hair getting into things, but the fuss they'd make, when all I wanted to do was pull it back off my face? Annoying. And the make-up? I ended up with terrible pimples for a while. But I have been trying to do better in terms of my personal appearance, because there's talk of another series.'

'That sounds exciting,' said Mavis.

Val nodded. 'I had some meetings in London last week, and it's looking quite hopeful, so I thought I'd make a bit of an effort. I treated myself to a new hairdo at that hairdressers' at the Ash Court Country House Hotel spa. I don't know if you know about it, but there's a girl there who…well, she's Australian, looks a bit scary, but the things she can make a person's hair do is amazing.'

Mavis nodded. 'Our Carol's just been there, and I have to say that whoever that Caz person is, she's a bit of a miracle worker. Yours looks as wonderful on you as Carol's does on her. Not cheap, though, is it?'

Val chuckled. 'Not at all. But who'll miss an arm or a leg when they've got their revitalized hair to look at? Mind you, the woman who was there at the same time as me wasn't as happy.'

Mavis perked up. 'Why? What happened?'

Val explained how a hairdryer had overheated, or something had gone wrong with one of the products, damaging the woman's hair to the extent that it had had to be cut again, to a much shorter length than she'd wanted. Mavis decided it was best to not mention Marjorie Pritchard's hands, and listened attentively, making all the expected sympathetic noises.

'And when was this?' Mavis leaned in. 'Your hair – when did you have that done?'

'Tuesday last week. Why?'

Mavis waved her hand. 'No reason – just interested.'

'What's interesting?' asked Althea, finally turning her attention from her daughter-in-law and grandson to Mavis and Val.

'Just chatting about Val's new hairstyle,' said Mavis.

'It's lovely,' enthused Althea. 'I often wonder if there's anyone out there who could possibly make what I've got look better. It's so much thinner than it ever used to be; I'd like it to have a bit more get up and go – instead of living with the reality that so much of it has got up and gone.'

'Your hair's very practical,' said Mavis.

'And I'm eighty, so that's all I should expect, you mean?'

Mavis patted Althea's hand. 'No need to be snippy, dear. What's got you in a tizz?'

Althea rolled her eyes toward Sheila and John Timbers. 'The Outlaws,' she hissed.

Mavis felt anxious, but Val smiled broadly and whispered, 'You know you're the Outlaw to them, don't you? My money's on you being the last one standing if there's a showdown, Althea. And you know I mean that in the nicest way possible.'

Althea's little face beamed. 'I do. Thank you, Val. And to what do we owe the pleasure of your company today? It's always lovely to see you, of course.'

'I haven't seen Stephanie much since the baby was born, so she invited me for lunch. I'll stay on a bit this afternoon.'

'It's difficult to talk about him when he hasn't a name, don't you think?' Althea dimpled at Val and Mavis.

Mavis warned, 'Not now, dear. We're having a nice lunch.'

'What do you think of Hector?' Althea asked Val, loudly.

Val gave the matter some thought. 'I quite like it. Hector Twyst. Is it a family name?'

Althea nodded. 'One of Henry's grandfather's names. As you're aware, we recently learned that Henry's great-grandfather, Harold, was a musical prodigy, which explains the names he gave his son: William Albert Hector Felix.'

Val looked surprised. 'Some unusual names there, I'd have thought, for a Welsh duke's son.'

Althea shrugged noncommittally. 'Harold Twyst – who became the fourteenth duke – never expected to inherit the title'

'Of course not, he gave up his career for it, didn't he?'

Althea replied, 'Indeed – if one expects one's child to live a private life, as Harold did, one names them as one wishes. Knowing what we do now about Harold, I suspect Felix was for Mendelssohn, Hector for Berlioz, and Albert was probably for Queen Victoria's Prince Consort, Albert. I, personally, would favor Hector over Felix, but both have a ring to them, don't you think, Henry?'

Mavis sighed as Henry turned to give his attention to his mother. 'Pardon? I didn't quite catch that, Mother.'

'I said I prefer Hector over Felix. Felix Twyst? No. Hector Twyst? Yes.' Althea beamed.

Henry gave Mavis a stare that spoke volumes, then said, surprisingly, 'Enjoy playing with names, but please don't let it worry you so, Mother. Stephanie and I will tell you when we've chosen a name for our son, once we've agreed it between ourselves. But, to everyone here who's made a suggestion, thank you.'

Mavis heard a new tone in the duke's voice, but couldn't be sure what it was. Could Henry have developed a backbone? Surely not. But there he was, smiling magnanimously at his luncheon guests, and indulgently at his son and wife. Mavis recalled what Althea had told her about his surprisingly adroit handling of the matter of the missing christening mugs, and allowed herself to wonder if Henry was one of those men who needed fatherhood to jolt them out of their expectation that they could go through life always being looked after. She'd met men like Henry before. Indeed, her role as an army nurse had often seen her acting almost *in loco parentis* for young recruits, though she reminded herself that Henry was in his fifties, and should long ago have realized the world didn't exist to coddle him.

'Don't you think, Mavis?'

Mavis snapped out of her reverie. 'Sorry, Althea, I was thinking of something else. What did you say?'

Althea looked miffed. 'I was saying that if I am not to be involved with the naming of the child, the organization of the service, the supplying of the christening gown or mug, nor the catering, I should at least be able to arrange the music for the gathering here at the Hall following the christening, don't you think?'

Mavis realized that everyone was looking at her. 'There's to be music here, for the reception?' She sounded as surprised as she was; the idea hadn't occurred to her, then she told herself that, of course, this was to be no 'normal' affair.

Henry and Althea nodded as though it were the most natural thing in the world; Sheila and John Timbers looked as puzzled as Mavis felt, and Val Jenkins seemed to be fascinated by the fruit in the winter pudding she'd been served.

Mavis felt more was expected of her. 'But no' as many people as you had performing for your wedding?' She asked her question of Henry, who appeared to consider the matter seriously.

He replied thoughtfully, 'Maybe not as many harpists – there were rather a lot of them – but maybe a string quartet?'

Althea clapped her little hands. 'Excellent. Please allow me to arrange it all? Henry? Please?'

Henry glanced at Stephanie, and they both nodded. 'Thank you, Mother, that would be most helpful. It would give the gathering a most delightful atmosphere. We'll want everything to be as calm as possible so that H...our son...is able to enjoy it without being overwhelmed by a cacophony.'

Mavis was delighted – for Althea's sake, and her own – that the dowager finally had something concrete to contribute to the christening.

Althea pulled on Mavis's arm and leaned in to whisper, 'Did you hear that? Henry almost named his son right there and then, and the name began with an H. I think he likes the idea of Hector, but doesn't want to say so in front of the Outlaws.'

Mavis whispered back, 'It's a possibility, dear. But I don't think you should keep referring to Stephanie's parents that way. They're right there, and it's a little disrespectful, do you no' think?'

Althea bristled. 'Not really.'

Mavis sighed, and returned her attention to Val. 'Will you be attending the christening, Val?'

Val chuckled, 'But of course. I've finally agreed to be...the baby's...godmother. Stephanie's been on at me about it for months, and I've given it a great deal of thought.'

'I'm sure you have,' said Mavis. Val looked serious.

She spoke thoughtfully, 'I'm not a great believer in organized religion, you see, but she and I have agreed that it's good for a child to have someone in their life who'll allow them to challenge the order of things, and I can be the one who'll listen, and allow them to think for themselves, even when it comes to spiritual matters.'

Mavis didn't have to turn to realize that Althea had heard the exchange, because the dowager's harrumphing was more than audible.

Althea asked loudly, 'Have you decided upon a godfather for the child yet, Henry? If Stephanie's chosen his godmother, one assumes you'll be selecting the godfather.'

Once again, Mavis felt the atmosphere become tense. This time, everyone turned to stare at Henry who didn't faff, as Mavis would have expected, but replied politely. 'I have made an approach, Mother, and believe it will be accepted. And Val's role as our son's godmother is something my wife and I agree upon; it is not her decision alone.'

Mavis couldn't help but notice how Stephanie glowed as she glanced at her husband, and she had a sneaking suspicion that this 'new Henry' was going to surprise quite a few people if he continued to be as confident in his decision-making as he was, recently, proving to be.

As the group rose to take coffee in the drawing room, Edward handed a note to Henry and spoke quietly to him, before helping the duchess and her charge to her feet.

Everyone stopped in their tracks when Henry exclaimed, 'Good grief. I say. Oh dear...' He looked flabbergasted.

'What's the matter, Henry?' Stephanie looked concerned. 'Not bad news, I hope.'

Henry gripped the back of the chair he'd just vacated and stared at his wife. 'Not really. Though it might be, I suppose. Or maybe not.'

Mavis hid a smile as the 'old Henry' made a guest appearance.

'It's not like Edward to stuff a secret missive into a person's hand, Henry – what does it say?' Althea sounded put out.

Henry stared at the note, then at his mother. 'It's from Alexander Bright. He asked Edward to pass this information to me as a matter of urgency, and I can see why. We must…I must…put even more effort into finding Father's old christening mug, it seems.'

Althea approached her son. 'And why is that, pray tell?'

Henry appeared to be gathering his thoughts, then blurted out, 'It seems that Father's christening mug was not only given to my great-grandfather by Tsar Alexander III, but it was also made for the tsar by the court jeweller, Fabergé, marked with the Imperial warrant, and, as such, would be a much sought-after piece of silver. Alexander wants me to know that a similar piece recently sold at auction for…and I have to admit that I am wondering if Edward has written this down correctly…but it says here two hundred thousand pounds. Two hundred thousand pounds? For something the same as Father's toothbrush holder? It beggars belief.'

'It's so funny that Alexander has found out all this about a mug that was presented to our family by another Alexander,' said Althea brightly. 'However, the sum you mention sounds ridiculous, Henry. The mug was so ugly.'

'Beauty is always in the eye of the beholder,' said Mavis, 'and it sounds as though the Twyst family has managed to lose something that could make any bank account look a lot more beautiful.'

CHAPTER TWENTY-ONE

It was five in the morning, and Christine was lying in bed wondering about her future. She and Alexander had talked when she'd returned to the cottage from the pub and, while she knew she'd been bubbling about the case she and Annie were working on when they started to chat, she realized she'd felt terribly sad by the time she'd hung up. Their conversation had morphed from one about how each of them was progressing in their professional endeavors, to how they were both feeling about the wedding plans – which seemed to have saturated the entirety of their personal lives.

It dawned on Christine that she'd almost forgotten what it was like to just relax with Alexander, either in person, or on the phone. She missed their chats about nothing of much consequence; missed the way they'd manage to solve world poverty, or at least come up with a much better way of running the country, by the end of a bottle of wine; missed the snuggling and nuzzling that allowed them to take comfort, and delight, in each other. Yes, she missed all that.

Now? Now there were lists, and scheduling requirements, and more lists. And then the big questions: where, and when? As Christine's mother had been at pains to point out, the where would probably dictate the when; since neither Christine nor Alexander had been able to say with any passion that there was a specific timeframe within which they wanted to become a married couple, why not choose their preferred location, and take it from there, depending upon its availability?

Now that was what they talked about. All the time. Where? And it was becoming more than irritating. The only thing they'd agreed upon as a couple was that neither of them had any strong feelings about it at all: at a church, or not; if a church, which one didn't matter; if not a church, then where? Somewhere that meant something to one of them, or both of them? And should it be hot or cold – or shouldn't that sway them? It was a circular conversation.

Christine squeezed her eyes shut, but couldn't stop visions of places she knew well, places she'd visited, and places she'd only ever seen on a screen or in a magazine, swirling in her head. She tried to drop herself, wearing bridal gear, into the vision of each place to see how she felt she fitted there…to no avail.

She really didn't want to get up – it was too early – but wondered if a glass of water might help her settle for another couple of hours, though she hadn't brought one down to her room with her the night before. Christine swung her feet out of bed and felt for her slippers, but couldn't find them. Determined to not wake herself up more than necessary, she didn't turn on the light, so padded up the stairs to the kitchen as quietly as possible in the dark; she could hear Annie and Gertie both gently snoring in Annie's bedroom, and didn't want to disturb them.

She shut the kitchen door, and hunted about for a mug, or glass, in the moonlight that peeped through the windows. She turned on the tap, but nothing happened. She turned on the hot tap, which also didn't respond. What was going on? For want of anything better to do, she hit both taps a couple of times, then tried again. Nothing.

Christine put down the mug and headed for the sitting room, where she believed they'd left the control pad for the cottage; there was a docking station on a shelf, together with some excellent, easy-to-understand instructions, and neither she nor Annie had encountered any problems controlling the heating, lights, curtains, or appliances with the pad. It really was an impressive system. Christine couldn't recall if it had anything to do with managing the water flow, but thought it was worth investigating.

She perched on a chair, scrolling through menus, and finally found something that talked about the hot water system, but that was to do with the temperature of the water being dispensed by the instant water-heater, rather than the actual level of flow of the water itself.

Christine felt a wave of panic as she realized that life could become unpleasant quite quickly in a place with no water. At least there were two loos – but they were due to host a guest later in the day.

She checked the time; no, far too early to phone their client.

Somewhere in the bowels of the cottage, there was a noise. Christine's body became rigid; it definitely wasn't Gertie, and it couldn't be Annie. This was a grinding sound…like one rock being dragged across another. Could it really be coming from inside the cottage? Christine strained to hear in the dim light of the moon-washed room, but the noise had stopped. Replacing the pad onto its charging spot, she went back into the kitchen and tried the cold tap again. The water came out of it with no problem at all. Same for the hot.

Was the grinding noise something in the pipes that had temporarily stopped the water from flowing? An air-block that had been shifted, maybe? While she – with Annie's help – possessed enough general knowledge to have managed third place in a pub quiz, she admitted knowing less than nothing about plumbing, but promised herself she'd reassess the list of all the plumbing problems that had been reported at the cottage, when she'd managed to get a couple more hours of sleep.

When Annie plodded into the kitchen at half eight, she looked surprised to find Christine hard at it, peering at her laptop, which had migrated from the sitting room to the kitchen table.

'The water went off and came back on again a few hours ago,' said Christine, 'and I'm trying to find out if it happens often.'

Annie didn't even try to understand. 'What? Explain more. Or better. Need caffeine.'

As Annie poured coffee, toasted bread, and managed to not trip over Gertie – who'd wolfed down her breakfast in record time – Christine talked.

Annie eventually held up her hands in surrender. 'Sorry, doll, I'm not feeling me best this morning. That beer I was drinking was a bit stronger that what I'm used to at Tude's, but I wasn't expecting this hangover. Jase might like to bang on about organic this and ethically-sourced that, but that lager I was drinking was wicked, and my head's telling me to stick to a long G & T in the future.'

'I won't say "Serves you right" then, eh?'

'Ta. Let me get more coffee, then give me the quick version.'

Christine was as patient as possible, then spoke slowly, explaining what had happened in the early hours, and what she was now doing about it. 'The list of problems at this cottage over the past couple of years contains seventeen instances of the water going off. Seventeen. Each time, a plumber was called, but – when they arrived – they turned on the taps and water came out. Not knowing how to diagnose or solve a problem that no longer existed, they each left having done nothing, except send an invoice for a call-out charge to our client. I've emailed Gemma Thomas who agrees it's an ongoing problem, but she feels she can't tell paying guests that the water always eventually comes back on, and to just keep trying it.'

Annie chewed her toast thoughtfully. 'Is it always the same plumber who comes…and gets paid for doing nothing?'

Christine smiled. 'Great minds think alike. I know what you mean; is there a regular plumber on call who knows they can make a good deal of money, for no effort, by somehow mucking about with the pipes? And the answer is…no. There've been eleven different plumbers who've attended, a few who've been here more than once, but no one regularly. And Gemma tells me that access to the stopcock is at the rear of the cottage, so anyone wanting to fiddle with the water that comes into the cottage from the water supplier would have to get over the fence to gain access, or walk up from the gate off the beach. I've been checking the camera that's at the front door and the one at the back, and I can't see anything of any use, which isn't a surprise as half the camera's view in the front is blocked by the wall around the garden, and the one at the back doesn't seem to work well in the dark.'

'You've been busy,' said Annie, sounding impressed by her friend's diligence. 'But there's water now. I used the bathroom, and there wasn't a problem. You said it came back after a few minutes, and it's been okay since then?'

Christine nodded.

Annie mused, 'Okay, so the worst type of problem – intermittent. And never when there's a plumber on the premises. That's…weird.'

Christine agreed. 'Like the power that goes off, until there's an electrician here, and the heating that comes on in the summer or goes off in the winter, until there's a technician here to fix it. I've gone through the lists looking for a pattern, and that's what I've found.'

'And have you told the client that?'

Christine nodded. 'She was delighted we'd pulled at least that much together, but still puts everything down to "the curse". I believe we've got at least a starting point: I think someone's somehow messing with the controls of the so-called smart house. An external party.'

Annie put her plate on the floor for Gertie to lick the crumbs off it, and scratched her scalp, all over. 'You know I'm no technical whizz, but even I can use that pad to turn things up, down, on, or off in the place; if it's that simple, I dare say all you'd need would be the password that allows you access to the system management thingy, and you could be anywhere with a wi-fi connection to be able to mess with everything.'

'But who?' Christine looked baffled.

'And why?' Annie looked cross. 'To make Gemma Thomas and her husband shell out for loads of call-out fees…increasing the costs of running this place so they'll want to sell? But she *does* want to sell, but won't, because of all the problems. So…has someone done too a good job of making her want to give up on the place?'

'Could be,' Christine mused. 'Tell you what, pass all of this on in your reports to Carol and Mavis, and let's try to find out from Cadog, when we meet him and Winnie down at the beach for a walk, if anyone's got, or ever had, a particular interest in owning this place. I think we're onto something here…but it's all a bit nebulous.'

Annie stretched and rose. 'Yes, you're right. But I tell you what, let's ask Car to bring us some of the equipment we keep at the office – the cameras we use sometimes. She'll be here tomorrow; we could have the entire outside, and even the inside, of this place under our own surveillance by the end of the day, with better stuff than what's already here.'

'Grand idea.'

Annie added, 'You ask Gemma Thomas if it's okay with her for us to install them, will you? You know what they're like…those suction pads don't cause any real damage. And I'll get hold of Car. Then we'll head off to meet Cadog, and point shiny lights at him until he breaks, and confesses all.'

Christine chuckled. 'He doesn't look the type to be standing outside with a tablet and a connection, taking control of the house. Not sure he'd even know what wi-fi is.'

Annie smiled. 'People can know more about today's technology than their age might suggest. Cadog isn't very good at the old "human interaction" thing, is he? The way he closes his eyes as he speaks suggests to me he's not truly comfortable in the presence of others; that might mean he lives a lot of his life online. But let's go – come on, if we don't get there to meet him, we won't have a chance to ask.'

Christine was already heading to the sitting room to put away her laptop when she said, 'Text from Jason. He can't make this afternoon, after all. Someone's phoned in sick, so he won't have cover.'

Annie shouted, 'Shame,' with such a sarcastic tone that Christine walked back into the kitchen.

'You don't like him, do you?' Christine was cross.

Annie gave her colleague her attention, and replied, 'Right – I'll be honest; there's something a little too confident – or maybe arrogant – about the man for my liking. And that's not just because he's been flirting with my obviously engaged chum. I can't put my finger on it, but there's something about him.' As she continued to prepare Gertie for the off, she added, 'Now *he's* someone I could believe would be able to use the technology needed to mess with this cottage…we should ask Cadog about him, too.'

Christine nibbled her lips. 'Thanks for being honest, Annie.' Then she wandered back into the sitting room to tidy away her things. 'Annie! Annie!'

Annie rushed into the sitting room, where Christine was staring at her laptop screen. She pointed at it. 'I came to close it down. And there's this.'

Annie looked at the screen. A skull and crossbones appeared at the top, beneath which the words appeared: 'STOP OR DIE'.

'What do you think it means?' Christine felt deeply shocked.

Annie replied, 'I'd have thought that was obvious. Hang on, let me check mine.'

Annie went downstairs to her room and brought her laptop up to the sitting room. When she woke it up, the same thing appeared on her screen that Christine had on hers.

'Not a curse, but a campaign, then?' Christine wasn't happy.

Annie nodded. 'I think I need to tell DCI Carys Llewellyn what's going on here; this is a clear threat. She should know about it. Now.'

SATURDAY 4ᵗʰ FEBRUARY

CHAPTER TWENTY-TWO

Mavis knew she looked as down as she felt when she took her seat at the breakfast table. She did her best to eat as quickly as possible, because she didn't feel she had the energy to spend too much time with Althea. Rhodri Lloyd had contacted her the previous evening to advise her that his client was still deciding how he wanted to proceed, which she'd thought kind of him. At least she felt she could now put The Case of the Invalid Invalid to the back of her mind...though, as she tried to shoehorn it in there, she realized that poor Ben Stirling was now a completely validated invalid, even if the cause of his incapacitation was not of her client's client's making.

She'd been down at dinner time, too, so Althea had all but bullied her into playing charades, in an attempt to alleviate Mavis's funk, she'd said. It had worked temporarily – because the sight of Althea Twyst gesticulating wildly as she tried to act out *Gone with the Wind,* *Toad of Toad Hall,* and – most confusingly – *All Quiet on the Western Front,* had left Mavis in stitches. However, she'd been utterly frustrated when Althea couldn't guess what she still believed was her excellent – and perfectly obvious – interpretation of *Jaws.*

Althea entered the dining room just as Mavis let out a sigh of utter frustration.

'Have you sprung a leak?' Althea smiled coquettishly, and took her seat at the table. 'Is the pot still warm?'

Mavis nodded. 'Been there no longer than five minutes. Cook knows when you're about to come down. Must be telepathic.'

Althea giggled. 'Don't be silly, I ring her so she knows. Though I decided to change my clothes after I'd rung, so I'm a bit behind.'

Mavis gave her attention to the dowager. 'Are you planning on going out?' She was used to Althea making more of an effort than usual whenever she was going to have to meet people; she wasn't aware they were expecting visitors, and Althea had certainly made an effort. Mavis had never seen the blue and white polka-dot blouse before, and the red-and-green striped skirt was something she believed the dowager hadn't worn for months. But it was the pearls that gave Althea away; they only came out when she was going to try to impress someone – and they always did, because they were three perfect rows of graduated pearls, with a diamond clasp.

Althea stroked her necklace as she poured tea. 'Yes. Young Ian is driving me into Builth Wells. I want to do a few things there.'

Mavis felt she needed to be on her guard. 'And what would they be?'

Althea waved airily. 'I just wanted a bit of a nose around the shops, that's all.'

Mavis stared across her teacup. 'Could you no' do that on a weekday? The place will be busier today – working folks needing to do all they can on a Saturday, and all that.'

'They put the best things out for the weekend.' Althea's eyes were wide and innocent as she buttered her toast.

'You mean the charity shops, don't you?' Mavis sighed. She didn't understand Althea's obsession with the places, but it existed, and accounted for most of the bizarre items she chose to wear. She didn't have the strength for a long discussion, so said, 'Enjoy that, then. Will you be back for lunch?'

Althea mumbled something about not being sure, so the pair agreed they'd possibly take tea together.

Mavis dreaded to think what she'd have to 'oh' and 'ah' about that Althea would be showing her upon her return, but set that to one side as she climbed the stairs to her room, where she intended to settle into her favourite armchair, and finish listening to her book.

A lovely, quiet Saturday stretched before her; she knew Carol, Annie, and Christine would all be together for the day at Port Beynon. Excellent.

And with Althea out of her hair, she wouldn't have to hear any more about those blessed christening mugs. Their loss, and the amount of money the Twysts now knew one of them to be worth, had energized Henry, it seemed, and had caused much discombobulation at the Hall. Althea had mentioned on several occasions how the Outlaws were helping with another search, this time to include the topmost floor of Chellingworth Hall, as well as the attics above the old servants' quarters. Mavis had to agree with her that the idea of them having a good excuse to poke and pry into every corner of Chellingworth Hall was, naturally, making her feel a little...invaded.

Mavis shut the door to her room, did her best to not think about how she wished she'd checked on Ben Stirling before she had done, and picked up her earphones.

CHAPTER TWENTY-THREE

Annie and Christine had tidied around the cottage – neither of them understanding where all the mess had come from – and were ready by ten for Carol, David, and Albert's arrival. The fact they didn't arrive until half past meant making a fresh pot of welcoming tea, because the women had drunk the one they'd prepared.

Everyone lent a hand to unload the car; boxes were laid out in the sitting room, on the kitchen table, and even on the kitchen floor – as Carol always said, delicate objects need plenty of packaging, and that was certainly the case for the cameras she'd brought with her.

'These are the ones we got at a knock-down price because we trialed them, and said nice things about them that the manufacturers used in their promotional materials.' Carol pointed at a grouping of packages with red tape sealing them. 'They have a sharper picture, and have an ability to record pretty well with night vision, though don't go expecting to be able to recognize a face, unless you know the person in the first place. So – good for the internal set-up in the dark or good for nighttime outside. The others, with the yellow tape, are really only of any use for daytime recording, or if an area is well-lit. Then they're great, and the pictures are much sharper than you'd imagine would be possible. Both the red and yellow ones are suitable for outdoor use. They all have suction pads, and the red-taped ones weigh a bit less than the others. Anything else?'

'Where do we plug them in?' Annie had been hunting for sockets in the places where she'd like to mount the cameras.

Carol rolled her eyes. 'I went over this months ago; they're all powered by rechargeable batteries. The charging station is in that bag. They should work for up to seventy-two hours; all the batteries are fully charged and the memories are empty now – but it doesn't hurt to check them before you set everything up, and don't forget you'll have to connect each one, individually, to the wi-fi. Okay?'

Annie and Christine enjoyed giving Carol four thumbs up, then Carol added, 'In that case, I'm taking my son and husband down to the beach for a walk. Look, Albert – it's not raining. Isn't that lovely? Yes. We can go for a nice long walk on the sands, and maybe Mam will get you a treat for lunch. Would you like that?'

Annie and Christine stood, patiently, as Carol did her mothering thing, then Christine said, 'We wondered if you could help us with something else, actually, Carol.' She twirled her hair as she spoke.

Carol looked from one friend to another. She didn't reply, instead calling out, 'David, would you be okay starting to walk down without me? Or would you prefer to take the car? That might be easier, given all Albert's stuff. I'll see you down there. Soon.'

A distant agreement floated to the three women, then Carol said, 'Right-o. Be quick. What's the matter?'

Christine showed Carol both laptops, each displaying the STOP OR DIE message. 'The messages just appeared, yesterday morning. Not in emails, or texts, they just appeared on our screens.'

Carol didn't even try to hide her horror. 'This is serious. Do you believe these messages are connected to this case?' Nodding. 'And what have you done about them? Have you told the police?' More nodding. 'Good, because this is not nice…and it's also not a simple thing for a person to do. It means they somehow had access to your laptop's system, not just your email or social media, or anything like that. Though they could have…' She paused, deep in thought, then added, 'Have either of you clicked on a link that didn't take you where you'd expected? I know you've both got good security on those devices, but it can still happen. So – either of you?' Shaking of heads. 'Good, but puzzling. Let me have a think.'

Annie and Christine stood in the kitchen as Carol wandered about the cottage. 'Is this the smart house control pad?' She came through from the sitting room waving the pad. Both nodded. 'And this hasn't left the house?' Shaking of heads. 'Have you two lost your voices?' Shaking of heads, and silent chuckling.

Carol tutted. 'You two are awful, you know that? Right, this is all I can say without carrying out a great deal of fiddling about, so it'll have to do for now: this pad is run on wi-fi, and is therefore connected to the wi-fi modem. Someone could have accessed your devices via the modem. It's not terribly secure, and I bet the password is something it's really easy to guess. Is it Sea View, or something like that?'

'Almost a bullseye,' said Annie. 'It's "seaviewcottage" – all lower case, all one word – then the numbers one, two, three, then an asterisk. So, yes, not hard to work out. And, in any case, it's printed on a card beside the modem itself, which even I thought wasn't the brightest idea.'

'Okay – so anyone who's ever been here could know it – or anyone with two brain cells could make a good guess. But who would want to do this? And why?' Christine was as close to whining as Carol and Annie were ever going to allow her to get.

'Obviously,' said Carol, 'someone wants you to drop this investigation, though I'd say it's unlikely they'd kill you if you don't. Killers don't usually use threats like that. Do they?'

The three women shrugged, and they all looked as uncomfortable and off-kilter as they felt.

'We wondered if you might be able to tell us who sent those messages, Car. We know that's your thing – but we also have another techy question for you: would it be difficult for someone to access this control pad to take over the house? You know, could they make heating come on when it's off, make the temperature of the water in the taps go up, that sort of thing. So hard? Easy? Scale of one to ten. Ten being hard.'

Carol looked at the tablet again, then put on an Arnold Schwarzenegger accent and mugged, 'I'll be back.'

She left through the front door, shut it, came back a few moments later, then left by the back doors, which she also shut. Then, eventually, she came indoors again.

Upon returning she said, 'Okay, first thing, this is a control pad as opposed to a voice-activated controller. I dare say our client Gemma prefers that because you have to touch it, not just be able to shout at it. Also, I can see by looking at it that, although this is high level, the entire cottage isn't as "smart" as it could be. For example, the place doesn't have smart light bulbs; yes, you can turn lights on and off with this pad, and you could add a program to your phone to do the same thing when you're not inside the cottage if you were the administrator, or account owner, but these are ordinary light bulbs, not those which automatically come on and go off when they sense movement, or the lack of it. Also, I see the kettle and coffee maker are not operated through the pad, though a robot vacuum cleaner on each floor is mentioned, and I don't see evidence of any, or their effects.' Carol looked around, somewhat pointedly.

'*Could* someone take it over?' Annie was agog.

Carol sighed, nodded, then shrugged. 'What we're talking about is referred to as the Internet of Things, or IoT, for short. In today's world, many things – in fact, almost anything – can be connected to the Internet. Again, this place has an ordinary fridge freezer, but there are smart ones with cameras inside the doors so you can check on your phone in the shop what you've got in your fridge, for example. Or you can play your music or TV through them.'

Annie said, 'Sounds all a bit too much – not sure I want to be able to see inside my fridge when I'm out. What if someone else can see it, too? Don't like that idea.'

Carol said, 'Well, in that case, you won't like what I'm about to tell you. You see, all these connected devices gather data about your usage of them, and pass that to the other systems. So your smart house, using the IoT, learns your habits and can accommodate them.'

'You're right,' said Annie, 'I don't like the sound of that at all. Gives me the creeps, that does.'

Carol continued, 'With so much connectivity everywhere, there are numerous opportunities for hackers. You see, a lot of people will "secure" their Internet, but they don't think of "securing" their kettle, or fridge, or even their robot vacuum.'

'Gordon Bennett,' said Annie, 'that's a job and a half.'

Carol nodded. 'You have to think about these things, and, yes, your smart house could have been hacked, taken over, or enslaved, via the Internet. I saw the satellite on the roof, then there's the wi-fi modem and wi-fi boosters inside the cottage. You might be able to get into the system via the wi-fi modem or boosters, or maybe even via several of the devices connected to the smart house system – they're incredibly easy to hack, as I've said – but you'd have to be inside the house to do that, not outside. I just checked – these are really thick walls – three feet in some places, at least a foot everywhere else. I couldn't pick up the wi-fi signal from the cottage once I was outside it, so, yes…inside the cottage to get in. But once you've got in, you've as good as "got in", if you see what I mean.'

'That could explain a lot,' said Annie.

'But I thought Gemma said the coffee maker exploded in her husband's face. That's not even connected to the system.' Christine sounded irritated.

Carol replied, 'Look, I'd like to catch up with David and Albert, so could we walk and talk?'

Her colleagues nodded, and they set off with Gertie.

'Why do you think Gemma doesn't have everything connected?' Christine was genuinely interested.

'I bet it's the water,' said Annie. Carol agreed. Christine looked puzzled.

Annie explained. 'If you turn on a coffee machine or a kettle and it hasn't got water in it, you're in trouble. I dare say there could be a sensor installed to tell a person there's no water in it, or not enough…but maybe she prefers to force people to have to fill them, then turn them on manually – less likely to cause a problem, with tenants.'

Christine nodded. 'Okay, but…well, could a hacker add them to the system without the owner knowing? Then turn them on when there's no water in them? That could cause all sorts of problems – dangerous, too.'

Carol puffed out her cheeks – and it had nothing to do with the chill in the air. 'Look, I'm not a hacker – at least, not a proper one. And I'll admit I don't know exactly what you could make the system do once you're inside it. But, if someone wants to make it appear that the house is "cursed", I dare say they could do enough mischief by hi-jacking the smart house system to impact the tenants in the ways you've been telling me.'

'And what about an e-bike? Can you hack one of them?' Annie was mindful of the fact they were nearly at the beach.

Carol gave the matter some thought. 'No idea. But I know someone I can ask. Interesting question, Annie. You're thinking of Brian Kelly's death?' Annie nodded. 'Okay,' said Carol, 'I'll look into that angle when we get home this evening. Now, let's find that son and husband of mine, shall we? A lovely, brisk walk, maybe a treat or two, then back to the cottage to help you install all those goodies I brought.' Carol winked.

'No need, Car, we can manage. There's a ladder, though one of us is tall enough to do most of the installing without needing one.' Annie raised her hand as far as it would go, showing off her impressive reach.

The joyful workmates had a fantastic time with Gertie, Albert, and David. The massive amount of fish and chips they carried back to the cottage was divided, and demolished, with Gertie only being allowed two chips, and absolutely no fish whatsoever.

Carol helped with the clearing up, while David burped his son, repeatedly offering to help Annie and Christine with the installation of the cameras.

They kept declining, so he handed his son to his wife and said, 'I'm going to reorganize the hatchback area in the car. I don't want things rattling around now we've emptied it.'

'Okay. I'll just change Albert, and we'll join you at the car, *cariad*,' replied Carol.

Annie and Christine left their colleague to it, making the most of wiping down every single surface in the kitchen…slowly.

A couple of minutes later there was an almighty crash outside the cottage. All three women, accompanied by a yelping Gertie and an instantly screaming Albert, rushed to the tiny front door to see what had happened. David was on the ground, his head bloody, his arms flailing – and the satellite dish was in pieces beside him.

CHAPTER TWENTY-FOUR

Althea Twyst had given a great deal of thought to how she could help her friend and housemate, Mavis, and she'd come up with what she believed was a perfect plan. Having spent months recovering from hip surgery there was one thing she had no doubt about: when a person was suffering from some sort of physical disability that impacted their mobility, their home would become cluttered with devices designed to aid them.

She was convinced that, if Ben Stirling was having to rely upon using a walking stick and had his knee braced, there'd be evidence of that in his house. Althea had also worked out a way to get into his home; knowing he was in hospital, she would wait until she was certain his wife was at home, then go to visit the poor woman to offer her wishes for his speedy recovery.

She'd tried on wigs, had plastered her face with make-up, and had even tried a body suit designed to make her appear much fatter than she really was – a real bargain at only a fiver! – but none of it had looked convincing. In the end she decided the best cover was to be…who she really was, and *she* was such a thoughtful person that a visit with a pot plant wouldn't be too out of character.

She told Ian Cottesloe exactly where to drop her off, though she realized he was going to ask again and again why she was going to visit this woman – because her actions were by no means normal, for her – so she gave him a version of the truth, and agreed he could wait outside for her.

Standing at the Stirling's front door, Althea had to stretch almost as high as she could to reach the doorbell. Pressing it a few times, she couldn't hear it making a sound. She allowed her finger to bounce on the button until the door flew open and a woman in a rather moth-eaten sweatshirt shouted, 'Forgotten your bloody key again, have you, Stuart?'

The woman adjusted her eyeline to look down at Althea. 'Who are you?'

'Althea, Dowager Duchess of Chellingworth. I've come about your husband.'

The woman looked her up and down, her eyes narrowing. She took in Althea's clothes, shoes, pot plant, and hat. 'Yeah, and I'm the Queen of Sheba. Who are you really?'

Althea fished in her handbag and pulled out a Christmas card – one of the official types she sent to acquaintances every year. It showed her, and McFli, standing beside a stile on the Chellingworth Estate, the Hall in the background, and it had her official greeting printed inside.

'I don't have calling cards. Will this do?' Althea smiled sweetly, as she recalled the photographer asking her to do on the day he'd taken the photo.

The woman at the door looked at the card, read the greeting – which named the dowager – looked at Althea, and raised both her eyebrows.

'And you're here for Ben?' Her expression told Althea she was struggling to connect any dots.

'Am I correct in believing you are Mrs Stirling?'

The woman nodded. 'Yes, I'm Julie Stirling. Why?' She pulled at the bottom of her sweatshirt.

'Your husband did some incredibly important restoration work for us up at Chellingworth Hall a while ago – might you recall that?' Althea was stretching the truth to snapping point, but this was all part of her plan.

'Umm…maybe. I don't remember the details, but I know he was out that way, yes.'

Althea pressed on. 'News reached me that he'd suffered a…medical incident recently, so I wanted to stop by to deliver this, with my heartfelt wishes for a speedy recovery.'

The woman stared at the plant again, and took it from Althea's outstretched hands. 'It's…interesting. What is it?'

Althea beamed. 'At the moment, not very much, but soon it'll become an elephant garlic. That's the top of it, the green bit. Excellent for the heart. Though not necessarily the most attractive plant in a pot, I do believe that giving cut flowers is a terrible thing – because they're already dying, aren't they? Whereas this? Eventually you can cook it up for him and know you're helping his heart. Our head gardener, Ivor, swears by the stuff, and he's incredibly fit for his age.' Althea shivered dramatically. 'Oh, I say, it's really quite chilly here on the doorstep, don't you think?'

Julie Stirling looked terrified – her eyes wide, panic oozing from every pore. 'Well, I wasn't expecting anyone, see…and I've been spending such a lot of time at the hospital that I haven't…'

Althea rubbed her arms with her gloved hands.

'Would you like to come inside, Your…Highness?' The bricklayer's wife's voice quavered as she spoke.

Althea didn't hesitate. She took one step forward and beamed. 'It's Your Grace, and thank you so much. I'm in desperate need of…facilities, too,' she hissed.

Even more surprised, Julie Stirling closed the door, and said, 'How about I pop the kettle on and you can…It's up at the top of the stairs, on the right.'

Althea turned to take the stairs, only to be stopped by the woman who ran up ahead of her, still holding the plant, shouting, 'Just hang on a minute down by there.'

She disappeared into what Althea assumed was the bathroom, which gave the dowager a chance to check the living room and kitchen for signs of…well, she wasn't quite sure what, but she'd know it when she saw it. She'd already spotted a walking stick in the umbrella stand inside the front door, but there was absolutely nothing anywhere else downstairs to suggest that someone was finding it difficult to get about.

All the furniture seemed to be where it had always been – there were no dents in the carpet from where it had been moved – and it was all quite close together, too.

Althea reckoned you'd have to sidle between a couple of pieces – well, *she* wouldn't...but a man the size of the one she'd seen in Althea's photos would.

The kitchen looked as though...well, as though someone had opened half the world's supply of packaging, and left it in a heap. There wasn't any evidence of actual food preparation.

'Hello?' Julie Stirling was back. 'I wondered where you'd gone.' The woman had changed her sweatshirt for a blouse, and she was now wearing what Althea assumed would be quite smart trousers, once they'd been introduced to an iron.

'You have a lovely home,' said Althea, beaming up at the woman. 'It's very...homey. Is it alright if I...?' She waved toward the stairs.

'Of course. I just wanted to clear a few things. At the top, on the right, like I said. I'll put the kettle on. Tea's alright for you, is it? I've only got ordinary tea. Nothing...um...'

'Tea would be wonderful, Julie – may I call you Julie?' Julie nodded. 'I very much enjoy a cup of good, strong tea. Thank you.'

Althea did her best on the stairs, which were much steeper than she was used to. She stuck her head inside the bathroom – no elevated seat, no contraption to help someone with a bad leg get off the toilet, or out of the bath. She noted the towel on the rail with a crease in it. *She put out a clean towel for me, how kind,* she thought.

Tiptoeing across the landing, she stuck her head inside the first room – which clearly belonged to the son. Althea rolled her eyes, and moved on. The door to the other bedroom squeaked a little, and she hoped her hostess hadn't heard it. She stepped inside, and looked around. Nothing at all out of the ordinary. Except for something poking out from beneath the bed that looked...odd. She dared the few steps she needed to take to knock the thing with her toe. Out slid a knee brace.

Excellent! Althea pulled her mobile phone from her handbag and took a few photos, then retraced her steps, photographed the bathroom, flushed the toilet, messed up the towel a little, and joined Julie Stirling in her sitting room.

Althea noted that the kitchen table was now cleared of rubbish, and there was a tablecloth on the small dining table, as well as a tea tray with a pot, milk in a jug, and sugar in a bowl.

'I've only got mugs.' Julie Stirling sounded devastated. 'And these are the only biscuits in the house. My son, Stuart, has been visiting Ben at the hospital, and I've phoned him to bring some more when he comes home. Nicer ones, you know? Will Malted Milk do for now?'

Althea sat on the seat she'd been offered, put her handbag on the seat next to it, and opened her coat. Judith stared when she saw Althea's blouse and skirt, which the dowager took to be a sign of delight.

'But of course – I love Malted Milk, though I always think of them as "cow biscuits", because of the little picture on them.' She dimpled at her hostess. 'So how is your husband, dear? Will they let him come home soon?'

Althea was practised in talking to those with whom she had nothing in common, but who expected her to want to know all about them – when what they really wanted to do was find out all about her. She knew that all she needed to do was keep asking questions to be able to extract information, then she'd be away from the place free and clear. And it seemed that Julie was only too happy to chatter on.

She told Althea about exactly how her darling Ben had had a close call, but that he'd be right as rain. In fact, she said, he was already looking better than he had done in some time, because he'd been limping about for months after a nasty accident at work. She reckoned all that had put a strain on his heart, and he agreed.

'What happened to injure him in the first place?' Althea made sure she used her 'innocent eyes' when she asked.

Julie was off: a heartless and careless client; a fall four months ago that had sent him to hospital; the agony he'd suffered; the fact he'd been unable to work all this time; how he got so bored, because he'd always worked so hard all his life; then, lately, trying to get his leg to mend by going to the physiotherapist at the hospital, and off for long walks on his own – contrary to his nature.

Althea sipped her tea, nibbled biscuits, and made soothing noises as the woman spoke. Sometimes she even uttered an actual word. 'Poor thing,' seemed appropriate most of the time, until Julie got to the bit about the long walks, when she enquired, 'Does he have a favourite route? I know I do. The walk from the Dower House to Chellingworth Hall is wonderful, you know.'

Julie admitted that she'd never visited Chellingworth Hall herself, but said there'd been mention of a bus trip being organized for the darts team her husband played for, and their spouses, next summer. She added that her husband had taken to walking around Hay-on-Wye; he claimed it was always an interesting walk because of the dozens and dozens of bookshops there. He also favored it because it was hilly, which was painful, but good for him, though he didn't notice too much because of the distractions of all the books, which he could stop and browse whenever he needed a bit of a break.

'You must let me know when you're coming to Chellingworth, I could invite you for tea in my home, to thank you for your hospitality.' Althea had emptied her mug, and was planning her exit.

The front door opened, and a lanky youth entered. 'There's some bloke sitting outside in a funny old car, Mam, and I've brought the biscuits you wanted, but why…' The young man stopped just inside the door of the sitting room, stared at his mother, Althea, and the tea tray.

'Got a visitor, I see,' he said. 'Are the biscuits for you?' Althea shrugged and dimpled. The youth chuckled. 'Well, whoever you are, you can come again because these are my favourites and we never have them. Don't eat too many, eh? Leave some for me?'

It was clear to Althea that his mother had no idea what to say, or how to handle the situation. Althea stood. 'You must be Stuart, Ben's son. Your mother mentioned your name, and your father often spoke of you when he was working at Chellingworth Hall,' she lied. 'I'm Althea, Dowager Duchess of Chellingworth, but I'm just leaving, as it happens, so you may have them all. Your mother's been a wonderful hostess, but now I must return home. I have appointments this afternoon.'

The boy stared, open-mouthed at his mother, who nodded at him, then looked at Althea again. 'Okay,' he said, 'Nice to meet you.'

Julie got up and shuffled around Althea, silently shooing her son out of the room. 'I'll just show you out then, shall I? Thank you for the...plant. I'm sure Ben will be pleased with it.'

'I'd keep it here, they don't like plants in hospitals these days, do they?' Althea tutted. 'And I hope he's back here soon to be able to enjoy it.'

Stuart announced excitedly, 'They're letting him out this afternoon. He told me, Mam. Said to pick him up at two. That's brilliant, isn't it? He's better than ever, isn't he, Mam? Must be all those hours and hours he's spent on his walks the past couple of months – that's done him good.'

Althea could tell the boy was genuinely happy that his father was being released from hospital. 'Maybe he'll take you on one of his walks; when a parent and child can spend time like that together, it's worth the world, you know. My son, the duke, never was much for walking. Painting is what he loves to do, which is very clever, but not terribly good for an accompanying parent, because one feels one is disturbing an artist. But a good, long walk? Just the ticket. And I bet they'll be telling him to walk as much as possible – it's the sort of thing doctors tell one to do whatever is wrong with one, it seems. Horrified if a person sits down for more than half an hour, these days, aren't they? Before you know it, they'll decide that walking's far too tough on the old joints, so we'll all have to learn to swim like fish, no doubt. Does your husband ever go swimming, Julie?'

Having reached the front door, Julie looked taken aback. She shook her head, looking at her son. 'He's been giving it a go, I know, for his leg, but not a big swimmer, is he, your father? Sitting in a deck chair is more his cup of tea, truth be told. Not that he'd be able to get into or out of one them with that blessed brace thing on his leg. Pleased to have got rid of it, he was.'

Althea's ears pricked up. 'He no longer needs a brace?'

'Not the one he was in. When they took him in with his heart, they said there was a better one for him – still firm, but softer on the inside. He's got some terrible sores because of the other one. I brought it home with me, and he reckons we can have a bonfire to burn it in the back garden, he's grown to hate it so much. But, there, you've got to do what doctors say, haven't you? Or else, if it all goes wrong, they always tell you they told you so.'

'Indeed,' said Althea, recalling her own surgeon's post-operative instructions, which haunted her still. 'A pleasure to have met you both. Good day.'

Ian held open the door to Althea's beloved, if ancient, Gilbern and she alighted. 'Let's get home, Ian, I have news for Mavis.'

CHAPTER TWENTY-FIVE

Carol was exhausted. She'd put Albert into his cot, and he'd settled, thank goodness, and now all she had to do was sort herself out, and let Annie and Christine know that she and her family were safely back in Anwen-by-Wye. It was gone ten, but they'd said to phone whatever time it was, so she got herself a glass of warm milk, and curled up on the sofa. She grabbed her phone and hit the button for Annie.

Answering almost instantly, her chum opened with a heartwarming, 'Hello doll, you all home safe and sound now? How's Dave, and Bertie? And you, of course? I'm on me own, so I've got all the time in the world.'

In a way Carol was relieved; her many years of friendship with Annie meant she felt she could be completely honest with her, and she was. She explained the worry she'd hidden from her chums as she'd packed her son and husband into their car to drive to the A & E, then talked about the hours of waiting, how good Albert had been – up to a point – and how helpless she'd felt as they assessed David, and had then given him a few stitches. Released with detailed instructions of what to look out for upon David's return home, she'd driven slowly – for David's sake – and was only now processing her thoughts.

'I can't even think about what might have happened if David had been carrying Albert out to the car when it happened,' said Carol. 'Even saying those words out loud terrifies me. He's so small, and delicate. Can you...imagine what might have happened?'

Annie said, 'Look, Car, I know this doesn't help at the moment but...it didn't happen, so try to not think about it.'

'Yes...yes, I know. And David was lucky, they said, just a mild concussion,' concluded Carol.

'Could have been a lot worse,' agreed Annie.

Carol sighed. 'I've got to be honest and say I thought Stephanie was making a ridiculous fuss about Henry when he cracked his head before Christmas, but now I understand. Head injuries are terribly dangerous. And with what David does for work, well, he's going to have to stop completely for a while – no screen time at all for a week, they said, just to be on the safe side. All he was bothered about was missing out on his wretched gaming, which is a good sign, I suppose. He's said he'll move around a few projects; there are a couple of blokes he's in a sort of casual alliance with, one in Los Angeles and one in Perth, Australia and they can cover every time zone between them, so juggle projects to suit. He reckons they'll be willing to pick up the slack for now, then he'll take on some extra contracts later on. So we should be alright. Financially.'

Annie had listened quietly, then asked, 'And how are you doing, Car? I know how Dave's doing makes the world of difference to you, as does little Bertie's well-being, but how are *you*?'

'Knackered, to be honest. I feel like a bus didn't just flatten me, but it reversed back over me again just to be sure I'd stay down. I'll warn you now, if David's out of commission completely, I'm going to have to pull back from things a bit at work to see to Albert and him.'

Annie's voice soothed Carol. 'Don't worry about a thing. It's only work. We can sort it. Your insistence that Chrissy and I didn't come to the hospital with you means we stayed here and at least got all the cameras installed on the walls, in the best possible spots. Then Chrissy decided to take herself off down to the pub, while I settled down to a small G & T, and a chat with Tude. Sadly, he wasn't too busy to chat – and it's a Saturday, which in't a good sign for his business. Anyway, you don't want to hear all about his problems.'

'What's drawn Christine to the pub? She's more a sort of wine bar person, I've always thought.'

Annie told Carol about Jason – including a detailed physical description – and mentioned the flirting. Carol was shocked, then realized she really wasn't that surprised.

She spoke thoughtfully. 'Christine's got something wild about her, hasn't she? Like an animal that allows you to get to know it, and allows you to believe it'll always be there for you – then it takes itself off and you never see it again.'

'Like a cat, you mean?'

Carol laughed, thankful for Annie's friendship. 'Not like a cat at all. My Bunty is the world's most doting, loyal creature. She's curled up on my lap at this very moment.' She stroked Bunty, who purred with contentment.

'If you say so, Car. Now Gert? She'll go where the snacks are, or the food. I know that. But dogs are different to cats in so many ways – and I've learned I'm a dog person. You? A cat person. Mave? Definitely copes well with both. Chrissy? She is, herself, a feral cat, masquerading as a domesticated one. That's what I think.'

Carol wondered about Christine. 'Think everything's alright between her and Alexander? We haven't seen much of him in Anwen since their engagement, have we?'

Annie explained about the big project he was working on. 'She's stressed about the whole wedding thing, no doubt about it. Hopefully, they can cut through the rubbish and focus on what matters. Not my monkeys, not my circus…except it sort of is, because she's me mate, and I like her. Anyway, there's not much I can do but be here when she needs me, and listen. Like this, with you – as useful as a chocolate teapot, me, but I can shut my gob and be supportive, sometimes.'

'Thanks, Annie.'

'I am officially the most chilled member of our team now – thanks to my counsellor.'

'I just wish I knew what had happened to David,' said Carol. 'He's got no idea. Just a smack on the head and down he went. No warning. Were you able to work out why the dish might have come down like that?'

Carol noticed that Annie didn't answer straight away.

Eventually her friend replied, 'I took a look up on the roof so I could tell the bloke who's coming to fit a new dish tomorrow what had happened – you know, so he knew what to expect, and could bring everything he needed with him to put it right. He's charging double the usual call-out fee, of course, because it's an emergency and a Sunday, and I didn't want him turning up and "not having the right part" because I'd given him the wrong information. Anyway, what I discovered was that there were brackets holding the satellite dish onto the wooden skirt thingy below the slate roof tiles…I can't remember the name of it now…anyway, the brackets had rusted a bit. Well, a lot, actually. The bloke I spoke to said it's not uncommon – all the salt in the air here, he reckoned. But, I've got to be honest and…hang on, let me send you some photos. You take a look for yourself.'

A couple of moments later, Carol was turning her phone this way and that. 'Thanks for getting up onto the roof to take these, Annie,' she said. 'I'm not imagining that cut mark, am I? Yes, overall that bracket's in a poor condition, but someone's been at it with some sort of rough-edged blade. Is that what you mean?'

Annie replied heavily, 'Yeah, Car. Someone went at it with what Christine and I reckon might have been a saw. I've sent the photos to DCI Carys Llewellyn, and we talked earlier. She's coming over tomorrow, so we can show her what's what here – on the spot, like. I've had to bribe her with the promise of a proper roast at the pub, but that's not too much of a pain. I like her. I'm hoping she can help.'

'Me too,' said Carol. 'I…I've got to be honest, I can't find all the words to express how I feel about this. I'm angry, of course, and incredibly grateful that David got off as lightly as he did.'

She tried to sigh away her anxieties, then refocused. 'Right then, let's turn our attention to work stuff, shall we, because I need something to sort my head out at the moment. I dare say I'm not going to be able to sleep tonight…'

'But you need to try. Promise me you'll try?'

Carol smiled. 'Yeah, I'll try. But, in the meantime, I still haven't found out anything of any note about those two old sisters who once lived there, sorry – but I shall. However, it's pretty clear this isn't a curse, but a person actually doing things, right now, to make that cottage a danger to…well, just men, by the looks of it. You and Christine haven't had any incidents there, except the water going off for a bit; David's there for an hour, and this happens.'

Carol could hear Annie whisper a curse. 'What is it, Annie? Everything okay?'

Annie replied, 'Yeah, everything's fine, except that I've actually got to get my bum up and out of the chair to turn on another light, because, with the satellite down, of course we haven't got a smart cottage any longer. It's just an ordinary, stupid one now…but that's not it. I just had a thought: if someone's doing this, which is certainly the case, then how did they know there'd even be a man here today? And how did they know exactly when the dish would fall down? I can understand cutting the brackets, knowing that something would happen to make the satellite dish fall down at some point – and that would be all well and good if what you wanted to do was inconvenience a tenant. Any tenant. At any time. But that thing came down right on poor David – the only man who'd been in the place since the one who was here to do the cleaning and got badly scalded. How did they manage that?'

Carol shook her head. 'No idea,' she said, feeling a wave of tiredness and helplessness wash over her. She yawned.

'Right, no more chatting, off to bed for you,' said Annie. 'Give all your attention to your family, and yourself, Mrs Carol Hill. And you know I'm being serious when I use your full name. I'll let you know if we make any progress here. Night night.'

SUNDAY 5th FEBRUARY

CHAPTER TWENTY-SIX

Mavis had napped a great deal the previous day, so she'd missed tea altogether, and had chosen to dine in her room, alone. She'd allowed herself to wallow in her guilt about Stirling, but she knew that wasn't healthy, so she strode into the dining room for breakfast having told herself to adjust her attitude, and approach the day with not a brave face, but one that told the world she had come to terms with the fact that she understood there were some things she just couldn't change.

Althea was already at the table, and looking perkier than usual, her eyes glinting with mischief of some sort. Mavis didn't know what was going on, but was certain something was up.

'Good morning, dear.' Althea greeted her brightly. 'Isn't it a lovely one?'

'Aye, that it is. I even opened my window this morning because it looks almost springlike out there. I've shut it again now, though, because looks can be deceptive; it's a nippy one.'

Althea crunched toast, while Mavis helped herself to tea from the pot. 'How are you feeling today, dear? Cook said she brought your food to your room last evening. Appetite doing well, but not wanting to mix?'

Mavis was used to Althea's solicitousness, but suspected the dowager was angling toward…what? 'Come on, out with it – I know you want to say something. You cannae hide much from me.'

Althea squared her small shoulders – encased in an eyewatering shade of lime – and said, 'I wanted to show you some photos.'
She pushed her phone across the tablecloth to Mavis, who stared at a photograph of an unknown bathroom, puzzled.

'Scroll on – there are more,' said Althea proudly.

Mavis did as Althea had suggested. 'Aye, well, whoever lives here could do with a bit of help about the house, I dare say. But why are you showing these to me?' Mavis slid the phone back to her housemate.

'I took them at Ben Stirling's house. Yesterday. And I think they prove he's not having any real problems getting about the place.'

Mavis allowed Althea's words to sink in. 'This is inside the Stirling home?' Althea nodded, her cheeks dimpling, eyes twinkling. 'And you were there, *inside* the house? Yesterday?' More nodding, and an attempt to prevent a grin breaking out. 'And how did you manage that, exactly?'

Althea burst out, 'I told her I was me, and she let me in. She made me tea, and that gave me a chance to case the joint. I took all those photos. Though I'm disappointed to report that the man's knee brace is under his bed because the hospital gave him a replacement. So I do understand that they don't provide you with the conclusive proof that he's lying, that you or I might have hoped for.'

Althea's face looked like that of a disappointed child, but Mavis couldn't let that dissuade her from what she felt bubbling up inside her. She was livid.

'Ach, I cannae believe you, Althea. You know you're not supposed to go meddling in our cases. We've been through this so many times. What we do is a job, a profession. We've all taken courses to be able to investigate properly, within the law. And you're telling me you've gone into someone's home, misrepresenting yourself, to take photographs where they have every expectation of privacy? You cannae be doing that – not even if you are a dowager duchess.' Mavis was aware that her voice had gone up an octave as she'd been speaking, but she was beyond caring; Althea had to understand she'd gone beyond the bounds of acceptable behaviour…and, probably, the law, too.

Mavis folded her arms tightly, and steeled herself as Althea shrunk into her seat, utterly deflated. She did her best to ignore the dowager's trembling chin and glazing eyes.

She told herself to pay no heed to the little fingers twisting a napkin until they were bloodless. She had to make herself immune to every device the woman used to get folks to forgive her, and forget her missteps.

A quiet 'I'm sorry' fell from Althea's lips, which she then nibbled and sucked. 'I was only trying to help. You seemed to need help. You've been so terribly down since that man had his heart attack, and you couldn't go back there yourself, you said. So I thought I could go for you.' She dared a glance in Mavis's direction. 'I said I was me. I didn't lie about that. And I took a pot plant. Well, a plant in a pot, to be more precise, but Ivor did a lovely job of it. Julie seemed to like it.'

Mavis tutted. 'On first name terms with my target's wife, now, are you? Can you no' see that what you did is wrong?' She was completely exasperated.

'I didn't find anything useful, that's all. What I did wasn't wrong. I was helping a friend out of a tight spot.' Mavis noticed that Althea stuck out her chin, then added a pout.

Mavis buried her face in her hands, and took stock. At least, she tried to, but she felt overwhelmed. The tears sneaked out, and she couldn't control them. Even as she told herself this was unacceptable behaviour, she felt Althea's arm around her back.

'Use my hanky. It's clean,' she said.

Althea stuffed a tiny square of fine linen, edged with delicate lace, into Mavis's hand as though it would be of some use. As she pushed it back toward Althea, and pulled a wad of tissues from her sleeve, Mavis suddenly felt the action was a metaphor for what was happening in her life: she was refusing help she knew would be inadequate, whereas what she should acknowledge was that help was being offered.

She grabbed the whisp of a hankie back, and sobbed quietly into her tissues.

Althea rubbed her back, soothing her with 'there, there' as she did so.

It took a few moments for Mavis to regain control, then she dried her eyes, blew her nose, and shooed Althea back to her seat.

'I'm so sorry, my dear, I didn't mean to upset you,' said the dowager quietly. 'All I wanted to do was help.'

Mavis took a deep breath, which shuddered through her body, then said, 'I understand, really I do. But you need to understand something too, Althea. I am not, nor have I ever been, a woman who asks for help. I've always been the strong one, the one who oversees the security and well-being of her family, the one who steps up and takes the lead. I had to leave my life of happy motherhood behind me when my husband was invalided out of the forces, so I trained as a nurse, where I took responsibility for the well-being of my charges, and now I do the same for my colleagues. I am, and always have been, the person everybody turns to looking for direction; I'm no' used to asking for help, and no' used to receiving it unbidden. I…am a strong woman. That means I need no help. Thank you.'

'Poppycock,' snapped Althea. 'Being a strong woman doesn't mean not asking for, or accepting help – it means knowing when to ask for it, and which to accept. There's such a lot of drivel talked, these days, about women having to be like superheroes. Well, that way lies madness. Everyone – every human being – needs help of some sort, at some time. Humans are social creatures – we've evolved acting as a community, not as individuals who cleave only to self-interest. It can be very selfish to not accept help offered – and short-sighted, too. Just think how much more we can all achieve – all we humans, and all we strong women – if we act with each other's interests at heart, because then we'd all be automatically helping each other all the time. There, that's my two pennyworth on the matter. Take it or leave it, as you will.'

Mavis nodded, wiped her eyes again, and gave her friend's words a great deal of thought as she poured more tea, and buttered some toast. As she crunched, she thought about the life she'd led, of the calls that had been made upon her by her family, and her profession. She didn't even taste the marmalade.

Finally, she said, 'Thank you, Althea. You're right. Strength comes in many forms, and accepting help is, indeed, one aspect of being strong. And the first thing I want to say is that I recognize the help you've given me in the past, so many times, and in so many ways – and I truly appreciate it all. Really. I value it. I'm sorry if what I just said made you feel otherwise.'

She patted the dowager's hand.

'It's just that I find that asking for help, when it's related to an area of my life where I have judged myself to have come up short, is no' something I've ever felt comfortable with. I need to…address that, you're right. You're a good friend to say what you did. Thank you. Now then – let's get our breakfast finished, and away to church, eh?'

Althea dimpled at her. 'Don't worry, we've got time yet. And thank you, Mavis. You're my best friend by far. I hate to see you unhappy. Which is why I…no, never mind.'

Mavis managed a small smile. 'I'm glad you didn't lie about who you were at the Stirlings', and I appreciate that the photographs are for our use only. You should delete them all, by the way. Though I'll take another look before you do that – now I know where you took them. As I keep telling you, it's wonderful to be able to talk through things about work with you, but you're no' a member of the team – you aren't involved with the business at all, except when specifically invited to contribute. And I didn't ask, knowing that the enquiries for this case are delicate.'

Althea rallied. 'Oh, I know that, dear, hence the pot plant. Gifts help with delicate matters. And she's really quite nice, Julie Stirling. The son looks a bit…well, those hoody things make anyone wearing them look as though they're up to no good, don't they? But he was polite. Which is more than you can say for a lot of them. He'll be home by now – did you know that?'

Mavis said, 'Who'll be home? They've let Ben Stirling out of the hospital? That seems a bit quick.'

'I hear on the news that they need the beds, so maybe that's it?'

Mavis raised an eyebrow. 'Aye, Mebbe.'

Althea continued, 'Anyway, both his son and wife seemed to think he'll be better than ever, now. Oh, and he likes to walk in Hay-on-Wye. That might be something. Though he doesn't swim very often.'

Mavis shook her head. 'Not following you, dear.'

'His wife said he's been trying out swimming, but I didn't find out where – which just goes to show there's a great deal of room for improvement when it comes to my interrogation techniques. If I'd managed to prise that information from her, we could have kept him in our crosshairs, and seen how he managed without his brace, because he'd have to take it off to use a swimming pool, wouldn't he?'

'Ah, yes. Very good. And the walks?'

Althea scratched her chin. 'Now that's a bit odd…though to be truthful, it didn't strike me as such until I realized something about the house. Of course, I've only seen the photos of Ben that you showed me, but he doesn't strike me as the sort of man who'd find walking about – for exercise – to be easier for him because of a load of bookshops. I'm trying to not do that nasty "profiling" thing – but he's a bricklayer, who likes motorbikes and heavy metal – you told me all that. Now, please forgive me if I'm being…judgemental…but that sort of life doesn't scream "book lover". Do you understand? And if I've said a bad thing, please don't tell anyone. I really do try to not be snobbish about people, you know that. One more thing – there weren't any books at all that I could see in the house. Which is why I think it's alright for me to say what I said. If he's a book lover, he'd have books in his house, wouldn't he?' Althea concluded her speech with a bright smile.

Mavis sighed. 'Aye, a book lover with no books is an unusual thing. Let me see those photos again, will you?'

Althea pushed her phone toward Mavis, and buttered herself another triangle of toast while humming tunelessly – which Mavis always found annoying, but didn't have the heart to complain about…after all, she was living in the woman's house.

'No' a bookshelf in the place, and no books scattered about, either. So, yes, long walks in Hay, because of the bookshops, seems odd. Well spotted.' Mavis checked her watch as they didn't want to be late for the service. 'Was there anything else?' She wondered if Althea was keeping something up her sleeve, because she was still twinkling.

'No, nothing else. I'm just looking forward to hearing Wendy playing today's hymns on the organ at church, that's all.'

'Wendy Jenkins?'

Althea nodded.

Mavis felt daring with her next comment. 'Are she and Ian Cottesloe...um...seeing each other? I thought I sensed something there over Christmas.'

Althea leaned in. 'I believe so, and I'm happy for both of them. But I want to talk to her about the christening. I've been put in charge of the music, as you know, and thought she could help.'

Mavis wavered, then decided she should speak her mind. 'She cannae bring the organ to Chellingworth Hall from St David's, and I'm no' sure that keyboard she used at the village hall at Christmas would be quite the ticket. By the way – is she related to Val Jenkins at all?'

Althea shook her head. 'No, she's from North Wales – completely different Jenkinses. Very common name, really. That gift to womanhood, Richard Burton, was a Jenkins originally, and if it was good enough for him...well, I don't have to say any more, do I?' She winked at Mavis, who replied with an eye roll. 'And I don't want to talk to Wendy about her and Ian, or about playing the organ...oh, never mind. I know what I mean. Come on, time to go.'

As they pulled on their coats at the door, Mavis hugged Althea, and they stepped out into the pale, wintry sunshine both strong in their friendship, and strong in themselves.

CHAPTER TWENTY-SEVEN

Christine had slept like a log, and got out of bed looking forward to spending time checking the recordings made by the cameras she and Annie had installed at the cottage the previous day…then realized there wouldn't be any, because the Internet would be down until the new satellite dish had been installed. By the time she got to the kitchen, Annie was already there, with both a pot of tea and a pot of coffee made. Gertie greeted her with her wonderful puppy-enthusiasm, which was only quieted when Christine got permission from Annie to give Gertie a treat.

'Late night?' Annie's tone wasn't accusing, but Christine felt a bit guilty in any case.

'I was in bed by eleven thirty, so not very. And yes, before you ask, it was mine, and I was alone. You've no need to worry about Jason and me – he's a nice bloke, and more than pleasant to look at, but I am, as you know, significantly aware of my status as an engaged person.' Christine hoped that would knock any plans Annie had to make more pointed remarks about Jason well and truly on the head before she even got started.

Annie's barbed response of 'Good' was something Christine knew she had to take, then she changed the subject.

'I saw the text you sent me about Carys Llewellyn visiting us today. Any idea when?'

Annie mumbled, 'About eleven,' through her breakfast cereal, then turned her attention to Gertie, who was salivating while she waited for Annie to finish, and pass the bowl to her.

With Gertie licking happily, Annie stared at her phone fiddled with it, then put it down. She couldn't make up her mind what to do for the best.

She said, 'I know I can use my mobile to access the Internet, but I don't want to gobble up all of my data before the bloke gets here to put up a new satellite.'

'I think I've already gone over my limit, which is annoying,' said Christine.

'We really should talk to Mavis about getting us all unlimited data packages again; this situation just goes to prove how important that is – and I think she's made a poor choice of where to cut costs with that one.'

'I agree with you about that. But it won't happen today, will it? The installer said about nine, right?' Christine was hoping it would be sorted out as soon as possible.

'Yeah, we're his first call of the day. I dare say you, me, *and* Gemma Thomas, all telling him how much of an emergency it was must have worked. If he turns up. I'm going to make sure I'm ready by half eight in any case, alright, doll? I'll hit the downstairs bathroom now – do you want it after me, or will you use upstairs?'

Christine gave it some thought. 'I fit in the shower up there just fine. You luxuriate, I'll nip upstairs in a minute.'

Annie left, and Gertie followed her, so Christine took advantage of having some time alone to drink coffee and stare through the windows in the sitting room. The dark clouds on the horizon were being pierced by the most magnificent shafts of soft, pale, yellow sunshine. She knew in her heart she'd love to wake to a sight like that every morning; having spent her childhood at a manor house that looked over a lake that felt as big as a sea to a small girl, she'd always been drawn to shorelines that were rugged, rather than endless sand. Maybe that was what she liked to much about Port Beynon; yes, it had sand, and it even had miles of dunes – which she also adored – but it was the rock pools that teemed with promise when the tide went out that she gravitated toward, because 'her' lake hadn't had anything like that, there being no tide to retreat. She loved the way the sea left behind all sorts of interesting creatures that needed to know how to survive in nothing more than a puddle until they were submerged beneath the waves again hours later, when they were able to resume their normal, seafaring ways.

Her phone buzzed.

It was Alexander.

Christine realized, with a sinking feeling, this wasn't the first time in the past few weeks that she'd hesitated about answering his call. She tried to work out why that was, and told herself she really knew the answer to that one.

She answered. 'Hello.'

'Christine?'

'Yes.'

Alexander sounded puzzled. 'You don't usually say that when you answer. No merry quip today?'

'Too tired. Late night,' she lied.

'Oh, sorry. Okay. Anything good? Fun with Annie and Gertie?' Christine could tell he was forcing himself to be jolly.

She told him about David's unfortunate run-in with a satellite dish, Annie's excursion to the roof, and the hours they'd spent setting up the cameras.

Alexander listened, then said quietly, 'That's not good news. But at least you've got the police involved. That's sensible.'

Christine was annoyed. 'Thanks. Do you think Annie and I aren't capable of working this all out on our own?'

Alexander gushed, 'Not at all. I know you can, and will. I'll give David a call, poor bloke.'

Christine agreed that was a good idea. 'So, what are you up to next week? Or even today?' As she asked she wondered if she really cared. She did.

'I'm just back from an invigorating run along the Thames. Not a bad day for it, but I was glad to sit in the sauna for a while afterwards; it's still chilly out there. And I'm off to Norwich later on; I thought I'd told you about that – the meeting with that bloke who's using similar business models to my own in the construction business. After that? Well, I'll just keep everything ticking over while I wait to hear back about this new project in London. I can't hurry them up, and I know I won't hear anything until Thursday at the earliest, because they've got presentations from my competitors scheduled until Wednesday. So I'll make the most of that time to clear the decks, because if it's a yes, then it'll be a fast start.'

'I really hope you get it,' said Christine. 'I know it means a great deal to you.'

When her fiancé replied she heard the weight in his voice. 'It does. But, enough about me – what about you? Lunch with the Swansea Police, then what? Anything nice? Curl up with a good book and a borrowed puppy?'

Christine managed a chuckle. 'Not sure. If we get the satellite sorted out, then maybe a bit of TV? I'm not enjoying either of the books I brought. And Annie keeps Gertie to herself, most of the time. Or maybe it's the other way around. We're hoping for some information about our client's uncle's death from Carys Llewellyn, and some more insights into the death of Brian Kelly, to be honest. But, please, don't worry about me. I'm perfectly fine. And I have Annie with me, of course.'

To Christine's ear, Alexander sounded distracted when he said, 'Of course.'

'I'll tell you one thing, Alexander,' she said, hoping to be able to find something that could cut through this weird feeling of disconnection between them she was experiencing, 'I just had the most wonderful experience – simple, but wonderful. I watched the sun poke through the clouds, and I've realized I'd like to get married beside the sea, with the surf pounding in the background, and the air full of invigorating ozone. What do you think?'

Alexander sounded incredibly relieved. 'I'm so pleased to hear that enthusiasm, and passion, in your voice. It seems to have disappeared of late. And if that's what you want, that's what you'll have. Now – were you thinking somewhere in Britain, or Bonaire? I know where the weather's better – always good, in fact. But it's not the sort of place that could accommodate a couple of hundred people. Well, I dare say it could accommodate a great deal more, but how many would come? And how would one of those "destination weddings" go down with your parents? They do seem pretty set on…let's call it "the more traditional route", don't they?'

Christine deflated. 'They do. And I don't think they'd care for it at all.'

'We could just up and go. Elope. It's been done…but it's still romantic. How about that? I could pick you up in Port Beynon tonight, and we could be on a beach before you know it, with a ring on your finger before the week's out. Up for it?'

Christine couldn't tell if Alexander was being serious or not. Was he testing the water, to find out what her reaction would be? And what *was* her reaction going to be?

She replied, 'Sorry to leave you this way, but there's a van outside; the man's here to install the new satellite, Annie's in the shower. Sorry. I've got to go. I…do love you, Alexander, you know that, don't you?'

'I do. And I love you too. Look after yourself, talk soon. Bye.'

It wasn't until a quarter to eleven that Christine finally managed to get herself showered, the installation of the new dish having proved much more challenging than anyone had imagined. She and Annie had also taken the chance to quiz the installer about the state of the one that had fallen, and he'd drawn in his breath, whistled, puffed out his cheeks…and agreed with them that something malicious had been done to the old brackets – though he was also unable to work out how any vandal might be able to control exactly when the dish would take a tumble.

When Carys Llewellyn arrived, Christine was still drying her hair, but decided to give it up as a bad job. She joined Annie and the senior detective in the sitting room, where she was surprised by Carys's appearance; she looked so much younger than she had when they'd met at police headquarters, and so much softer, and more vulnerable, now that she was wearing a fleecy, pale pink sweater.

'I see you've both got tea, I'll just grab one and join you,' said Christine. She could hear Annie explaining that the Internet was now working again, how all the smart home features had been reconnected, and that – although it had taken a while – each of the new cameras was now also connected to the wi-fi. It was also clear that she'd already shown Carys the death threat they'd both received on their laptops, because Annie was passing on the explanation about the Internet of Things that Carol had shared with them.

'I'd like a look at those brackets you reckon were cut through,' said Carys as Christine finally joined the pair.

'I'll bring you the relevant bits,' said Christine, and she popped outside to collect the brackets. She hunted about in the remnants of the old dish; the installer had said he'd take all the large parts to dispose of them safely, and she swore to herself when she realized he might have also taken the critical pieces.

'Did you put them somewhere, Annie, or did that bloke take them with him?' She sounded as cross as she felt when she asked.

'Oh no.' Annie slumped. 'That's a great way for professional detectives to work – let someone walk off with the evidence. Sorry, Carys.'

'We've got the photos you took of the brackets,' offered Christine, so they checked those, and Carys's concerns increased.

'Okay, that looks like sabotage to me,' she said, 'and I need you to bring me up to speed with everything else, too. I'll have a quick look around, but how about we get out for that lunch you've promised me? Then maybe you can point out to me where Brian Kelly came off his bike, because I'm afraid the bits of brambly bank that appear in the photographs of his road traffic accident look very much like any other.'

Twenty minutes later, Carys had taken dozens of photos of the cottage, and Christine was pointing out the area where the accident had taken the life of Brian Kelly. The threesome had walked up and down the hill a few times – accompanied by a very confused-looking Gertie – then finally headed toward the beach.

Carys said, 'I agree there's every likelihood that Kelly lost control of the e-bike before he reached that curve, then careened right past the cottage. Terrible. Poor man. At least I can picture that for myself, now. So, tell me everything you've discovered so far.'

Christine and Annie took it in turns to tell Carys about their beliefs, and proofs, that a human hand was at work, even if only to enact the supposed curse put on the cottage by its two previous inhabitants. It didn't take long, because Annie had been sending information through to Carys on an ongoing basis.

'Do you have anything for us about the death of our client's uncle, Ted Thomas?' Christine really hoped she did.

Carys sighed. 'All I can do is confirm he died of carbon monoxide poisoning, which is puzzling, now that I've seen the cottage. There's no gas there at all – everything's electric. Can you find out from your client if there was gas there before, when he lived…and died…there, please? Maybe right now?'

Annie offered to make the call, taking Gertie to one side with her, so Christine and Carys dawdled as they waited. Carys asked, 'Do you enjoy your work?'

Christine didn't have to think before she answered. 'Love it. It's so varied, and it keeps me on my toes. It's grand to learn new things all the time, and to be able to help people. That's the best part of it, helping out. And I work with great people, too. Annie's quite a card, and Mavis is a rock. Carol's our calm center…and me? Well, I'm the youngest, so they expect me to be the maddest – but I get the job done. What about you?'

Carys nodded thoughtfully. 'I can't imagine myself being anything other than a police detective. I admire the work my brother does…but I prefer detection over policing, so I'm glad I chose the path I did. He might end up going further, but I don't have to deal with all the external politics he does, which suits me. Mind you, there's enough politics internally to keep me busy – which is what's come up with this case, a bit. Not that that should worry or concern you…ah, here she is.'

Annie announced, 'Yes there was a propane-fuelled boiler in the cottage before Gemma installed all new electric systems. She had the old propane tanks taken away from behind the cottage when she had the cellars under the house transformed into the two extra bedrooms and bathroom. So there was, in fact, a potential source of carbon monoxide at the cottage back then. Was anything said about the boiler being broken or malfunctioning at Ted Thomas's inquest, Carys? That's where that sort of thing would come up, right?'

Carys scratched her head. 'Yes. But I haven't had the report, yet. Politics. Right, anything else?' Carys was all business.

'The neighbours seem harmless, no one appears to have a reason to want to hurt just men who are staying at the cottage, and we're as much at a loss as we were when we started,' admitted Christine, 'which isn't good for our client, and doesn't look good for us.'

The threesome entered the pub, which was already quite full. Christine smiled at Cadog and Winnie, sitting with Amy, Glyn, and Llew Francis – and they all exchanged waves. Jason was behind the bar; she spotted him as he spotted her, and she threw him a coquettish smile – there was no harm in it, she knew that. He waved, and she waggled her fingers in his direction.

The aroma of roasting meats made Christine's mouth water, and the warmth of the pub compared with the chill of the seaside air made her feel cozy, and safe. 'There's a table, over there,' she said, waving an arm toward a corner.

With Gertie tucked under the table, and the women settled, Christine hoped that the arrival of a water bowl wouldn't be far behind. She kept glancing about, then finally said, 'I'll get some menus from the bar for everyone.' Jason had disappeared; she reckoned he'd be in the kitchen overseeing the lunch service – which looked brisk.

'Here you go,' she said brightly, plopping the menus in front of Carys and Annie. Annie's expression puzzled her – she looked as though she'd lost a pound and found a penny. 'What is it, Annie, what's the matter?'

Annie nodded at Carys. 'Listen up,' she said, sounding grim.

Carys leaned in and whispered, 'I was just saying to Annie, it's a small world, they say, and it's true, especially when you're in my job.'

She paused, then chuckled. 'I've got to be honest, and say you'd never think it to look at this place from the outside, but there are three people in here I've arrested on different occasions in the past, one of whom I've actually tried my damnedest to put away a couple of times. Three. Right here, in this little place. You'd never believe it, would you?'

Christine leaned in too. 'Arrested for anything that might have a bearing on our case? Anything similar? Sabotage, that sort of thing?'

She still couldn't fathom Annie's expression. 'What? What am I missing, Annie?'

Annie smiled sadly. 'Sorry, doll, it's that Jase of yours. I knew there was something off about him.'

Christine tutted. 'First, he's Jason, not Jase. Second, he's not "mine". And third – what do you mean "off"? Is he one of the one's you've arrested before, Carys?'

Carys shrugged. 'He's the one I've tried to put away a couple of times, though I never knew him as "Jason".' The DCI chewed her upper lip. 'And now I'm in a bit of a quandary – because no charges were brought on either occasion, so he's not legally guilty of anything…and I'm ethically bound to not tell you what I think of him. Because he's never done anything wrong, as far as the law is concerned.'

Annie nodded sagely. 'I told you so.'

Christine felt herself getting hot. 'No, you didn't. You just didn't like it that we were indulging in a bit of completely harmless flirting. So, come on, what did you think he'd done, Carys? Or what do you believe he did, but couldn't prove?'

Carys shook her head. 'There's nothing between you and him? Really?'

Christine waggled her engagement ring at the officer. 'Engaged to be married, and very happy about it,' she said. 'Nothing to worry about here. So, can you tell us now?'

Carys sighed. 'If there's nothing at all going on, there's nothing you need to know. Now why don't we order something? I'm starving.'

'Jason is the one in the kitchen, you know,' Christine said. 'Might he have recognized you, and spit in your food?' She'd hoped to raise a smile, but failed, recognizing that her poor attempt at a joke had fallen more than completely flat when Annie kicked her under the table.

Carys looked at Christine through narrowed eyes. 'I've risked more, for less. So I'll have the beef.'

Annie rose. 'Right beef for you, and me. Chrissy?'

Christine mumbled, 'Yes, beef, please. And a pint of the dark stuff.'

'Drink for you, Carys? I'll be G & T'ing. You?'

Carys smiled. 'Driving, so fizzy water, please. No fruit. I hate it when they force you to have fruit.'

Annie chuckled as she left.

Christine said quietly, 'I promise you there's nothing between me and Jason, but I don't believe you can't say what he's been up to. Was it something...violent?'

Carys's brow furrowed, then cleared. 'Nothing violent, no. I believed, because I'd been told by people I came to know and learned to trust, that he'd used his...masculinity...to get people to do things they shouldn't have done. Indeed, they knew they shouldn't have done what he'd asked almost as soon as they'd done it, but felt too ashamed to admit they'd been so foolish. Two lovely, vibrant women, who were tricked into parting with large sums of money. Then, when it came to the crunch, they wouldn't go through with backing up what they'd said to me about him, so everything fell flat on its face. Myself included. See, in a way he duped me as badly as he duped them, and I'm not the forgiving type, Christine. But, legally, there's nothing against him.'

Annie had been hovering, then popped drinks in front of everyone and said, 'Okay, I got the gist of that, but what about the others here you've arrested? Come on, I think a roast beef dinner with all the trimmings is worth that much.'

Christine hid a smile as Annie put on her poor little lost girl expression.

Carys shook her head. 'I didn't realize the tables would be so close together, nor that the place would be so popular.'

'Come from all over for the Sunday lunches here, they do.'

Christine hadn't seen Cadog Smith approach from behind her, so snorted stout all over the table and dribbled it onto the floor when he presented himself at their table, booming loudly. Annie didn't comment, but passed her a hanky, while Gertie cleaned up the floor.

'Nice to see you Constable – though I think it's Detective, now; I heard you'd given up your uniform a while back. Quite a while, actually. Not your usual neck of the woods, is it?'

Christine noted that, for once, Cadog actually kept his eyes open as he talked to Carys, and she smiled broadly at him. She wondered how they knew each other, but didn't feel it appropriate to ask.

Carys replied, 'Hello again, Mr Smith. And how are you and your wife, these days? Well, I hope.'

'Well, not chained to any trees, are we, so that's a start in your book, I suppose.' Cadog chuckled.

Yes, Christine could imagine him taking a stand for an ancient tree or two.

'Wife's not up to it these days, in any case,' he added sadly. 'But there, we had our moment, didn't we? And the trees are still there.'

'Except for the ones that blew down in that storm a few months after you and your wife "saved" them, Mr Smith. The tree surgeon said they were unsafe, which is why the landowner wanted them cut down…before they fell down onto his house. Which is exactly what they did.' Carys tutted and wagged her finger.

Cadog wrinkled his nose and whispered, 'But it was a newish house, and they were very old trees. And some of them are still there. And he rebuilt down the hill a bit, didn't he? No harm done.'

Carys replied, 'A man's home, over two hundred years old, was wrecked.'

'See? Like I said, a relatively new house, compared with the trees. Not much of a loss. Anyway, enough about that. How have you been? You're looking well. I see you're wearing a ring. Did you marry that bloke you were seeing at the time?'

Christine couldn't imagine how Cadog Smith knew so much about the DCI's past, though watching the two of them together made it clear there was a significant, and possibly even warm, history.

Carys explained. 'Mr Smith and his wife lived in a tree for a couple of months about twenty years ago. I was one of the constables assigned to ensure their safety while in said tree, and I was required to do all I could to encourage them to vacate.'

Cadog smiled. 'Bit of a waiting game we played, didn't we?'

Carys nodded. 'Indeed we did. Talked a lot, back then, didn't we, Cadog? They eventually saw sense, as did I; they climbed down, and I moved to CID.' She nodded at Cadog. 'Detective Chief Inspector Llewellyn. Pleased to meet you.' She held out her hand, smiling broadly.

Christine felt the genuine warmth in the way Cadog held Carys's hand in both of his and said, 'Ah, not Constable Carys James any more then, eh? Good for you. You must have been as good as me and the wife always thought you were.' He leaned in and whispered, 'Used to bring us soup when it got cold, she did, in her own Thermos.'

Christine looked at Carys with fresh eyes; Carys was operating at a high level in what was essentially a man's world, the same way she'd been doing when she'd worked in the City of London. She wondered how Carys had managed to do that for more than twenty years, because having to be twice as good as the men all the time had grated on Christine's nerves.

'Are you sticking to the plan – twenty-five years in, then out…retirement?' Cadog winked at Carys. 'Can't be far off now, can you?'

'We'll see,' replied the officer as a harassed-looking server approached with a large tray, so Cadog stepped away. 'My regards to your wife, Cadog.'

'Three beefs,' said the girl, and placed the plates in front of each woman. 'Cutlery's over there.'

'Sorry, I forgot that,' said Annie, leaping to her feet, and getting caught in Gertie's lead as she came to sniff at the food.

Christine got up. 'I'm closer. You sort Gertie.' As she fiddled with bundles of cutlery, and little packets of mustard and horseradish, Christine scanned the bar, and even dared a peep through the roundel of glass in the swing door that led to the kitchen. No sign of Jason.

She wondered if he had, in fact, caught sight of Carys and had made himself scarce.

She didn't like what Carys had said about him – not just because it sounded as though what he'd done had been truly dreadful, but because she hadn't spotted anything amiss about him. How could she not have felt what Annie had – that something was 'off'? And, for all her bleating, she was fully aware that Annie really had warned her about him.

Returning to the table, she knew she'd missed something important, because Annie was giving her that look again.

'What now?' She placed all the little packets in the middle of the table. 'Tell me.'

Annie leaned close to her ear. 'You know Carys said she'd arrested three people in the pub before?' Christine nodded. 'Well, one was Jason – aka John, aka Simon…real name Melvin, by the way – the other was Cadog Smith, though she didn't take in his wife. And you'll never guess the other one. Go on, guess.'

Christine liked Annie, but sometimes her playful enthusiasm was a bit wearing. 'I'll never guess, will I? So just tell me. Oh, go on then, the least likely person here – Amy Francis.'

Annie patted her on the back. 'On the nose. Yeah, imagine that. Amy Francis – terror of the pub quiz, magical baker of apple tarts, and…get this…hacker of government websites.'

Christine couldn't hide her amazement. 'What? Really? Why? I mean…she's not your usual geek type, is she?'

She stared at Carys, who shrugged. 'You can never tell, can you? It was only the library website, but it's supposed to be a secure part of the local authority's online presence, and she broke into it and stole – or downloaded – a whole lot of online books.'

'So she knows how to hack,' mused Christine, ripping the top off two packets of horseradish sauce at once. 'That's interesting – especially when it comes to the death threats Annie and I received.'

'And, if what Carys told me about Jason, aka Melvin, is true,' said Annie, 'then he certainly knows his way around online banking and so forth, so might be able to stretch to a bit of smart home intrusion.'

Annie pulled her bottle of hot sauce from her handbag and splattered it all over her meal.

When she saw Carys's expression Christine realized she'd forgotten how odd some people thought Annie's actions were.

Carys leaned in, 'And I suppose I should tell you that Cadog Smith isn't backwards in coming forwards when a bit of online manipulation is concerned,' she whispered, picking up a packet of mustard. 'He was quite a web-warrior long before the online world became what it is today; he might have kept up with technological developments.'

The three women tucked in to their lunch, and Christine was pleasantly surprised by the tenderness of the meat, as well as the fluffiness of the massive Yorkshire pudding.

They had three possible whos, but still no why, and that was really bothering her. She said, 'I think we need to talk to Gemma, our client. She'd know if anyone had shown an interest in buying the house when it passed from her uncle to her. I'd have thought she'd have mentioned it, but I'm not sure any of us asked her outright.'

'Good idea, Chrissy. Are you not eating those roast potatoes? Because, if you're not, I'll have 'em.'

Christine smiled at her friend. 'Annie, they're yours.'

MONDAY 6th FEBRUARY

CHAPTER TWENTY-EIGHT

Carol didn't panic when she woke and her husband wasn't next to her, but she panicked when she got downstairs and found him fast asleep on the sofa, with Albert snuggled beside him. Had she slept through him needing to bring Albert to the sitting room to sleep for some reason? How could she have done that?

Her son stirred, and so did her husband.

'How long have you two been here? And why are you here?' Carol didn't understand.

'This one had the screaming ab-dabs at about three this morning, so we snuggled here for a while, and it appears we're still here now at…wow, nearly seven. Good boy, Albert.' David kissed his son's cheek. 'You can change him, though. There you go.'

Carol picked up her son. 'Are you feeling alright? Head okay? Stitches not hurting?' She was worried about David's head injury, and couldn't imagine how she'd slept so deeply. Yes, she'd done a lot of research online last night, and, yes, she'd been at it until gone midnight – but that wasn't unusual for her; she'd wanted to make up for lost time and had done a huge amount of crosschecking of the data she'd inputted for The Case of the Dangerous Day Spa. She'd also gathered a great deal of background information about the Gorst sisters of Port Beynon, one of whom had turned out to not be named Gorst at all, having married a man called Williams. She'd sent Annie and Christine a package of information before she went to bed, feeling quite pleased with herself.

Now, however, she was cross with herself; she was the one who was supposed to be looking after her family, and she'd slept through them both needing her.

Carol realized that, if she was getting that tired keeping up with work, she'd have to take some time off, just to make sure David didn't do too much while he was recovering.

'I'll see to him, and you can have the bathroom while I make us all breakfast. Leave it to me,' she said, and beetled off to attend to her son's needs.

Over scrambled eggs on toast, David asked, 'What time's your appointment, I've forgotten.'

Carol had no idea what he was talking about, and told him so.

'Your appointment at the spa. Isn't it hands and feet day today? I'm sure that's what you said last week. Hands and feet on Monday, then you'll have been done from top to toe.'

Carol remembered. 'I'll phone them to cancel. I'm certainly not leaving you alone with Albert. You have a slight concussion; they said to limit your bending, and you know what it's like with him – you're bending all the time with an infant. Up and down like a yo-yo he is.'

David put down his knife and fork and stared at Carol. 'You know I love you, don't you?'

Carol smiled. 'Yes, I do.'

'And I know you love me.' David smiled back. 'But I don't think you're aware of what that means to me. I want to see you happy, Carol. To see that lovely face of yours beam with radiance, not scowl because you're worn out. And do you know when you've been at your most radiant, recently?'

Carol couldn't imagine.

'When you were posing at yourself in the bathroom mirror with that new hairdo of yours.'

Carol felt immediately ashamed. 'I didn't know you could see me. I was just playing, you know, making faces, like they do on the telly when they're on the red carpet. Just a bit of fun.'

David placed his hand on hers, just as Albert decided to spit up some of his breakfast mush. 'Very attractive, Albert. No, don't wipe it up, love, just ignore him for a minute; he doesn't care about his bib being messy.'

Carol nodded, knowing her husband was right.

David touched her hand, gently, 'I promise to sit beside him, with him in his cot in his room, while you're out. He can play or doze. I won't have to lift him from the floor, and I can relax. No screen time at all. And you go. Allow yourself to spend a bit of time focusing on yourself. See, no matter what I say, you don't seem to be able to *feel* like the beautiful woman I love with all my heart. And if sitting with someone fiddling with your extremities for an hour *can* help you feel that way, like it did with your hair, then please do it? Besides, it's something you can usefully do for work, which means you're more likely to be able to justify it to yourself…which I'll never understand, by the way, but that's you as well.'

Carol felt her eyebrows head for her hairline. 'You want me to go that much?'

'I do.' David mugged an expression of heartfelt pleading. 'For the sake of our marriage – go and get a mani-pedi, and find some joy in your fingers and toes.'

Carol thumped him playfully, then glanced at her feet as she pulled them out of her slippers. She shrugged. 'You're sure you'll take it easy? And you'll text me if there are any problems?' David nodded and crossed his heart, silently. 'The appointment's at ten. I'd only be out for a couple of hours. If you're sure…I have been noticing how the hard skin on my heels has got really rough through the winter; I keep catching the sheets with it, so I dare say they could benefit from a bit of attention.'

'Exactly – you'd be removing any chance of accidentally slicing the skin off my shins during the night. You must go, Carol, for my sake, if not yours.' He grinned broadly, and she gave in.

Now quite accustomed to finding her way to the spa, Carol walked up to the receptionist – the brunette – and gave her name. As she entered the spa itself, expecting to be greeted by Willow, she was treated, instead, to a woman going on and on in a comedic Scottish accent proclaiming the wonders of the place…to its manager.

Willow was standing behind her reception desk, looking like a trapped animal, her eyes wide, and anxious.

The woman who sounded as though she belonged in a music hall act was wafting a gloved hand – which Carol thought odd, given the circumstance – and talking to Willow as though she'd never so much as seen the place she actually managed. The woman waxed lyrical about the delightfulness of each facility – listing them, in her painful accent. Carol couldn't believe it; did any Scottish people really talk like that? Mavis didn't, and no others Carol had met in her life did, either. Yes, Mavis used the odd Scottish word or two, but Carol could always understand her. This woman? She was gibbering.

Carol looked the woman up and down: nice clothes, if too tight; a scarf that clashed with her blouse, but she knew more than one person who liked to dress that way; brown cotton gloves, which she still thought was an odd thing to be wearing; bare legs and strappy sandals – even odder than the gloves, given the time of year, but at least they gave Carol a clear view of the woman's bunions, and painted toenails.

Immediately she saw her feet, Carol was in no doubt that this was the woman she'd seen at the spa the previous week who had – at that time – sounded Russian, and claimed to be a hotel guest who'd got lost. Now here she was pretending to be Scottish, and – apparently – having just finished the guided tour.

The woman finally left, giving Carol a small smile as she disappeared through the smoked-glass door. Carol had seen the smile before – flashed at her by the redhead who'd been having her nails done the previous week.

Is that why she's wearing gloves? Carol thought.

With the woman finally gone, Carol barked at Willow, 'Who was that?' She didn't want to lose any time. 'Quick – what's her name?'

Willow looked flustered and poked at the screen where she kept a list of appointments, scrolling madly. 'Sorry – I can't find it,' she said.

'Good grief,' said Carol under her breath. 'Ever seen her before?'

Willow shook her head. 'Just a show-round. I don't think she'll be back. Seemed like a bit of a time-waster. Not like you. And you're a bit early. Lovely. I'll just get Jasmine. Please, take a seat.'

Willow headed toward the nail bar, while Carol slipped out through the smoked-glass door, and scampered to the end of the corridor. No sight of 'Mrs Bunion', which was good, because it allowed Carol to race along the corridor that led to the hotel's main reception, where she caught sight of her quarry descending the stone steps that led to the car park.

Carol exited the building, pulled out her phone, and increased the magnification on her camera as much as possible to photograph the woman and the car she got into. She pulled off her coat, folded it inside-out over her arm, then yanked out the pale pink pashmina she always carried in her bag and swooshed it around her head and face; she looked as different as possible from the way she had when the bunion woman had smiled right at her in the spa. She didn't think she'd be recognized as she, too, crossed the car park, and got into her car, ready to follow wherever the woman went…within reason.

She'd snapped surreptitiously as she'd come quite close to the woman's vehicle and was certain she had the number plate in focus. Then she waited…and waited…and waited. What was the women doing? Was she ever going to leave? Carol bobbed her head about. Right, the woman was on the phone, laughing. Eventually she set off.

Unfortunately, Carol had no choice but to immediately follow the woman's car to be sure she didn't lose her when she turned onto the main road at the end of the drive. She comforted herself that, after that, at least the bunion-woman's hatchback would be easy to spot, it being a mustardy-yellow, and one of the more hideous colors Carol had ever seen.

At the end of the drive, the car took the road Carol knew led toward Hay-on-Wye, which she realized could make things tricky for her in some ways, but maybe less so in others; the road didn't allow for overtaking in many spots, so it wasn't unusual for a line of cars to have to drive behind each other for miles, which could work in her favor.

Carol stayed back as far as she dared. When Mrs Bunion took the turning for Hay itself, she was on full alert, because she didn't know the roads and little side streets in the area terribly well.

Knots of people ambled about browsing the myriad bookshops for which Hay-on-Wye was – quite rightly – world famous. She passed Val Jenkins's shop, and could even see Val inside it, upstairs; she'd kept the crime books downstairs even when she'd bought her father out of the place, and her cookery section was above it, so the massive sign across the front of the old, stone building reading CROOKS & COOKS was still valid.

Carol saw the target's car turn into a residential street that was narrow, and had a NO THROUGH ROAD sign, which gave her some sense of comfort because Hay was noted for not having a great deal of parking availability. She drove to a small car park beside the River Wye, grabbed her ticket, then her bag, a lightweight mac that had been tossed onto the floor behind the passenger seat, and two hats that had been gathering dust on the parcel shelf for some time; she liked to have as many potential ways to change her appearance as possible if she was on someone's trail.

She cantered all the way to the street into which Mrs Bunion had turned, and was relieved to see her enter the last house on the street, though her car was located a few doors down, in what had been the only remaining space in the residents' only parking area. Carol sauntered along the street admiring the stone facades of the terrace, noted the number of the house and the name of the street, and realized that a metal barrier was the only thing preventing it from being a thoroughfare.

Carol walked to the corner and turned it, so she was beside the wall of the back garden of the house Mrs Bunion had entered. It was a waist-high wall, with shrubs providing some illusion of privacy for the inhabitants; they were lilacs, just putting out fresh, green buds.

Carol could clearly see a washing-up bottle on a windowsill, so assumed she might at least have a chance of peeping into the kitchen window.

She paused, pulled out her phone and fake-dialled, which allowed her a reason to loiter at the wall peering over some branches, half-smiling, and fake-chatting into her phone every time someone walked past – just so that she didn't look too suspicious.

Finally, she spotted someone bobbing about at what she was certain was the kitchen sink. She watched, and snapped, as the back door opened and out stepped a now blonde, as opposed to brunette, version of the 'Scottish Mrs Bunion' in a leopard-print leisure suit, and gold trainers. She was followed by a well-built man. The pair made their way to a shed that was perilously close to Carol's position, but she held her ground, snapping away.

As the couple approached, she picked up on a North Walian accent from the woman – so, not a Scot, after all, what a surprise! – and the man's accent suggested he was local. From what she could overhear of their playful and innuendo-filled conversation, they were planning on pulling something out of the shed that needed the two of them to do it. Carol discovered they meant a large planter that she reckoned must have been made of fiberglass, though it was supposed to look like stone. They carried both parts of it to the opposite corner of the small garden, snapped them together to form an alarmingly large structure, then the man dumped a large sack of what Carol deduced was potting compost into a wheelbarrow, and pushed it across the grass, where the pair set about filling the planter. Carol reckoned they'd need more soil. A lot more.

Standing in the street watching the couple – and couple they were, Carol had no doubt about that – she felt some satisfaction; clearly the woman had been pretending to be someone other than she was at the spa on more than one occasion, and Carol now had her address, her car details, and knew she was from North Wales. That wasn't a bad start. She assumed the man was the woman's husband; why else would he be helping with gardening jobs, in what appeared to be gardening clothes?

She headed back to her car; the mani-pedi hadn't happened, but she'd made some useful discoveries, and told herself her nails weren't that bad after all…then promised herself to give the pumice stone a good workout on her heels that evening.

Before she started her engine, she sent an email and a couple of the photos she'd taken of the woman – in both her guises – to Els van Beek, the hotel manager, then set off to get back to her family.

CHAPTER TWENTY-NINE

Noticing that it was already gone eight, Annie looked up from her laptop as Christine arrived in the kitchen. Her usually sleek chum was looking dishevelled.

Cheerily, she said, 'Mornin', doll. We got a brain-dump from Car last night; you'd better get some of that coffee down you before you even open your inbox.'

Christine nodded, petted Gertie, then sat at the table sipping coffee, making noises not dissimilar to a small, woodland creature.

Annie read on, taking in the facts and insights Carol had sent through. She nipped into the sitting room, took a good look out of the window, then returned.

'What are you doing?' Christine sounded annoyed.

Annie replied, 'Don't be snappy. I told you not to open that second bottle of red last night. Take some painkillers and don't expect any sympathy from me. I want to get back to Anwen, Chrissy; I don't want to be stuck here forever, lovely though it is. Tude and I are missing each other something rotten. I know I'm away from him quite often, and at least Gert's with me here, but this is different. See, I really don't think anything bad is going to happen while it's just us in the cottage. It's not like we can lure a man here hoping something life-threatening happens to him – just so that we can try to catch whoever is doing these things in the act. Which means I really think we need to tell Gemma Thomas that we can't help, after all. That said, I want to read all this stuff from Carol first, in case there's anything useful here.'

Christine sighed, and poured more coffee. 'Grand. Do what you like.'

Annie did, and kept reading. Eventually she couldn't ignore Christine's sighs any longer. She set aside her laptop and said, 'Right, out with it. This isn't just a hangover, it's something else. What's happened?'

Christine put her head in her hands. 'I think I texted Alexander last night, about not being too happy with the way things are between us at the moment.'

The penny dropped for Annie. 'Think you did? Or did?'

Christine shrugged, looking helpless. 'My phone was completely dead when I woke up this morning, and, when I plugged it in, I couldn't find an outgoing text from me. I think I must have deleted it. Anyway, there were loads there from Alexander which…suggest…I must have told him exactly how I've been feeling. I can't even look at them any more; I've left the blessed thing downstairs, hoping that out of sight can eventually become out of mind. But it's not working so far.' She rubbed her hands over her face. 'I think I've been very foolish, Annie. Any advice?'

Annie's heart softened. 'Look, doll, we've all done something we wish we hadn't when we've had a few too many. Especially when a person's your age. Don't be so hard on yourself; your twenties are a time when you're supposed to be able to make mistakes, and learn from them. It's just that, these days, that's made all the more complicated because of instant communication, social media and – heaven help us – video calling and so forth. Poor decisions can become a lifelong albatross around your neck, because of the way the Internet never forgets anything. But, at its core, this really is just about you and your fiancé having to work through some stuff. Why don't you phone him and explain? If you were texting him, he probably guessed from your spelling and so forth that you'd had a few, in any case. He'll understand. But the lesson is – put your phone away and don't text when you're drunk. Got it?'

Christine nodded contritely. 'You're right. Though I wish I knew what I'd said. His texts are…a bit…well, he sounds hurt, and worried. Oh Annie – what if I've really gone and messed everything up? I love him so much.' She collapsed in a teary mess onto the table.

Gertie tried to help, putting her front paws onto Christine's thigh, to offer kisses and licks, while Annie hunted down a box of tissues in the sitting room.

'There, there, get it all out. You'll feel better when you do – and when those painkillers kick in,' said Annie sagely. 'Down now, Gert – let me get you a treat.'

It took a while for Christine to stop sobbing, then – because Alexander wasn't answering his phone – Annie packed her off to the shower, convincing her it would help her feel better.

Alone in the kitchen, Annie cleared away the breakfast dishes, put the kettle on, and took a moment to enjoy the view down to the beach through the window above the sink. She was happily picturing herself and Tudor taking Gertie for a good, long walk down there, when she became aware of a car pulling up on the parking pad beside the cottage. She looked out of the front window, but couldn't see who it was. A knock at the door followed almost immediately.

'Alexander. Nice to see you. How are you?' Annie could tell exactly how he was without him needing to answer: he had deep circles beneath his eyes, which were red and puffy; his skin had taken on a chalkiness, and his chin was stubbly, suggesting he hadn't been able to indulge in his normal morning grooming routines. Also, his clothes were a crumpled mess – which was noteworthy for the man who was always one of the best turned-out Annie had ever seen.

'Is she here? Is she alright? She hasn't gone and done anything stupid, has she?' Alexander's eyes were wild as he pushed past Annie.

'Hang on there a minute,' said Annie, a bit taken aback. 'She's upstairs in the shower. Other than an almighty hangover, made worse by a massive dollop of guilt about what she might have texted you last night – and you should know right now that she has no recollection, or record, of what that was – she's fine. You, on the other hand? Have you slept in those clothes? Have you even slept?'

Alexander's shoulders unhunched. 'Thanks…good, she's alright. I thought…never mind. What? Have I slept? Not much. She texted me at two this morning, in a right state. Said she…she couldn't cope with it all any more. I was at a business thing in Norwich. It's taken me until now to drive here. But she's okay you say?'

Annie rubbed his back, while Gertie welcomed him excitedly. Alexander reached down to pet the puppy as Annie said, 'There'll be a cuppa ready in minute. Come and wait for her in the kitchen, with me.'

Alexander nodded, and Annie could see the tension disappear from his body when he slumped onto a chair, shaking his head. 'Thanks, Annie. Thanks.'

With tea and some toast in front of him, it was a no-less crumpled, but most definitely more relieved, version of Alexander Bright who greeted his fiancée with an all-encompassing hug when she appeared with wet hair, and a tired smile.

Annie said, 'I'll just take this one for a turn around the garden while you two…yeah…come on, Gert, let's make ourselves scarce.'

Happy to be out and about with her human, Gertie enjoyed frolicking around the grass, nosing into corners, and pawing at tufts here and there. Annie beamed at her, and gave herself over to taking in the wonderful scenery, wistfully imagining getting back home to Anwen-by-Wye…then she realized she'd lost sight of Gertie altogether.

'Oi, Gert, where've you got to?' Annie called. She got no response until a yelp floated up on the sea breeze from the bottom of the garden. Annie headed off down the slope, but couldn't spot Gertie until she was close to her, because the puppy was giving her full attention, and every ounce of her energy, to digging a hole she'd already made into a deep pit.

Moles, thought Annie, who'd already noticed Gertie's ability to sniff along a mole run until she reckoned she knew where it was – then make a determined effort to get to it. None of this was good news when it came to leaving divots all over the village green in Anwen, and Annie was just as concerned about her client's back garden. She strode out to pull Gertie away from the surprisingly large depression she'd managed to make. When she got there, she realized that Gertie wasn't after a mole at all, but had managed to uncover a large rock, and was well on her way to uncovering another.

Annie bent down. 'What's that there then, Gert? Oh look – it's all the way along here.' Annie went so far as to point at another patch to encourage Gertie to dig there, which she did – with glee. As Gertie scraped excitedly, Annie helped by shoving soil out of the way, then finally by moving it in great handfuls.

Standing back to take stock of what she and Gertie had achieved, she was surprised to see a more-or-less straight run of rocks with mortar between them heading from the beach to the cottage. The further up the slope the rocks were, the deeper they went, so she pulled Gertie off and called her as she ran up the slope, trying to get her to follow.

Rushing into the kitchen with filthy hands, and accompanied by a dog with a muddy face and paws, Christine and Alexander helped clean everyone and everything up as Annie explained her discovery with excitement.

'I think I know what it is,' said Annie as she wiped her face with a piece of damp kitchen roll. 'In them notes Car sent, there was a lot about a load of smugglers who ran a big network from this village. Down on the beach there, along to the right, remember them ruins, Chrissy?' Christine nodded, while Alexander sat at the table looking bemused. 'That's where the head smuggler lived, and they said – well, it said in Car's notes that everyone around here believed at the time – he had dug and reinforced tunnels all over the place to get the stuff he'd taken from ships stopped in the bay here away from the beach. In case he was raided, you know? What if there's a tunnel leading to this cottage from down there? Wouldn't that be…well, something. I'm not sure if it's a good or bad thing, but it might explain—'

'How someone is able to get in here without using the doors, or being spotted by Gemma's cameras?' Alexander smiled. 'Christine's been bringing me up to speed.'

Annie was surprised that the couple had nothing better to talk about – considering the state they'd both been in half an hour earlier – but was glad she didn't have to go through everything with yet another person.

'Exactly,' said Annie triumphantly. 'I'm going to review what Car sent, hoping I might spot something I missed, and I'll text Gemma Thomas asking about any hidden doors or anything like that they might have found when they were renovating this place. By the way, Chrissy, have you also told Alexander that he's in mortal danger – possibly literally – every moment he's here?'

Alexander spluttered tea. 'She mentioned something about a so-called curse thing, and I feel the same way she does about it – it's all rubbish. No such thing as curses.'

Annie shrugged. 'You might not be wrong about that, because one thing I did learn from Car's most recent notes was the history of the two old women who lived here…the pair we've been made to think of as a pair of old crones who possibly made human sacrifices out in the garden.'

'You tell Christine all about that while I take the chance to shower and change my clothes, will you? I brought the overnight bag I had with me, so I'll make myself a bit more presentable, eh? I'll just get it from the car, then hit the shower.'

Annie explained the comparative dimensions of the two bathrooms in the cottage to Alexander, and he agreed he'd probably fare better in the one on the lower floor, then left the women to get his bag, and headed downstairs.

'So what's the story with the two spinster sisters who lived here, who enjoyed spitting at all the men who dared pass their door?' Christine finally had a bit of color in her cheeks, which Annie was pleased to see.

Annie poured the last cup from the pot and settled herself. 'Well, that's the thing, they weren't both spinsters. One of them was married, which is why Car had a bit of a time of it. Lil Gorst wasn't – she was Lillian Williams. Yes, I know – but it was her married name, and we can't choose who to love based on what our name will end up being, can we? Oh, before I go on – and because it's only just occurred to me – are you going to change your name to Christine Bright when you two get married, or not?'

Christine sighed and rolled her eyes. 'Pass. Under discussion, not yet decided. It's…complicated. Mammy and Daddy "have opinions". Let's talk about the Gorst sisters…more interesting. Please.'

Annie patted her chum's hand, and continued, 'Lillian married a John Williams, but he died right at the beginning of the First World War. She never remarried. Her sister, Elizabeth – known as Bess – didn't ever marry. The two sisters are buried in the graveyard of St…hang on, I've been practising…St Illtyd's Church, in Oxwich. There – did you like that?'

Annie had made the best attempt she could manage at pronouncing the Welsh double 'l' sound, so was hoping for more than the shaking shoulders and 'Well, you did your best' that she got from Christine.

Ignoring her friend's jibes, she pressed on. 'Anyway, they did sell a farm in Slade Cross, around the bay, and they bought this cottage in the 1920s from a family that had been using it for their sheep. Now I'm guessing the women were young and fit enough to do the place up a fair bit, because they then ran the local post office out of it for twenty years from 1937…in what's now the sitting room, if you can believe it. Then the post box outside was used, for collections only, until 1974. Lillian Williams died in 1973, her sister, Elizabeth Gorst, died in 1975. The cottage – known at that time as The Post House – went into probate, and from there, as Amy told us, the Overton family bought it. They rented it out to the Francis family, then sold it to Gemma's uncle, Ted Thomas and, when he died, he left it to Gemma in his will, so no lengthy probate period this time around. And we know all about it from that time. The "Gorst Sisters" are women about whom little is recorded, Carol said, but they were running a post office, so must have been assessed as trustworthy to be able to do that, she reckons.'

Christine mused, 'No mention of late-night shenanigans with Satanic rites, then?'

Annie chuckled. 'Nah. Not a surprise that, though, eh?'

'I suppose not.'

'Anyway, Carol mentioned that Lillian's husband didn't even make it to war in 1914, he was killed during training, in England. I can imagine Lillian might have taken against men after that – hence the spitting that Cadog mentioned, but, other than all the local gossip and rumors, they lived lives that were unremarkable. Of course, they were two women running a business from the 1930s until the 1950s – so, right through the war years – which I can't imagine was a common thing back then. Maybe all the witchcraft rumors began because it was the only way the locals could cope with the idea of two women doing what I dare say most would have thought of as men's work.'

Christine said, 'Oh, I don't know. A lot of women were doing things most people had believed could only be done by men at that time. All the men were at war, so they had no choice but to get on with it, and there were all the jobs associated directly with the war effort, too. I don't know why rumors start, but I do know they're difficult to stop once they get going, no matter how unfounded they might be. I say this given there were quite a few choice ones that used to do the rounds about our family back in Ireland – which I dare say is to be expected when you're an absent viscount, living in England, but owning swathes of land in an Ireland that's all but bleeding to death.'

Annie gave her colleague a sideways look, and carried on. 'Well, whatever it was that labelled the women as witches, it stuck. But I get what you mean; it could have been because of something stupid like one of them having a big, hairy mole, or because they weren't churchgoers, like Cadog claimed. But it's clearly something that's been whispered about for a long time. Bless them – they managed to make a life for themselves, and that's what they get.'

Christine said, 'I dare say you've faced obstacles within your life that neither they, nor I, could ever imagine.'

Annie sighed. 'You're right, you've no idea. And not just because I'm black, but also because I'm a woman.'

'Oh yes, those City types? They can be…bad.'

'You're not kidding. During my days in the City, I know for a fact that the assumption had already been made that I wouldn't amount to much because I was a woman before some people even met me face to face and found out I was black. Some of the expressions on the faces of people arriving at the office for a meeting, when we'd been talking on the phone for weeks, was priceless. Only a few ever actually said the words, "I didn't know you were black", but they'd all known I was a woman, and had already treated me as "less" because of that. How did you cope with it, Chrissy? Being female, in the City. Or is it a world of difference for a young, white, good-looking daughter of an Irish viscount?' Annie laughed.

Christine chuckled wryly. 'Yeah, just a bit. To be honest, I always believed I was treated the way I was mainly because Daddy was a viscount. We worked in the same field, so everyone who knew him knew me, and vice-versa. We were often viewed as a "team", though we never worked together. Now that I'm out of that world? Well…maybe now I have a slightly better understanding of what it's like to be assessed purely on the basis of my gender, because I mix so much more often with folks who have no idea who my father is. But I've learned that a great deal depends upon who's doing the assessing. Age makes a difference, for example; there really is a completely different set of expectations among the young these days, don't you think?'

Annie snorted. 'Oh, Chrissy, doll, you are "the young" to me. I'm almost twice your age, so bear that in mind. But there's one thing I'll tell you – it doesn't matter about your gender when it comes to assumptions made about a person based upon their age. And I'm as guilty of that as anyone. When Carys Llewellyn told us yesterday that she'd once arrested both Cadog Smith and Amy Francis, I remember thinking that must have been in their youth, because they're both too old to do anything arrest-worthy at their ages.'

Christine nodded. 'Me too.'

Annie said, 'But see, that's as wrong-headed as others thinking I'm not going to be capable of something because I'm a woman who's black.'

'I know. You're right.'

Annie added, 'See, to my way of thinking, there are good people and bad people of all sorts, and goodness or badness in't just linked to any aspect of gender, age, or ethnicity.'

'But what about upbringing, Annie? That plays a part. Life experience can send a person toward the light, or the dark. And I know that for a fact...'

'Bit of a serious conversation going on here, I'm guessing,' said Alexander, returning – freshly attired – to the kitchen. 'Anyone interested in the opinion of someone with a white, alcoholic mother, and an unknown – but obviously black – father, who grew up not in a manor house with a title, nor in the bosom of a loving, working-class family? No? Thought not. Okay – what's on the agenda for today then? I'll disappear if you two need more private time, but, otherwise, I'm good to go. Or stay. Which is what I'd prefer.'

'You could help us hunt about for possible access points to an old smuggling tunnel,' suggested Annie. 'With what Gert dug up out in the garden, and Car's notes about the history of this place, I'm wondering if there's an entrance to a tunnel somewhere down in the two bedrooms and bathroom that are now housed in what used to be the cellars. Gemma's replied to my query saying she knows nothing about any such thing, but that doesn't mean it's not there.'

Christine sat up like a meerkat. 'Go banging on all the walls and floors until we find something that sounds hollow, you mean? *Three Go Mad in Port Beynon*...and we've even got a dog to make us four. Will there be lashings of ginger beer for tea, I wonder?'

Annie and Alexander chuckled.

'How about lunch at the pub instead?' Annie made her remark in all innocence, and realized, too late, that she might have put her foot in it as far as Christine was concerned.

Even Alexander noticed the change in his fiancée. 'You okay?' he asked. 'Is the pub a bit of a horror show?'

'It's very nice,' said Christine quietly.

Annie bit her tongue on the matter, turning her attention instead to Gertie. 'Come on, Gert, let's go exploring.'

Half an hour later, three deflated humans and one rather bored puppy made their way back into the kitchen, agreeing there was nothing to be found in the basement other than solid walls and floors.

'I have food prep skills, but a desire for a pie and pint. Any chance they might offer that at your lovely seaside pub?' Alexander was waiting to take his turn to wash his hands at the sink; having moved every piece of furniture on the lower floor just to be sure they didn't miss any possible trap doors, they all felt a little grubby.

'Not sure about pies, but there'll be something, and none of us will have to make it or clear away afterwards, so there's that,' said Annie, wiping her hands.

'Yes, let's go,' said Christine, sticking out her chin toward Annie, who took the chance of Alexander having his back turned to give her chum the universal sign of: Sorry, what can I do?.

As they left, they were met at the door by Amy Francis, holding an apple tart. 'I spotted a new arrival so rushed over,' she said. 'I missed my chance on Saturday, so didn't want to miss out again. It's still hot.'

General greetings were exchanged, and she was introduced to Alexander. Christine thanked her, and explained that tart would make a good dessert after the group had returned from their planned lunch at the pub.

Having put the tart in the kitchen, the group finally walked down the hill in what was only a slight drizzle. Gertie barked excitedly when Cadog and Winnie came into sight, walking toward them. Fortunately, they all met up where there was a relatively wide bit of pavement, so could stop for the dogs to do their doggy, sniffy things, and for the humans to exchange more socially acceptable ways of greeting each other.

'He seems pleasant enough,' said Alexander as they all went in their own direction, 'and it's good to know the pies at the pub have a good reputation, I'm pleased about that.'

Annie grinned. 'I can feel me mouth watering already.'

Alexander leaned in, 'Tell me, was it just me he couldn't look at, or does he always talk with his eyes closed? I knew a bloke like that once, but he only had one eye in any case, so maybe that was it.'

'Cadog always seems to do it,' replied Christine. Annie reckoned she was forcing a jovial tone.

'Here we are then,' said Annie, as they entered the pub's porch. 'It looks quiet.' She pushed the door open, and was delighted to smell some sort of meaty deliciousness. 'Something's cooking, which is good,' she said, feeling her tummy rumble.

The women settled themselves while Alexander grabbed a couple of menus from the bar, which was deserted. By the time he took his seat, he'd already made up his mind.

'I'm for the pie and chips. No mushy peas for me, though,' he said.

'Yes, me too. And I'll have your peas,' said Christine, who appeared to Annie to be trying to sink into her seat.

'Me three,' said Annie. 'And I'll have me own peas, ta.'

Alexander looked around. 'Do I order at the bar and get some drinks while I'm at it? Oh, hang on, here comes someone now.'

Annie could feel herself grow tense, almost one muscle at a time, as Jason approached, a tea towel over his shoulder, and a smile a mile wide on his face.

'And how's my gorgeous gal, today?' He beamed at Christine.

'I'm fine, ta, Jase. You?' said Annie – maybe too quickly.

Alexander looked up at Jason, smiling – Annie read it as 'coldly' – then he looked at Christine, whose face was an emotionless mask, then he returned his gaze to Jason.

Eventually, he said, 'A pleasure to meet you, Jase. I've been told you have good pies, so we're all having that. Each, of course, though it appears I'll be donating my mushy peas to my fiancée.' He pulled Christine's hand from her lap, and held it in his, then smooshed it against his cheek. 'Anything to keep her happy, you know.'

Jason shrugged. 'If you say so. Three pies it is, and I'm guessing a pint of the dark stuff for you, a G & T for you, and, what will sir be having?'

Annie felt her toes curl at Jason's condescending tone. He had no idea who he was dealing with; she reckoned Alexander knew at least half a dozen people who could make Jason vanish off the face of the earth if asked to do it, and she was half-convinced that he was capable of doing as much himself.

Alexander stood, and smoothed down his immaculately-tailored shirt. He was a couple of inches shorter than Jason, but that didn't seem to matter as he patted the pub manager on the back in the friendliest of manners saying, 'Why don't you show me what you have on tap at the bar, Jase?'

He steered the man away, his head nodding as he commented upon the décor of his surroundings, and his appreciation of local brews.

Christine whispered dejectedly, 'Nice try, Annie, thanks, but I think Alexander might have guessed that Jason is my…type. Oh well – nothing happened except for a bit of friendly banter, with the odd bit of innuendo thrown in for good measure. All I have to do is tell him that, and he'll believe me. Won't he?'

Annie didn't know what to say; she couldn't take her eyes off the two men who were standing so close together at the bar that they would have looked like great friends who hadn't seen each other in years to anyone entering at that moment. Indeed, the bonhomie radiating from the pair wasn't even drawing the attention of the handful of others at tables much closer to where they were standing. She hoped that was a good sign.

When Alexander returned he was all smiles, and delivered the drinks with a flourish. 'Jason was telling me you were in here with a police officer yesterday I'm guessing was Carys Llewellyn. Was she able to help you much?'

Annie decided to dive in, filling in all the blanks it seemed Christine had left in the full story of their time at Port Beynon, including the details of all the ills that had befallen men at the cottage.

She was flabbergasted when Alexander stood to attention and mugged a salute.

He said, 'Well, if you need to have a man around the place to see if anything else "happens" then I'm him. You know I can be alert when required, and can handle myself in most situations. How about it? I want to do whatever I can so that you two can clear this all up, and get back to a more "normal" life.'

'We're used to being away for work,' said Christine.

Alexander replied quickly, 'I know – of course I do – that you both have to get away for work sometimes, but this is sounding as though your observation period here could go on forever, if things only happen when a man's about. I'm missing our times together, Christine, and I bet Annie's missing Tudor. I know he's missing her.'

Annie allowed her surprise to show when she said, 'You've talked to Tude? When?'

Alexander replied lightly, 'I saw him actually, when I nipped over to Chellingworth Hall at Henry's request to take a look at a trove of silver pieces that had been discovered – or rediscovered I should say, because they've always been there – when they were hunting about for their missing christening mugs.'

Annie chuckled, 'Good job with naming a case there, Alexander – I'll give you credit for it when it matters. And why did Henry do that? I'm aware that you and Bill Coggins know your onions when it comes to antiques, but I thought you were a silent partner in that business now. Was this just to help Henry out of a tight spot he'd somehow managed to get himself into?'

Alexander's eyes narrowed as he replied, 'Yes, that's what I suspected, but, no…for once, Henry was taking a long-term planning view. Discovering that he was in possession of a collection of silver mug-like objects, all of which were listed somewhat generically on the documentation produced by the insurance folks, he invited me in to talk him through what he was really looking at. It's as though the scales have fallen from the man's eyes, in some ways.'

'Sounds like it,' said Annie.

'Maybe it takes a jolt – a sudden change of perspective – for that to happen to a person.'

He paused, but Annie didn't think he'd finished his thought.

'Henry's a father now, maybe that's it,' said Alexander somberly. 'Yes, maybe it really does take a significant occurrence for a person to see a situation…more clearly.'

He casually glanced at Christine who leaned forward and hissed,

'All I did was flirt with Jason a bit, alright? I like flirting, it's fun. And I may never stop doing it my entire life. So I suggest you come to terms with it.'

Alexander smiled – Annie thought it was a genuine, warm smile. 'Christine, I don't ever want you to be anyone but your true self, my darling. I love you, and want you to be happy. And if flirting makes you happy, then carry on. But you didn't seem very happy when you texted me in the early hours. So, if you're just acting that way because the idea of being my wife is making you miserable, then we'll stop planning the wedding.'

'It's not the idea of being your wife that's making me unhappy,' whispered Christine angrily, 'what's making me unhappy is that it's not really you and me planning our wedding, it's Mammy and Daddy telling us what they expect us to do…and you going along with it all.'

Alexander sat back in his seat. 'You don't want us to do what they want?'

'Correct.'

'So why didn't you say that? I've been agreeing with everything because you have been. I've got no family of my own so this won't be a joining of families, it'll be me joining yours. I honestly thought your stress levels were through the roof just because of the planning, not because of…what was being planned. Oh, you know what I mean.'

Annie was feeling completely uncomfortable about getting caught in the middle of what was obviously a deeply personal, and possibly pivotal, conversation, and tried to think of some excuse to leave the table. She sighed with relief when she saw the server approaching with their food.

'Pies are up,' she said cheerily, and possibly too loudly. Not that Gertie needed to be told.

The puppy shot out from her position under the table. Her lead caught around one of the legs, shifting the table upon which Annie was leaning so that she collapsed onto Christine. She fell back on her chair into the path of the server, whose tray ended up on the floor, where the only one to benefit from the food at all was Gertie, who launched herself at the pies as they rolled away under the table, exactly where she'd started out in the first place.

The entire disaster only took about ten seconds, but the mess was tremendous, with everyone's clothes covered with splatters of mushy peas, stout, or the gravy from the one pie that had exploded upon impact with the edge of a chair.

The server burst into tears, Annie tried to stop Gertie eating absolutely everything, and Christine and Alexander sat looking at each other, sitting there covered in all sorts…and they both began to roar with laughter.

'Well, I'm glad you think it's funny,' snapped Annie.

Christine managed a reply. 'I don't – we're in a right old state, so we are. Like life. Would you look at us now.' Annie couldn't tell if her chum was laughing or crying any more. 'I want this – I want laughter and friendship and a mess that can be cleaned up by a puppy's tongue. Alexander, I love you.' She launched herself at her fiancé, ignoring the fact that the two of them would end up with double the amount of food on their clothes.

Annie rubbed her head anxiously as she looked at Gertie, who'd managed to gobble up two pies, most of the chips, and was licking mushy peas off the leg of the table. 'Oh, Gert – what shall we do with you?'

Gertie's delighted expression and wagging tail suggested that congratulations, and petting, were expected.

It was about an hour and a half later that Annie, Christine, Alexander, and a less than playful Gertie, made their way back up the hill to the cottage. They'd helped clear up, were served with replacement meals and drinks, and had tipped their server generously.

Jason hadn't made a second appearance – despite the chaos – and Annie had been grateful for that; she suspected both Christine and Aleander shared her sentiments.

As they finally got to the cottage Annie bent to attend to Gertie because she just didn't seem to be her usual, happy self. 'You bad girl – you're paying for eating all that human food, I bet.' She stood, having administered a good petting and saw that both Christine and Alexander had stopped beside his car. 'What? What is it?' Annie couldn't see anything wrong.

'My tires,' said Alexander quietly.

Annie looked. Because they were so slim in any case, it was hard to tell, but, yes, two of them were definitely flatter than the other pair. And the holes in the sides of them was another giveaway.

'Somebody has slashed two of the tires on my Aston.' Alexander spoke as though a loved one had died, which struck Annie as odd – though she at least grasped the sense of violation.

Christine said, 'Let's check the cameras, while you get hold of some replacements.'

Alexander looked dazed. 'Replacements? These tires? That might take a while.'

Was Alexander close to tears? Annie couldn't tell. But he was most definitely upset.

'Who would do this? And why?' He sounded devastated, and completely nonplussed.

CHAPTER THIRTY

It was gone four before Els van Beek returned Carol's phones calls, by which time Carol had begun to wonder if she'd ever get in touch again at all.

The photographs Carol had taken of the woman doing a bit of gardening in her back garden in Hay-on-Wye were good enough for the hotel manager to identify the subject as Celia Brown. She'd worked at the hotel for a couple of years, until she'd left a few months earlier. She'd been what had once been referred to as a 'Chambermaid' but was now designated by the Ash Court Country House Hotel as a 'Customer Comfort Expert'.

Immediately Els had told Carol the mysterious woman's name, Carol could tell she was being given the brushoff. Again.

'We can deal with the matter from here, thank you,' said Else abruptly. 'There is no need for you or your colleagues to be concerned.'

Carol didn't like the sound of that, and was convinced Els was keeping something from her. So she pushed, and cajoled, and was syrupy sweet, until Els finally snapped.

'I want nobody knowing this, you are clear about that? Nothing is to be said about it, unless I do the saying. Do you agree?' Els sounded almost comically serious.

Carol said yes, of course she did. As she replied, it suddenly dawned upon her that she'd made a significant emotional investment into the case already, and needed to know the whole story – which she hoped Els would reveal.

'Very good.' Els paused, and sighed heavily. 'The hotel has been receiving threats, and an attempt has been made to blackmail us.'

Carol felt vindicated; she knew the woman had been hiding something.

Els continued, 'The threats state that guests will be put off coming here because of the increasingly poor reputation of the hotel and its spa as the result of a scheme of actions that will be taken against us; the campaign will be stopped only if we agree to pay out a sum of one hundred thousand pounds. The blackmail letters have been posted from many different local areas all around us, and we were told we had to put an advertisement into the local newspaper stating we were ready to pay up, using some sort of silly code. And, before you ask, no, we have not informed the police, because...well, those above me, on the board of the group that owns this place and several others like it around the UK and Europe, did not want word to get out about it. They feared there would be implications for more of their properties.'

Carol heard herself tut aloud. 'You could have told me this sooner. It might have helped. As I told you, a friend of ours is one of the victims of this so-called campaign; if you're so keen to maintain a spotless reputation, why on earth wouldn't you or Willow at the spa act upon her perfectly reasonable request for at least a refund of the money she'd spent?'

Els sounded puzzled when she replied, 'I have agreed with Willow that any of her spa clients are to be dealt with by her, while I focus on hotel guests who have complained about problems. We have also agreed that each would give aid, extra services, or refunds, as necessary. I am very sorry to hear she hasn't done this. I shall look into that specific matter, but for now, you wanted to know what has been happening here. Fully. Which is what I am telling you.'

'Right; you've been blackmailed, and now you believe the person blackmailing you is Celia Brown, because I've been able to identify her as a person who's been at the spa at least three times, to my certain knowledge, always heavily disguised. Correct?'

Els agreed. 'I have checked our records; the address at which you said this woman is living was the address we had for Celia Brown. And I can see why she might have done what she has. Thank you for that.'

'Hang about, you're not stopping there – you said you'd tell me what's been going on…so tell me. Why has Celia Brown been doing this? I don't get it.'

Els sighed. 'It is complicated.'

'I bet it is. She's put people's livelihoods, and even lives, in danger…I can't imagine what's made her do it – except to get her hands on a hundred thousand smackeroos, of course.'

'Smackeroos? Ah, pounds. I see. Yes, it has always been about the money for Celia. She is a woman who is owed a living.'

'Tell me everything. Please.' Carol was frustrated.

'I told you that a syndicate of workers here won the lottery. Celia would have been one of the winners, except that she had not paid her portion of the ticket price that week. There was a great deal of bad blood about it, as you can imagine. I'm sorry to say that Celia was never really…popular with her fellow workers, because she liked to do something the quickest way, not necessarily the best way. Also, the group had a written agreement, which they had all signed, and it clearly stated that there was no "discretion" allowed…that only those who had paid their portion of any winning ticket price were allowed to receive a share. Celia was very unhappy about this. She made her opinions clear to all her colleagues every chance she had. I know I told you we lost several staff members at the time – they were pleased to get away from Celia's horrible comments, but, even then, she did not stop. Eventually she became a figure of fun – it was a…coping mechanism for those who had nothing to do with the syndicate, but had to put up with her self-pity, her belief that she had "been robbed", and her very unpleasant comments about her ex-co-workers. It came to a head, and I dismissed her. She found a position as a cleaning operative at the local hospital very shortly thereafter. I gave a good reference.'

'But you didn't put two and two together? To work out that Celia was the one doing the blackmailing?' Carol found it hard to believe.

Els cleared her throat. 'I did not think she was…clever enough to come up with such a scheme. Nor would she have the energy to follow it through.'

Carol noticed the flush creeping up the woman's neck.

The manager hurriedly added, 'I realize this was wrong of me. She must have always been more intelligent than I had imagined. Or at least more cunning than I had expected.'

'Maybe her husband is the driving force,' said Carol.

'Her husband? Celia Brown is single.'

Carol wondered who the bloke in the photos was. 'Okay then, maybe he's her boyfriend; maybe he's the brains of the operation, and Celia's the one with access. It's got to be much easier for a woman to disguise herself to get into the spa than for a man to do it.'

'Though he might have used our swimming pool,' said Els sounding as though she'd just had the idea.

'Good thinking,' replied Carol. 'He's in the photographs I sent you of Celia – could you get your people at the pool to tell you if they recognize him? I can't imagine he'd have bothered with any disguises – pools and disguises don't really mix well, do they? But maybe a swimming cap and goggles? If you could come up with just one date when he was there, you'd know which day's-worth of CCTV to check to see when he arrived. I know the lists you gave me show the time someone gets checked in at the hotel's reception desk – once we know that, we might be able to come up with a name. Which would be a start.'

'I shall do that, but, for now, all this information is only for our own use, here at the hotel. But thank you for your offer of help.'

Els then made it quite clear to Carol that she was to do nothing – take no action at all – until the hotel security team had checked through their CCTV footage. Els said she would also take her concerns about Celia to Willow Richards so they could discuss the possibilities. Carol asked her to get in touch when she had some answers, which the manager promised she would do.

When she ended her call, Carol admitted to herself that the lack of closure wasn't sitting well with her. She felt frustrated.

With David and Albert playing nicely – and gently – in the sitting room, she phoned a chum who shared her passion for quilting – and also happened to be a local police officer.

Constable Llinos Trevelyan's number was programmed into Carol's phone, but she knew she didn't always get an answer when she rang it. This time she did.

'Hiya, it's Carol. How are you, Llinos? At work?'

Llinos laughed. 'No, I'm on later. Not long before I'm out of the door, to be honest. Is this about quilting…or policing? If it's policing, let me get going, and I'll phone you back, hands-free, of course, when I'm on my way in. Otherwise, maybe we could have a proper chat tomorrow?'

'It's policing,' admitted Carol. 'How about I give you half an hour?'

'Half an hour.'

With Albert changed, fed, burped, and back in his father's arms, Carol settled to talk to a woman with whom she felt a bond, *As only those who share a delight in quilting can*, she thought to herself.

She answered her phone before the second ring.

'You're keen,' said Llinos. 'Just tell me all about it, and I'll listen.'

Carol liked the way she didn't beat about the bush. 'This is all hypothetical,' she began.

Llinos laughed. 'Isn't it always?'

Carol chuckled her agreement, then explained the 'hypothetical' situation.

Llinos was a good listener. 'So you know who's doing something, and you believe you know why, but you're not sure exactly what, though the upshot has been – you believe, and as far as you're aware – a nasty hand infection sustained by Marjorie Pritchard and a broken fibula sustained by Selina, the personal trainer employed at the spa. Poor Marjorie – that must be taking its toll.'

'I get the impression she's being what she sees as a trooper, but, yes, not nice,' agreed Carol. 'So what would that be? Bodily harm? Grievous bodily harm? What's the categorization, here?'

Llinos half chuckled as she replied, 'The answer to that will depend upon the specific circumstances, so I can't tell you, even hypothetically. Sorry.'

'Can you explain a bit more, please?'

'Well, what I can tell you is that any case would have to be based upon proof that the person in question undertook an action that led directly to the harm caused. Until you have that, you have nothing. Sorry. So – hypothetically – if you've got an identifiable person undertaking an action on film or in photographs, or having left behind physical evidence of undertaking an action, which then led to the harm being sustained, you're onto a winner. At least, you're onto the beginning of a winner, because further investigation by the police might still lead to no charges being brought, if it's felt that another course of action is possible.'

Carol mulled Llinos's words. 'I get it that we need proof, but I think it's going to be hard to get. See, for example, I think I've – hypothetically – worked out how Marjorie could have come into contact with something that could have caused her infection, but I couldn't see any cameras in the area where "the action" might have taken place, and any evidence of it happening would now be long gone. And as for the personal trainer? Again, I'm not aware of there being any cameras in the gym, so it's unlikely there'd be evidence, other than the fact that I saw a person I believe to have been the suspect in an area which would have allowed them easy access to the gym at the relevant time. Oh yes, and she was wet, as were the dumbbells I picked up.'

Llinos replied, 'There's not much more I can say, really, Carol. Sorry. And I'm nearly at work now. Tell you what, if there's anything you think of that I can do to help, let me know, alright? Marjorie's a good person, even if she's a bit of a pain – she doesn't deserve this.'

'You're right, she doesn't, which is why the WISE women are supporting me in this.'

'What's Annie called it, by the way? This hypothetical case.'

'The Case of the Dangerous Day Spa.' Carol smiled as she spoke. 'I hope she's getting on better in Port Beynon than I am here. But I'll let you go now. Thanks. Talking through it with you has really helped.'

'You're welcome. We'll chat in the comment threads on our quilting message boards soon, I dare say.'

Carol sat back flicking through the photographs of Celia Brown, who'd taken care to disguise herself on at least three occasions that Carol had witnessed. She couldn't help but wonder how many other times she'd done it. At least once, if she'd been the cause of Marjorie's problems.

Hoping Els would get in touch, but knowing that staring at a phone didn't make it ring, Carol got on with preparing dinner for her family. The peas were just coming to the boil when her phone lit up, and she could see it was Els Van Beek.

Typical, she thought to herself as she turned down the heat under the saucepan, answered her phone, shoved it under her chin, and stirred the parsley sauce she was willing to thicken.

'Have you got anything?' Carol didn't see any point in messing about.

'We have found Celia on recordings from the camera at the reception area of the spa when you arrived this morning, which is a start,' opened Els.

'Where's the camera there? I didn't see one.' Carol was puzzled.

Els replied tartly, 'You're not supposed to; all our security devices are discreet.'

And hardly effective, was what Carol wanted to say, but didn't. 'So it's hidden?' It gave her an unpleasant feeling to say the words.

'Not hidden, but unobtrusive. There's a sign as you enter the hotel alerting all guests and clients that they might be filmed, for security reasons. Our legal department assures us this is an adequate warning. Nothing's filmed or recorded in sensitive areas; the camera in the reception area of the spa is directed toward the desk and seating area – nowhere where clients would be less than fully clothed.' Els sounded as though she'd rehearsed her speech, or was reading it.

'Can you tell me the name she was using earlier today, when I saw her?' Willow had referred to the disguised Celia Brown as a first-time visitor, and Carol was interested to know what she'd been calling herself – it might be illuminating.

'Yes, it was Karen MacDonald.'

Carol couldn't help but laugh.

'Is this amusing?' Els sounded truly puzzled.

'I have a colleague with the same surname,' explained Carol, not sure Mavis would see the funny side. 'Have you managed to find Celia Brown on film when she was using any other names?'

Els sounded triumphant. 'We have. The day you say you saw her looking for her way back to the hotel from the pool, she was signed in as Candice Stowe. I have also checked our files for the day your friend had her manicure, but neither of those names is there.'

Something stirred in Carol's memory banks, and she rushed into the sitting room to sit at her desk – also known as the dining table. She shushed David as she hunted through the spreadsheets on her screen, checking – again – the date Marjorie had been at the spa. *Got it!*

She tried to keep her voice calm as she said, 'I have a lead. The name Celia used on the day my friend was injured was, I believe, Judith Roberts. I can't believe it – she's a Corrie freak, like me. She's using names of characters from *Coronation Street* – and pretty minor ones at that…nothing too obvious.'

'I do not understand.' Els sounded confused.

Carol felt the excitement rise in her tummy. 'Don't worry, I do. Let me take another look at these lists of names, and I'll email you some dates to help you work out when to check your security footage. When exactly did Celia leave your employment?' Els read out the date. 'Thanks. Does your CCTV data go back that far?'

'Yes, it all gets archived in the cloud, I believe, for a year.'

'Excellent – I'll get back to you.'

Carol sat back feeling satisfied.

'See that look on your mam's face, Albert?' David was on his feet, cradling his son. 'That's there because she knows she's had a breakthrough about something. I fell for that look when she was my boss – that spark she gets when she's solved a knotty problem. Your mam's a very clever woman, Albert.'

Carol shot out of her chair and headed for the kitchen. 'A very clever woman who can smell that she might have burned the parsley sauce a little bit. Sorry – don't panic, I'll sort it.' And she did.

TUESDAY 7th FEBRUARY

CHAPTER THIRTY-ONE

Carol was ready for her meeting with Mavis five minutes early, so tidied her desk, and made sure she was absolutely set. She was feeling rather pleased with herself, even though she knew she didn't have the best possible news to report. Good? Yes. Best possible? No. Not yet.

Mavis appeared promptly, but looking a bit less bright-eyed than her usual self; Carol thought her pleasantries left something to be desired, too.

They caught up, briefly, on the personal front, then Mavis said, 'I've nothing to report, I'm afraid. At all. I'm awaiting news from Rhodri Lloyd, having put everything about Ben Stirling in front of him, including the information Althea managed to gather.'

'Althea? She's involved?' Carol was surprised, and then a little alarmed when Mavis told her about the dowager's sortie to the Stirling home. 'I do hope she doesn't think she can do this sort of thing on a regular basis, Mavis.'

Mavis said, 'Ach, I believe I've made as much clear to her. Thank you. Anyway, I trust our client will get in touch promptly when he receives instructions from his client, so we'll wait for that. But do bear in mind there's an outside chance you might have to become involved, Carol, to possibly take over with our watching brief.'

Carol's heart fell a little. 'Of course,' she said.

Mavis continued, 'Now, we've no' spoken for a couple of days, so tell me what's what with this spa thing you've been looking into. You've no' been giving it all your time, have you? You're still supporting Annie and Christine with their case, as required, correct? That's our paying client, after all.'

Carol avoided an eye roll, replaced it with a fixed smile, and replied, 'Yes, I am. Though I have to say they seem a bit all over the place with things down there. Witches, smugglers, potential Internet and smart home hackers – none of it seems to be making any sense. Anyway, that's for them to sort out, so it's not my problem at the moment, whereas the spa is…and I had a bit of a breakthrough yesterday.'

She explained how she'd followed the suspicious woman, how Els had been able to reveal her real identity, and how Carol had then been able to find seventeen additional names of minor characters from *Coronation Street* that appeared in the lists of non-hotel guests allowed access to either the pool, or the spa.

Mavis nodded as she listened, and her smile grew with each piece of news. 'Good job, Carol. I'm sure the hotel manager will be pleased to have your insights to allow her to narrow down the times when they need to try to spot the woman on camera there. Any idea when she'll get back to you?'

Carol hesitated. 'No, not really. But there is something I want to talk through with you. I had a word with Llinos Trevelyan about a "hypothetical" situation, and she said there could be charges to answer, if we can gather enough non-circumstantial evidence about this Celia Brown. So I was wondering if you had an opinion about when we should walk away. Should I allow the hotel manager, and presumably the management and legal types within the group to which the hotel belongs, to take this forward from here on? I mean, we don't have a client as such – this was something we took on as a favor for Marjorie.'

Mavis looked thoughtful. 'Aye, I agree. Though it's much more satisfying to keep at a case until it reaches its conclusion, you know as well as I do that we cannae always do it. Parts of the process take time, or have to be handed over to the proper authorities, meaning we need to walk away and move on, having set the wheels in motion.'

Carol sighed, knowing her colleague was right.

Mavis added, 'It can mean there's less satisfaction for us, but hopefully it's justice that's satisfied at the end of the day.'

'Of course,' said Carol, already feeling the frustration.

Mavis added, 'I say we'll wait to hear back from the hotel manager, but we'll no' say anything to Marjorie at this point.'

Carol agreed. 'Oh no, not at all. Half the world would know who we suspected before tea time if we did that, and that wouldn't be good. And that's all we really have at this time – suspicions. You know, Mavis, the things people will do never ceases to amaze me; I mean, to look at Celia Brown, you wouldn't think she could be that brazen, or so cruel. That poor personal trainer is going to be off work for months. Does this look like a cold-blooded saboteur?'

Carol held up one of the photos she'd taken of Celia Brown in her back garden. 'Up to all sorts of mischief, then happily doing a bit of planting with her hubby...well, he's not her husband, because she's not married – so I'll call him her "significant other". All the bottom-patting and sweet-talking going on between them told me they're at least that to each other.'

'Could you send that photo through to me, Carol, please? And the others you took. There's something familiar about that man. Is it the way he carries himself, mebbe? Ach...I cannae get it from that. Let me see them.'

There was a pause in the conversation as Carol sent the photos, and Mavis received and opened them. Carol watched from her dining table as Mavis examined the photos in the office. With only Mavis there, the place looked dark and cavernous behind her, and the Scotswoman looked small, and very isolated.

'Well, would you look at that.' Mavis was close to the screen, and fiddling about. 'You say she was working in the garden with this man? That they acted like a couple?'

'They did – all a bit sickly, if you ask me. He looked at ease, and as though he were on his own turf. If you scroll though you'll see some shots of him close up – in wellies and shorts, hauling that planter and potting compost out of the shed in a wheelbarrow. No idea why the shorts – it wasn't that warm. But maybe they were his gardening shorts – I know I have gardening leggings.'

Mavis surprised Carol by giving a little round of applause. 'You've got him for us, you clever woman.'

Carol was confused. 'Got who?'

'You've got Ben Stirling – that's him in the shorts and wellies…no knee brace, no stick, and carrying stuff I dare say his cardiologist wouldnae want him to. No' so soon after having stents put in, in any case.'

Carol said, 'You're kidding. How would a married bricklayer from Builth get to know an ex-chambermaid from a posh hotel, who lives in Hay-on-Wye?'

'I cannae say, but maybe if we look at everything we know about the two of them we might be able to work out where their paths crossed. However, I need you to answer me this right now: would you say these two had an expectation of privacy at the time you took these photos?' Mavis was very close to the camera as she spoke.

Carol gave it some thought. 'The shrubbery was almost as high as my shoulder; it was a row of young lilacs, not a plant noted for its hedging properties, so I'd say that the rear garden was relatively easy to see into – as is evidenced by the photos. I didn't have to make any particular effort to take them, and no tele-photo lenses were used, just my normal zoom. I'd say anyone walking along that street on that day, at that time, would have seen the same as me. Not a private spot, though on privately owned property.'

'Hmm…right-o, leave it with me. I'll be off to talk to Rhodri Lloyd now, he'll be better than us with the legal aspects of this. Carol?'

'Yes?'

'Thank you. This is a piece of good fortune, and I appreciate it.'

'It all goes to show that we're at our best when we work as a team, I'd say,' said Carol thoughtfully. 'Sharing information across cases can lead to…well, this sort of thing. You're welcome. Must go now. See you this afternoon for our video-chat with Annie and Christine. Bye.'

Knowing she had the conference call coming up, but some time before she had to get ready for it, Carol filled her next hour with as much domestic activity as she dared.

Eventually, she stuck her head into the sitting room to see how her husband and son were doing.

'Hey, no screentime for you,' she said. Carol couldn't believe that David was watching TV.

'They meant computers, not the telly. Besides, it's for him, not me. He loves this sort of stuff.'

Carol watched her son's face beaming as some reckless youths dared each other to perform ridiculous and dangerous stunts – like jumping off a shed roof onto a waterbed, or trying to ride a bicycle over a brick wall – all of which ended in predictable, and, she could only assume, painful disaster. Which her infant son found hilarious.

Albert watched the screen, rapt, waggling his arms in glee, while David watched his son's face, rapt, and glowing with delight.

Carol watched them both for a moment, shaking her head in disbelief, and finally said, 'Well, not too long then,' and left them to it.

Finally able to give her attention to the notes that Annie had sent through, Carol tried to make sense of the situation in Port Beynon. All the facts that had been gathered so far seemed...annoyingly disjointed.

Carol liked order, and frequently told herself there was nothing wrong with that. Mavis always supported her marshalling of data, and she found that alone helped her take pride in her work. Though she also enjoyed the part of her job that was more spontaneous – like taking off after the duplicitous Celia Brown – it was the delight of data processing that really gave her satisfaction. The order of it. The security of it...

Carol heard a distant bell ring in her head. Annie's report had mentioned Carys Llewellyn's revelation that Amy Francis had hacked the local library system, that Cadog Smith had been a one-time web-warrior, and that Jason, aka Melvin, at the pub had been getting into online banking systems that weren't his own. She needed to find out more about those three people in particular.

She texted Annie to find out if she knew the pub landlord's surname, so that she could delve into whatever online footprint he'd created. The reply was swift: 'Don't know. Will ask Carys. Might be a while.'

Carol plodded on, wading through notes, making her own summaries, entering information into spreadsheets on her screen, and sorting it all out in her head.

Smugglers and their hidey-holes, with evidence of a tunnel in the garden, but no entry point inside the cottage. Smart home system problems, suggesting someone with computing skills – which covered the death threat on the laptops, too. The physical interference with the satellite dish and, possibly, Brian Kelly's e-bike – though her research had told her the only hacking that might impact such a vehicle was of its GPS, and that wasn't what had made the man crash to his death. Rumors about witchcraft and a curse – but she'd already discovered a great deal about the Gorst sisters which proved they were anything but witchy – indeed, they sounded like two women living lives so independent that they were out of step with their time. And where did Ted Thomas's death fit in?

Carol sat back and stared at her notes on The Case of the Cursed Cottage. She'd arranged them in different colored blocks of type within a spreadsheet, setting everything out in front of her on one screen, exactly the same way she liked to do things with her quilting – getting all the potential fabrics sorted, making sure there was the best possible variety and blend of colors and patterns, then fitting them together in the way that worked best for the entire design.

She chuckled to herself – no wonder she enjoyed quilting – even that was about organization, order, and then repetitive, though ultimately satisfying, tasks. Making sure the whole, overall design worked because of, or maybe despite, the beginnings of disparate parts – that's what she enjoyed. A cog rolled around in her mind...then another.

She checked the notes Annie had sent her once more, and noticed a gap in the data.

She dashed off a text asking where the details were about what had been found on the camera footage during the period immediately following the satellite having fallen on David's head.

Annie replied, 'No recordings. Remember the satellite dish was down?! On David's head!? Cameras online only after new dish went up.'

Carol started to type…then picked up her phone. 'Hiya, it's me,' she said when Annie answered. 'The cameras I brought down to the cottage record to their own internal memory when the Internet's down. Have you checked that?'

Silence. Muffled voices. 'Did we know that?' Annie sounded unsure.

Carol sighed. 'Yes, I'm certain I told you – and there were the leaflets that I made sure I'd left in all the boxes to help you with the installation…they mention it too.'

More muffled voices. 'Sorry, Car, we must have missed that. We were a bit discombobulated because of David's noggin, you know? Like you were, of course. And him. But – no, we haven't checked. Christine's digging out the leaflets now…um…will they tell us how to access that memory?'

Carol replied as patiently as possible. 'Yes, they will, so I won't bother explaining, but, if you need help, phone me back and I'll talk you through it. And don't forget our video-call later today. Mavis is off for lunch at Chellingworth, so she'll have to make a special effort to be back at the office in time for it, so none of us can be late. Bye.'

Carol reassessed her theories about what was happening at Sea View Cottage. She'd need to spend the next few hours searching various online databases – both publicly accessible ones and some where she'd set up accounts with special privileges because of the nature of the WISE Enquiries Agency's work – and maybe then she'd feel more confident about her ideas. But she'd also need the Gower contingent to undertake some specific tasks for her. She sent another text – and imagined the reaction it was likely to get in Port Beynon.

CHAPTER THIRTY-TWO

Henry was seated at the head of the dining table as though he were holding court. His wife and son were at his right hand, his mother at his left, with Mavis MacDonald beside her. His mother- and father-in-law were sitting along from their daughter. All was almost right with the world.

One person was missing: his sister wasn't there, and he wasn't surprised. With no one having been able to reach her for weeks, Stephanie had received a text from Clementine out of the blue – his wife, not him! – asking if she could visit. Stephanie had responded with an open welcome, and this date and time had been agreed. But now? Now she hadn't arrived. Typical.

Irked, Henry had decided to press on with the planned luncheon in any case. Clementine would just have to find out about his announcements at another time.

A tasty chicken consommé was followed by grilled local trout, served with a julienne of winter greens, and followed by one of his – and his mother's – favorites, lemon posset. A perfectly delicious luncheon, and well within the confines of his weight-loss regime, he felt. He'd asked for fruit and coffee to be served at the table, because, once she was all set up with their son, that seemed to be the best arrangement for the duchess.

Delighted that the atmosphere at the table had been almost convivial, he gradually wondered if that was because not one single person had mentioned any of the arrangements for the christening. He suspected it was, and dreaded breaking the spell – but knew he had to. He hoped the coffee would fortify him when the moment came.

Just as he was adding the merest splash of cream to his cup, the door of the dining room opened, and Clementine appeared.

'Clemmie, how good of you to join us. We've just finished,' he said archly. 'You're looking…well.'

His mother spoke more directly. 'Good heavens, Clementine – it's wonderful to see you, of course, but…what on earth have you done to your hair? I mean – where's it all gone? Oh no – oh Clemmie, my dear, you haven't got…you're not suffering from…is that why no one could reach you?'

'Hello, everyone. Don't panic, Mother, there's nothing wrong with me. I shaved all my hair off, voluntarily. An artist friend of mine is having chemotherapy, and hers started to fall out in clumps, so a crowd of us shaved our heads in support of her; one bald woman among many bald women means she won't be singled out, pitied, nor judged, that's what we all felt. It's a small thing to do, and my hats have found a new lease of life.' She kissed her mother on the cheek, and pressed her hand on Mavis's shoulder. 'Mother. Mavis.'

She stood beside Henry and kissed his cheek too, which took him aback; his sister wasn't the type for cheek-pecking, as a rule.

He watched her face as she looked at his son, and felt his heart swell with pride. 'Magnificent, isn't he?' He didn't dare do more than whisper, because his son – his perfect son, with a slightly long, but otherwise perfectly normal head – was asleep.

Clementine nodded. 'Well done, Stephanie.' She beamed as she spoke.

Henry felt as though he were waiting for a shoe to drop – or two at once. Something about his sister was…different. And it was more than the hair thing. She had a glint in her eye that made him worry. She was up to something. He looked at his mother, whose face was a picture of innocence – no, she didn't know what it was.

'Sorry I'm so late, everyone –' Clementine spoke in low tones as she walked around the table to take a seat beside Mavis – 'but I think you'll agree with me that it was worth the wait. I had to drive the van I rented ever so slowly to get here, so that I didn't do any damage. I've brought you a present, brother dear. Edward organized some help to get it set up in the Great Hall. I thought that was where it should wait – until you've seen it.'

Henry was cross. How was it that his sister always seemed to steal his thunder?

This luncheon was supposed to be about him and Stephanie, and their son – now it was going to become all about her. He tried to sigh away his annoyance.

'You want us all to come out there to see…whatever it is?' He didn't mean to snap, but knew he had.

Clementine nodded. 'If that's not too much trouble. How are you doing with that hip of yours now, Mother? All mended? Good. And Stephanie – if it's too difficult for you to get out there, maybe we could wait until everyone is ready to leave the table, and you're on the move anyway. Yes, why don't we do that?'

Henry was feeling increasingly uncomfortable. What was his blessed sister playing at?

Turning to his wife he said, 'I'd rather find out what's going on now – would you mind very much if I went to take a look?'

He adored the way Stephanie had a warm smile on her face when she replied, 'Go, Henry, and go now. You won't be able to settle to make your announcement – our announcement – until you have done. I'll come too. I can't sit glued to a chair just because he's asleep in his carry cot beside me. It's designed for him to be safe in it; if we're just slipping away from the table for a few moments I dare say he'll survive. Besides, Edward will be here. Shall we?'

Stephanie rose, so Henry shot to his feet and helped her up, as Mavis did the same for his mother, and John did for Sheila Timbers. Clementine led the way, all but skipping, and clearly fizzing with excitement.

The Great Hall was its usual cavernous self, except that, near the bottom of the grand staircase, there was a massive 'something' covered over with what Henry took to be a couple of old sheets.

His sister squeezed his arm as she said, 'I do hope you like it, Henry. Really I do. I should have brought it two or three weeks ago, but I had a bit of an idea, so asked for a few changes to be made. I think it was worth it.'

She scampered to stand beside the object and flung back the sheeting to reveal an almost life-sized portrait of Henry himself.

The entire group gasped. Henry felt a bit woozy. It was the strangest sensation; he was looking at an incredibly realistic image of himself standing at one of the windows of the Long Gallery with the elegant Capability Brown landscape of the Chellingworth Estate beyond. Quite how the artist had created such a realistic effect for the glass in the windows Henry had no idea, so he approached the canvas to use his experienced eye to try to work it out. Up close, the work was even more entrancing. The brush strokes! The skill! Amazing. He stood back again, and took in the rest of the picture. The artist had taken a few liberties with the exact location of items in the Long Gallery, so Henry was delighted to see a glimpse of his own father's portrait in the background of his, and there – on a shelf that didn't exist in reality – was a row of silver christening mugs: his father's, his own, and even his sister's. Once again, the ability of the portraitist to create hyper-realistic renderings of complex reflective surfaces – an enormous challenge, Henry knew – was astonishing.

'The mugs,' he exclaimed. 'At least we have them preserved here, in oils, even if we can't find them in real life.'

Clementine was at his elbow. 'Don't panic, I've got them all.' She waggled a knitted bag under his nose. 'I borrowed them so Vince Blanch could paint them in. When you finally decided – after all those lengthy conversations – that you'd like to be portrayed in the Long Gallery, surrounded by your family, and showing as much of the Twyst heritage as possible, I got the idea. Those mugs partially represent the family line. See? I bagged them just after you commissioned the piece, in November.'

Henry was, literally, lost for words.

His sister continued bubbling, 'Look, he's done it so that Father's portrait is shown in the background – I dare say you've spotted that. And, also, if you look out of the window – even though you can't see it from there in real life – I got him to paint in the folly…your new studio, that Stephanie sorted out for you for Christmas. That's why the portrait is so late – the new bits weren't dry. Sorry.'

Still speechless, Henry just stared as his sister darted about, pointing at the portrait.

'Can you see, Mother,' she was almost jabbering, 'there – beneath Father's portrait – there are ballet shoes with their ribbons unfurled, and red tap shoes? Those represent your having metaphorically taken off your dancing shoes to marry Father, and to have us two. Me? Well, I'm sort of everything in it – because, you know, art and all that. And Stephanie, you? Your name comes from the Greek for garland, or crown – see over there?' Clementine pointed to a floral crown lying beside the ballet shoes. 'That's you – a crown of yellow roses.'

Henry was agog. His eyes roamed the canvas; there was a mass of detail in the painting. He stepped back and forth, seeing new wonders and wanting to examine them. Even the folds in his silk pocket square bore further scrutiny. And the bow tie? It was his favourite, and exquisitely executed.

It was several moments before he became aware of the fact that no one was saying anything; everyone was watching him, silently.

He turned to face his family, and smiled. 'It's magnificent. I shall very much enjoy looking at it, for the rest of my life. And that's not just because it's of me,' he chuckled, 'but because it encapsulates everything I value and cherish about my life: my home, and my family.'

His mother clapped her little hands with glee and his sister actually hugged him – not an experience with which he was overly familiar.

'I say,' was all he could manage, then he stepped back to allow everyone else a chance to study the detail of the piece that would take its place beside his father's portrait, and hang there for…well, who knew how long?

The earliest representation of one of his ancestors had been commissioned in 1510, so had been on display for more than half a millennium. The mere thought almost dazed him, and he felt the emotion of the moment getting the better of him.

Of course he'd known the portrait was being painted – he'd stood about for long enough for sketches, then photographs. What he hadn't been prepared for was how seeing it in its finished state would make him feel.

He knew how he adored the portrait of his late father, and couldn't help but wonder what his son would, one day – and even for the rest of his life – think about this one, of him.

'I must telephone Vince Blanch to thank him for his work,' said Henry. 'I wish I could talk to him about the techniques he used for some of those marvellous effects.'

'You can do that at the christening,' said Clementine brightly. 'Whenever it is, he'll be my guest. I knew you'd want to talk to him about it, so I've invited him for a few days, and when you set the date, I'll let him know. Unless you want to have him to stay sooner.'

Henry replied – more thoughtfully than might otherwise have been the case, 'We've been trying to get in touch with you. It's all set for the first of March. And of course he can come, but the day will be about our son, so maybe he and I could spend a little time out in my studio another day.'

'That soon? Okay. I'll phone him.' Clementine seemed immediately distracted. 'Has Mother been fretting about those christening mugs? She's hardly said a word to me. I didn't mean to upset anyone. No one ever paid them much attention anyway.'

Henry sighed. 'Ah yes, the christening mugs – they've caused us quite a bit of bother. Which reminds me…' He raised his voice a little. 'Would everyone please join me back in the dining room, please, I've some things I want to tell you.'

Clementine stared at him. 'How very forceful you sound, brother dear. What's got into you?'

Henry faltered, he wanted to say so much, but contented himself with, 'Just let's all return to the dining room, shall we?'

Once everyone appeared to be as settled as they were going to be, and with every face full of anticipation, Henry began.

'As you know, there's been a certain amount of …activity…about the place as we all did our best to try to find the missing christening mugs.' His sister opened her mouth to speak, but he continued, 'Yes, I know you didn't mean to upset anyone by taking them, Clemmie, and no, nobody was ever very interested in them in any case.'

'I was,' grumbled his mother.

'Actually, you weren't,' said Henry evenly. 'You probably hadn't even thought of them for donkey's years, Mother, and it was only when you did that you became fixated upon them.'

Henry noticed how Mavis patted his mother's hand on the table, which seemed to calm her down a little; he was grateful to Mavis, and tried to convey as much with his eyes.

He continued, 'It has come to light, through the investigations that we've made, that at least one of the mugs that was temporarily not where it might have been expected to be, has a history attached to it that makes it much more valuable than had been suggested by its rather generic listing in the insurance records held in Chellingworth's Estate Office. To discover that what was listed as simply "a nineteenth-century silver cup with embossed figures and coronated lid" is, in fact, a piece of Imperial Fabergé worth hundreds of thousands of pounds is something which made me take pause. How many other items in the place have been similarly misrepresented?'

Clementine gushed, 'Hang on a minute, Henry. You're telling me that Daddy's old toothbrush mug is worth a fortune?' Henry nodded. 'Good grief, wait until I tell Vince – he had them all just sitting about in his studio. He'll love that story. Anyway – sorry, carry on. I didn't mean to interrupt.'

'We know you didn't, Clementine,' said Althea, 'but since you did, I have to say two things: Clementine – Henry found your passport in your rooms here, and I thought you'd like to know that it's safe; Henry – the same firm has done the insurance assessment here for many decades, and while I believe continuity is good, it might be that they've become a little…less than diligent?'

'Well put, Mother. My feelings exactly. Which is why I am announcing that I am going to commission a Grand Inventory to be made. Not just a relisting, but a total reassessment of every item that belongs to the Twyst family. And that means not just here at Chellingworth Hall, but also at the London and Scotland properties. It will take time, and it will be somewhat annoying on occasion, I am sure. But it needs to be done.'

His mother said, 'Quite,' in what he felt was a reassuring manner.

Buoyed by this support, he continued, 'I don't want my son – our son – to end up having to do it; he should know what he's inheriting. Wherever possible, full details of how the object entered our family will also be recorded. Some of this information exists already, of course, but I think the simple example of my father's christening mug proves that there might be much we don't know about an object. Family stories are all well and good, but there are gaps in knowledge, and when something is being used as a toothbrush mug why would one expect it to be a priceless piece?'

Stephanie said, 'There'll be cost implications, won't there, dear? Not just to do it, but for the insurance, going forward?'

Henry nodded. 'Indeed.' He felt it the right moment to stand, so moved to be beside the fireplace, shoving his thumbs into the pockets of his waistcoat, because he never knew what to do with them otherwise.

'Alexander Bright has met with me – which was kind of him – and I learned a great deal in a short time. Since I see the value of continuity, Mother, I have approached our current insurers with a proposition; if they would like to continue to retain our business, they'll supply whatever experts are required for this task. They are considering their response.'

'Very charitable of them.' Henry thought his mother's tone was just a little sharp.

He pressed on, 'If they decline, we still have the best part of a year to undertake the process ourselves, at our expense, with Alexander having agreed to find the appropriate experts for various types of items. I have faith in his ability to do so.'

'I'm sure he'll do a good job,' noted Mavis to his mother.

Henry ignored them both. 'Once we know exactly what it is that we need to insure, we will then move ahead with seeking quotes for the task. I am already mindful of the fact that Christine Wilson-Smythe has the experience needed to advise us on how to deal with Lloyds of London, should we choose that road.'

'I'm sure she'll help, if she can,' said Mavis MacDonald, smiling.

Henry nodded at her, then added, 'The venerable firm who've been our insurers for, as Mother said, a very long time indeed – since Victoria herself was on the throne, in fact – might no longer be our best option.'

'All very commendable, Henry,' said his mother, smiling broadly at him. 'I'd be happy to go up to Scotland while whomever does whatever they need there; I haven't spent any time at that house for some years. Your father and I were extremely happy there. Always looked good in a kilt, did your father. Excellent knees.' She turned to Mavis and said, 'A man needs good knees to be able to carry off a kilt, don't you think?'

Henry noted how Mavis was always patient with his mother. 'Aye, that's true, though many that wear them cannae boast of such. More's the pity.'

Concerned he was losing momentum, Henry added forcefully, 'That's kind of you, Mother, but I think it's a process better overseen by our housekeeper, and it will be done during the period when the house is not open to the public, so it might be a bit nippy for you. Despite the fact you have happy memories of the place, my recollection is that you found it draughty, and damp.'

Ignoring his mother's disdainful expression, he continued, 'And now for something else.'

His mother tittered, and asked pointedly, 'Is it something *completely different*, dear?'

Even Henry was aware of the association between the phrase and her blessed Monty Python people. 'Not entirely, because all of this has to do with family, our seat, and my son. Our son.' He nodded at Stephanie, who sat upright and nodded back. '*Our* son…who will be christened Hugo.'

Stephanie smiled, Hugo gurgled, and everyone around the table looked…still a little apprehensive, and – maybe? – underwhelmed.

'It's a good name,' said his mother, nodding at Mavis. 'And what will his others be?'

Henry replied, 'He will be named Henry and Devereaux, of course.'

'Of course, the Twyst tradition,' said his mother quietly.

Henry nodded. 'And, as I'm sure you'll all understand, we want to acknowledge Stephanie's lineage too, so he will also bear the name John…for you, John.' He nodded at his father-in-law, who was sitting open-mouthed, and yet still managing to smile.

Turning again to his mother, he added, 'And, because it has not been done to date, we thought it was high time that your place within the Twyst family, Mother, and *your* lineage, should be marked. Your grandfather's name was Arnold, and our son will carry that name forward, too. Hugo Henry Devereaux John Arnold Twyst. Our son.'

A spontaneous round of applause broke out, led by his mother. Mavis fussed with a tissue as his mother began to cry, and he felt the warmth in his heart as Sheila and John Timbers beamed at each other, then both got up and rushed to their daughter, who accepted their hugs and kisses with a truly happy face.

'Isn't it wonderful,' said Sheila Timbers to his mother, 'my John having his name as part of Hugo's…a future duke. And you get Arnold, which is lovely, too. But why didn't Henry choose your father's name for his boy? Didn't they get along?'

Even Henry could hear a slight edge of something in his mother-in-law's tone. Was she gloating? Surely not, he told himself.

His mother set aside her tissues long enough to reply. 'They got along very well, dear. And I think it's wonderful that I will have so many connections with my grandson's name; as Henry said, there'll be Arnold, for my grandfather, and – of course – I was the wife of one Henry and the mother of another, so I'm delighted he's chosen to stick with that one, and then…well, my father was John, you see, so that makes three for me, I believe.'

Henry loved it when his mother smiled sweetly, as she did at that very moment at Sheila. He couldn't quite work out what his mother-in-law's expression meant.

Turning to his wife, who gave him a supportive, if nervous, grin, he looked at his son's delightful face, and whispered, 'I think your father did well today, Hugo.'

Yes – that was most definitely who his son was: Hugo Twyst.

CHAPTER THIRTY-THREE

Mavis was feeling a bit wiped out by the time she settled herself at her desk in the office. Lunch at Chellingworth Hall had been a more draining experience than she'd been expecting, but she knew that now she had to focus her attention on the meeting between the entire team – there were many loose ends to be tied up.

She was ready to go: a mug of tea, all her paperwork sorted, her phone beside her in case any texts came in – when would she hear back from Rhodri Lloyd, she wondered? – and absolute peace and quiet to allow her to concentrate. Well, almost. Althea had insisted upon joining her at the office, but had promised to be as quiet as a mouse. She was currently sitting on the sofa keeping McFli entertained, though Mavis had no idea how long that would last.

A few moments remained before she was due to connect with her colleagues, so she had time to read a message that pinged in from Rhodri: his client was delighted with the photographic evidence of Ben Stirling's lies, and he was going to move forward with what he had. Rhodri would let her know what transpired. She was glad about that; always ready to step back if a differently-equipped specialist was able to take the lead, she knew that The Case of the Invalid Invalid was, indeed, that, and was glad it had never needed to be renamed The Case of the Belligerent Bricklayer. She couldn't help but wonder, however, how Stirling would react when he found out about the photographs of him without his brace. Mavis also allowed herself to muse about why the relationship between him and Celia Brown looked so comfortable. She suspected the woman was his mistress, which meant that – even if those photographs had shown him needing a knee brace – he might have been happy to drop his suit against Rhodri's client to prevent his wife from seeing them. Mavis felt a shadow of concern cross her horizon; was that so very different to blackmail?

Her laptop dinged into life, and her Pavlovian response was to click; there was Carol at her dining-room table in Anwen-by-Wye top left, Annie and Christine were sharing a camera in Port Beynon, top right, and there she was, bottom middle. All set.

'Thanks for all being on time,' began Mavis. 'This is going to be an important meeting, in many ways. First of all, I'll invite Carol to update you on The Case of the Dangerous Day Spa.'

Carol made quick work of her report, as she concluded, 'Because of the direction I was able to give her, Els van Beek and her team have already found eleven more instances of Celia Brown appearing on CCTV using the pool or the spa, and, shortly after each occasion, Els has located a customer complaint either from a hotel guest or a client using the spa. The nature of the complaints range in scope from disgusting slime having found its way onto clothes stored in lockers at the pool, for example, to incidents like Marjorie's with her hands, or the results of faulty chemicals being used by the hair stylists. We've talked through how those things might have happened, and have agreed that Celia could easily have dropped a noxious substance onto the "welcoming hand wipes" in the spa affecting Marjorie, as I suggested to Els, swapped styling or soaking chemicals in storage cupboards, or in the case of the pool lockers – the doors of which Els admitted don't have a tight fit – squirting smelly goo into the closed units. All quite "petty" stuff, if you believe that potentially burning someone's scalp, or incapacitating them for weeks because they can't use their hands or feet in comfort, is petty. The collapse of the rack holding the weights which injured the trainer was an escalation; Els believes Celia was becoming frustrated that the hotel was weathering the storm of complaints too well, and not posting the advertisement that would tell her they were prepared to pay the "reputation ransom" being demanded. Els is taking this forward as an official matter, naming Celia Brown. I've put her in touch with Constable Llinos Trevelyan. For us, therefore, that aspect of the case is closed, unless and until I'm called upon to give a statement to the police, and, possibly, evidence at any proceedings thereafter.'

Carol accepted her plaudits, then Mavis took up where she had left off, explaining how Carol's surveillance efforts had led to a break in her own case. Again, applause rang out through Mavis's laptop speaker in the office.

Carol waggled a hand and added, 'I've think I've also managed to work out where Ben Stirling and Celia Brown met up, Mavis; Celia got a job as a cleaner at the hospital where Ben received his physiotherapy. Now I can only surmise this, but, with Celia being noted as someone only too ready to complain about how she was unjustly robbed of what she felt was her rightful portion of the lottery winnings, and Ben Stirling having always – by the looks of it – been a bit of a chancer, I suspect we're seeing the product of two people coming together who both felt the world "owed" them, and finding a common goal – that being fleecing whomever they could, for as much as possible. I think it's no coincidence that the amount mentioned as the blackmail amount in the letters sent to the hotel, and the sum Stirling was suing Rhodri's client for, are one and the same; a hundred thousand pounds. Even better if they could nab two hundred thousand between them – that could set up the lovebirds very nicely.'

Mavis asked, 'Do you think the wife, Julie Stirling, had anything to do with any of this?'

Carol shook her head. 'I don't get the impression she did – and bear in mind I was the one who saw Stirling and Brown together. Definitely a close couple. I reckon his "long walks" were a cover for adulterous behavior.'

Althea shouted from the sofa in the office, 'Julie Stirling is a delightful woman. You should tell her about her husband. She deserves to know.'

Mavis didn't turn, but shushed her friend. 'That's no' our place, Althea. We'll talk about it later. Besides, if this all comes to court, everything will have to come out. Now, with thanks to Carol, that brings us to—'

'May I?'

Mavis jumped; Althea had popped up on her screen, and was standing right behind her, peering over her shoulder. 'Ach would you no' do that? What is it now?'

Althea waved to Carol, Annie, and Christine. 'Is Alexander there with you in Gower?'

Alexander appeared behind the two women in Port Beynon. 'Still here, still alive and kicking. I am bait that has not yet been taken.'

Althea dimpled at the camera. 'Oh good. I just wanted to congratulate you all on doing such good jobs, but I wanted to tell you something too. Is that alright?'

A general nodding of heads was rounded off with Mavis saying, 'Get on with it.'

Althea cleared her throat. 'First of all, thanks to Alexander for agreeing to help Henry with the Chellingworth re-evaluation, if needed. It's a great comfort to me. And I wanted you all to know that The Case of the Missing Christening Mugs has been solved. Clementine borrowed them. They weren't stolen. Nor lost. Just borrowed. And they're back now. And have been beautifully incorporated into the most wonderful portrait of my son. Thank you. The end.'

Mavis stifled a smile as Althea bowed at the laptop, then sidled back to the sofa, upon which McFli was fast asleep. She hoped she'd stay there.

Mavis returned her attention to the screen. 'Aye, well, there you are then. All done and dusted. It's just the wee matter of The Case of the Cursed Cottage we have to grapple with. Over to our Gower contingent.'

Carol waggled an arm. 'If I may, Mavis.' Mavis shrugged. Carol continued, 'Thanks. Right – were you three able to find what I asked you to look for?'

Three nodding heads. Annie said, 'I don't know how you did it, Car, but, yeah, we found exactly what you said we would, where you said we would. So come on, how did you do that?'

Carol looked delighted.

Mavis was mystified. 'What did you find? Where? Don't be playing any games with me, you lot, I'll no' be having that.' She smiled. 'Out with it.'

Annie replied, 'Carol got us to go out to the road, just where it bends before you get to the cottage – up the hill, the way Brian Kelly would have ridden his e-bike home from Fairwood Common. She told us to look for broken branches or ones with some specific types of markings, on both sides of the road, across from each other – and we found them. I took loads of photos, Car – I just in't had time to send them through. Now, we've got our own theories here, but you tell us – go on, have your moment of glory...we all know you deserve it, 'cause it looks like you're the star of the team at the moment.'

Carol twirled a curl and mugged a coquettish 'Oh, you are awful' at the screen, before she leaned forward to begin.

Mavis found Carol's intensity fascinating – and knew how lucky the team was to have her.

Carol began, 'It was quilting that made me think of it. And, I suppose, because of what I've done all my professional life too. I like patterns: I can spot them on a screen, I love them in systems management, and admire them in code. And they're an important part of my leisure time, when I'm quilting. When I'm doing that, I make sense of the way different patterns work together to form an overall design. For example, I spotted a pattern in the mass of data about people who'd gained access to the hotel pool and spa. I believe it's what we all do when we're working on a case – try to spot a pattern that suggests a lead we can research. However, I think patterns can be dangerous too, if we read too much into them. And we allowed ourselves to accept an overall design that our client, Gemma Thomas, had noted – and labelled as a "curse" – to color our investigations at Sea View Cottage.'

Annie said, 'When you say "our", you really mean "our", don't you?' She pointed at herself and Christine.

Alexander's disembodied voice said, 'I think Carol's trying to say you've been working from the wrong starting point. Is that right?'

Carol said, 'Thanks, Alexander, that's just what I mean. Honestly, I'm not criticizing you two, we were all guilty of it. But, when I thought about quilting, I looked at the overall "design" that Gemma presented us with quite differently. You see, a quilt is one big design that looks the way it does because of the way you bring together little pieces of other patterns. So, instead of seeing one big bundle of incidents at the cottage, I separated them out, and discovered different sets of incidents. First, and most seriously, the death of Brian Kelly, and the satellite dish hitting David – those two things required some sort of mechanical, physical intervention.'

'Yeah, we know that, Car,' said Annie shifting.

Carol smiled. 'I know. Then there are a host of other incidents that involve the failure or malfunction of appliances or systems connected to – or which can be connected to – the smart home management set-up…and I'll add the death threat on your laptops to this group, too. These can be seen as a different pattern.'

Alexander's voice could be heard shouting, 'Don't forget the tires on my Aston Martin, Carol. Part of the first pattern, right?'

'Wrong. That's an outlier – I'll come back to that.'

Christine looked away from the camera to where, as Mavis judged it, her fiancé was sitting. She giggled, then returned her attention to the screen.

'So come on then, Car – tell us what's going on.' Annie wagged her finger at her colleague.

'Okay, let's deal with the murder of Brian Kelly – and, yes, it was a murder. It was the worst thing that happened, and it ties in with David's injury too. First of all, I didn't believe there was any way for anyone to mess about with the brackets of a satellite dish and be able to be certain of exactly when it would fall – that was my starting point.'

Everyone nodded, accepting Carol's judgment.

She continued, 'Yes, that's where I started, with my own husband – sorry, but he's one of my main concerns in life.'

''Course he is, Car,' said Annie, nodding, and poking Christine, who also nodded.

Carol smiled. 'Ta. Anyway, once I accepted that, I tried to work out *who* could have fiddled with it. You had to get up onto the roof to see what had happened to it, Annie, so anyone wanting to damage it would have had to do the same thing. Now the satellite dish was mounted at the front of the house, to one side; it hit David when he was heading to the car on the parking pad. Anyone fiddling with it would be easily seen from the road – unless they did it at night, and, even if they did it in the dark, they'd be likely to be noticed by Amy or Glyn Francis; they couldn't miss spotting someone on the roof of the cottage they overlook. Neither of them mentioned seeing someone doing it, which I found suspicious—'

'One of them did it?' Annie sounded incredulous. 'But they're...' She looked at Mavis and said quietly, 'They're both getting on a bit to be up on roofs.'

Mavis allowed herself to raise both eyebrows as she said, 'I'm just about ten years or so older than you, and you were up there.'

'Amy and Glyn have a son,' said Christine forcefully, 'and he's certainly young enough to do it. I know he might be a bit nerdy, creating apps in his bedroom as they said, but it's a possibility. But then we're back to why, again.'

'Ah, yes, Llew Francis. A fascinating subject for my research. You do know who he is, don't you?' Carol twinkled at her colleagues.

'Nah – who is he, Car?'

Carol chuckled, 'Llew Francis has developed some apps, yes, but he's best known as a game designer. His parents might think they're giving a home to a beloved, if somewhat underachieving, son who needs a nest, but what they don't realize is that he owns a company that's worth a couple of million. It has a cult following. And his company's name? Sea View Dragon. Even David's heard of it. The company logo is a Welsh dragon with its "arm" wrapped protectively around Sea View Cottage.'

Annie and Christine exchanged a telling look. 'That could have been him on the camera,' said Christine. 'Hoody, trainers, jeans. The right build, I suppose.'

'What person on the cameras? Doing what? When? This is the first I'm hearing of this. There's nothing in your reports about this.' Mavis felt she'd missed a lot and wondered why.

'Sorry, Mave,' said Annie, 'you're right, it wasn't in any of our reports. Which is our fault. It wasn't until Car told us that the cameras would have recorded even when the Internet was down that we checked each camera, and told each one to upload its internal memory to the cloud. That's when we saw him; he came through the front door when Chrissy was down the pub, and I was walking Gert around the garden waiting for her to…you know, find the right spot. He was wearing dark colors, with a hoody pulled down over his face. He went everywhere, poking about. It gave me the creeps when I saw it. And I agree – the build is right for Llew Francis…but why on earth would Llew Francis want to make the satellite fall on David? I don't get it, Car.'

'Okay, everyone stop for a minute,' said Carol firmly. 'Llew Francis didn't. Brian Kelly's wife, Sara Kelly, did it.'

Mavis grappled with what Carol had said, but couldn't make sense of it, nor could her colleagues in Gower, either, judging by the looks on their faces.

Althea shouted, 'That's confusing. Tell Carol to explain.'

Mavis turned. 'You said you'd be quiet.'

'I can't help but hear, can I?'

Mavis said patiently, 'Please explain, Carol. Quick as you can, but leave nothing out.'

Carol smiled. 'Of course. Thanks to Carys Llewellyn, who unearthed this information – when I told her where to dig – we now know that Sara Kelly had called the police in Liverpool to the Kelly house on several occasions where a "disturbance" was recorded each time, and then again when the couple had moved to Amersham, outside London. No charges were ever brought, in either region, by the way. Carys also told me that this is, sadly, not unusual in situations when domestic abuse is suspected, which it was.'

Looks of anger and resignation were shared across the miles.

Carol pressed on. 'Amy Francis told you the couple rowed, spectacularly and publicly, and also told you that she'd chatted to "the wife" about Internet problems they'd had at the cottage, and how impressed she was that "the wife" had fixed them. How might "the wife" have done that? Or – should I say – how might Sara Kelly have explained her reason for being on the roof to someone who had seen her there?'

Christine said, 'But why on earth would she do that? I mean – what was she trying to achieve?'

Carol replied, 'I think we can all agree there really is no way to predict when a bracket that's been almost cut through will fail. We know it didn't fail until it hit David – many weeks after Sara damaged it – but maybe she believed it would fail right after she'd cut through it, killing her abusive husband in the process. However, it didn't.'

'So you're saying she tried to kill her husband with the dish...but when it didn't work – what? She tried again? But...how?' Mavis was trying to piece everything together in her head but wasn't having much luck.

Carol smiled. 'I had a theory, based upon one of those stupid stunt things on TV that David had been watching with Albert. Seeing that inspired me to dig around a bit on the Internet for a video that might explain how Sara managed it. And I found what I was looking for – which is why I asked you folks to check all the trees along the road there. I believe Sara Kelly waited for her husband to return to the cottage on his e-bike from his event, ran a length of rope, or something like it, across the road, using a tree branch on one side to tie it off, and another on the other side to help pull it tight. That's about the only way to have made the bike somersault, as the reports about Kelly's body and bike said happened...an immediate stoppage, mid-body, with the bike and its passenger flipping forward, down the hill. Blackly amusing when it's a few teens messing about in their back garden on a video they've posted online, but deadly for Brian Kelly.'

Christine mused. 'That's...well, I'm not sure that clever is the right word. I suppose "cold" would be better. And...risky.'

Carol said, 'Risky? Yes, but she really did get away with murder – until now. However, to be fair, you two gathered information that gave me another big clue to her guilt: Sara Kelly told Amy Francis that her husband wouldn't answer his phone when she tried him – indeed, it was something she mentioned so often that Amy found it memorable. But think about it – wouldn't you at least go out and have a general look around if your loved one didn't come home? I'd do that if it was Bunty missing, let alone if it were David. And her husband's body was discovered very close to the cottage...she could have spotted it, if she'd looked. When I considered the dish and the bike together, I saw a pattern – two acts with the same desired outcome, undertaken by the same person; physical actions by Sara Kelly, who wanted her abusive husband gone. Oh, and Alexander – no, I don't think she returned to damage your tires for some bizarre reason, I think that was done by Jason from the pub, aka Melvin. Anyone got a surname for him yet?'

'Melvin Roberts,' said Annie, 'several aliases. To be fair, Jason is his father's name.'

Carol smiled. 'There – Melvin Roberts, a jealous man, used to being able to manipulate vulnerable women, thwarted and enraged, he lashed – or slashed – out.'

Alexander shouted, 'Sounds like a dangerous nutter. Not bad looking though, in a sort of surfing lumberjack way.'

Althea called out, 'That should have been a good clue in itself, then. Lumberjacks aren't always what they seem to be.' She started singing the famous Monty Python song.

Mavis feared frivolity might break out at any moment so said, 'Shush, now, will you. Have you passed on your ideas and thoughts about all this to...anyone, Carol?'

Carol nodded. 'All sent to Carys Llewellyn, as well as the information I was finally able to get from the company that owns the software used to run the smart home systems for the cottage. The system has indeed been enslaved by someone with an IP address registered at the house opposite Sea View Cottage, and by "someone" I'm certain it's Llew, not Amy or Glyn.'

'But not because his parents are too old, eh?' Annie smiled, but her point fell flat.

'No,' said Carol. 'It's because the IP address is connected to his company. He's been able to sit at home and use his laptop or even his phone to control the water supply, electrical appliances, heating and lighting, and gain access to the place through the front door. I also believe that when there have been plumbing problems due to blockages and so forth it's been because he's entered the property – as you saw him do – and has dropped something down a toilet that would cause a blockage later on.'

Annie tried to get Carol's attention without interrupting her.

Carol said, 'And as for why…yes, stop waggling at me, Annie…I'm getting to that. Sadly, I think it's quite simple.'

'I bet it's money,' shouted Althea.

Mavis shushed her.

Carol said, 'No, not money – but covetousness. I believe he wants to own the cottage. He lived through some of the most formative years of his life there – then he was taken away from it…or maybe he believes it was taken away from him. And now? Well, he's had to sit there looking at other people enjoying *his* sea view, *his* direct access to the beach, for all these years. He's got the blessed thing on his company logo for heaven's sake – and that dragon might not be protecting it, but grabbing it. I just don't think it occurred to him that Gemma Thomas wouldn't be prepared to sell until she knew what was going on there; I think he assumed she'd just get rid of it. He out-gamed himself on that one. Because of the injuries his actions caused to that poor cleaner, as well as my husband, I have also passed all my findings about him to Carys Llewellyn, too.'

Annie looked a bit peeved, thought Mavis, then she spoke up, proving she was. 'So what was the point of us lot being here all the time, eh? Can we leave now? I'd like to sleep in my own bed, having enjoyed dinner with Tudor, thank you very much.'

'You sure about that?' Christine nudged Annie playfully.

Annie smiled back. 'You know very well what I mean. Anyway, Car – why just men? Why did only men get hurt? And what about Gemma's uncle? Did Llew Francis kill him with carbon monoxide somehow? He was the first on the scene, after all. Remember – his mother told us it was him who called her and Glyn over to the cottage. Was that Llew trying to get the house then? Not knowing her uncle had left it to Gemma?'

'Hold your horses, there, Annie. First of all, I really think this is where Gemma led us astray – but not intentionally. See, when you think there's a pattern, you tend to see that pattern again and again, whether it's there or not. Carys Llewellyn finally managed to get hold of the inquest report about Ted Thomas's death; it stated that the gas heating system had malfunctioned due to its age, and the wear and tear of being in an environment where there was a high salt content in the air. So I suppose at least Gemma was right about that in a way – the cottage did, sort of, kill her uncle'

Annie noted, 'As Carys said, when we met her.'

Carol replied, 'Perceptive of her. Now then - the death of Brian Kelly? Nothing to do with Llew. David being hit by the satellite dish? Also not Llew. And Alexander's tires? Again, not Llew. I believe that because her husband had the kettle explode in his face, and maybe she'd had complaints from several male tenants, plus the thing with her uncle…Gemma only saw the *male* thing, and we all accepted that, and took it on board. Then we all added in the unfortunate scalding of a male cleaner to that perceived pattern. Not her fault, and not ours – but I don't think it was Llew's intention to target men specifically.'

'And what about the two aged sisters who spat at boys as they walked past? Not witches, just independent women? Cadog Smith with maybe one bad memory that stuck with him…that he liked to talk about…a lot?' Annie looked as though she knew the answer.

Carol nodded. 'I think so.'

Mavis said, 'Annie and Christine, you've been on the spot there doing an excellent job of gathering critical information. Without you doing that, we'd have no' had the insights you passed to Carol.'

Annie and Christine shrugged, and smiled.

Mavis continued, 'And you've sorted that information, interpreted it, and done further research, Carol. This was a true team effort. Thank you all. I'm sorry I was no' as involved with this case as I'd have liked to have been, but I had my own case to work on, which I'd no' have solved without Carol either, *and* she's the one who did all the work at the spa. Now I understand you may think I'm losing my marbles when I say this, but—'

'Three cheers for Carol,' shouted Althea into Mavis's ear.

'Exactly.'

WEDNESDAY 1ˢᵗ MARCH

CHAPTER THIRTY-FOUR

It was as though the daffodils lining the drive to Chellingworth Hall knew it was St David's Day, and were bobbing gaily in the almost warm sunshine beneath the clear blue sky. The procession of vehicles from the church to the Hall had been quite something, with the duke, duchess, and their son Hugo in the leading car – the best Bentley, for the occasion. They greeted their guests as they arrived and entered the Great Hall, where the reception was being held. Almost everyone commented upon the delightful service, which had been officiated by a glowing Reverend Ebenezer Roberts who'd given a heartwarming, and blessedly brief, sermon.

Of course, the chance to see the future duke up close was high on every attendee's list of priorities, so it had been arranged that Stephanie would be seated, allowing people to look down at Hugo, without her having to stand holding him for what turned out to be the best part of an hour.

'Did you see Henry's face when he came into the Great Hall, Mavis?' Althea was buzzing with excitement. 'He's impressed, isn't he?'

Mavis nodded. 'That's what he said, and I can only imagine everyone else is too. Where on earth did you manage to find a dozen harps and harpists, dear? I thought you were asked to hunt down a string quartet.'

Althea waved away Mavis's comment with a dismissive gesture. 'No, not right for this at all, dear. They can be a little screechy, I find. No, not right at all. You recall that I found six harpists for Henry's wedding, exactly one year ago?'

'How could I forget?' Mavis smiled warmly.

Althea bristled a little. 'Well, I got in touch with the same people and asked if they could rustle up another six. They couldn't, but then I asked Wendy Jenkins, and she got in touch with some of her old chums from the music college, and Bob's your uncle. A whole dozen of them. The harps were delivered during the service. And don't they sound wonderful? So rich, yet calm, and not too piercing, which might have disturbed Hugo.'

'It's perfect, Althea. Very thoughtful and clever. Well done. And well done with the christening gown, too. I know you offered to help when it arrived and everyone agreed it looked too "new". How did you manage to make it look just right for today?'

Althea dimpled, then whispered, 'Tea. I got Cook Davies to soak it in tea. We kept dipping it in and out until it was just the right color…we had to make lots of pots of different strengths, then, when it was perfect we set it, and let it dry naturally. Good colour, isn't it?'

Mavis smiled. 'Again, perfect. And how did you know that would work, pray tell?'

Althea hissed, 'It's what the Royal family did for the Honiton gown. They had the same problem we did – a family heirloom past its prime, so they had a new one made, but it looked all wrong, so – tea! There are very few problems in life that can't be solved, or at least helped along, by tea, don't you think, dear?'

Mavis shook her head slowly. 'You might be right, Althea. And I say that knowing that it's over our many cups that you've helped me understand that I'm not a lone actor in my life, but that I have friends who will help lift me up when I'm a bit down. Thank you for that. Now – speaking of tea, how about a cuppa?'

'I'd prefer a sherry; time enough for tea. Today's a celebration, let's indulge.'

'Sherry and cake it is, then,' said Mavis, and the pair made their way toward tables that were groaning beneath the weight of silver platters mounded with sandwiches, sausage rolls, and more Welshcakes than Mavis believed she'd ever seen in one place since the duke and duchess's wedding.

As they made their choices, they were greeted excitedly by Marjorie Pritchard. Mavis thought it peculiar that she appeared to be attempting to shake hands with everyone in the place and, when she reached Mavis, she twirled her beautifully manicured fingers in front of her.

'Look,' she said happily waggling both hands, 'better than ever. Both of them. Thanks to all of you for everything you did, Mavis. Willow and Jasmine at the spa have been telling me all about it. Imagine that Celia person doing all those horrible things, just because she wanted money out of them. They were quite right to not pay up. I'm pleased she's got her comeuppance, anyway.'

'Aye,' said Mavis, 'that tends to happen when you cause innocent people to be harmed.'

Marjorie nodded vehemently, and leaned in. 'Jasmine was telling me that they arrested Celia at her house in Hay-on-Wye, and they also carted off her boyfriend, who was involved in some way too. Married he is, it turns out, but the wife has slung him out, so Jasmine said. And did you know they said I can have free manicures for a year? Lovely, isn't it?'

When they were alone again, Althea asked, 'Did your client's client drop his suit in The Case of the Invalid Invalid, by the way? You haven't told me. Ben Stirling must be on shaky ground if he's been taken into custody because of that trouble at the spa.'

Mavis chuckled, 'My client's client is now no longer facing being sued by the invalid invalid, thank you. And I'd no' noticed that delightful double play on words, my dear.'

Althea nodded graciously. 'You're very...very welcome.' She dimpled. 'But tell me, Marjorie's nails looked odd, to me. Why did they have that little white stripe at the top? Was that supposed to represent her nail above its bed? It looked a bit...well, luminous, in a way.'

'It's called a French manicure, dear, and it's quite popular, I believe, with those who prefer to look as though they're not wearing nail varnish.'

Althea looked unconvinced. 'I don't know why a person would be afraid of using a vivid colour on their nails – it often looks quite decorative, I think. Clementine does it all the time – which is much better than the black she used to insist upon wearing right through her teen years.'

Althea sighed, and waggled her fingers across the Great Hall at her daughter and her guest, the portraitist Vince Blanch.

It had been decided to keep the new painting of the duke on display for all to see until after the reception, so that the artist would be able to accept the praise for his efforts from more than just the sitter. However, it appeared he wasn't really enjoying the process, because he and Clementine were clearly sneaking away to…somewhere.

Althea shrugged as her daughter disappeared from view. 'At least she was never a wishy-washy girl. Never gone for insipid colors, has Clementine. And she's a little too old for them now, I'd say. One mustn't be snobbish, or ageist, but I do think The Female Outlaw is getting on a bit to be wearing that baby-blue flouncy thing; it's like something out of a Doris Day film. And she's even got her husband to wear a shirt and tie – both of the same color. Just too much matchy-matchy going on there.'

Mavis dared to remark, 'Too matchy-matchy? No' your style at all, that, as I know. That turquoise dress you're wearing today is quite vivid, and with the red shoes and orange tights it makes for quite a non-matchy-matchy outfit.'

Althea preened a little. 'One mustn't always do the expected, must one?'

'No' much chance of anyone ever accusing you of that, dear.'

'Excellent,' said Althea. She stuffed an entire Welshcake into her mouth, then tried to not giggle.

Carol was pleased that Albert had taken his cue from baby Hugo and had been an absolute angel since the family had left their house in Bunty's charge earlier in the day. She'd refreshed him for the afternoon's reception, but knew it wouldn't be long before he'd be tired of being contained in her arms, or his pushchair, and would need some time ranging around their own sitting-room floor with his toys; his scooting was now up to quite a speed.

'Does today make you want to get this one dunked?' David beamed at his son, and kissed his wife on the cheek as he handed her a cup of tea.

Carol tutted. 'Shh, the vicar can hear you. And, no, I still want to wait until he's a bit older. That's usual for our family, and I'll stick to our normal, not be pressured by someone else's, thanks. But we should start to talk about godparents before too long, because that can be a nightmare. Val Jenkins did well, didn't she?'

David nodded, brushing crumbs of cake from his tie. 'I thought Tudor did brilliantly, too. I've got to say, that was a surprise. I wasn't even aware that he and Henry knew each other that well, or, if they did, that they got on. Always at loggerheads at the annual croquet tournament, if you believe all the stories. I've only been the once, of course, and it did all get a bit heated.'

'I think they call that good clean fun, *cariad*. And yes, it was a surprise, though I knew something was up when Annie said her mum and dad were coming for the christening. I know they came for the wedding last year, but this is different. Did you notice how Annie looked at Tudor when he was beside the font, making his statements and affirmations? Annie's happy, and deeply in love. It might not be long before those two are in church together again, but for a different reason.'

David spat cake. 'Annie and Tudor? Get married? Do you think they'd bother?'

Carol smiled. 'You have no idea how much of a romantic Annie is. And, from what she's told me about Tudor, he's just as bad, I'd say. But, maybe you're right, in a way – maybe a church wedding wouldn't be their style. Though neither of them has been married before, so it would be their first – and hopefully only – experience of getting married, so...oh, I don't know. Anyway, let's not talk about them – let's talk about us. We'll be off in a few weeks, won't we? And Albert will get his first chance to spend days at the beach while his dad builds sandcastles. Thanks to you getting the all-clear to be able to fly. Just as well your skull's so thick, eh? Jersey's got nice beaches, they say. I hope the weather's good, that's all.'

'Wherever we are, the sun shines from you,' said David.

Carol rolled her eyes, but let him kiss her anyway.

Annie had begun to introduce her mother to people, but Eustelle had taken herself off to find some cake and hadn't returned, which had left her father to strike up a conversation with Tudor...and now she couldn't get a word in edgeways.

Standing a little apart from the two men she loved most in the world allowed her to consider their similarities, and differences. Both steady, both calm, both hard working, both having done what they needed to do to make a better life for themselves and – in her father's case – for his family.

She'd been delighted when Tudor had told her about Henry's invitation to become Hugo's godfather. He himself had been surprised, then pleased, then worried; she knew how seriously he would take his responsibilities, and was absolutely certain that Hugo would benefit from getting to know Tudor. He was the epitome of what people always called 'the salt of the earth', and she knew in her heart what a great deal that meant; reliability was an underrated trait.

'He's a kind looking man, child, and good at heart, too.' Eustelle Parker was at her daughter's elbow.

'He is, in't he,' mused Annie. 'Glad you can see it in him.'

'It's been wonderful for your father and me to see you two together again. It's been a while. Don't leave it so long next time. We could both squeeze into that spare room of yours, if we snuggled enough.' Eustelle looked mischievous. 'It was very kind of the duchess to invite us to stay here for the night this time, though, and I can't wait for all my friends to see the photos we've taken of our room. Your father's said he'll take them along to show around at his club, too. Now come on, child, let's get someone to take some snaps of the four of us together; we're all in our finery, and I mustn't let this new hat go to waste. I had a terrible time finding it – they don't seem to make proper hats anymore – just those little fascinator things, and they're not a bit of use to me. A hat's got to be a decent size to make a statement.'

Annie smiled at her mother. 'And that one's saying a lot, in't it?' She reached to hug her mother around the waist.

As Eustelle tried to find the perfect spot for the photos to be taken, Annie's father ambled behind her, and Annie grabbed Tudor.

She whispered, 'Thanks for chatting with Dad. He likes it, and you.'

'Having a chinwag with Rodney is the only reason I'm going out with his daughter,' said Tudor with a wink. He leaned in. 'Did I do alright? Could you understand what I was saying in the service?'

'You did yourself, and everyone who loves you, proud.'

'So you were proud?'

'Couldn't have been more so.'

The couple hugged.

'It's nice for you to have a reason to be proud of me, for a change.' Tudor was sipping a glass of port, and surveying the scene.

'How do you mean?' Annie asked. 'There are lots of reasons for me to be proud of you – just look at how you keep that pub afloat.'

Tudor shrugged. 'Yes, but compared with you, I just do normal things. You? You're a woman bringing down justice on the heads of the guilty.'

Annie smiled. 'I'm not sure that's how I see myself, Tude. That all sounds a bit…well, biblical, or classical for me. I just help people.'

Tudor replied, 'But you do. Like that bloke down in Gower – Llew Francis. Now that's a very nasty piece of work, if you ask me. Imagine being so covetous that you'd do all those terrible things to people, just because you want a particular house, or cottage in this case.'

Annie nodded. 'I know, I don't get it either. Carys Llewellyn tells me that his solicitor is making noises about him trying to make out he wasn't of sound mind when he did it all. Apparently, he's claiming the cottage was his spiritual home, and the source of all his inspiration for his work. That the universe told him it was supposed to be his, by rights. But I can't believe that'll stand up in court, because it was such a sustained campaign of…well, terror, for our client. To do all that? Dreadful. I mean, it was a very nice cottage, and the view was spectacular – but his "spiritual home"? Nah.'

Tudor looked at Annie sideways. 'Can't imagine it would be worth doing what he did for any home. Awful, as you said.'

Annie sighed. 'Yes, it was a nice cottage, and the seafront was magnificent…but, I don't know, Tude, the village itself wasn't like Anwen. It seemed to be missing a heart. And I think that was because the pub was so…well, I told you it was nicely decorated, but it didn't have any soul. Not like your place. The Lamb and Flag is a genuine delight at the center of our village – and it makes such a difference to the place. Someone needs to tell you that.'

Tudor smiled, then flushed a little. He nodded toward Henry. 'He's been saying as much. Never comes in himself, of course, but he says he's been listening to what folks say about the place…and we're having a meeting in a couple of weeks about it. He's looking to build more links between the village and the Hall.'

Annie rolled her eyes. 'Sounds a bit feudal when you say it like that.'

'Hmm…well, we'll see what he's got to say for himself. I'm the godfather of his son now, you know – so maybe I'll get my own way about the pub, even though I lease it from the Estate.'

Annie laughed, and only just avoided knocking Tudor's port all over the front of his best waistcoat.

She chuckled. 'Yeah, Tudor Evans, the powerful pub landlord, that's you. But don't expect me to be anyone other than the person I am, right?'

'I wouldn't want you to change one little bit.'

Annie kissed Tudor's cheek. 'Good, 'cause changing is not on my agenda. Not any more...I need to stop and take stock a bit now, I reckon.'

They hugged and wandered off to join Eustelle and Rodney Parker beside the fireplace, for photographs.

Christine and Alexander had found a relatively quiet corner, where they sat sipping champagne, enjoying the harp music.

'It's dreamy,' said Christine. 'I like dreamy music.'

'And classic rock, and Sinatra, and rap, sometimes. Eclectic, that's you – in oh-so-many ways. And I love your eclecticness.' He kissed her.

'And I love your...everything.'

Christine gazed at the crowd, noting that Mavis and Althea had settled down with a couple of sherries, that Carol and David were fussing over Albert – who'd been very good all day, and then she spotted Annie and Tudor shuffling about in front of the fireplace with Annie's parents.

She could tell that Stephanie and Henry had finally finished their greeting duties; she noticed that Stephanie looked a bit tired, and was allowing her husband and parents to help her with her son. Then she looked at Alexander, and her heart swelled.

She mused, 'It's wonderful to see people you care about being happy – truly happy. Connected to others who matter deeply to them. But sometimes...oh, I don't know, Alexander...how do things go so badly wrong for some people? Were they never really happy to start with? Or do they just slide into unhappiness without noticing until...well, until the only resolution they can see to their problems is to murder someone they once said they'd love forever?'

Alexander looked into Christine's sad face. 'Well, that's put a different spin on the day, I must say.'

'Sorry.'

'It's okay, really. But it sounds really quite specific. Are you talking about Sara Kelly killing her husband? She's confessed, right? I only heard a part of what Annie was whispering at the back of the church.'

Christine nodded. 'Yes. She walked into a police station near Amersham last week and told them she'd killed her husband. Said she hadn't expected to feel so awful about having done it. That she missed him, if you can believe it. Carys Llewellyn's area has picked up the case, due to it having happened on their patch, and, of course, she's having to oversee things now because there was no suspicion of foul play at the time – a bit of a problem for her to sort out down there, it seems. Anyway – yes – I mean how does that happen? Can love really turn to murderous hate just like that?'

Alexander shifted on his seat. 'Again, not fully up to speed on this one – but I clearly recall there was mention of domestic abuse, sustained over a long period. It sounded to me as though the man was a monster – and she snapped.'

'Yes, that's what Sara Kelly said when she confessed, apparently; said she'd hoped things would be different when she and her husband were away from home, but they carried their problems with them to Port Beynon, and that was where she realized he'd never be any different.'

'So hardly love turning to hate on a whim, was it?' Alexander held Christine's hand in his. 'I'd say the poor woman was responding to an unbearable situation the man himself had created – but, to be honest, I'm not really qualified to weigh in on the female perspective with this one. Just…just don't let it worry you. You know it's not something that will ever happen to us. We're us, not them. Be here, with me, now. Enjoy this.'

Christine still couldn't raise much of a smile. 'We'll be alright, won't we?'

Alexander hugged her. 'Of course we will. But how do you mean, exactly?'

'I mean since we talked to Mammy and Daddy and made it clear we're not getting married for at least a year, and that no one is to even mention weddings to us.'

'Ah, right. Yes, of course. It was a good decision, all round.'

'Yes. I think that's just what we need. Let's just be us, Alexander? Just you and me, finding out who we are as us…so we can be better together going forward.'

'I'll drink to that.'

'Me too.'

Hugo had been fed and changed, and was making sleepy, truffling noises in his cot beside his parents' bed.

'What a day, Henry. I still can't believe it all went as well as it did. Everyone was happy, including Hugo…who was just the most wonderful baby in the world. Your mother was her best self; she did a great job with the harps, as well as having managed to save the day as far as the new christening gown was concerned. And she really loved the christening mug you designed for our boy, didn't she? I'm so pleased. I adore it too; simple, elegant, yet not severe. Well done, Henry.'

Henry had burrowed under the covers, and was staring at the ceiling. He felt as though he'd climbed Mount Snowdon: exhausted, but proud to have reached the summit.

He said, 'I'm relieved that your parents and my mother appear to have buried the hatchet – and not in each other. Mavis took lots of photos of the three of them with their grandson, which is wonderful. You were right to hire a professional photographer, dear, but the snaps tend to show the real smiles, don't you think?'

'Indeed, though the official portraits will become an important part of the Twyst archive. Our heritage. Hugo's heritage.'

'Indeed. Family, friends, and heritage; we did all three proud today. Oh, and happy first anniversary, dear. I didn't want to take away from today, so there might be a little surprise memento for you in the morning – as we begin our second year of marriage.'

'Why Henry, that's very sweet and thoughtful of you, dear. And you might find I'm ready to reciprocate. Neither of us could have imagined what would happen to us during our first year of marriage. I wonder what our second will bring.'

'Who knows, my dear? Not I. But I know that facing whatever it might be with you and Hugo beside me will make it so much…better than without you.'

'Indeed.'

ACKNOWLEDGEMENTS

My thanks to my mum, sister, and husband, for their unwavering support, which allows me to continue with my writing. My thanks to Anna Harrisson, my editor, and Sue Vincent, my proofer; we've all tried to make this the best possible version of this story. My thanks, too, to every blogger, reviewer, librarian, bookseller, and social media user who might have helped – in any way – to allow this book to find its way into your hands. Finally, thank *you* for choosing to spend time with the women of the WISE Enquiries Agency.

(PS: Port Beynon in this book was inspired by – but is not the same place as, nor does it have the same inhabitants as – Port Eynon, in Gower, Wales. The real Port Eynon is lovely, so please don't think that all the dodgy people and places of my Port Beynon are anything like the real thing – they are all entirely my own invention. *Cathy Ace*)

ABOUT THE AUTHOR

CATHY ACE was born and raised in Swansea, Wales, and migrated to British Columbia, Canada aged forty. She is the author of The Cait Morgan Mysteries, The WISE Enquiries Agency Mysteries, the standalone novel of psychological suspense, The Wrong Boy, and collections of short stories and novellas. As well as being passionate about writing crime fiction, she's also a keen gardener.

You can find out more about Cathy and her work at her website: www.cathyace.com